THE PARALLAX VIEW

Eamonn Vincent

ARBUTHNOT BOOKS

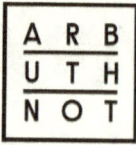

This edition published by Arbuthnot Books

https://www.arbuthnot-books.com

ISBN: 978-1-0687038-3-6

Cover illustration: Eamonn Vincent

Also by Eamonn Vincent

Non-Fiction

Me Neither – A Memoir

Fiction

Who Was Nightshade?
Foul Papers

The Thieves of Time

Book 1: Event/Horizon
Book 2: Palace of Tears
Book 3: The Parallax View

Poetry

Only More So
Even More So

For Maia and Cecilia

"This is the situation: The head of one of our departments, one of the most celebrated detectives in Europe, has long been of opinion that a purely intellectual conspiracy would soon threaten the very existence of civilisation. He is certain that the scientific and artistic worlds are silently bound in a crusade against the Family and the State. He has, therefore, formed a special corps of policemen, policemen who are also philosophers."

– The Man Who Was Thursday, G. K. Chesterton

"The rage to recognize in works of imagination the individuals whom one meets with in the world, is for these works a real plague. It degrades them, gives them a false direction, destroys their interest, annihilates their utility. To seek for allusions in a romance, is to prefer slander to nature, and to substitute mere gossip for observation of the human heart."

– Adolphe, Benjamin Constant

CONTENTS

Week Zero

27 September – 3 October 1976

MI6 – Borough – Monday

SHEENA FERGUSON, DIRECTOR OF the department, had called her assistant, Jeremy Collingwood, into her office in Borough to discuss an operation that did not seem to be bearing fruit. She was leafing through a slim folder. 'Jeremy, maybe it was a mistake to employ Grace Mitchell to watch Müller.'

'You know how it is, ma'am, we have no brief to monitor internal threats. That's for our sister agency. So we have to do it informally.'

'But Harry Larkin? For God's sake! He's the criminologist, isn't he? That's not going to help him establish a rapport with Müller or Doyle. They probably don't even know what criminology is.'

'Few people do, ma'am. Sir Leon Radzinowicz, at Trinity, seems to have been the *onlie begetter* of the subject.'

'Larkin doesn't strike me as being a Trinity man.'

'No, he holds the Ashby Research Fellowship at King's. I'm not sure that's the best entrée to St Rad's High Table either. So we are rather dependent on Dr Mitchell.'

'We've had precious little back from her.'

'Perhaps there is nothing to report. After all, we do not have incontrovertible evidence that the Stasi turned him.'

'I find that hard to believe. Even so, I would have thought he would have been in touch with one or two people of interest to us.'

'He seems to have thrown himself into his work, spending long hours in the University Library.'

'Where he could bump into all sorts of ne'er-do-wells in the stacks, and we'd be none the wiser.'

'I really don't think that Dr Mitchell could be expected to dog his footsteps in the UL. She has her own academic workload.'

'Well, it's all very unsatisfactory. I had also rather expected Grace to offer him accommodation. I thought there was a spark between them.'

'I believe she did, but for entirely understandable reasons, he found the prospect of rooms in St Rad's more agreeable. But when the flame is not guttering, they do appear to have intimate moments at Glisson Road.'

'I think you're being far too understanding, Jeremy. I am attending a *Preparing for Armageddon* conference in Cambridge shortly and having a look around the command centre there. I thought I might ask Grace to meet me afterwards. It would be nice to have something to prod her with. Does anything come to mind?'

'Well, it's perhaps somewhat tangential, but we understand that Ulrike Schmidt, whom we knew as Inge, the young woman who was Steve Percival's contact and who was arrested and given a custodial sentence for her part in Müller's exfiltration – has, somewhat surprisingly, been included in the latest batch of dissidents ransomed by the West German government.'

'Well, that is odd. They don't normally let people out so quickly.'

'It is not unknown, ma'am, especially when Honecker's D-Mark account is running low.'

'Good. Please let me have a report and, in particular, any information on what motivated our friends in relation to – what was her name? Ah, yes – Ulrike.'

'Certainly, ma'am.'

Sheena – Kennington – Tuesday

STEVE RANG THE DOORBELL of the imposing house in Kennington, to which Sheena Ferguson had invited him. A few moments later the door opened to reveal Sheena's smiling face, not an expression he associated with her, based on their two previous meetings.

'Steve, so nice to see you. Come in.'

Steve stepped into the spacious but gloomy entrance hall.

He held out, somewhat bashfully, the posy of flowers he had brought. Sheena whisked them out of his hands. 'How lovely! Thank you, we'll deal with those later. First, let me give you a hug.'

Sheena was not a large woman, but she was a commanding presence, and Steve meekly submitted to her embrace.

Letting go of him, she pointed to a door on the left. 'You can hang your coat up in there; we're in the drawing room on the right.'

Having deposited his coat, Steve followed her through to the drawing room, wondering who else was there. But he soon realised that the first person plural pronoun applied just to the two of them, and, possibly, even just to Sheena herself.

'What would you like to drink? A sherry? White wine? A cold beer?'

Steve opted for a glass of white wine, while Sheena served herself a small glass of sherry. She pointed to the sofa, invited him to sit and then settled into a small armchair next to the fire.

'I am so sorry that I haven't been in touch sooner.'

'Sheena, I didn't expect you to be. But I am grateful for all you did when I got back from Germany.'

'And how have you been since then?'

'I've been okay. I still occasionally think that Mavis is on an overseas posting and she'll be back soon. It's always a shock to realise that she won't be.'

'I know exactly what you mean. But you've moved back into the flat?'

'Yes, I haven't changed anything in it. So it looks just the same as it did when she was alive.'

'Steve, you can't keep it as a shrine.'

'I know. I did get a girlfriend to help me take Mavis's clothes to a charity shop.'

'Is that the young actress who starred in your play?'

'Yes, Becky. We've been together since I left Cambridge. Her acting career has been going from strength to strength recently. She is appearing as Rosalind in a long run of *As You Like It* at Stratford. So I've seen very little of her. In fact she phoned me the other day to say that she's fallen in love with her co-lead and feels that it's a good moment to end our relationship.'

'I'm sorry to hear that, Steve. *Fie on Orlando!*'

'Even without Orlando's entrance, I'd been coming to the conclusion that the relationship had run its course.'

'I do hope you are not brooding too much.'

'No, I'm pretending to write a novel.'

'Pretending?'

'Well, I'm not sure if that's what it actually is.'

'But this is as distinct from poetry and drama, which are forms you've already had some success with?'

'I'm not sure that success is quite the word I would choose.'

'Artistic success is a relative concept. What do you do to keep the wolf from the door?'

'I live pretty frugally and, thanks to arrangements made by the department, my outgoings are minimal. But I've also got a job as a sub-editor on a rock music magazine. It's essentially beer money, but I'm learning a useful skill.'

'You have probably realised that there is an ulterior motive behind my concern, acting *in loco parentis*, for how you're keeping body and soul together.'

'I wondered.'

'To an extent, you are already on our books, but I would like to make it a little more formal.'

'What would that involve?'

'Several things. Firstly, I would like you to re-establish contact with Grace Mitchell and Professor Müller.'

'I thought Grace was keeping an eye on Müller. Wasn't that the whole idea of getting me out of the picture?'

'You are correct. Grace is doing her best, but Müller is a wily old devil. He refuses to cohabit with her, says he prefers his rooms in St Rad's, pretends to prefer the monastic peace it affords him. I think that Grace is perhaps a little overawed by his academic pre-eminence and is failing to keep close tabs on him. I would welcome an independent view of what is going on there as a useful corrective to the bland reports we are currently receiving. There is no need to rush into action. Try and find a natural way to resume contact.'

'Okay.'

'Secondly, I need someone who can keep an eye on Collingwood.'

'Surely you don't have any doubts about Jeremy?'

'No one's above suspicion in our world, Steve. There are some worries about leaks in the organisation. There always are, of course.'

'Jeremy's hardly likely to confide in me.'

'Not directly, of course, but people often give themselves away by forgetting what they're not meant to know or by saying something which conflicts with an earlier statement.'

'But I like Jeremy. It will feel awkward.'

'If it's any consolation, I'll be asking him to do the same to you.'

'I have no secrets.'

'No one has *no* secrets, Steve. That is the first lesson to learn.'

Steve thought but dared not say that the axiom must also apply to Sheena herself. From the glint in her eye, he had little doubt that she had intuited the direction of his thoughts. Feeling even less at ease than he had been on his arrival, he said, 'Of course, I have what might be considered personal secrets. I meant secrets of a state security nature.'

'I'm glad you made that clarification. Even so, sometimes the two realms overlap or intermingle. That is often where it all goes wrong.'

'What would I have to do?'

'Just see Collingwood socially. Invite him out for a drink. Jeremy is a bit of a loner and that worries me. If you become aware that he frequents certain clubs, let us say, or there is evidence of a friend who we know nothing about, please let me know. Above all, be his friend.'

'Maybe Jeremy would misinterpret my interest in him.'

'I'm not suggesting you go to bed with him unless you particularly want to. Once again, I just want you to mention to me anything that seems out of the ordinary.'

'How do I report to you without going through Jeremy himself?'

'I will give you my direct line. Please memorise it. Do not put it in your notebook. If you are unable to come round, please leave a message on my answering machine. You will call yourself Leslie for such purposes. If I call you, I will be Georgia.'

She had him repeat her private number several times to memorise it. 'Good, I will soon be asking Jeremy to brief you on a particular matter. He is a very willing workhorse, but he is not entirely in his element in certain situations.'

Steve wasn't sure what Sheena was referring to. He didn't suppose that Jeremy would be much cop in a shoot-out, but Steve himself would be even less of a dead-eye Dick.

'I can't think of any situation in which my abilities would be superior to Jeremy's.'

'With the young ladies, my dear.'

Embarrassed and bashful, Steve said, 'Oh, I see what you mean…'

'You two make a good team. And, yes, Jeremy is much more experienced other than in that one particular. It is quite hard to fake such matters.'

'Does that mean you foresee something of the sort coming to pass?'

'It is quite likely.'

'I'm not sure I did particularly well last time. If I may be candid, I had some difficulty performing initially. I think nerves and tension played a part.'

'You men are fragile creatures, so it's brave of you to admit it. But I have to tell you from years of dealing with agents that it's the ones who feel the fear that are the best. The thick-skinned ones tend not to last long. I admit that one does not expect to be having this conversation with one's ward, but you are a grown man. And one who has a winning way with women.'

'Sheena, I can probably revive friendly relations with Grace and Dieter and see Jeremy socially, but I am reluctant to be deployed as the British equivalent of a Stasi Romeo.'

'Of course, and it may not come to that. But it is helpful that you are no longer bound to Becky. I do not need a reply right now. You have until Friday to decide. Ring me on the number you have just memorised. If I am not available, leave a message with your decision. Furthermore, neither of us will mention this *tête-à-tête* to Collingwood. Please confirm that you understand that.'

Steve did not feel comfortable about deceiving Jeremy, but in practice he really had no option but to agree to her request. 'Yes, of course.'

'Good. And, in fact, it would be useful if you could maintain the somewhat truculent manner that we have come to expect from you when you are at the office, despite the rapprochement that you and I have reached this evening.'

Steve was faintly amused that he had a reputation for being truculent, but Sheena was making a mistake if she thought he was so easily won over. On the other hand, ought he to take her concerns about Collingwood seriously. He would have to tread carefully. 'That should be easy enough.'

Sheena laughed and rose from her chair. 'And now we are going to stop all this shop talk and have a pleasant evening. Let us go next door. I have prepared a Boeuf Stroganoff and selected one of my favourite wines from the cellar.'

She then embarked on what amounted to an elaborate piece of supper-table theatre by decanting the wine which Steve noticed was a 1966 Haut-Brion into a heavy cut-glass decanter. Whether the use of a candle to check for sediment was entirely necessary or not, it was beyond doubt that the Haut-Brion was intense and startling on the palate.

After he had savoured the first mouthful, Sheena asked him to describe it excluding the usual referents for Haut-Brion like blackcurrant and leather. All he could come up with was that it had the taste of the aroma of a cigar, a necessary circumlocution since he had never actually smoked a cigar. She was evidently pleased with his effort and told him that she would make an oenophile of him yet.

The dish, which she had prepared herself, was delicious, the cream, mushroom and paprika expertly balanced. After the main course, she produced a platter of cheeses and walnuts, insisting he have a small glass of port with the cheese. Having retrieved a bottle of Graham's 1963 from a cabinet, she assured him he'd find it far superior to anything he might have had at St Rad's. She'd been keeping it for a special occasion such as this. She poured two glasses and then proposed a toast to the memory of Steve's mother and her own former lover. Noticing the tear in his eye, she reached out and squeezed his hand. He felt immensely grateful to her and profoundly sad at the same time.

She allowed him time to compose himself and then said, 'Let's move back to the drawing room.'

Steve followed her through to the drawing room with its high ceilings, dark panelled walls, lamplight catching the gilt edges of maritime paintings and dusty glass. Steve stood by the window, glass of port in hand, listening to the tick of the longcase clock. The aroma of beef, cream and paprika still hung in the air, softened now by wood polish and the faint mineral edge of a smouldering fire.

Sheena crossed the room with feline certainty to the mahogany sideboard – a piece of furniture so large and solid it almost seemed to be a structural element of the house. She unlocked and pulled open a narrow drawer, revealing a wooden humidor lined with cedar. The scent rose instantly: a hint of leather and summer hay.

'Could I offer you a cigar?'

Steve smiled. 'I wouldn't know what to do with it.'

'That's fine, but I hope you don't mind if I smoke. It is my evening ritual.'

'Not at all.'

She selected a torpedo-shaped cigar from the humidor; it seemed far too big for such a small woman. She handled it with something approaching reverence. Laying it on a small silver tray, she picked up a guillotine cutter, placed the cigar inside the aperture, and with a clean, practiced motion, sliced off the end.

Next she eased off the band – the decorative label bearing a fleur-de-lys design in red and gold – by rolling the cigar between her fingers to loosen the glue. Holding the cigar to her nose, she closed her eyes and inhaled. Satisfied with her choice, she struck a flame from a small lighter. Rotating the cigar slowly, she began to toast it, making sure not to let the flame of the lighter come into direct contact with it. When the tip had finally begun to glow, she put the cigar to her lips and drew in a mouthful of smoke, savouring its aroma, before exhaling slowly, letting the smoke drift upwards.

'I've always found cigars more honest than people, particularly Montecristo cigars,' she said. 'They burn predictably, and you know when they're finished.'

Steve took a sip of his port and said nothing. What could he possibly say? No one could accuse Steve of being particularly reliable. The room, for a moment, was nothing but smoke and silence.

Sheena lowered herself into an armchair by the fire, crossing her legs in a manly fashion. The cigar was now fully lit, its tip glowing softly with each draw. She held the cigar near the base, fingers lightly apart, taking care not to let the ash fall onto her clothes. Her other hand rested along the carved arm of the chair, a ring on her right ring finger glinting under the lamplight. She invited Steve to sit.

Once he was settled into the chair she had indicated, she caught his gaze and, smiling faintly, said, 'Do I disgust you?'

Taken aback, Steve blinked. 'Not at all.'

'I don't mean the cigar smoking.'

'I know what you mean and, no, you don't.'

'But you must find the thought that your mother and I were lovers distasteful.'

'I really don't. I'm glad she finally found someone she could love.'

'Well, I am grateful for your words, even if I don't entirely believe them.'

'Sheena, we hardly know each other. You are a powerful person. I am your subordinate. We have not had much time to develop the relationship. Things will probably get easier as time goes by. I might even ask you to introduce me to the mystery of cigars.'

Sheena smiled. 'Now that is a project I would enjoy; I may well hold you to it.'

Later, as he was taking his leave, she said she had something she'd like to give him. It was a small photograph in a silver frame of Mavis and Sheena holding hands. He was touched by the gesture but felt awkward about taking the photograph. It was as if he were intruding on a private moment but Sheena insisted. He also felt she was using the photograph to bind him to her, which troubled him more than a little. And yet it had been a memorable evening. He'd felt flattered by the attention she'd given him and impressed by how open she was about her sexuality.

As he stepped onto the street, he looked back at the tiny but powerful woman, Montecristo cigar still in her right hand, standing on the threshold of her impressive house. She gave an almost Churchillian wave and called out, 'Remember, I need your reply by close of play this Friday.'

Steve waved weakly in acknowledgement and realised in the same moment that he would do what Sheena had asked. She had in effect done a number on him.

Sheena & Grace – Cambridge – Wednesday

SHEENA FERGUSON TAPPED THE ash from the tip of her small cigar into the ashtray on the table of the Cambridge wine bar, in which she and Grace Mitchell were sitting. 'Thank you, Grace, for agreeing to meet me at such short notice. I have been attending a security conference in Cambridge to discuss arrangements in the event of a nuclear war. You are probably aware that Cambridge is one of the regional command centres.'

Grace sipped her glass of white wine. 'I had heard something of the sort, but I am not sure that gives me a great deal of comfort.'

'Unfortunately, some of us have to think the unthinkable.'

'Well, I am sure you are not here to seek my views on how best to preserve scholarly life after the apocalypse.'

'Indeed, I am here to see how you are getting on with Professor Müller, and to update you on one or two developments in that connection.'

'As you know, he declined my offer to lodge with me.'

'Were you not able to offer him the service he was used to in East Berlin?'

'I'm considerably older than the female graduate students he lorded it over at Humboldt.'

'But, if I may say so, you have lost none of your charms. Admittedly, that's from a female perspective. Was he resistant or were his tastes somewhat recondite?'

'It is not for want of trying, I can assure you. But he is getting on a bit and is having trouble in that regard. He really just wants me to get my clothes off and stroll around. Occasionally, it triggers something, and then I do whatever is necessary to make him feel there is still life in the old dog.'

'Ah, men, such simple creatures.'

'Dieter is complex in other ways.'

'Indeed, and the opportunity to have you strolling around in the buff has not persuaded him to move in with you?'

'I think he prefers the cloistered life and High Table conversation at St Rad's, with only the occasional foray to Glisson Road. Despite our best efforts, women are still regarded as intrusive at the older colleges.'

'Fools – they will soon come to regret their primitive attitudes.'

'Well, Sheena, I can't believe that is the real reason you have sought me out.'

'You are correct. It has come to my attention that Dieter has been in touch with the West German government, and has per-suaded them to ransom Steve Percival's contact – the young wo-man we knew as Inge – from the DDR. Has Müller made any mention of it?'

'No.'

'The girl has been released and is recovering at her aunt's in Frankfurt. She apparently suffered some harsh treatment. I imagine the Stasi assumed she would be with them for some considerable time.'

'Oh, poor girl. What persuaded them to change their minds?'

'Lots of D-Marks is usually the reason. If Müller has indeed been involved in any way or if the girl tries to contact him, I'd like to know. We believe that she will try to make contact with Steve Percival, which may lead to Steve getting in touch with you. I know things ended badly there, but I'd like you to assist Steve.'

'In what way?'

'In helping him bring Müller and the girl together. You never know: if things go well, you might find you no longer have to be so attentive to Müller.'

Grace & Müller – Cambridge – Thursday

MÜLLER HEAVED HIMSELF OFF Grace's supine body. 'I'm sorry, my dear, that was rather unsatisfactory.'

'Oh, nonsense, Dieter. It doesn't have to be fireworks every time.'

'It's very kind of you to say so, but I don't think it's ever been fireworks during the time we've been together.'

'I can assure you that you attended to my needs more than adequately. I am sorry that I was unable to do the same for you.'

'And I can assure you simply seeing you in your naked beauty is joy enough.'

'It's lovely of you to say so, but I'm not sure I believe you. I have put on quite a lot of weight in the last year, since I gave up running.'

'I cannot agree. And if you have, it suits you. Your curves are sublime.'

Grace laughed. 'There was a time when I longed for curves. For many years, they were only implicit, and then suddenly I was Rubenesque.'

'Well, this older male is not complaining.'

'Would you care for a postcoital cup of tea?'

'What I'd really like is a cigar, but your British doctors have forbidden it.'

'Coitus or smoking?'

'Both, in effect, but smoking absolutely. So, a cup of tea would be very welcome and much more refined.'

Grace put her robe on and returned a few minutes later with a tray bearing teapot, milk jug and cups. As they were sipping their tea, Müller said, 'I had a surprising letter today.'

'From anyone I know?'

'I don't think you know her, but I do think you know *of* her. She was known to your people as Inge, although her name is actually Ulrike.'

Grace thought it best not to let on that she had had some forewarning of this fact. 'I'm not sure what you mean by *your people*.'

'Come, come, my dear, I know you have been asked to watch me. When we first met at poor Mavis's funeral, everyone in the congregation was a member of the intelligence community.'

'I was there as the girlfriend of the deceased's son.'

'True enough, a son who was already following in his mother's footsteps. Perhaps it will not entirely surprise you to learn that Mavis mentioned you to me before she died, not by name, but everything else she said about her son's lover is you.'

'It seems rather unprofessional of her to have spoken to you in that way.'

'Remember, we had known each other when we were idealistic young lovers just after the war. Anyway, we used to meet at Ulrike's flat. Normally, Ulrike would absent herself and let us get on with renewing our relationship. But inevitably there came a time when Mavis and Ulrike coincided in my absence and they became friends.'

'When you say *friends*, you mean something intimate?'

'Yes.'

'How do you know this?'

'Mavis confided in me shortly before she died.'

'Why tell me this now?'

'Well, Ulrike was arrested shortly after I got out and, after a period of interrogation, given a custodial sentence. From what I've heard, she was traced through a couple of blunders of Steve's while in East Berlin.'

'Like what?'

'He left some D-Marks in her room. The Grepo had noted the serial number and Steve had a receipt in his wallet from the bar he and Ulrike met in, which was confiscated on his exit from the DDR.'

'Oh, poor Steve. He must feel terrible.'

'I'm not sure he knows.'

'How do *you* know then?'

'Don't worry, I'm not being controlled by a Stasi handler. It was in the letter from Ulrike.'

'But surely she wouldn't want to put such details in a letter from prison?'

'Ulrike is no longer in prison. She was writing from her aunt's in Frankfurt am Main. When she was being considered for ransom, the West German government contacted me and asked me to vouch for her, which I was happy to do. I told them she was a brilliant student with a bright future – and that is true. Once she was released, they gave her my address and now she has written to me.'

'So she has been free for only a short while?'

'That is correct. She said that now she was a West German citizen she hoped to continue her studies with me in Great Britain and wondered if I might be able to put her up until she had worked out some way of affording a place of her own. I, of course, said that was impossible. I live in a men-only college and, since I have no formal teaching role, I could not supervise her studies. But for other reasons, which I'd rather not go into, I do not want to have a close personal relationship with her again. You are more than enough for me.'

'So why are you telling me all this, given that you know I have been asked to keep an eye on you? This puts me in a difficult position.'

'Because Ulrike is a brilliant intellect and the person who ought to be her teacher is you.'

'I'm not sure how I could do that without her being a member of the university and therefore a member of a college.'

'Well, I suppose all I'm asking for in the first place is that you agree to meet her and assess her suitability as a PhD candidate.'

'Does that mean she's going to turn up on my doorstep?'

'Not unexpectedly. I have given her Steve's contact details.'

'I didn't know you knew them.'

'Doyle obliged me.'

'I am hoping that he will keep her at arm's length from me, but agree to introduce her to you.'

'Don't you think you ought to warn Steve, not least because she knew him as Tom?'

'I imagine she has figured that out by now.'

'Dieter, this seems a little improper and rather convoluted.'

'Grace, don't prejudge her. Just agree to talk to her. Whether you decide to pass this on to your masters or warn Steve is up to you.'

The most worrying aspect of Müller's words was that Sheena seemed to have had some foreknowledge of what was afoot. And she had explicitly asked to be informed if Grace got wind of such developments from Müller, and to assist Steve in bringing Müller and the girl together. So she would have to report back to Sheena the following day.

But what did Sheena hope to achieve by facilitating the reunion of Müller, Steve and Ulrike? She seldom did anything without some wider strategic purpose in mind. Nor would it be easy to persuade Müller to countenance a meeting with the girl, given his antipathy to resuming even a pedagogical relationship with his former student. On top of that, Steve and Grace had not been in contact since they had, under pressure from Sheena, ended their relationship. No doubt Steve was still very angry with Grace, in particular for the clumsy and hurtful way that she had acceded to Sheena's pressure. Grace did not relish the thought of being the one to make the first call.

Ginny & Steve – Frognal – Friday

'THANK YOU, STEVE, FOR accepting my invitation.'

'It's lovely to see you, Ginny. So is this the house you and Peter bought when your father died?'

'No, I inherited the house. This is where I grew up.'

'Ainsworth Street must have felt cramped compared to this. I would have thought the entire floorspace there was less than this single room.'

'That doesn't necessarily make living more comfortable. Not that I'm a fan of snug and cosy.'

'So what's this all about?'

'I'll tell you that over a drink. But before that, I'd like you to meet someone.'

Ginny rang a bell. A few moments later, a maid appeared. 'Juanita, please ask Nanny to bring Amelia down if it's a convenient moment.'

'Amelia, your daughter?'

'Yes, I know men are not that interested in babies, but I am inordinately proud of her. It will only be for a few minutes, and then Nanny will whisk her off to bed.'

'Ginny, any child of yours would be of interest to me.'

'Bless you. That's very lovely of you to say so, Steve.'

A few moments later, there was a tap on the door, and a rather prim middle-aged woman entered with a small child in her arms. Once inside, she put the little girl down and said, 'Go and give your Mama a kiss, Amelia.'

The little girl tottered across the room with a smile on her face, arms outstretched. Ginny scooped her up and received her daughter's kiss. She then said, 'Amelia, I want you to meet an old friend of mine. This is Steve. I knew him before you were born. I hope you and he will be friends too.'

Amelia babbled something and buried her head in her mother's chest. Ginny laughed. 'Who's suddenly all shy?'

Amelia peeked out at Steve and then smiled tentatively.

'You're doing well, Steve. Here, why don't you hold her?'

'I'm not very familiar with the technique.'

'You'll get the hang of it.'

Without waiting for his reply, Ginny held Amelia out and placed her in Steve's arms. He was expecting Amelia to protest or struggle to return to her mother. But after a brief moment of doubt, the child decided that Steve was no threat and snuggled into his embrace.

'Oh, Ginny. She's beautiful. She's got your looks. I don't see much of Peter in her.'

'Oh, those traits will probably emerge later. She can certainly be stubborn like him.'

Steve thought that it would be hard to say who was the more stubborn of the two – Peter or Ginny – but refrained from voicing the thought.

He stroked Amelia's head. 'Her skin is so soft, and her hair so fine.'

'She's definitely turning into a little princess. When she was born, she was much more like a frog.'

'How long has she been walking?'

'A couple of months. She can really move quite fast now, which can be rather troublesome for poor Nanny.'

Nanny laughed. 'A nuisance is the last thing Amelia is, ma'am. I have cared for a number of children, as you know, and I can safely say that Amelia is a delight.'

Steve said, 'This is the first time I've ever held a child, but I can completely agree with, er, Nanny.'

He felt uneasy referring to her simply as *Nanny*, but asking her name would likely breach protocol. Before he could dwell on it, Ginny said, 'She loves your voice, Steve. I notice that every time you speak, she quivers with pleasure.'

Whether this was true or not, Steve was absurdly pleased by the observation. But at this point, Amelia twisted around in his arms and reached out for the nanny, who stepped forward and took charge of the little bundle of warmth.

'I'll take her back up to the nursery, ma'am, if that's appropriate.'

'Yes, thank you, Nanny. I know it's already past her bedtime. We don't want her getting into bad habits.'

As the nanny turned and walked towards the door, Steve noticed Amelia peeking over her shoulder. Just before they passed through the doorway, she made a little wave, whether to her mother or her new friend, wasn't entirely clear.

'I'm so glad you got here before she really had to be put to bed. You've made a friend there, Steve. She doesn't take to everyone.'

'She's absolutely delightful, Ginny. I don't know anything about babies, but because she's yours, she feels very special to me.'

Ginny smiled warmly. 'Thank you, Steve. She *is* very special.'

'Does Nanny have a name?'

'Yes, Mary, but it's simpler to call her Nanny. It'll be less confusing for Amelia as she gets older.'

Steve nodded. It was not for him to query why the rich chose to raise their children in this way. The thought of delegating something so intimate felt alien to him, but he had no right to judge. He was just about to let it go when Ginny, smiling wryly, said, 'I'm sure you disapprove, but that's the deal Pete and I made.'

'Of course, I'm not being critical. But if she were mine, I'd want as much time with her as possible.'

'Well, that does you credit, Steve.' Ginny's voice was light, with the faintest hesitation before she went on. 'Dino has prepared us a light supper. It should be ready at six-thirty. In the meantime, what would you like to drink?'

'A glass of white wine would be nice.'

Ginny rang the bell again. Shortly, Juanita reappeared. 'Would you bring up the white wine Dino selected and some caviar with blinis?' she said.

'Of course, ma'am.' Juanita disappeared, and Ginny turned back to Steve with a small smile. 'It's not quite Ainsworth Street, is it?'

Steve chuckled. 'No. Back then, it was more whatever cheap red plonk we could find and a packet of crisps. Are we celebrating anything special?'

'My thirtieth birthday.'

'Your thirtieth? I thought you were younger than that.'

'You've not forgotten how to charm a woman, Steve.'

'I meant it. I didn't even know when your birthday was. We weren't together long enough. I'm sorry I haven't brought you a gift.'

'Steve, you're the best gift I could ask for.'

Steve felt a little uncomfortable. 'I presume Peter will be joining us.'

'I'm afraid not. He's in the States. I didn't want him to change his schedule. He's in the middle of a big deal.'

It was a relief not to have to encounter Peter, but his absence was almost as troubling.

A few minutes later, Juanita returned with a silver tray bearing a small crystal cruet of caviar resting in crushed ice with a mother-of-pearl spoon; a plate of warm blinis; a dish of soured cream; ramekins of finely chopped egg yolk and egg white; and a few lemon wedges. She placed the tray on a side table, left, and re-turned minutes later with a bottle of white Burgundy in a silver cooler, condensation beading its surface.

Ginny picked up the spoon and scooped some caviar onto a blini, adding a touch of soured cream before taking a bite. 'Dino gets terribly distressed if we don't start with caviar. It's an occupational hazard of keeping a French chef.'

Steve laughed. 'From his name, you'd think he was Italian.'

'Actually, he's Australian. Dean, really, but we call him Dino. He trained with Bocuse and also worked for the Troisgros brothers. So he's French by assimilation.'

'Ginny, this is a very different world from the one I'm used to.'

Steve watched her load another blini with caviar and soured cream, briefly hesitating before following suit. The taste was extraordinary, rich and briny, silk on his tongue. He glanced at the bottle, noticing the words *Puligny-Montrachet* before Ginny reached forward and turned it slightly away.

'I know. It's nonsense really, but nice to share with friends. What do you think?' she asked, her eyes sparkling with amusement.

Steve swallowed. 'Delicious, strangely familiar.'

Something flickered in her expression, as though she understood exactly what he meant.

She took a sip of her wine. 'I'm sorry I haven't been in touch sooner. I hear things didn't end well with Grace, and you moved back into your mother's flat?'

'Who did you hear that from?'

'Jude. She continues to make herself indispensable at Inflexion Books. She's with Peter on the trip to the American Booksellers Association convention.'

Steve was well aware of Peter's reputation. 'Does that worry you?'

'It doesn't worry me. I have no real problem with Jude. She tells me every time she succumbs. But I don't suppose you really want to hear that, do you?'

No, he didn't. Absurdly, he'd been allowing himself to think that Jude was keeping herself for him. But why on earth should she? He had made absolutely no commitment to her. 'I haven't heard from her since the day Grace kicked me out. I went round to see Jude. I thought she might let me stay with her for a while, but she wasn't keen on the idea. I was feeling a bit sorry for myself at the time.'

'She was right. She is a refreshingly direct woman.'

'Even if she and Peter are having a thing?'

'I don't think she'll let it get out of hand. In the end, both she and Pete are more interested in making money. They get more of a thrill from that than from a furtive clinch.'

At that moment, Juanita re-entered and announced that supper was ready. Steve followed Ginny through to the dining room, admiring her figure and catching a trace of her perfume – jasmine with a back note of something darker.

Two places were set on opposite sides of a long dining table. Juanita had followed them in with the wine. 'Is the white okay for you, Steve?'

'Perfect.'

They took their seats and Ginny indicated that Juanita should fill the glasses. Steve noticed that there was a menu card by his place setting. He glanced at it. It was decidedly French. The first item was an *amuse bouche*, *Gougères*, which were helpfully described in Dino's note as delicate cheese puffs, warm from the oven, infused with a hint of Comté.

Steve popped it in his mouth. It was an airy but delicious nothing. Dabbing the crumbs from his lips with a napkin, he said, 'Do you eat like this every day?'

Ginny despatched her own airy nothing and said, 'No, mostly it's cottage pie or spaghetti bolognese, admittedly with a Dino twist. This is a special meal to celebrate my birthday and an excuse for you to meet Amelia.'

'I wish you'd told me. I haven't brought anything for you, nor for Amelia, and I don't feel I've dressed for the occasion properly.'

'Steve, you look fine and your presence is gift enough.'

Juanita brought in the starter, a langoustine salad with fennel and segments of blood orange.

'So Jude wouldn't have you, but I'm sure there were other takers.'

Steve laughed. 'I wouldn't say they were lining up. Actually, I got together with Becky, the girl who played Freya in my play. She's been using my flat as a London base. I went up to Stratford to see her in *As You Like It* recently and she informed me she'd met someone else. Not entirely surprising.'

'And now there's a vacancy in Steve Percival's heart?'

'There's no vacancy, Ginny. My heart belongs to you. Anyone else will always be a substitute.'

'But you know we can never be together.'

'I know. I've accepted that, but I've learned to enjoy those fleeting moments when we are together.'

'Like now?'

'I have no expectations. I am not going to ask why it has to be like this. I am just happy to be here with you.'

'As I am happy to be with you. But I hope you do not deny yourself between times.'

'One's not entirely in control of these things, but I'm getting on well with Sally, one of my colleagues at *Buzz*. Not that we've quite got to that stage yet.'

'Come on, Steve. I thought you were quicker off the mark than that.'

Juanita cleared the starter plates and brought the main course which Steve saw from the menu card was pan-seared sea bass, baby carrots, *haricots verts*, and zucchini.

'I'm sure that even with a nanny, looking after a small child and running a place like this doesn't leave you with much time for anything else, but I was wondering whether you had kept on with your art.'

'As a matter of fact, I have.'

'I'm so glad to hear it.'

'After dinner, I will show you my studio.'

'I look forward to that.'

'And what about you, I hope you are still writing.'

'Well, I am, but I'm not sure what it is. It's supposed to be a novel, but it doesn't feel like a novel. Also the job is full-time, nine to five, well ten to six mostly.'

'I'm pretty certain that's not all you're up to, Steve. I sense you're tangled up in something complex. If you're ever stuck or can't see a way out, please think of confiding in me. I doubt I will have an axe to grind in whatever world you're involved in. And I also have a vested interest in you. I am here to help.'

Ginny had always had a way of reading his thoughts and unsettling him with her enigmatic comments. He couldn't for one moment imagine what her vested interest in him was, though he would have welcomed her advice on how to handle Sheena's proposal. She would undoubtedly have despatched his temporizing in short order. But something told him to let the purpose of her unexpected and sudden invitation to supper become more apparent before offering too many hostages to fortune.

Juanita cleared the fish course and asked Ginny what she'd like to drink with the dessert. 'I think we'll each have a small glass of demi-sec Vouvray.'

The dessert was apple tart with whipped vanilla cream or *Tarte Fine aux Pommes avec Crème Légère à la Vanille* as it was described on the menu card.

Over their coffees, after the table had been cleared, Ginny said, 'Let me show you the work I've been doing in my studio.'

When the cab had dropped Steve off, the sweeping driveway and the dark bulk of the building in the gloaming had made it clear that Ginny and Peter's home was large. But now as he followed her through to the back of the house, he realised that it was even bigger than he had imagined. They reached a door to the back garden. She unlocked it and said, 'It's out here. I had it built in the garden as a place for me to escape to. I also had this covered walkway built, so that I can get out there even in bad weather. Otherwise it's really just a garden room.'

She unlocked the door to the studio and switched on the lights. Steve looked around. Calling it a garden room was a serious understatement. The studio was a sleek wooden and glass modernist structure. At the back of the room was a large cabinet whose shelves were loaded with materials and against which canvases were propped. At one end of the main space was a dais covered with drapes. The wall behind the dais had a large velvet curtain hanging from a brass curtain pole. In the centre of the room was a wooden easel with a canvas on it, which bore the image of a standing female nude, blocked out in neutral tones. At the other end was a daybed and a low table.

Steve said, 'What a fabulous space. And I see you're working with a live model.'

'Yes. That's mainly what I do now. I had the studio built so it faces away from the house, which means my models can relax with their clothes off without feeling they're being observed from the house. There's a lavatory and shower through there and a space where they can undress and leave their clothes.'

'May I look at some of the more finished work?'

'Of course, help yourself. In fact, I will just use the lavatory while you're doing that.'

Ginny went through to the room at the back and Steve flipped through the canvases. When Ginny returned, Steve said, 'Ginny, this work is fantastic.'

'Thank you, Steve, but enough of admiring my daubings. Please unzip my dress.'

As ever, Ginny had the power to perturb Steve. 'Not here, Ginny.'

Ginny laughed. 'It's a little chilly outside for what I have in mind.'

'But someone might see us.'

'As I explained, no one can see in. And even if they could, I don't care. Come on, Steve. I thought we'd got past this stage a long time ago. Anyway, you owe me a birthday present.'

Suddenly, Steve was determined not to be bashful. He unzipped her dress and as she let it drop he reached around with both hands and caressed her breasts through her flimsy bra. She turned around, unbuttoned his shirt and ran her hands over his chest. 'I'm glad to see you've been keeping yourself in shape.'

A little later as they lay on the daybed with a throw over them, Ginny said, 'That's exactly the kind of birthday present I was hoping for. Thank you.'

'Will Nanny and Juanita know I'm still here?'

'Probably, it's still rather early. Nanny has a bedroom and sitting room at the top of the house next to the nursery and Juanita has a flat in the basement. Dino will already be out on the town. But so what? Even if they do suspect something, they work for me, not Peter. Anyway, Peter doesn't have a leg to stand on. As I mentioned, he's been busy blotting his own copybook.'

'That doesn't surprise me.'

'I'm sorry that I mentioned who his partner in crime was.'

'I don't feel regretful about Jude. At one stage I did think she might be the one, but time has passed and one gets involved with other people.'

'Becky until recently, it seems?'

'Yes.'

'If I remember her from the play, a very pert young woman.'

'Exactly that. Not much mystery there, but fun while it lasted.'

'It sounds to me as if you're getting the hang of this.'

'I wouldn't say that. I'm in a bit of a pickle at the moment.'

'Can you tell me about it?'

'It's a long story.'

'The longer, the better, but in that case I think we need some refreshment. I will ask Juanita to bring a bottle of champagne over.'

'That sounds nice. I'll just get dressed.'

'No need to get dressed. I'm not suggesting you flaunt yourself, though. She will be discreet.'

'Okay, if you're sure. It's all a bit out of my comfort zone.'

'You'll get used to it.'

Ginny rose from the daybed, went over to an intercom by the door of the studio, and asked Juanita to bring over a bottle of Pol Roger and a couple of ordinary white wine glasses. The sight of a naked Ginny walking nonchalantly back to the daybed outweighed by far any potential embarrassment consequent on his own state of undress. Not many minutes after she had rejoined him under the throw, there was a tap on the door of the studio and Juanita came in carrying a silver tray bearing glasses and a bottle of champagne.

'Thank you, Juanita. Just put it on the table. You can finish for the evening now. I will lock up.'

Juanita nodded silently, but flashed what seemed to be a sympathetic smile at Steve, who was attempting, not very successfully, to make himself invisible.

Once Juanita had retreated, Ginny said, 'Please do the honours, Steve.'

Steve knew he would be inviting ridicule if he dressed even partially before attending to the champagne and so strode as purposefully as a naked man can across the room and, removing the foil and wire cage, popped the cork and poured the creamy, foaming liquid into the glasses on the tray.

He brought them over to the daybed and handed one to Ginny. Clinking his glass against Ginny's, he took a sip, enjoying the biscuity flavour and the soft bubbles, before climbing back in beside her.

Ginny, having tasted the champagne, nodded appreciatively and placed her glass on the low table behind their heads.

'Right, I want the whole story. No holding back.'

Steve told her about how Grace had asked him to help her have a child. He then moved on to the news of his mother's accident and his trip to West Berlin, the encounter with Inge in East Berlin, and how it had come about. He also told her how sexy it had been, but how anxiety or fear had impaired his performance to begin with. She had laughed joyfully at the details that Steve provided. He told her about Müller and Collingwood. He even told her about Sheena, the nature of her job, the quasi-pastoral relationship she had assumed towards Steve and the way that she had broken up his relationship with Grace, at which point she said, 'When did Grace know I was pregnant?'

'Not until the first night of the play.'

'Although you already knew, when we had that little fling at the Great Eastern.'

'I didn't think it was for me to tell anyone about your news. I also thought it might upset Grace. She and Peter had rowed about having children. His position wasn't that it was the wrong time; he just didn't want to be a parent. So if the first thing that happens when you and he get together is that you become pregnant, you can see how Grace might consider that a slap in the face.'

'Yes, I do. And I had no idea that was the deal between you and her. You didn't mention it at the Great Eastern. I must say you have exercised extreme discretion in both directions. I congratulate you. But in the pesky way of these things, perhaps it would have been better, had you been more open, both to me and Grace.'

'But surely that would have resulted in upset all round.'

'You may be right, but life cannot be lived without plentiful helpings of upset. I am not criticising you here. I'm the one who is at fault. I knew that I had lost you to Grace even when we were together in Ainsworth Street.'

Steve was enjoying being reunited with Ginny, but he felt her justification for going off with Peter didn't hold up to scrutiny. 'How could you have known? Grace and I were not together. I didn't sleep with her until some time after you had moved out. And that was just a one-night stand until several months later, when she came up with the idea of asking me to be her donor. She made it clear that she didn't expect me to hang around forever, although she did want me to acknowledge my paternity of the child.'

'I knew, Steve, in the way I know things. What I did was not very nice to someone as kind and loving as you. But, for reasons that are impossible for me to go into, I felt I had to yield to Peter's pursuit of me.'

'I didn't know he was pursuing you.'

'I know. Let's not go too deeply into that aspect of the situation. But had you told me in the Great Eastern that Grace had asked you to be the father of her child, I would have insisted you tell her that you were already the father of my child.'

It took a moment for Steve to register what Ginny had just said. Haltingly, he said, 'I'm not Amelia's father.'

'I'm pleased to say that you are. Peter couldn't have been her father. He'd had a vasectomy several years previously. He didn't tell Grace and that was why he couldn't give her a child, even if he'd wanted to, which he didn't.'

'But then he must know that he's not Amelia's father.'

'He does.'

'And does he know that I'm the father?'

'Yes, he knows that too.'

'I can't imagine Peter agreeing to something like that.'

'He was initially pretty pissed off and wanted me to have an abortion. But I explained to him that my father would free me from the terms of the trust he'd set up to control my access to his wealth if he understood that I was expecting Peter's child and that we would get married as soon as he got his divorce from Grace.'

'So you deceived your father?'

'A little, although what my father really wanted was that I marry a man of whom he approved. And he very much approved of Peter. I understood that as soon as I met Peter. I'm afraid he would never have approved of you, Steve.'

Steve gave a sullen laugh. 'Well, thanks.'

'That's not what I think, Steve. I infinitely prefer you. But I was locked in a battle with my father.'

'You could have told me.'

'I couldn't. It would have broken us.'

'But hasn't it anyway?'

'Is this being broken?'

'Well, not at the moment.'

'And you are the father of my lovely daughter.'

'Whom I've only met for the first time today.'

'I accept that. But I promise you I will involve you more. It just needed careful handling.'

'I don't know. I'm finding it hard to adjust to this.'

Ginny got up, slipped her dress over her head and scooped up her underwear. Steve looked bemused. 'What's happening?'

'It's getting cold. We'll go up to my bedroom. You're staying with me tonight, and we're going to sort this out.'

'I'm not sure that's a good idea, Ginny.'

'Pshaw. Get your togs on and follow me. And don't forget the bottle.'

Back in the house, Ginny asked Steve to wait while she locked the doors and switched off the lights. He sat down and reflected on the revelations of earlier. The truth of the matter was that he wasn't sure how he felt about being Amelia's father or indeed whether it was even true.

How probable was it that Peter would agree to such a thing? He did not strike Steve as the kind of man who would accept another man's child, even if it granted him access to enormous wealth. And what did Ginny expect Steve to do with this knowledge? He could hardly pop up once a year on Amelia's birthday or take a close interest in her education with the saturnine Peter in residence. Perhaps Ginny was simply trying to bind Steve to her. But if so, surely she must realise that he was already bound?

On the other hand, if what she was saying really was true, it was certainly ironic. In the closing stages of their relationship, sexual relations between them had been limited, and yet she had conceived. By contrast he and Grace had subsequently taken an extremely methodical but, as it turned out, futile approach to their attempts to beget a child, a fact which he had in some way felt was his fault. He wished now that he'd asked Ginny when she'd first discovered that Peter had had the vasectomy. Or was that also part of the deception?

In the many conversations Steve had had with Grace on the subject of her becoming pregnant, she had never once mentioned Peter having had a vasectomy. She had simply said that he had been adamantly opposed to her longstanding desire to be a mother. Which admittedly squared with Ginny's assertion that Peter hadn't told Grace. Nor, with the way things currently stood with Grace, was Steve in a position to corroborate the matter.

Even if they had been on speaking terms, any such question now risked revealing the fact that Steve was the father of Ginny's child. Given Grace's reaction to the revelation of Ginny's pregnancy the previous year, which Steve felt had been the decisive factor in bringing his and Grace's relationship to an end, one could only imagine her reaction to the news that Amelia was Steve's daughter. No, this was one of those things that Steve was going to have to keep under his hat if, in furtherance of Sheena's wishes, he and Grace resumed friendly relations. Not that he had yet given much thought to how this was going to be managed. Not for the first time, it seemed to Steve that he was a mere plaything between the women in his life.

A short while later, front door locked, downstairs lights extinguished, Ginny ushered Steve into her bedroom. As with the parts of the house that Steve had already seen, the room was understatedly elegant, although there were one or two signs of the hippie style that Steve associated with Ginny as well as some striking examples of her own work.

Steve was fascinated to be allowed once again into Ginny's inner sanctum, but also a little apprehensive. Supposing Peter returned unexpectedly? 'Won't Peter realise I've been here?'

'I doubt it. The housekeeper will have changed the sheets long before he's back. Anyway, he only comes in here when he's feeling a bit sex-starved, which is not often these days. Mostly he sticks to his own room.'

Steve wanted to say that he was sorry to hear that. But that would have been absurd. He wasn't in the least sorry. It just seemed a pity that Peter and Ginny's relationship had become cold and unloving.

Ginny pointed to a door. 'That's the *en suite*. Let's have a bath together and start again.'

Steve remembered when they used to have baths together, in the days when their bathroom was on the ground floor at the back of the little house they had shared.

'Okay, as long as I'm allowed to soap every part of you.'

'I expect no less.'

A quarter of an hour later, cleansed and fragrant with the scent of Floris Rose Geranium Bath Essence, a bath oil that reminded Ginny of her mother (or so Ginny said), she and Steve moved to her bed.

'Let us now attend to other matters.'

'But I need to get home.'

'Stop trying to be somewhere else. You're staying with me to-night.'

Steve knew it was pointless to fight against what she had decided. In truth, he was not struggling that much. 'Okay, you win.'

'That's right, Steve. I have. I do.'

As ever, Steve was completely mystified by the things that Ginny said. How could he not love her?

She kissed him tenderly. 'And remember, Steve, you can have whoever you want – .'

'I want you.'

' – other than me. Choose wisely.'

Week One

4 October – 10 October 1976

MI6 – Borough – Monday

STEVE WAS SITTING IN Sheena Ferguson's office, holding a mug of strong black coffee in both hands. Sheena put down the sheaf of papers she had been reading, and said, 'Thank you for coming in so promptly, Steve. If you don't mind, we'll skip the chit-chat.'

Steve shook his head silently to indicate that he had absolutely no objection to the absence of chit-chat.

Sheena tapped her fingertips together pensively. 'It has come to our attention that a young woman whom you knew in East Berlin as Inge has recently been released from a Stasi jail and has now arrived in London. We think it possible, indeed likely, that she will seek to make contact with you.'

Steve, realising this must have been on Sheena's mind when she invited him to supper, said, 'But why was she in jail? You told me last year you were under the impression she was a Stasi operative.'

Sheena, with just the hint of a raised eyebrow, looked carefully at Steve over her steepled fingers. 'Perhaps we were wrong, but we don't think so.'

'But it's almost impossible to leave the DDR.'

'Not if the DDR actually wants you to leave for some reason, which is often hard currency related, but is also sometimes for reasons of political meddling. And not if the West German state can be persuaded to cough up that hard currency for you.'

'So West Germany has paid a ransom for Inge?'

'Yes, that does seem to be the case.'

'Is she considered that important?'

'That is the problem; she is not. So how is it that she has been included in a batch of much higher-profile dissidents?'

'Her spell in prison was a ruse, and she is on a mission for the external department of the Stasi.'

'In a nutshell. Collingwood is always saying good things about how quick you are.'

'And her task is to hook up with Müller?'

'You really are getting the hang of this.'

'How do I come into this?'

'If she were to immediately set up shop with Müller, it would arouse suspicions. So she needs to have an alternative reason to be here. And that reason is that she fell in love with you that very wet day in East Berlin. In that sense, you're an intermediate step on her way to Müller. They will then reprise their roles for public consumption as eminent intellectual and star student, while getting up to no good on behalf of the Stasi.'

'And it is my job to thwart her?'

'Quite the opposite. It is your job to assist her as plausibly as possible. It is convenient, therefore, that the relationship you have been conducting with the young actress since you left Cambridge has now come to an end.'

'In what way?'

'I am aware that you are what is called successful with women. But I would like you to refrain from finding a substitute for the actress until we have brought this Müller business to a successful conclusion.'

'Are you saying I shouldn't have other girlfriends?'

'Well, that would be the ideal, but I know you may find that an unnatural restriction on your libidinal rights. So what I am saying is that you shouldn't bring other women back to your flat.'

'Are you watching my flat?'

'We're not the only ones. So be sensible. Once we have sorted this matter out, you can have as much pussy as you want.'

Steve was taken aback by Sheena's sudden bluntness and perturbed that his first formal job for the service required him to limit his sexual encounters, the exact inverse of the James Bond model. 'Well, how long is the operation likely to take?'

'No idea. The sooner we can help them get the show on the road, the sooner we can bust them. And while we're on the subject, let us, for the purposes of this conversation, call her Ulrike.'

'Is that her real name?'

'Who knows, but that's what's on her West German passport.'

'How will she find me? She only knows me as Tom, a student of architecture.'

Sheena now broke out in peals of laughter. 'Steve, I think you're underestimating this girl. A frequent error made by male members of the intelligence community. She will find you, have no fear.'

'Sheena…'

'In these offices, you address me as *ma'am*. Understood?'

Shocked by the sudden note of authority in her voice, Steve nodded weakly.

'Good. Now go off and have breakfast with Collingwood and he will tell you more.'

In a much less confident tone of voice, Steve said, 'I've got to get to work.'

Still imperious, Sheena said, 'This is your work. Your role at that toddlers' playground that calls itself a magazine is your cover. So until this operation is over, make sure you hold on to the job. And if your bosses chide you because you are late in today, tell them you've been to the clap clinic. It always works. And when Ulrike does catch up with you, remember to call her Inge, until she has brought you up to date with her current identity.'

Steve was speechless. Sheena rose from her armchair and strode to her desk. Even Collingwood, silent throughout the conversation, was staring at her in amazement.

Without looking up from her desk, Sheena said, 'Don't stand there like a couple of showroom dummies. Go and get reacquainted.'

The two young men looked at each other and stepped silently into the corridor.

Buzz – Soho – Monday

WHEN STEVE ARRIVED AT the *Buzz* offices on the corner of Beak Street and Carnaby Street, the office was certainly not empty. The ad sales people were already working the phones; Leslie and Betty, who comprised the accounts department, were trying to bring some semblance of order to the financial records of Groove Time Ltd, *Buzz*'s publisher; and Nick Harker, the magazine's production manager, was looking mournfully at page layouts for the forthcoming issue with Sally Scott, his assistant. But there was not a single person from the editorial department, which, for a magazine operating in the heady world of the music industry, was only to be expected.

Philip Peterkin, the editor; Jamie Jameson, his deputy; John Gilligan, *Buzz*'s star writer, who single-handedly wrote more than half of those sections of the magazine not commissioned from stringers and freelancers; and Sarah O'Grady, who wrote much of the rest, were nowhere to be seen. All four of them would have been at gigs the previous evening, and then, no doubt, the after-gig ligs, which was when the real work was done, the gathering of tittle-tattle from the nonentities, sycophants and hangers-on who surrounded those artists who were currently in the ascendancy.

Steve, who had been appointed as the magazine's assistant subeditor a few months earlier, liked to think of himself as part of the editorial department, but, in point of fact, his boss was Nick Harker, the production manager. So technically he was a member of the production department. But he sat with the editorial team as did Sally, because it was quicker that way to check on a phrase or point of detail as they worked on the writers' copy. Sally was an experienced sub and had already taught Steve a lot about the craft. Increasingly, she was allowing him to produce editorial fillers and write pocket reviews of those records that everyone else had rejected. But what Steve really aspired to was to review gigs and ultimately interview artists. Sadly, those assignments were strictly within the purview of Phil and Jamie and were jealously guarded by the editorial team, together with the right to keep far from conventional office hours.

To be in early, therefore, was to identify oneself as one of the drudges of the production or business departments rather than one of the hipsters of the editorial department. And this fine morning it had not gone unnoticed by Nick and Sally that the somewhat erudite new sub-editor was at his desk unusually early and looking a good deal less bedraggled than normal.

Nick stopped by Steve's desk on his way to the little kitchen to get Sally and himself mugs of Nescafé to fuel them through the remainder of their layout conference. 'You alright, Steve? You look almost smart.'

Steve was momentarily lost for words. 'Bank. Had to go to the bank. Manager wanted to tick me off about my overdraft.'

Nick nodded. 'Blood-suckers. What happened?'

'Agreed to extend it.'

'Blimey, result. How come?'

'Not sure. Perhaps she fancied me.'

'Ooh, female bank manager. Fondled your overdraft, did she?'

'Let's just say that she was impressed by how quickly I'd run it up.'

'Does Sarah know you're having a thing with your bank manager?'

'Sarah? I had no idea she even knew I existed.'

'That's not how I hear it.'

Steve found Nick's rejoinder somewhat troubling. He knew that Nick and Sarah were close outside the office context, but had divergent sexualities. Affecting an insouciance he didn't feel, Steve said, 'Thanks for the tip.'

Eyes twinkling, Nick said, 'None of my business really. But I'm glad you're in early. It's going to be a scramble this week with the increased page count. It'd be good if we could get Letters to the Editor off to the typesetters before lunch.'

Steve picked up the pile of typescripts that had been left on his desk and waved them in the air. 'I'm on it, guv.'

'Good man. Wanna coffee?'

'Nah, I'm good.'

Steve rather liked subbing. It wouldn't have been to everyone's taste, but he relished the challenge of tidying up a writer's copy without compromising the individual voice or style. It was not lost on him that he probably put more effort into his subbing than the journalists had spent on writing the pieces in the first place. He also liked the fact that he was expected to go to the typesetters on Tuesday and Wednesday each week and see the magazine through the page make-up process. This meant he was legitimately out of the office for two days a week.

For the first few weeks, Sally had gone with him to show him the ropes, but soon he was seeing the paper to bed by himself. Thereafter on Tuesdays and Wednesdays, he'd get to the office around mid-morning, pick up any new copy that needed to go across to the typesetters, walk up to Oxford Street and catch a 55 bus to Clerkenwell, hopping off just before the bus got to the St John Street crossing. Xpress Photoset, the typesetters that *Buzz* used, was one of the more go-ahead type shops, using phototypesetting technology in a district which still contained a number of traditional hot metal firms. Xpress were very proud of their Compugraphic machine which enabled them to set directly to photographic paper. The text was input from a keyboard that looked like a large typewriter and the processor output strips of photographic paper a little wider than the column width of the magazine. Scalpel-wielding paste-up artists then positioned the strips on sheets of white card cut to the dimensions of the publication, securing the strips in place with wax adhesive.

At Nick's prompting, writers were under strict instructions from Philip and Jamie to write to specific lengths, but they seldom stuck to their brief. It was therefore up to Steve and Sally to sub their copy to the correct length. Even so the process was more of an art than a science and articles often ran too long and occasionally fell too short.

On such occasions, one of the paste-up artists would call Steve over and indicate that five or six lines needed to be cut or, less often, added. If it was not too close to the print deadline, Steve would edit the piece on the fly and get it reset. But not infrequently it would be too late to reset and, looking over the paste-up artist's shoulder, he would indicate the lines and sometimes individual words that needed to be removed, which the artist would then literally cut with his scalpel, reassembling the surviving bits and pieces on the pasteboard. Steve never ceased to marvel at how deft the paste-up artists were, sliding the tiny pieces of paper into place by eye. He hoped they were equally impressed with the skill it took to sub a piece of text in such pressured circumstances and still end up with something coherent, but somehow he doubted that they really gave much thought to whether what a scuzzy new rock magazine was saying made sense or not.

Even so, there was a real sense of exhilaration as he signed off the last page each week. It had never occurred to him that collaboration could be so enjoyable. His only previous experience of working with a group of people had been his brief stint at the Festival Theatre when his play *Palace of Tears* had been in production. But that early experiment in collaboration had soon come to grief. Indeed, for reasons that were still unclear to him, he had been ostracized shortly after the first night and the play's run had literally ended in tears.

By contrast, every Wednesday evening now was a kind of celebration. He'd jump the 55 bus back to Soho and join the rest of the *Buzz* crew in the John Snow in Broadwick Street. By the time he got there, most of them were on their second or third drink and one or two of the more notorious members of the staff already high on dope or speed. By rights, the Old Coffee Shop should have been the *Buzz* staff's local pub, being almost next door to the office, but the John Snow was the music business pub. The Warner Bros offices were just up the road and there were studios and venues all around. It was not unusual to see musicians, managers and A&R people loosening up before the evening's gigs. There was no us and them. It was very much a case of rubbing shoulders. A pub was a public house, after all. In any case the star writers of the various music journals were as much in demand as the artists themselves. That was the position that Steve now hoped to attain in the near future if he played his cards right. In the meantime he was happy to soak up the vibe and learn the trade. The intellectual pretensions of St Rad's and the other Cambridge colleges seemed a million miles away.

Before long, the editorial crew started to drift in. First was Phil, the editor. He looked grey and his greeting to the still underpopulated general office was more of a groan than a cheery good morning.

He immediately disappeared into his office, not emerging for a further half an hour. In the meantime, Sally and Nick had finished their layout conference and Sally emerged from Nick's office with several copies of that week's page plan. She tapped on Phil's door and quickly put one on his desk, pulling the door shut quietly behind her. She then walked over to Steve's desk and before giving him a copy, jerked her head backward in the direction of Phil's office and said, 'Fast asleep.'

Steve laughed. 'Probably just dreaming up a great new feature.'

Sally perched her neat bottom on the corner of Steve's desk. 'You're looking nicely buffed up this morning. Something on?'

'I told Nick, had to go in to see the bank manager.'

Sally looked concerned. 'If you're short of cash, I can help out.'

Steve winced, but was touched. 'Thanks, Sal. No need. They've extended my overdraft.'

'OK, but I've got a bit tucked away – '

Steve was beginning to wish he'd never mentioned the bank manager. On the other hand he could hardly say that he'd been in to see the head of MI6. Still, there was no need to be so blunt. 'Thank you, I'll bear that in mind.'

Sally smiled at him and twisted a lock of hair. 'It's going to be a struggle to get this special issue to press on time. I think we'd both better go to the typesetters tomorrow and see where we are on Wednesday morning.'

'Okay, it's only another eight pages, isn't it?'

'For which we have very little copy yet. I'll have to get Phil to crack the whip.'

'Phil couldn't even crack a joke at the moment.'

Sally laughed. 'Very good. Can I use that?'

'Be my guest.'

Sally narrowed her eyes. 'What are you doing here, Steve? You're far too clever for a place like this.'

'Hey, cracking jokes about cracking jokes is not being clever.'

'What would you say, if I told you I've got a few friends on the staff of the London College of Printing and none of them can remember you.'

Steve was suddenly alarmed. When he'd seen the ad for a sub-editor on a new music magazine, he'd figured that saying he was a

Cambridge graduate was unlikely to enhance his chances of getting hired. So, remembering what Jude had told him about her letterpress course at the London College of Printing, he had embellished the truth in his letter of application. Well, actually he'd lied and said that he'd done a course there. But it had got him an interview, during which he had succeeded in convincing Greg, the managing director of Groove Time, that not only could he spell, but his knowledge of the Pink Floyd corpus was extensive. Furthermore, he'd made it clear that he was prepared to work for a pittance. This was actually because he had inherited his mother's flat and a small financial bequest when she had died the previous year. He'd been careful, however, not to mention this fact. After a bit of chit-chat, Greg had asked him whether he had any objections to working for a business that didn't recognise unions. Shamefully, he had replied that he'd never been a member of a union, which was actually true, though it did not reflect his political inclinations. Nevertheless, this last affirmation seemed to clinch the matter and Greg had asked whether he could start the following week.

The problem now with Sally's remark about his being unknown at the London College of Printing was that she was technically his line manager and therefore the person he worked most closely with. Unfortunately, it now seemed that she realised that Steve was not all he appeared to be. This hint of mystery had piqued her interest, which she had followed up by making a few enquiries.

In the normal run of things, if there was such a state of affairs in the life of Steve Percival, he would have come clean and cheerfully admitted that he had lied. He had, after all, been holding down the job for several months now and it was fairly clear that his colleagues, especially the managers, thought he was doing well, not that he'd had to submit to any kind of formal performance review. But Greg was an unpredictable type and if he felt he'd been manipulated or deceived, there was a slim but not non-existent chance that he might dismiss Steve forthwith.

So, he needed to forestall Sally's suspicions. But how? He'd need to give it some thought. Buying time, he said, 'Yes, well, it's all a bit complicated. Please keep it to yourself for now and I'll tell you everything when we've finished at the typesetters tomorrow.'

Sally's eyes twinkled. She liked a mystery and it gave her a bit of a thrill to think that she might have acquired some power over Steve. She was looking forward to playing this one for all it was worth. 'You'd better, otherwise I'll have to consider whether to share my suspicions with Greg.'

Steve was quite amused by this unabashed power-play. It was kid's stuff compared to the kind of thing he'd had from Ginny and Grace. He knew from those relationships that the proper way to deal with having the moves put on you was defiance not appeasement. But he didn't want to blow his cover, and not just because he feared Sheena's wrath more than public shaming at *Buzz* and the loss of his job. The real reason he didn't want to screw up the operation was because he was intrigued by the idea of re-encountering Inge or Ulrike or whoever she now was.

Sally stood up from her perch on the corner of Steve's desk and, as she went over to her own desk, ran her hand across the back of his head, which brought an amused smile to his lips.

A few moments later, Jamie, the deputy editor, announced his arrival with a cheerful greeting to the two subs. 'Is Phil in yet?'

Sally said over her shoulder, 'He's comatose or he was when I took the new page plans in.'

But at that moment the door to Phil's office opened and, standing on the threshold, he said, 'I am not. I was just summoning up the old voodoo for my editorial.'

Jamie laughed. 'Care to share what the spirit has vouchsafed?'

'Not yet. You'll have to wait until I've typed it up.'

'Okay. What time did you leave the Nashville last night?'

'Not sure. Not sure I did leave. I feel like I'm just an emanation.'

'Can emanations suffer from hangovers?'

'Good point. You wouldn't consider making me a cup of the strongest coffee known to man, would you?'

'Doesn't matter how many teaspoons of Nescafé you use, it's never going to be strong.'

'Do your best.'

Steve turned around from his desk. 'I could get you a double espresso from Mario's.'

'Would you mind? I'd be eternally grateful.'

'Not at all. Anyone else want one?'

Unsurprisingly, Jamie and Sally also decided they needed some stimulation. Steve put his jean jacket on and went down to the little Italian snack bar, which did excellent Italian coffee from a gleaming, old-fashioned Gaggia machine. When he got back with the coffees, John and Sarah had finally made it to the workplace, both nursing coffees they'd brought in with them. Steve handed out the coffees. Phil said dramatically, 'You've saved my life.'

Jamie laughed and disappeared into his room and Sally said, 'Creep.'

Steve winked at her and said, 'I know my place.'

And so the working day at *Buzz* began in earnest, or an approximation thereof.

Xpress Photoset – Clerkenwell – Tuesday

THE TUESDAY SESSION AT the typesetters went well. Steve and Sally had cleared all the pages by six o'clock. As Sally put her coat on, she said to Steve, 'Okay, Percival, time to spill the beans. The Sekforde does a nice pint of Young's Bitter – let's go there.'

Sally was an enthusiastic beer drinker, able to match most of the guys in the office pint for pint. Soon she was wiping her lips with the back of her hand, having taken several large mouthfuls of beer. 'So, you weren't at the LCP?'

Steve put his glass down and pondered for a moment what to say. He had come to no conclusion about how to handle the situation in the intervening hours since Sally had first challenged him on the subject. He would just have to improvise. 'No, I wasn't.'

'Why did you say it then?'

'I thought I had a better chance of getting an interview. And I knew someone who did a course there.'

'Because otherwise you were unqualified?'

'Yes.'

'But you're not actually unqualified, are you?'

'Well, I've listened to a lot of Pink Floyd and the Incredible String Band.'

Sally laughed. 'Really? That's an odd coupling.'

'I didn't feel that either specialism, but particularly the latter, was likely to land me the interview.'

'But in fact you are highly literate. The readability of John and Sarah's pieces has improved beyond measure since you've been subbing them. I've started to feel a little eclipsed by your speed and deftness.'

'You've taught me everything I know.'

'About production matters perhaps, but not about subbing.'

'Then we make a good team.'

'Yes, we do. But if we're going to continue working in harmony, you need to tell me what your true credentials are.'

'Maybe I have none.'

'Well, I imagine you have some A-Levels at least, and not just in the lyrics of the Increds. You spell better than anyone in the office, yet I've never seen you consult a dictionary.'

'Some people are just good at spelling.'

'And your knowledge of matters beyond the narrow world of popular music has been remarked upon by a number of people in the office. John said that he thought you must have actually read *The Mass Psychology of Fascism* when you queried something he'd written about Wilhelm Reich in one of his typically rambling and under-researched pieces about Kraftwerk.'

'Flicked through a battered old Penguin copy in a secondhand bookshop.'

'Of course you did. Typical behaviour of an inky hack.'

'Look, I couldn't do the reviews and interviews the editorial team handle. I couldn't generate the sheer tonnage of words they produce, nor have the bottle to puncture the posturing of rock stars when interviewing them. I have a different set of skills altogether.'

'But some of the reviews you've done when we needed to fill space have been brilliant.'

'About LPs no one is interested in or has ever heard of, to fill space where an ad has been pulled at the last moment.'

'That in itself is an art.'

'Maybe. The more insignificant something is, the better I am with it.'

'And that's the other thing, the crippling lack of self-confidence masked by enigmatic pronouncements, something others have noticed too.'

'Have you been deputed to ask me to modify my behaviour?'

'No, I haven't been asked to do anything. I've taken it upon myself to get to the bottom of you.'

'Good luck with that. But why?'

'Because we work together and because I like you.'

'I like you too. And enjoy working with you. You're a good boss.'

'Thank you. So are you going to tell me what the LCP is a disguise for then?'

'If I tell you, will you keep it to yourself?'

'Unless it's Wormwood Scrubs.'

'Aren't offenders entitled to an opportunity for rehabilitation?'

'Quibbles aside, yes.'

'I read, as we say at Cambridge, Modern and Mediaeval Languages.'

Sally was silent for a moment as she digested this news. 'All of them?'

'What?'

'Which languages?'

'French and German.'

'No kidding.'

'No.'

'What college?'

'St Rad's'

'Oh, my goodness. Where did you go to school?'

'City of London.'

'So we've been infiltrated by a member of the haute bourgeoisie.'

'CLS wasn't like that. And in any case I gather that Jamie's father is a High Court judge.'

'Really? Okay.'

'And there's money in Greg's background. How do you think Groove Time is funded? It's certainly not making a profit.'

'True.'

'So I'm not exactly a viper in the bosom of the workers' co-operative that calls itself *Buzz*.'

'I'm not sure that follows from your premisses.'

'Who's giving their intellectual credentials away now?'

'Fair cop.'

'Where?'

'Philosophy at the LSE.'

'Nice. So there we are. Am I safe now from being outed?'

'There may be other conditions.'

'Like what?'

'I'll tell you later.'

'Later?'

'Back at my place. You could stay over.'

'Sal, I don't think I could do that.'

'I'm not asking you to share my bed. Unless things work out that way, of course.'

'To be honest, I'd love to go to bed with you, but I'm in a tight spot at the moment.'

'I'm not going to shop you to Becky.'

Steve hadn't mentioned that he and Becky were no longer together. It hadn't seemed necessary. But now it might serve as useful cover for whatever might be involved in any re-encounter with Inge. 'I didn't think you would, but I need to sort things out with her first.'

'What, ask her permission to have a tumble with me? Last time I looked this was 1976 and you're allowed to overlap a bit, try before you buy.'

He would have preferred to project himself as the self-confident, masterful ladies' man, but he realised that he must be coming across as the tentative, conscience-stricken lover. Which was not how he really wanted to be seen by Sally. He liked her, and they got on well. He found her attractive enough to daydream a number of times about what she looked like without her clothes on. And he had been wondering from early on in his time as her assistant whether the circumstances might arise which would result in them going to bed together. If her present offer, oblique as it was, had been made the previous week, he would have had no hesitation in taking her up on it.

'No, it's not that, but I can't go into details.'

'Hey, kid, you might not get the offer twice.'

'Please don't write me off, Sal. I'm sure we can work something out.'

'It makes me feel a bit uncomfortable that I opened up to you.'

They finished their drinks and went their separate ways. As he was travelling home, Steve wondered whether he had been unnecessarily cautious. What was the likelihood that a fling with Sally would intersect in a disastrous way with whatever might be involved in keeping an eye on Inge while she was in the country, and which presumably would be for a relatively short time? Well, it was too late now.

Sally was nothing like the women he'd recently been involved with; not as impossibly sexy, intelligent or beautiful as Ginny, Grace or Angie; nor as pert and pretty as Becky. She was none of those things, but she was good-looking, open, generous and direct. Surely that was a good thing. The person she most reminded him of was Jude. Ah, Jude! With a pang of regret, he wondered how she was.

He had imagined, when he first moved down to London, that at some point Jude would probably be in touch with him. They'd go for a drink and one thing might lead to another. But in the event, he'd not heard from her in the fourteen or fifteen months since he'd left Cambridge. This was hardly surprising. He'd not really treated her well. In fact, he'd rather taken her for granted. And now to rub salt in the self-inflicted wound, she had fallen into the arms of Peter Newman, the only consolation for which was that Steve had recently had one blissful night with Ginny.

The John Snow – Soho – Wednesday

WHEN STEVE AND SALLY met up at the typesetters the next day, they were too busy to revisit the previous evening's discussion. By the time they got to the John Snow later on, most of their colleagues were already well into celebrations for having got the special issue to the printers on time. Even Greg, the managing director, had dropped in, a rare event. Someone got them some drinks. They found a table in the corner of the bar and started to unwind. This session was probably going to go on until late and might well get messy.

Sarah came over and, looking straight at Sally, said, 'Didn't take you long to get your claws into the new boy, Sal.'

So Nick's comment about Sarah having her eye on him had not been without foundation. You wait the best part of a year to get off with one of your female colleagues and then two come along at once.

Sally laughed. 'No claws needed.'

Steve wasn't used to being fought over, but even as he framed that thought he recognised it was actually far from the case. He felt he should say something to make it clear that he too had a say in such matters, but what? Sarah was certainly no stranger to him, but his knowledge of her was derived almost entirely from her writing, which was scrappily dynamic and to the point. There had been few personal interactions between them.

Actually, if he were being honest, she scared him a bit. She had a reputation for being fearless, a skill which she mainly deployed in getting rock musicians to say things they would later come to regret. She could hold her drink and was an enthusiastic user of drugs. Steve wasn't entirely sure which. She was also, in Jon Chapman's terminology, undoubtedly hot, presumably a useful asset when coaxing pretentious musicians to spill the beans. But she was also a little shop-soiled as a consequence, with lank hair and damaged skin under the thick layer of makeup she wore. This was the first time that Steve had been so close to her. She smelled of gin, patchouli and cigarette smoke, was snake thin and wore the tightest of jeans. And it was almost impossible not to notice that she was not wearing a bra under the gauzy blouse that gaped beneath her leather jacket.

She smiled down at Steve and winked, all too aware of the effect she was having on him. 'Maybe another time. Anyway, well done you two. It must have been a slog at the typesetters.'

Steve was absurdly grateful for the plaudit, but Sally was irritated by the condescension. 'It would have been easier if everybody's copy had been on time.'

But Sarah was already walking away, swinging her hips like a catwalk model. Sally noticed how Steve's eyes followed the transit of her backside across the bar. 'Steve, you'll be doing yourself no favours if you get tied up with her. There's overlap and there's stupidity.'

Steve nodded. 'Yeah, it's just it's the first time she's really talked to me.'

At that moment the street door opened and a couple walked in. The guy was tall, broad-shouldered and blond; the girl was small, skinny and dark. Something about them troubled Steve. Neither of them looked like the usual Broadwick Street irregulars, but somehow the girl looked vaguely familiar. And then, with a sudden knotting deep in the pit of his stomach, he realised that the girl was Inge. While she scanned the room, presumably looking for Steve, the blond guy went to the bar and ordered some drinks. Fortunately, the pub was crowded and he and Sally were sitting in a alcove, which gave him a moment to get his thoughts in order.

Since his meeting with Sheena, Steve had been working through the different ways that Inge might contact him and trying to convince himself that she was just a research student trying to find a way to continue studying with her professor. In none of the scenarios had she been accompanied by a large man who looked as though he could handle himself. Suddenly, Steve wasn't sure he wanted to be spotted and particularly not with Sally on hand. He sat there in ghastly anticipation.

Sally noticed that he had become tense and that the blood had drained from his face. 'Steve, what's happening? You look as if you've seen a ghost.'

That was exactly how he felt. He wanted to say something, anything, but his mouth was too dry.

Sally followed his eyes across the room. 'That's not Becky, is it?'

Steve took a sip of his beer. 'No, it's a girl I knew in Germany.'

'And things didn't end well between you?'

'I can't talk about it right now.'

'She seems to have a bodyguard. Do you owe her money?'

'No.'

'Got her pregnant?'

'No.'

At that moment Steve and Inge's eyes met. Steve had enough presence of mind to know that he must not act as if he were expecting to encounter her, but what the fuck would be the appropriate expression to adopt? Shock, surprise, disbelief, gradually dawning realisation? He wasn't sure. Sally, who was now almost as alarmed as Steve, suddenly pointed in Inge's direction and said, 'She's seen you.'

Steve was initially irritated by Sally's intervention, but actually her gesture must have looked quite natural. Inge's eyes widened, a shy smile spread across her face and she waved.

Steve knew he had to make a move. He opened his arms wide palms upward in a gesture of amazement and then waved her over.

A moment later, she was by their table. Speaking in lightly accented English, she said, 'Tom, how marvellous to see you.'

'Inge, what are you doing here?'

'It's a long story.'

Steve stood up. What should he do? Shake her hand, kiss her? Just then the big guy joined them with the drinks. 'Tom, this is my friend, Werner. Werner this is the boy I told you about who was so kind to me in Berlin.'

Steve wasn't sure what part of his involvement in Inge's life could be described as kindness. Werner leaned forward and offered his hand and said in much more accented English, 'Pleased to meet you, Tom.'

Sally was following this exchange in disbelief. Why were they calling Steve Tom? Steve, aware of how strange the encounter must seem to Sally, said, 'And this is my friend, Sally. We work together on a magazine.'

Inge laughed. 'An architecture magazine?'

Steve shook his head. 'No. Sally is my boss and we are the subeditors on *Buzz*, a rock music magazine.'

In the ensuing pause, Inge took a packet of cigarettes out of her bag and, having put one in her mouth, waved the packet around, inviting any other smokers in the group to take a cigarette. In the absence of any takers, she put the packet back in her bag and lit her own cigarette with a yellow plastic Bic lighter.

Sally was standing now too, and, sensing that Steve was feeling out of his depth, slipped her arm protectively around his waist. She began to suspect the couple were German drug dealers or gangsters, and that Steve had got on the wrong side of them or perhaps had ripped them off. What a silly boy!

Well, if they wanted Steve, they were going to have to deal with her too. 'Are you here on holiday?'

Inge exhaled a plume of smoke. 'Oh, no, we're students. I'm here to do some research in the British Library. Werner's an engineer and studying at Imperial College.'

Sally thought that neither of them looked anything like postgraduate students. Admittedly, she hadn't actually met any German students, although she was aware that they tended to graduate at a more advanced age than their British counterparts. Even so, the way these two comported themselves and the menace they were exuding was palpable.

Steve, for his part, was still finding it difficult to know what to say. It was little more than a year since he'd shared a dangerous and sexually thrilling evening with Inge, but she had changed almost beyond recognition. She was no longer as painfully thin as when he had gone to bed with her; her hair was neatly cut and conditioned, and she was smartly dressed and made up.

Sally was still happy to make the conversational running. 'Are you here for long?'

Inge nodded and said lightly, 'Just a few weeks. I'm hoping to apply to a British university to complete my PhD. Werner is already a graduate student at Imperial.'

Suddenly, Steve found his tongue. 'How did you find me?'

Inge laughed. 'I wasn't looking for you. I did hope I might catch up with you during my time here, but Werner and I are just exploring the pubs of Soho and trying to get used to the *lauwarmes Bier*.'

Steve managed to say, 'Ah yes, room-temperature beer takes some getting used to, especially Sam Smith's.'

Werner looked puzzled. 'Sam Smith's?'

'Yes, the beer in this pub is from Yorkshire, not typical of London in general.'

'But it is ale?'

'Yes.'

Inge intervened. 'Tom, I am very pleased to see you again. But I see you are having an evening with your girlfriend. Do you have a telephone number I can reach you on? I'd like your advice.'

Steve didn't really want to offer up the number at his flat, but he supposed that in reality she already knew it. 'Of course. And maybe I could get your number in return?'

'I'm staying in student lodgings. I'm afraid I don't have access to a personal telephone.'

Steve tore a page from his notebook and jotted down his number. As an afterthought, he also jotted down his address. The Stasi almost certainly had that too, so it would be as well not to act in a suspicious manner.

Inge tucked the note in her bag and leaned in towards Steve and gave him a kiss on the cheek. 'So lovely to see you again, Tom.'

With that, the couple turned and left the pub. When they'd gone Sally said, 'Well, Tom, you've got a lot of explaining to do. The LCP story pales into insignificance compared to this.'

'Not here, Sal.'

'No, okay. But I've got a feeling it would be better if we discussed this back at my place.'

Steve was grateful for the suggestion. He had been thinking along much the same lines. 'Yes, you're right. Would you mind if we went now?'

But he needn't have appended the request for Sally was already buttoning her coat and moving towards the door. As she did so, Sarah, who had noticed the encounter in the corner of the pub, called out, 'Ooh, that looked a bit heavy!' Sally acted as if she had not heard and propelled Steve through the pub doors. Out on the street, she said, 'Your friends didn't even finish their drinks.'

Later back at her flat, Sally opened a bottle of red wine and said, 'Right, hiding your Cambridge background is one thing; being known as Tom by a couple of German heavies quite another.'

Steve took the glass of wine she offered him and said, 'Sally, this is very tricky. I'm not quite sure what to say.'

Sally sipped her own wine. 'Are they drug dealers? Do you owe them money?'

'No, I wasn't involved in anything criminal. I was asked to deliver something to East Berlin. Inge was the person I was delivering to.'

'What was this something?'

'I can't tell you.'

'You looked terrified when Inge turned up in the pub.'

'I wasn't expecting to see her there and especially not with a minder.'

'Werner certainly didn't look like a bundle of laughs. But you were expecting to see her somewhere or at some point?'

'Yes,'

'So why the terror?'

'She looked very different from when I last saw her.'

'Changed her hair style?'

'Changed everything. That's why I didn't recognise her immediately.'

'From a female perspective, she looked like serious competition, if a little on the scrawny side.'

'She was a lot scrawnier when I met her.'

'The diet in East Berlin perhaps?'

'Yes, I think so.'

'A place that is infamously difficult to get out of if you are an East German.'

Steve could see where Sally was going with this. Cautiously, he said, 'Yes.'

'Yet, here she is, a year or so later, in London applying to universities.'

'Yes, I'm pretty amazed.'

'But not completely so, it would seem. Not to the extent that you felt compelled to ask her how she got out. Perhaps because you had some foreknowledge?'

'Sally, I am really constrained as to what I can say.'

'Does that mean that this job at Buzz is some kind of cover?'

'Well, not in the sense that I lied about my LCP experience.'

'But in a more general sense.'

'Let's just say it's convenient that I'm doing the job I'm doing.'

'So just putting two and two together here, you're undercover?'

Steve shrugged.

'A cop? A journalist? A spook?'

Steve shrugged again.

'Okay. Is Steve Percival not your real name?'

'No, it's my real name.'

'Okay, so Tom is your operational name?'

'Was.'

'Tom what?'

'Just Tom.'

'And Inge isn't Inge.'

'Apparently not.'

'But Tom and Inge have been asked to get together again? No way that she was just sampling the pubs of Soho looking for the perfect pint of bitter with her heavy. She was actually looking for you, wasn't she?'

Steve nodded mournfully. 'Yes.'

'Steve, you don't really come across as a Harry Palmer, even less as a James Bond.'

'Look, Sal, this has all gone off very wrong. I'm sorry to have got you mixed up in it.'

'You could do with a wingman, well, wingwoman.'

'I don't think I can do that. I will get into terrible trouble.'

'It seems to me you're in trouble already. Do you think Inge was surprised to see me.'

'Initially, she must have thought you were Becky. I'm pretty sure she knows about Becky.'

'How?'

Steve had said more than he meant to. While he was trying to come up with a suitably evasive answer, Sally said, 'Because she's a German spook. Not just a German spook, an East German spook.'

'Sally, you've got to keep this to yourself.'

'What do you think I'm going to do? Go into the office and say "Guess what! Steve's not a sub, Steve's a spook and he's battling the Stasi on the streets of Soho!"'

'Sal, it's not funny. Sheena will kebab me.'

'Okay. Who's Sheena? Your boss?'

Steve shrugged. 'Steve, you're safe here. No one's listening to us. They don't know about me.'

'I'm afraid they do.'

'You told them?'

'No, they just know about these things.'

'Bloody hell, Steve, this all sounds a bit oppressive.'

'I know. It's not something I chose to do.'

'Are you being blackmailed?'

'No, it's more complicated than that, but once again I can't go into details.'

'So, what are we going to do?'

'I'll stay here tonight, if that's okay. And then I'll go home to-morrow after work and wait for her phone call.'

'I could come over to your place tomorrow?'

'That wouldn't be a good idea. I'm meant to get close to her.'

'I don't fancy your chances with that big blond hunk she hangs out with.'

'No, I think she wants to connect with me and the hunk knows that.'

'So, they're both Stasi and you're MI6.'

'She's not officially Stasi, and I'm not officially what you just said.'

'So what's she here for?'

'We don't know. That's what I've got to find out.'

'So now you've just explained your mission.'

'Sal, you've got to treat this with the utmost discretion. Please don't let me down.'

'When I set my eyes on you I thought my opponent was a beautiful actress. If I can believe you, she seems to have left the field of battle. Then Sarah makes a half-hearted pitch. But now I find my opponent is an East German spy. Is that why you wouldn't go to bed with me?'

'Yes.'

'Okay, I give you full credit for that. Supposing I were to say that, if we were to go to bed, I wouldn't hold it against you if things don't work out. And I won't get in the way of whatever you've got to do in the near future. Or be jealous. But I will look out for you.'

'I would be immensely grateful.'

'Okay, we don't need to go public. Just let me know when I need to back off. And they can't stop us from working together.'

'No.'

'My goodness, Steve, you are a dark horse.'

'I'm not. I'm a bloody fool.'

'In that case, why don't you just say to – Sheena, was it? – that you want out.'

'I can't tell you now, but if we get through this, I promise I'll tell you.'

'You'd better, buddy, otherwise I'll – '

'What?'

'I don't know, but I'll think of something. But for now, let's get to know each other better before we enter the looking-glass world.'

The George - Borough – Thursday

PUBLICATION DAY WAS GENERALLY a low-key day in the office, with everyone exhausted from the dash to get the magazine out and several sporting terrible hangovers. Normally, Steve tried to get ahead of the game by subbing the features that were already lined up for the following week's edition. But his heart wasn't really in it this particular Thursday. Dreading a return to his own flat, he felt safer at Sally's, even though he suspected that her flat was probably being watched by now as well. It was just that she was such a sensible, reassuring presence. They had held hands on the 38 bus into work and throughout the morning found reasons to be in close proximity to each other: a page layout conference, a subbing problem, a fresh cup of coffee.

Steve was jumpy all day. Every time the phone on his desk rang, he was certain that it was Inge. But how could it be? He had given her the telephone number at his flat. Ostensibly she knew neither his work number nor his real name. He was pretty certain, though, that she had found out or been told what it was by her handlers. Not surprisingly, the calls were all routine queries from Stan or Tina at the typesetters checking details in the copy he had sent over on the morning courier. At the end of the working day, Sally suggested that they get a quick drink before they went their separate ways. But even though Steve could not be sure that Inge would phone him that evening, he thought it best to remain sober. In truth, he was reluctant to go home. He now felt vulnerable there. He would gladly have abandoned his flat and moved in with Sally for the long-term.

But back home, his mood lightened a little. It was good to be in a familiar space. He looked at his watch. With luck he had time for a bath and a change of clothes. He stripped off, took a quick dip and put on a set of clean clothes. It then occurred to him that his fridge was almost completely empty. He'd dash out and pick up some things at the corner shop. But, just as he was putting his coat on, the phone rang. It was Inge.

'Tom, it's Inge. It was so great to see you yesterday evening.'

Steve sat down on the wooden chair by the telephone table in the entrance hall. 'It was great to see you too, Inge. But I must admit that I was very surprised.'

Inge laughed. 'I'm sorry. You looked like you'd seen a ghost.'

Steve said, 'That's what Sally said.'

'Sally, your girlfriend?'

'No, Sally's the colleague I was with in the pub. She's a friend too, of course. My girlfriend's called Becky Spalding.'

'And you and she live together?'

'We used to, but we broke up recently.'

'Well, in that case, I was wondering if we could meet this evening. It's still early. I checked your address on the A-Z map and I could get to London Bridge station quite quickly from my lodgings. Is there a pub we could meet at?'

'There's the George on Borough High Street. It's only a short walk from the station.'

'Okay. Could we meet there at seven-thirty?'

'That's easy for me, but I don't know where you're coming from.'

'I'm living in Huntley Street, between Tottenham Court Road and Gower Street.'

'That's a tricky journey.'

'Don't worry, I'll be there. I'm getting quite familiar with the curious bus routes you have in London.'

Steve laughed. 'Yeah, we don't make it easy. Sort of secret knowledge.'

'Okay, I'll see you there. Do you think you'll recognise me?'

'I hope so. With luck you haven't changed too much from last night.'

Three-quarters of an hour later, Steve was sitting in the George in one of the bars nearest the street. He was nervous. He had been trying to envisage how the conversation might go and what he could and couldn't say. Once again, Collingwood's briefing had been sketchy to say the least. Inge knew that he had been acting on behalf of British intelligence when he was in Berlin. But to say that he had been working for them would have been an exaggeration.

Whether Inge now knew that he had been reactivated by Sheena and Collingwood was, however, another matter. Presumably, it would be best to act on the assumption that this information had already leaked out, while sticking to his cover story that he was a sub-editor on *Buzz* magazine. Fortunately, that last detail was relatively easy to substantiate. It would also make sense to appear to buy into Inge's cover story of being a visiting graduate student, while assuming she was an active Stasi operative.

But what he was expected to do beyond that was still not clear to him. Sheena had said that she wanted him to assist Inge to hook up with Müller. But not only was Müller now in Cambridge, he was also in some kind of relationship with Grace, Steve's own former lover. That hardly made his task easier or more palatable. He also feared that he would get confused by the different levels of simulation and dissimulation.

Lost in such lugubrious thoughts, it took him a moment to realise that Inge was now standing in front of him smiling broadly. Furthermore, there was no sign of Werner, unless he was getting the drinks. Steve jumped to his feet, and this time embraced Inge. She did not resist. 'Inge, it's so lovely to see you.'

'And I am very pleased to see you, Tom. But before we go any further, let's use our real names. I'm really Ulrike Schmidt. And you are Steve Percival.'

Steve released her and took a step backwards. If she really was working for the Stasi, she would clearly know his real name. But why give away what that implied so early in the encounter? 'How do you know that?'

'Dieter Müller told me in a letter.'

So she had already been in touch with him. 'How is he?'

'Enjoying Cambridge, although he says he has not seen you for more than a year.'

'No, I moved down from Cambridge shortly after I got back from Berlin.'

'I imagine Sally was a little puzzled to hear me calling you Tom yesterday. How did you deal with that?'

'I told her that my real name was Thomas Steven Percival, but that I preferred to be called Steve.'

'Is that true?'

Steve knew he had to be careful here. Ulrike might have been briefed on his passport details. 'About my real name? No.'

'Did she believe you?'

'She seemed to. No one in my office knows very much about me. I lied about my qualifications to get the job.'

'Was that necessary?'

'I thought so at the time.'

'What is your academic background then?'

'I studied French and German at Cambridge.'

'*Lieber Steve, du bist ein stilles Wasser*. What is the equivalent expression in English?'

'A dark horse, I suppose. But look, before we get any further in this curious conversation, let me get you a drink. What would you like?'

'A glass of white wine, please.'

'Take a seat. I'll be right back.'

When Steve got back with the drinks, Ulrike had taken her coat off and lit a cigarette. She pushed the packet of Marlboro across the table towards Steve. 'You smoke?'

Steve shook his head.

She retrieved the packet. 'Do you mind if I do?'

'Of course not. Most of the people I work with smoke. I don't smoke because I think of myself as a runner; not that I have done much running recently.'

Ulrike released a cloud of smoke. 'So where do we begin?'

'Well, I have answered a few of your questions. Perhaps you could answer some of mine.'

'I will do my best.'

'I, of course, know that Professor Müller, Dieter, got out, but I heard that you were arrested.'

'I was. I was treated brutally as such people are, kept in a tiny cell, deprived of sleep, questioned relentlessly, beaten, raped.'

'Yet here you are fifteen months later in London?'

'You are suspicious?'

'How did that happen?'

'Dieter has friends in high places in the West German administration. He persuaded them to ransom me.'

Steve was familiar with the scheme, but felt it best to feign ignorance. 'Ransom you?'

'It's something that happens a lot. It's one of the main ways that the DDR gets hard western currency. Admittedly the hostage normally has to spend a good deal longer than I did in prison. But when influential people are involved, these things can be speeded up.'

'Is Müller that influential?'

'He is.'

'And are you still in love with him?'

'I was never in love with him. Sometimes I submitted to his grubby demands. A man in his position can have his pick of the female students.'

She stubbed out her cigarette. 'I hope you do not think too badly of me.'

'No, I understand how these things work.'

'But I owe him a huge debt of gratitude. You met Dieter, I take it?'

'Yes, briefly, while he was still in West Berlin.'

'And what did you think?'

'Well, I am sure he is a leading figure in his field, but I did not take to him. He seemed far too pleased with himself.'

'Perhaps he was just relieved to have made it to the West. Anyway, even if you don't like him, it is good that you have met.'

'In what way?'

'I would like you to take me to Cambridge to meet him.'

'Why would I need to go with you? Couldn't you just write to him and say you'd like to meet up?'

'I have and he refused. He probably thinks I will cause him trouble.'

'He helped you get out of the DDR.'

'That didn't involve him having to deal with me directly. And he did not think I would follow him to England. I was meant to live at my aunt's in Frankfurt am Main and enrol at the university there.'

'But why would my going with you make any difference?'

'If he thinks I have come to England to be with you, that we are now lovers, then he might not feel so threatened by me and might be prepared to help me.'

'Which is how?'

'To enable me to continue my studies at Cambridge.'

'I'm not sure that's something he could easily do, eminent though he is.'

'Even if I couldn't formally be his student, there might be some arrangement by which I could use the University Library as a private scholar.'

'The thing is that Cambridge has a collegiate system. To be awarded a PhD you have to be a member of the University. To be a member of the University you have to be a member of a college. Most of the colleges are for male students only. Müller is attached to St Radegund's, which is actually the college I went to. There are only three women's colleges. And there are now a handful of colleges that are co-educational. You would be better off applying to one of the women's colleges.'

'But how would I go about doing that?'

'Well, I might actually be able to help there. My former supervisor is a senior member of Newnham, one of the women's colleges. I haven't been in touch with her for a while. We were briefly lovers but it didn't work out. But I could introduce you to her. She is also a close colleague of Müller's. In fact I think *they* may be lovers.'

'Would you do that?'

'I'll certainly contact her if you'll allow me. Obviously, I can't guarantee that she will do anything for you or even be prepared to see us.'

'Won't that be difficult for you considering the relationship ended badly and that she is now with Dieter?'

'It will feel a bit strange, but maybe it's time for us to meet again.'

'Steve, you're my only hope. And we did fall in love a bit that day.'

Steve nodded. 'Yes, we did. I've thought about you a lot.'

'So, would you be prepared to pretend that we are in love?'

'Yes, of course. One problem in introducing you to Grace is that I have a full-time job, so I can only be out of London at weekends.'

'I understand, but I only have enough money to stay in London for six weeks and I've already been here for a week. How soon will you be able to speak to her?'

'I will try and do it tomorrow.'

'Okay, Steve, let's try that approach first. Thank you. You are a good friend.'

'Would you like a coffee back at my place? It's quite close to Borough Tube station.'

'Yes, I think that would be a good idea.'

Steve showed Ulrike into the flat. She looked around. 'Oh, Steve, this is a beautiful apartment. But it does not seem like a young man's place.'

'Well, it was my mother's. I grew up here and, when she died, I inherited it. I haven't had the heart to change anything. It took me a long time just to donate her clothes to charity.'

'I'm so sorry.'

'I miss her terribly, but there's nothing to be done about it. It'd probably make sense for me to move. But that's a big decision.'

'I do not wish to minimise your grief, but I too have lost both my parents, my mother only last year.'

'Then we are in the same situation. Let me open a bottle of wine and we'll drink a toast to our parents.'

'That's a lovely idea.'

Once they had both made somewhat mawkish toasts to their mothers, Ulrike insisted on being shown all the rooms of the flat. When they got to Steve's bedroom, Ulrike said, 'Perhaps we should practise before we have to perform in public.'

Steve wasn't sure what she was saying. 'Practise what?'

'Being lovers. When we were in Prenzlauer Berg, you asked me to take my clothes off. Why don't you do that now?'

Later when they were having a reviving cup of tea, Ulrike said, 'Do you think we'll be able to convince Müller that we're in love?'

Taking a sip of tea, Steve said, 'I'm not sure. I think we might need a little more practice. Why don't you stay over?'

Ulrike laughed. 'I'd like to, but I have to get back tonight. Werner is taking me to Oxford. We are setting off early and won't be back until late on Sunday evening.'

'Oxford?'

'In case Cambridge doesn't work out.'

'He has a point.'

'I will phone you at your work on Monday to see whether your teacher is prepared to meet me.'

Steve had a restless night, replaying the conversation with Ulrike. Something felt off, but he couldn't pinpoint the detail causing his unease. On the face of it, her stated ambition to complete her PhD at Cambridge fitted with what little he knew about her, but going through Müller was probably not the best way to achieve those ambitions, whether he was prepared to see her or not. He had simply not been in Cambridge long enough to understand the niceties of academic preferment in that connection. Grace was a much better bet. But whether she would be prepared to speak to Steve was another matter. With luck she would understand that it was Sheena related and she too had obligations in that connection.

On the other hand, the resumption of intimate relations with the woman now calling herself Ulrike had been delightful. For a start, there hadn't been the terrible feeling of jeopardy, which, as she had not failed to remind him, had initially impeded his performance in East Berlin. Moreover, she was now a more fragrant and better-nourished young woman, while still remaining charmingly immodest. All the same, he was left with a vague feeling of libidinal dissonance. It was as if they had always been lovers; yet, at the same time, it was as if he had never made love to her before. He told himself it must be because his main sexual partner for the last year had been Becky, who, although a luscious handful, had never behaved as if she was totally committed.

Buzz – Soho – Friday

THE NEXT MORNING IN the *Buzz* office, Sally said, 'Did you hear from Inge?'

'Ulrike.'

'What?'

'Her name's really Ulrike.'

'Do you actually believe that?'

'Probably not. But *what's in a name?* as someone said.'

'You're right, Tom. What happens next?'

'She wants me to take her to Cambridge.'

'That seems easy enough.'

'I can't give you all the details, but that's the last thing it is.'

'Do you think you're cut out for this kind of thing?'

'No.'

Just then Steve's telephone rang. It was Collingwood. 'Steve, could you come into the office on your way home?'

'Jeremy, it's Friday night.'

'Have you made arrangements?'

'No, ideally on Friday nights, things just develop.'

'Well, maybe they'll develop once we've had a brief word. Will your work let you get away early? It'd be good if you could be here by five-thirty.'

With that Collingwood hung up.

Sally looked at Steve. 'Who was that?'

'I suppose you'd call him my handler. He wants me to drop by the office.'

'Where's that?'

'Can't tell you.'

'You could come back to my place this evening after you've seen your boss.'

'He's not my boss. You are.'

'Yeah, yeah. I suppose you're waiting for Ulrike to come round?'

'No, she's gone to Oxford for the weekend.'

'So what's to stop you coming to my place?'

'Nothing really.'

'Good, that's a deal, then.'

Steve left the office at four o'clock. Before he got the bus for London Bridge, he stepped into a telephone box and, without thinking too deeply about it, rang Newnham College and asked for Dr Grace Mitchell. He couldn't be certain she'd be there, but he remembered that she often used to drop into her college rooms to pick up any messages and catch up with colleagues. A few moments later, he was put through.

Grace thought it best not to indicate that she had been expecting to hear from him. 'Steve, what a pleasant surprise.'

'Hi, Grace, sorry to ring without any warning.'

'Much the best way, I think. How are you?'

'Fine. And you?'

'I'm fine too. Are you ringing from a phone box?'

'Yes.'

'Very sensible. Give me the number. I'll ring back if the pips go.'

He did as she asked.

'So, what is this call about? I don't imagine you're phoning to find out how my book on the existentialists is selling.'

'Inge has turned up in London and wants to make contact with Müller.'

'Okay, Steve. Stop right there. This is a conversation we need to have face-to-face. Could we meet over the weekend? I have a lunch appointment in London on Sunday. Could you meet me at the bar of the Great Eastern at five o'clock that day?'

'Sure.'

'Okay. See you then.'

Steve put the phone down in pensive mood. That was not how he had been expecting the conversation to go. On his way to Borough, Steve decided that he wouldn't mention this conversation to Collingwood.

MI6 – Borough – Friday

STEVE GOT TO THE Borough offices just before five-thirty and was shown up to the reception area on the fourth floor. He didn't have long to wait for Collingwood to come and fetch him. 'Thank you for coming in, Steve. Let's go in here.'

He showed Steve into a small meeting room.

'So we know you met Ulrike on Wednesday evening, but we're not clear what the lead-up to that was.'

'She tracked me down to the pub where everyone at work goes after we've signed off the magazine for the week.'

'That was bold.'

'She even used my operational name from Berlin, Tom.'

'Goodness me!'

'Well, using my real name would have involved telling me she'd got it from another source.'

'Which is what she told you subsequently?'

'Yes.'

'And the source was?'

'Müller. She also had a big hunk with her.'

'Really? That's not the normal protocol either. By the way, did anyone else hear you being addressed as Tom or anything else sensitive?'

'Yes, unfortunately, I was with a colleague called Sally. She seemed to think Ulrike and her minder were gangsters and that I owed them money.'

'Could be worse. Is that what she still thinks?'

'I'm afraid not. For quite other reasons, Sally has her suspicions about me.'

'Could you explain what you mean by that?'

'When I applied for the job, I thought saying I had a degree from Cambridge might not enhance my application, so I claimed to have gone to the London College of Printing. Sally made some enquiries and found that to be a lie. In a jokey kind of way, she threatened to expose me to the big boss.'

'Unless what?'

'Unless I slept with her.' Steve knew that this wasn't quite how things had happened, but it gave Collingwood some idea that Sally was more than just a colleague.

'Steve, how on earth do you get yourself into these scrapes?'

'No idea.'

'Won't it complicate things with Ulrike?'

'I don't think so. Sally's a bit of a free spirit. We're at the try before you buy stage.'

For a moment the expression on Collingwood's face was one of distaste.

'I'm sorry, Jeremy, I know you don't approve of the way I live my life. I just offer the information so that you're fully in the picture.'

'Thank you, Steve. I appreciate that.'

'What I'm trying to say is that when Sally asked me why they were calling me Tom, my explanations just made her even more suspicious.'

'How much did you tell her?'

'A bit.'

'Is she reliable?'

'I tell you what, it's she who should be working for you, not me.'

'Hmm, okay. I'm afraid I'm going to have to look into Sally's background. You also met Ulrike at the George in Borough the following evening.'

'Yes, she also asked me how Sally had reacted to her calling me Tom. I told her that I'd told Sally that the name on my passport was Thomas Steven Percival and that I'd misrepresented my qualifications to my current employers. If you recall, my cover for the East Berlin jaunt was that I was an architecture student, which she had remembered. I assumed that she knew what my real background was, so I owned up to it. I think that really interested her, because of course Müller is now attached to St Rad's.'

'Anything else?'

'She said that she'd been arrested, but is grateful that Müller pulled some strings to get her ransomed. She also said her relationship with him had been on a *droit de seigneur* basis. She had never loved him.'

'And did she offer any reason why she had sought you out other than to encounter once again your mercurial charm?'

'She said she wants me to take her up to Cambridge to meet Müller.'

'Couldn't she just contact him directly?'

'That's what I said. She said that he had refused to see her. In his new life he doesn't want a lovelorn former student hanging around his neck. Also it sounds like he'd fixed her up at an aunt's in Frankfurt.'

Collingwood made a note. 'Hm, that might be worth looking into. Does she actually have a reason for seeing him apart from wanting to thank him or go to bed with him?'

'She wants to finish her PhD at Cambridge and she thinks he might be able to help. Her plan is that if he believes that she and I are lovers, he might not feel so threatened by her and will help her find a place.'

'I see. There is a certain logic to her story. Please let me know when and if there is a date for you to meet Müller.'

'I will.'

'Did she stay over with you?'

'No, but we got a bit of practice in.'

'Practice?'

'At being lovers.'

'Oh, jolly good. Was it a satisfactory experience?'

'It was at the purely physical level, but then she had a bath and went back to her digs.'

'Were you disappointed?'

'I was a bit but also a little relieved.'

'Did she give a reason?'

'Werner is taking her to Oxford for the weekend. Apparently Werner thinks it would be a better place for her at which to study.'

'What a ridiculous idea!'

'Quite.'

'So what are your plans for the weekend?'

'I'm spending it with Sally in Islington.'

'My first impulse was to ask you if that was wise, but actually it might be quite handy. Could we arrange what would seem to be a chance meeting over the weekend? Do you know the King's Head on Upper Street?'

Steve nodded.

'Let's meet there accidentally, as it were, around one o'clock tomorrow.'

'Okay. Does that mean you also live in Islington, Jeremy?'

'I'm afraid I can't say.'

Steve laughed. 'I bet you've got one of those huge places in Barnsbury or Canonbury.'

'Sorry, Steve. Can neither confirm nor deny.'

'Jez, this profession's going to have to come up with a better phrase than that.'

'You're right there, and please don't call me Jez.'

Sally & Steve – Islington – Friday

LATER AT SALLY'S FLAT in Islington, as they were eating their fish and chips straight from the paper bags using the newspaper in which the food had been wrapped as a tablecloth, Steve did his best to fend off Sally's questions about why he had been called in for a meeting with his handler.

'They just wanted to know how things went with Ulrike.'

'And what did you say?'

'Pretty much what I told you in the office this morning.'

'I can't believe that's all that was spoken about.'

'Well, *you* were mentioned.'

'Me?'

'I'm afraid so. He wanted to know what my movements were over the weekend. I said I was spending it with you.'

'So I've got you to myself for the whole weekend?'

'Well, I'm afraid I'm meeting Grace on Sunday evening.'

'Hang on a moment. Who's Grace?'

Steve realised, not for the first time, that, if he couldn't even keep in mind who knew what and what any particular person ought not to know, he really wasn't cut out for the world of espionage. 'Grace was my girlfriend before Becky.'

'Any overlapping?'

'No, as a matter of fact.' Absurdly, Steve almost felt proud of himself.

'Could you tell me a little about Grace?'

'Grace was my teacher. She is thirty-six. We got together when her husband left her. She asked me to help her have a child.'

'In the conventional way?'

'Yes.'

'But if there was no overlapping with Becky, then presumably things didn't work out. Or are you now the father of a young child?'

To say that he was not the father of *her* child would not help matters. 'No, it didn't work out.'

'Who terminated the arrangement?'

'She did.'

'To find another donor?'

'No, not really, but I don't want to go into all that.'

'Steve, based on the little you've told me, it's clear your life is not like other people's. I was already a little apprehensive about getting involved with you, what with little Ulrike and her unsmiling sidekick floating around the place and your working for the spooks. And now I discover that there are battalions of other women I know nothing about.'

'I'm sorry. Maybe I haven't thought this through properly. But you were the one who talked about overlapping and it being 1976.'

'Okay, but that was before I knew the things I now know. And I've got a feeling that there is more to come. Is this how you normally operate, having two or three girlfriends on the go at any one time?'

'No, no…' Suddenly, an image of his life in Cambridge came into his mind.

Sally noticed the hesitation. 'In the sense of yes, yes?'

'Well, not by design, but I suppose things could be seen in that light.'

'I'm not sure, Steve, that I want to be the backstop when sundry other girls are otherwise indisposed.'

'No, it wouldn't be like that, but, you know, I might have to see Ulrike quite a lot in the short term.'

'In defence of the realm?'

'I suppose so.'

'But I've got you this weekend, have I?'

'Yes, something like that, apart from Sunday evening. And only if you want me here.'

'Okay, let's take it a step at a time and we'll see how things develop. But I should tell you that I'm not sure I want to have a relationship on this basis.'

'I completely understand. Would you mind passing the vinegar?'

They woke late the next morning. After a shower, Steve went out to Upper Street and picked up bacon, eggs, fresh bread, orange juice and a copy of the Guardian. A little later, the breakfast things cleared away, and the Guardian read, Steve felt at a loose end. Earlier he had suggested, as previously agreed with Collingwood, that he and Sally have lunch in the King's Head around one o'clock, to which she had immediately agreed. Steve was well aware that had he mentioned they were going to *bump into* Collingwood, she might not have been quite so keen on the suggestion.

That meant, however, that there were still a couple of hours to kill. Normally, in such situations, Steve would reach for his guitar, but in the absence of a guitar he decided to continue with his exploration of Sally's extensive collection of LPs. No doubt even a sub-editor on a music magazine was likely to develop a wider knowledge of the current music scene than the average music fan. And Sally was certainly up to date with recent releases, including LPs by artists Steve had never heard of. What, for example, was *Music from the Penguin Café*? Intrigued, he slipped the disc out of its sleeve and put it on the turntable. The room filled with what sounded like the members of string quartet fooling around before a recording session, but there was also something agreeably hypnotic about the music they were playing. Mainstream it was not, however.

Sally looked up from the Guardian's cryptic crossword, in which she was engrossed, and said, 'Good choice. Do you like Eno's stuff?'

'This is Eno?'

'It's his label. He's the producer.'

Steve could see that he was going to have to upgrade his knowledge of the music scene if he wanted to be taken seriously at *Buzz* and not just thought of as a good sub-editor. 'You're going to have to give me a crash course in what's hip in the music world. This makes the String Band seem distinctly conventional.'

'It will be my pleasure. But I expect my students to get their essays in on time.'

'Not my forte.'

'There may well be detention for repeated transgressions. I would like five hundred words on the album we are currently listening to by breakfast time tomorrow.'

Steve laughed, prompting Sally to say, 'Not a laughing matter, Steve.'

She picked up her crossword again. Before returning his attention to the music, Steve noticed that, Sally, clearly a seasoned puzzler, had made considerable progress in the short time she'd been working on the puzzle. As she rapidly filled in the grid, he listened to the remainder of the tracks on side one of the disc. How indeed would one sum up an album like this? It resisted the usual music paper clichés.

The arm of the record player swung back to its cradle with a soft clunk. Sally put her newspaper down. It seemed that she had got as far as she could in a first pass at solving the puzzle. She went over to the sideboard and picked up a spiral-bound pad and a biro and handed them to Steve. 'You can get something down on paper while I work out what I'm going to wear to the King's Head.'

Steve took the pen and pad without comment. He didn't really like being given tasks, but he supposed he ought to show willing. Sally disappeared into the bedroom and some minutes later appeared in a dove-grey, pleated maxi skirt with a black close-fitting, scoop-neck top. 'What do you think?'

What he thought was that she looked much more sophisticated than the woman he worked with on a daily basis.

'You look amazing, but we're going to a pub, not a swanky restaurant.'

'But this works for you?'

'It certainly does.'

Sally started to pull the top over her head. 'How are you getting on with your assignment?'

'I'm thinking about it.'

'Perhaps you should aim to get it done before we go to the pub'

'But you said breakfast tomorrow.'

'I've changed my mind. You've got to learn how to do hot takes.'

She went back into the bedroom. Steve could hear the sounds of cupboards and drawers being opened. He jotted down some notes, but nothing he wrote seemed to describe the record. His vague resentment at being given a task was getting in the way of his critical faculties. Maybe it would help if he listened the other side as well. He turned the record over and returned to his notes.

Something about 'The Sound of Someone You Love Who's Going Away and It Doesn't Matter', the long first track on side two of the record, triggered a mood of melancholy in him. Suddenly he had an idea and started scribbling, oblivious to the fact that Sally seemed to be having difficulties in finding an alternative to the outfit he had rejected. She did not re-emerge from the bedroom until the end of side two. She had changed out of the grey maxi skirt and black top into a pink floral-printed maxi skirt with a simple close-fitting white top.

'What about this?'

Steve looked up from the writing pad. 'Beautiful, very elegant. But it's essentially the same thing in brighter colours. Haven't you got something a bit more boho or with a peasant vibe? I believe embroidery is quite big these days or something in earth colours.'

'Blimey, you might be having difficulty writing a record review, but you seem to have the fashion lingo down. Did you do work experience at Condé Nast?'

'No, but for the last year I've been living with an actress who mainlines Vogue.'

'Ah, yes.' Sally unzipped the skirt and stepped out of it. 'So, any further progress with your review?'

'I've got a few words down.'

Sally pulled the white t-shirt over her head. 'Well, read it out then.'

Steve felt somewhat embarrassed. It was almost as if Sally were his supervisor, although one who conducted supervisions in her underclothes. He cleared his throat. 'At a time when disco and prog rock firmly dominate the charts, Simon Jeffes, the genius behind the Penguin Café Orchestra, comes along to upset the behemoths of the contemporary music scene. With his singularly idiosyncratic approach to composition and, no doubt, with some help from the enigmatic Brian Eno, Jeffes has conjured up an album which is at once intimate, pastoral, and genre-defying. The result is a sequence of pieces that are simultaneously timeless and sharply contemporary, and which, improbably, combine whimsicality and sophistication. The mood of *Music from the Penguin Café* is both warm and enigmatic, blending an almost folkloric simplicity with a structural playfulness. Acoustic textures dominate, with guitars, ukuleles, and pianos intertwining in gently hypnotic patterns. There is an unmistakable sense of freedom and joy, a playful looseness that gives the music an almost improvisatory air, even as it is carefully composed. The pieces unfold in a way that resists conventional song structures, instead moving like a dream sequence – each track feeling like a fragment of an imagined landscape, imbued with both nostalgia and gentle absurdity.'

'Bloody hell, Steve…'

'Yeah, I know, bullshit.'

'But top notch bullshit. How many words is that?'

'Dunno, coupla hundred.'

'Well, I think you can consider your assignment completed. More words are not going to improve it.'

'I'll take that as a compliment, though it could be read differently. You, on the other hand, have not completed your own assignment which is to find something to wear, appropriate to lunch at the King's Head. Not that I particularly object to your standing around in your underwear.'

Sally returned once again to the bedroom and re-appeared a few minutes later in a new outfit. This time she was wearing a loose, blue blouse with three-quarter sleeves and an ethnic design in orange and blue on the front over hip-hugging, flared blue jeans. Steve studied her closely for a few moments. 'Much better. You don't have a black leather jacket, do you?'

Sally nodded. Steve was suddenly decisive. 'Okay, the close-fitting white t-shirt from the second outfit, with the jeans from this one topped off with the leather jacket and some Converse sneakers, if you have some.'

Without a word Sally returned to the bedroom and a short while later re-appeared as prescribed. She turned around slowly so that he could appraise her from all angles. 'Lovely, your bum looks great in those jeans.'

Sally turned back to face him. 'I thought it was my top you were concentrating on. I know that peasant blouse doesn't enhance my figure, but it cost a fortune.'

'I'm sure there's a time and a place for it.'

'Steve, I'm starting to think you might be taking the piss.'

Steve got to his feet and took her in his arms. 'Sal, I haven't had so much fun for ages. You looked beautiful in all the outfits. I thoroughly enjoyed the private fashion show. If we weren't heading out for a lunchtime pint, I would be taking you straight back to bed.'

The King's Head was busy. It was, after all, Saturday lunchtime. Luckily a table became free just as they got there. Steve was amused that the pub still showed their prices in pre-decimalisation amounts, despite the increasing difficulty of matching the new currency to prices, affected by the raging inflation that had been precipitated by the oil crisis of three years earlier.

He caught Sally's eye and smiled at her. This was lovely. Maybe he should just tell Collingwood to get lost, and the whole lot of them, Sheena, Ulrike, and Grace. He and Sally were made for each other. He even preferred being at her flat to his own. Hers might be smaller and somewhat sparsely furnished, but it was airy and comfortable. Most of all, it was not filled with sad memories.

No doubt he should have made a more determined effort to change things at Trinity Church Square. Becky had helped him take his mother's clothes to a charity shop, but he had done nothing to change the interior. Furniture, fittings and decor remained as they had been for as long as he could remember. Perhaps he could sell the flat and move in with Sally. Sadly, there were quite a few things to sort out before any radical move of that sort could be made, even assuming that Sally would agree.

She noticed that he seemed abstracted. 'What are you thinking about?'

'How much I like being with you. I wish all the other stuff would go away.'

'So do I, Steve. Your life is so complicated. I don't know if it would be wise for me to get involved.'

'You're already involved.'

'But not to the extent that I couldn't withdraw.'

'I've only just found you.'

'Leaving aside who found whom, the obligations we owe each other are minimal, whereas you already seem to have an extensive web of obligations to sundry others.'

'You're right, but you're the only person who can help me free myself from that web.'

'I wish I thought that was the case.'

While Steve and Sally were having this poignant exchange, Collingwood entered the pub. Having spotted Steve, who had not yet noticed his arrival, he bought himself a pint and then, waiting for a lull in the couple's conversation, presented himself at their table. 'Steve, fancy meeting you here.'

Steve looked up. 'Jeremy! Nice to see you. You don't strike me as a typical King's Head patron.'

'Oh, you'd be surprised. But I'm sorry. I can see that I'm inter-rupting a tender moment.'

'Oh, no. Please join us. Jeremy, this is Sally. She's my boss.' Then, addressing Sally, 'Jeremy went to the same college as me at Cam-bridge, a bit before my time, though.'

Jeremy drew up a chair and sat down. 'Not that much before your time, Steve. I'm not that old.'

If Sally was irritated by this interruption of her lunch with Steve, she didn't show it. 'And what do you do now, Jeremy?'

'Oh, I work for the Foreign Office, but in a rather humble capa-city, certainly not on track to be in the diplomatic corps.'

Privately, Steve thought it was high time the department came up with another way of answering that question too, but Sally seemed to take it at face value. In any case, Collingwood was intent on reversing the polarity of enquiry. 'And since you are Steve's boss, you must also be a member of *Buzz* magazine's staff?'

'I am indeed.'

'And are you a Cambridge alumna too?'

'Certainly not. The LSE.'

'Ah! A much more radical institution. And are you an economist?'

'No, I did philosophy.'

'And were you involved in student politics?'

Steve thought that Collingwood was going in a bit hard, but Sally seemed completely unfazed. 'Naturally.'

'Anything interesting.'

'The IMG.'

Steve was surprised. This had not come up so far in their own conversations.

Collingwood chortled. 'Oh, jolly good.'

Sally was puzzled. 'You approve?'

'Well, not of the organization's aims as such. But it is refreshing to meet someone who was actually involved and doesn't just make the claim in order to add a bit of brio to their CV.'

Sally pursed her lips. 'Jeremy, I know exactly what working for the Foreign Office really means and, no, I will not be telling you who I knew and what we did.'

Steve was startled by Sally's poise and quick-witted retort. He felt he ought to intervene, but had no idea what he should say. Oddly, both Sally and Collingwood seemed to be enjoying the encounter.

With a twinkle in his eye, Collingwood said, 'Nor would I expect you to.'

He swivelled around and, having assured himself that there wasn't anyone else in their immediate vicinity, said, 'Steve told me that you were with him when Ulrike made contact. She seems to have been under the impression initially that you were Becky, Steve's sometime girlfriend. And then, of course, I understand that she called Steve Tom, because, of course, what else could she have called him? To have used his real name at that moment would have given away the fact that she must have got the information from her handlers. But that then meant that Steve had to explain to you later on the kind of thing that he was mixed up in. When he told me this I asked him if I might meet you because it's impossible for you to unknow what you now know.'

'And you want me to promise not to talk about this to any of my former comrades?'

'No, not at all. That's entirely up to you. Somehow I think you won't, but if you do that is something that we will have to live with. I'm not sure it would make much difference to the situation that Steve is dealing with.'

'So, why did you want to meet?'

'Let me say first that this meeting was not Steve's idea. It was mine. So please do not be too annoyed with him. I have put him in an impossible position. But I think he is getting used to that. Secondly, Steve will need some back-up which we will not be in a position to supply without showing our hand. You, on the other hand, are already *in situ* and ideally placed to stay close to him. Thirdly, despite your student affiliations, I do not think that you actually approve of the Stasi even if you approve of the idea of a socialist state.'

Steve was waiting for the inevitable explosion of anger and contempt from Sally. He had been expecting Collingwood to use this supposedly chance encounter to run his slide-rule over Sally without giving away what he was about, not to offer her the job of his minder. He was not looking forward to the dressing down that he was going to get when they got back to the flat when he would no doubt also be given his marching orders. But there was no explosion, not yet at least.

'From what I gather,' Sally said, 'Steve is being asked to have an affair with Ulrike. That immediately limits my access to him.'

'But you work together, quite closely as I understand it, and our friends know that.'

'They know about me?'

'If they didn't, they do now. But the proximity you have with Steve is explicable and if they do run a background search on you, you will be revealed as a former IMG member, which will give them some comfort.'

'Supposing I refuse.'

'Then you refuse. Everything remains the same. Steve will just be more exposed than he might otherwise have been.'

'Can we go on being lovers?'

'Most certainly, with the obvious proviso that Steve will have to be with Ulrike from time to time.'

'And will I be in any danger myself?'

At last Steve felt he could contribute to the conversation. 'Jeremy will say the risks are negligible, when in fact they will be far from negligible.'

'Oh, Steve is exaggerating. Let me assure you that we will never be too far away. I will give you a number to ring, but only in a real emergency. So what do you think?'

'I don't know. I'm rather annoyed with Steve and I'm going to give him a very hard time when we get back to the flat. But I think he's a honest guy and I do rather like him. I just wonder how he got mixed up in all this?'

'I am sure he will tell you and please don't give him too much of a hard time until you have heard his story.'

Steve looked at Collingwood. 'Do you really mean that?'

'I leave it to you, as you see fit. If we're asking Sally for help, she has to trust you and by extension trust us, because as you know, Steve, you are now one of us. Another drink anyone?'

'Back in Berlin, you told me that things were on a need to know basis.'

'That still applies.'

Back at her flat with mugs of tea on the table between them, Sally said, 'If you ever do that again, I'll – '

'What?'

'I'll think of something.'

'Let me know when you do and we'll add it to the list.'

'The whole lunch in the King's Head thing was totally underhand.'

'That's the world I live in. If I'd told you we were going to meet my handler, you would have refused to come.'

'But now I'm mixed up in the same goddam business.'

'I had no idea he was going to ask you to be my back-up.'

'But you obviously said something about me.'

'Very little. I didn't know you were at the LSE or in the IMG.'

'He didn't seem particularly surprised.'

'Sal, he's MI6. He probably asked his colleagues in MI5 what they had on you.'

'On me?'

'You were in the IMG. They will know practically everything about you. That's their job.'

'It's outrageous.'

'Some of those who flirt with radical political positions as students go on to become dangerous people. Any state has a right to protect itself against enemies, including internal ones.'

'I had no idea that you were so conservative.'

'The truth is neither of us knows much about the other.'

'Okay, well it seems you now have carte blanche to tell me how you got mixed up in all this.'

Steve groaned. 'My mother was a senior officer in the intelligence service. Last year she was posted to Berlin, but it seems that she had been flying in and out for the previous couple of years. She was running an operation to exfiltrate one of our agents from East Berlin.'

'Did you know this?'

'Of course not. I'd understood since I was a boy that my mother worked for the Foreign Office. I knew that she was getting transferred to Berlin but not why. Anyway, as I mentioned, I was living with Grace, my former teacher, and we got a phone call one Sunday saying that my mother had been knocked over in a hit and run accident in West Berlin and was in a coma. I flew out there but she died a few days later.'

Sally reached for his hand. 'Oh, Steve, I'm so sorry.'

He sniffed and took a moment to recompose himself. 'My father died when I was a baby. My mother had been everything to me.'

Sally squeezed his hand. 'You should have told me.'

'There hasn't been time.'

'Did they catch the driver?'

'No and the supposition is that it was an assassination. Anyway, I was then asked, by Jeremy, as a matter of fact, if I would go across to East Berlin and take some travel documents to a person who would get them to the agent.'

'And that person was Ulrike or Inge as she was called at that point?'

'Yes, you're getting the picture. She was posing as a sex worker and I was a sex tourist. A lot of that sort of thing goes on and it was thought that it would distract from what we were really up to.'

'So you and Ulrike got down to business? I thought there was a bit of electricity between you.'

'The whole thing was very weird, very scary and, yes, very sexy.'

'I can see that. So did the agent get out?'

'Yes, but Inge was arrested. It was suggested to me after the operation that she was a Stasi officer. They didn't tell me she had been arrested.'

'What did you think? Is she Stasi?'

'How could I tell one way or the other? And even if I could there was nothing I could do about it.'

'So what changed?'

'Last week, Sheena pulled me in – '

'Who's Sheena? Oh, I remember. She's the woman who was going to kebab you.'

'Yeah. Sheena Ferguson is Jeremy's boss, everyone's boss as far as I can see.'

'Okay.'

'Sheena told me that Inge was in London and was now called Ulrike Schmidt. She had in fact been in prison and her release had been secured by the West German government.'

'Really?'

'They do it all the time. It's one of the main ways that the East gets hard Western currency.'

'So that's good, isn't it?'

'Maybe. But Sheena thinks there's something fishy about it. So now they still think that Ulrike is Stasi and that she is over here for a purpose.'

'And what is that purpose?'

'If Sheena knows, she's not telling, but she's asked me to keep tabs on Ulrike. She wants me to get close to her, and exploit our previous brief sexual relationship.'

'Can she make you do that?'

'No, but Sheena is very scary and, more importantly, she was my mother's lover.'

'Golly, Steve, it doesn't get any less incredible.'

'I know. There's some other stuff I'll fill you in on another time. I don't think I've got the energy to tell all at one fell swoop.'

'But I don't understand what Jeremy actually wants me to do.'

'Join the club. That seems to be the way that he and Sheena work.'

'When are you seeing Ulrike again?'

'No idea. She said she'd be back from Oxford late tomorrow. I'm waiting for her to make a move. Other than that it's subbing at *Buzz* as usual.'

'So why are suddenly meeting up with your old teacher tomorrow? Is Grace somehow tied up in all this as well?'

Steve realised there was no point holding back. 'Yes.'

Sally squeezed his hand. 'Before you start, let's get something stronger than tea.'

A few minutes later with a glass of red wine to hand, Sally said, 'Okay, how does Grace, the woman you failed to impregnate fit in?'

'Well, as I mentioned, she supervised me for two years of my degree course, which means I wrote her an essay on various aspects of French literature and thought once a week for two years. Admittedly, terms are quite short at Cambridge. And there were some weeks when I failed to produce an essay.'

'Didn't you get sanctioned?'

'Sanctions were available, but she was kind enough to bear with me. After graduation, I found myself living in her part of the city and we became friends with her and her husband.'

'Who's we?'

'Ginny and I. Ginny was my girlfriend at the time.'

'Is there no end to the string of girlfriends?'

'It is definitely a finite list, but there have been quite a few changes in a relatively short space of time. Anyway, Ginny was a former catwalk model and rather striking looking in the way those women are.'

'And she fell for scruffy old Steve?'

'Oddly, yes. But Grace's husband had other ideas and broke up his marriage to be with Ginny.'

'And you and Grace consoled each other in her bed?'

'Yes.'

'And she said, Steve, I want you to set to work and give me a baby?'

'More or less.'

'And you went to work with a will?'

Steve nodded.

'But pregnancy came there none?'

'Not so much as a phantom pregnancy or a missed period.'

'Oh dear. So then she said, sorry, lad, you've had your chance.'

'Yes. Grace was with me for some of the time in Berlin. The documents I gave to Inge were for Dieter Müller, an East German

Professor. That side of things worked and Müller attended my mother's funeral. It turned out he and Grace knew of each other, had read each other's books.'

'And hit it off?'

'Not exactly. But Müller got a fellowship at Cambridge and Grace was asked to keep an eye on him.'

'Asked by whom?'

'Sheena.'

'She can do that?'

'There are special reasons, but, yeah.'

'Blimey, I hope Sheena doesn't get to hear about me.'

'It's quite likely she already has. Anyway, the consequence of Sheena getting involved meant that Grace and I were over. There is a bit more to it than that, but that's the nub of the matter.'

'And then this was when Becky came along?'

'Yeah.'

'And Grace and Müller got together?'

'To some extent. I'm not sure of the precise details.'

'Why has she agreed to meet you, then?'

'Because I phoned her and told her about Ulrike. I thought she could meet Müller at Grace's place. She said she'd need to know more. She's up in London for a meeting tomorrow and suggested we meet to talk the idea through.'

'Wow, wow, wow! Your life seems very complicated, Steve. I think we had better go to bed before you are whisked off by some new diva and I never see you again.'

Great Eastern Hotel – Liverpool St – Sunday

WHEN STEVE GOT TO the bar of the Great Eastern Hotel, Grace was already sitting in a comfortable chair with a large glass of red wine in front of her and a manuscript on her lap, which she appeared to be correcting. She was so engrossed in her work that she had failed to see him enter the bar. For a few moments, Steve just stood there, drinking in her beauty, feeling an immense sense of loss. She must have felt the energy of his gaze. She looked up; their eyes met, and a smile spread across her face like the sun rising on a summer's morning. He suddenly felt that all was well and everything was possible. He crossed the room. By the time he had reached her table, she had put her work to one side and risen to her feet. Steve took her in his arms and kissed her hard. After a second or two, she pushed him gently but firmly away. 'Not here, Steve.'

Absurdly, he was buoyed by this formulation. 'Grace, it's so lovely to see you. Thanks for agreeing to meet.'

She invited him to sit and waved over a waiter. 'Two more of these, please,' she said, pointing at her glass.

Studying his face closely, she said, 'Does anyone else know you're meeting me here?'

'No.'

'Honestly? You didn't tell Collingwood? Or Inge?'

He didn't feel good about it, but there was no sense in mentioning Sally. 'I did tell Inge that I was going to try and contact you, which was last Thursday evening, but I haven't seen her since then. Nor do I have a contact number or address for her.'

'So, she initiates contacts?'

'Yes.'

'Have you slept with her?'

'Yes'

'Why am I not surprised? There's something very odd going on here, Steve.'

'You can say that again. Including the way you kicked me out.'

'We can't get into that now. Not if you want me to help you bring Inge and Dieter together.'

'Are you making that a condition?'

'Yes. When the time is right, I will beg your forgiveness and try and explain how I got it so wrong. But right now, we're the ones who have got to deal with a tricky situation.'

'But I don't actually know what's going on. Last year, Sheena and Collingwood led me to believe that Inge was a Stasi officer. Now they tell me she has been in a Stasi prison and was ransomed through the good offices of Müller, who they'd previously said was a double agent. Now, I've been asked to help Inge, who is really called Ulrike, as best I can.'

'So now she's guilt-tripping you and you can make it up to her by getting her and Dieter together.'

'Yes.'

'It all sounds a bit too convenient. What does she say?'

'She's grateful to Müller for getting her ransomed. She has an aunt in Frankfurt and I think his idea was that she continue her studies there. But she would really like to complete her PhD in the UK, preferably at Cambridge. She thinks Müller is reluctant to assist her to come to Cambridge because he sees her as a lovelorn former student, which is why she wants me to pose as her lover. It might make him more open to her academic ambitions.'

'Is she a genuine PhD candidate?'

'I'm not in a position to answer that. Müller would know. And you could probably suss her out pretty quickly.'

'And have you mentioned me?'

'Not by name.'

'And does she know that Dieter and I are an item?'

'Yes.'

'Well, let me tell you what I know. Dieter did receive a letter from Ulrike saying that she was coming to England for a few weeks and would like to see him. He was not happy about it and wrote back to her and told her he did not wish to see her for the same reasons you mentioned. He also gave her your real name and contact details.'

'I wondered how she tracked me down. Does he not want her around because he's living with you at Glisson Road?'

'No, he has rooms in college. He does stay over from time to time, however. Stop torturing yourself, Steve.'

'Have you been briefed on this by Sheena?'

'Only in the vaguest terms.'

'I don't trust that woman.'

'Neither do I. I think she uses people and doesn't worry too much if they get hurt.'

This shocked Steve, but was very much what he was beginning to think. 'So what do we do here?'

'I can't force Dieter to see the girl. I can try and persuade him. Do you know what her area of study is? I'm sure Dieter does, but I don't want to have to ask him.'

'No, but I can find out.'

'Do that and let me know. I'm in my office in college most after-noons between four and five. Ring me there, preferably before Friday.'

'Okay.'

'And, forgive the vulgarity, but she's definitely the same girl you fucked in East Berlin.'

'I suppose so.'

'Come on, Steve. You said you've already slept with her since she's been in London. Hair colour, size, body shape, sexual tech-nique.'

'Well, in those terms, it's definitely the same girl.'

'But?'

'I don't know. Perhaps it was just the change of environment. Instead of being in a squalid flat in East Berlin with the thought uppermost in my mind that we were being filmed and recorded by the Stasi, we were in my mother's flat in Borough with hot water and red wine and the curtains drawn.'

'And is her behaviour, her manner the same?'

'Well, she was very decisive, took the initiative as she had in Berlin.'

'Which is just how you like it, isn't it?'

Steve shrugged. 'I suppose so.'

'Okay, this is what we'll do. I'll tell Dieter that Ulrike has been in touch with you and that you are now together. Presumably, Ulrike is the name by which he knows her. You and Ulrike will be my guests at Glisson Road. I will try to persuade Dieter to join us for supper. With luck, by then I will know something about her re-search and how relevant it is to her chances of getting a place at Newnham. Then we will see what proceeds from that.'

With that, Grace stood up. 'My train back to Cambridge leaves in forty-five minutes. Time for one more drink, I think. Could you order, Steve? I just need to powder my nose.'

He watched her cross the room. She moved with elegant self-confidence.

He caught the waiter's eye and ordered another round of drinks. As he did so, it occurred to him that the last time he had been in the bar of the Great Eastern was when he had been assisting Gary at auditions for the Festival season and Ginny had appeared out of nowhere. He had been a resident at the hotel for those few days and Ginny, who was in the early stages of her pregnancy, had asked to use his room because of her morning sickness. At her request they had then made love. Steve had felt uncomfortable at the thought of making love to a woman pregnant by, as he thought at that time, another man. But she had been insistent. The experience had been magical as his interactions with Ginny often were. When she was leaving, she had, in the enigmatic way that Ginny favoured, called down blessings on his head.

As he was letting his thoughts drift over those moments with Ginny, Grace returned. She noticed the sadly pensive look on his face. She touched his arm lightly. 'Are you okay, Steve?'

'Yeah, just thinking about how crazy everything is.'

Grace resumed her seat. 'What are you doing now in the way of work?'

'I'm a sub-editor on a music magazine. It's fun, quite a nice bunch of people.'

'Are you writing?'

'Only photo captions, headlines and the occasional pocket review of LPs no one has ever heard of.'

'I'm sure that helps polish one's fluency and style.'

'Maybe, but there's very little thought involved.'

'I can't believe you haven't got some private project on the go.'

'Well, I still scribble in notebooks, but nothing coherent.'

'In our time together, I often noticed that you seemed to be unaware that you were actually at work on a new project in its early stages. Allowing the unconscious to do its work, I suppose.'

'Well, the job at *Buzz* is full-time and there also tends to be a social aspect to it. Press day each week is rather like a first night. We're so amazed to have got the new edition off to the printers that we spend the rest of the night in the pub.'

'Sounds fun. Good colleagues?'

'A crazy bunch, but Sally, my immediate boss, has taught me a lot about magazine production. I'm not sure how long things will last. The magazine is in permanent financial crisis.'

'It sounds like useful experience.'

'How are things going for you?'

'The existentialists book got pretty good reviews. Thanks for your help on that. I'm working on a new book focusing on the poetic movements in Europe in the first half of the twentieth century.'

'Sounds amazing.'

'I've nearly finished a first draft. Perhaps you could read it when I've completed it.'

'I'd love to, but I know even less about that subject than I did about existentialism.'

'You read with a different eye, which is what makes your take so valuable. You don't have a professional axe to grind.'

Steve accepted the plaudit silently, not sure if he was happy to be a token member of the laity. They continued their conversation for a few more minutes until Grace, looking at her watch, noticed the time. She drained her glass and stood up. 'It's been lovely seeing you, Steve. Ring me by Thursday if you and Ulrike can come up to Cambridge on Friday. Otherwise it will have to be the following weekend.'

Steve rose and kissed her. She let him hold for a few moments, then headed for the door of the bar. Steve watched her until she disappeared from view. He called the waiter over and asked for the bill, but then decided to have one more glass of wine before heading back to Borough.

Week Two

11 October – 17 October 1976

Buzz – Soho – Monday

AT WORK ON THE Monday morning, Sally said to Steve, 'How did the meeting with your old teacher go?'

'Fine. She's agreed that Ulrike and I can stay with her this coming weekend, as a couple, I'm afraid.'

'Will you be sharing a room?'

'That's what being a couple means.'

Sally harrumphed quietly, sat back down at her desk, and stared out of the window across Carnaby Street, her arms folded across her chest and a sullen look on her face.

Steve leaned across towards her and said in a loud whisper, 'I'm sorry, Sal, I don't know what else to do. The other day you said you wouldn't be jealous and you'd look out for me.'

'But you're not giving me a chance to do so. What does Ulrike think? Is she pleased?'

'She doesn't know yet. I am waiting to hear from her.'

'I think you're having second thoughts about me?'

'No, it's just everything is so complicated.'

'I might be starting to have second thoughts about you.'

'I wouldn't blame you if you did.'

'And what I also think is that you're going to fall in love with this girl. She's probably got you already.'

Steve shook his head silently. She was probably right.

The lunchtime session at the Star and Garter in Poland Street was just getting started. Ulrike hadn't wanted to meet at the John Snow. When Steve arrived, she was already sitting at a table in the corner, calmly smoking a Marlboro with an empty glass in front of her. It looked like she'd been there for some time. Steve greeted her and then asked her what she would like to drink. A few minutes later he returned with the drinks and said, 'How was Oxford?'

'It was beautiful, so unspoiled.'

'It wasn't bombed during the war. Hitler gave orders that it shouldn't be touched.'

'Really?'

'He was going to make it his administrative centre once he'd successfully invaded. Other historic cities were not so lucky.'

'Is Cambridge as beautiful?'

'Yes, I think so, although it has a different feel to it. It's on the edge of the Fens, which means it's very low-lying and damp.'

'That does not seem so good.'

'No, perhaps I'm not selling it very well.'

'How was your weekend?'

'Very relaxing. I caught up with some friends. But I also managed to speak to my former teacher. She is prepared to let us stay with her this weekend. She will try and persuade Müller to join us for supper on Friday evening.'

'Do you think he will?'

'I have no idea, but I am going to speak to Grace again on Thursday. Are you okay for this weekend?'

'Yes.'

'She wanted to know what your area of research is.'

'The poetry of resistance in the first half of the twentieth century – particularly the ways in which poets responded to political oppression, war, and exile. I am interested in how language itself becomes an act of defiance, whether through formal experimentation, coded symbolism, or the simple act of writing in a suppressed tongue.'

'That sounds intimidatingly high-powered. Could you give me a couple of names of particular poets?'

'You could mention René Char and Paul Celan.'

'Okay, at least those two names mean something to me. Thank you.'

Steve & Ulrike – Trinity Church Square – Tuesday

THE TUESDAY SESSION AT the typesetters went reasonably smoothly, helped by the fact that Sally had, once again, accompanied him, making it easier to talk. Now that she had a better idea of the mess he was in, she accepted that her interactions with him for the next few days or so were going to have to be confined to the workplace. They kissed passionately outside the typesetters before going their separate ways.

Back at the flat, Steve tidied up a bit, put an LP on the hifi and then lay down on the sofa to mull over recent events. He hadn't got very far with his mulling when the phone rang. He went out into the hall and picked up the receiver. 'Hello?'

'Steve, it's Ulrike.'

'Hi, Ulrike. You sound a bit shaky. Are you okay?'

'Not really. Can I come around to the flat?'

'Of course.'

'I'll be there in about an hour.'

Steve was worried by Ulrike's tone of voice. She sounded very tense.

A little less than an hour later the doorbell rang. Steve pressed the switch that opened the street door and went down to meet Ulrike. She was standing on the doormat in the communal hall, looking very bedraggled and upset.

'Ulrike, what's happened?'

'I was mugged. They took my shoulder bag with my wallet and passport in it. And my ticket back to Frankfurt.'

'Oh, no. Come in, come in.'

He led the way upstairs. Inside the flat, he took her coat. It was soaking. Her skirt was covered in mud and her blouse was torn and gaping open. Her face was pale and drawn, and it looked as if she had the beginnings of a black eye.

'Where did this happen?'

'In Camden. I was crossing a park. There were two of them. They dragged me into some bushes. One of them was trying to get his hands up my skirt. I screamed and kicked him. Fortunately, there was someone walking a dog, so the other one hit me and took my bag instead.'

'Have you reported it yet?'

'No, I don't know how to go about it.'

'Okay, we'll do that later. You need a drink. Come in and sit down. What would you like? A cup of tea or a glass of whisky?'

She chose whisky. Steve poured them each a tot.

'Ulrike, your clothes are filthy. They're covered in mud and so are you. We need to get you cleaned up. I'll run a bath.'

'But I have no clean clothes with me. I'll just sit here for a bit. It'll probably dry up.'

'Don't be silly. You can borrow some of Becky's. She's got enough here to stock Selfridge's.'

He knelt down and unbuckled her shoes. 'I'll put these outside on the doormat and run a bath. Just sit here.'

A few minutes later he was back with a dressing gown and a bath towel over his arm. 'Come on, let's get you into that bath.'

As he took her by the arm to help her up, she yelped. 'I fell on my shoulder.'

'I'm sorry.'

He went around to her other side and helped her stand. 'Just through here.'

He led her into the bathroom. 'Right, get these clothes off. There's a towel here and a dressing gown you can use. I'll wait outside. Call me when you've got the dressing gown on and I'll put the dirty clothes straight in the washing machine.'

He stepped outside the room and pulled the door to. A few minutes later, she called out. 'You can take the clothes now.'

He opened the door. She was sitting on the seat of the lavatory with the dressing gown tied loosely around her, shivering and looking exhausted. She nodded at the clothes on the floor. He was about to scoop them up, when she said, 'I'm sorry to ask you, but could you help me into the bath? I'm not feeling too steady.'

'Of course, if you don't mind.'

'Steve, it won't be the first time you've seen me naked.'

It was true, but the circumstances were different. He helped her stand and take two steps to the edge of the bath, ready to catch her if she fell. She undid the belt of the dressing gown. 'Please take the dressing gown off my shoulders, but be careful of my right arm.'

Gently he removed the dressing gown, pulling it carefully off her arms, and said, 'Okay, step into the bath, but check that the water's not too hot for you. I'll make sure you don't fall.'

She swirled the water with her hand and then carefully put her right foot into the water. Carefully holding her by the left arm, he helped her to bring the other foot in. 'Okay, turn around and sit down slowly. I'll hold your left arm and have my other hand around your shoulders.'

He lowered her into the water, getting wet himself in the process. 'How does that feel?'

'Much better. Thank you.'

As she stretched out in the bath, he noticed that she had a large bruise on her ribs under her right breast. He stood there for a few moments not knowing what to do or say.

She looked up at him. 'Do you have any shampoo?'

He took a bottle of Clairol Herbal Essences off the shelf. 'Is this okay? It's what Becky uses.'

'Yes, but would you mind doing it?'

He rolled up his sleeves and wet her hair with the hose attachment. He then poured some of the shampoo into his hands and started working it into her hair. 'I'm not getting it into your eyes, am I?'

'No, you're doing it very well.'

'Right, a rinse now. I think Becky's got some conditioner here somewhere.'

'Don't worry about that. And thank you, I'm feeling a lot better.'

'Right, stay here. Run some more hot water if you need it. I'm going to get these dirty things into the washing machine. I'll be back shortly.'

When he got back, she said, 'I'm ready to get out now. Could you help me?'

He put a bath mat on the floor next to the bath and one of the bath towels over his shoulder. 'Okay, reverse order. I'll hold your left arm with my right hand and put my left arm around your shoulders. Just move very slowly.'

'I'm sorry. You're going to get wet.'

'It doesn't matter.'

He got her standing. 'Same process, but stepping over the side of the bath. Once you're securely on the bath mat, I'll put this towel around your shoulders.'

She patted herself dry. 'Could you dry my back?'

'Can I rub?'

'Gently.'

'What happened to your ribs?'

'The guy who was trying to get my pants off kneed me in the side.'

'Oh, Ulrike, I'm so sorry.'

'It's not what I expected to happen in Great Britain.'

Steve didn't know what to say. He handed her a pair of Becky's floral pyjamas. 'I know it's probably not your style, but it's just for now.'

She put them on. 'Oh, they're so comfortable. I've never worn satin before.'

'Are you warm enough? If you're not, there's the dressing gown.'

'No this is fine.'

Steve pulled the plug out and let the bath drain. 'Right, let's get you some supper. I'm afraid I haven't got much in, but we can have a bit of a fry-up.'

'That will be lovely.'

'And I've got a nice bottle of red wine.'

'Thank you, Steve, I'm sorry I was horrible to you just now.'

'No, I understand. We'll discuss things later. Let's just get something to eat and report the assault and theft to the police.'

'Steve, I don't want to report the assault. They will want to do a physical examination. I don't want that.'

'Okay, I understand, but it's possible your bag will be handed in. Those scumbags just want the cash so they can score.'

'What's that mean?'

'Buy drugs.'

They went into the kitchen. Steve poured them each a glass of wine, then got to work on the supper. Fifteen minutes later they sat down to bacon, two fried eggs each, a tin of baked beans and several pieces of toast.

When they had finished eating, Steve said, 'So explain to me what happened.'

'I came out of the place I've been staying in late this afternoon.'

'Is that Werner's place?'

'No, I only know Werner slightly. I stayed in a youth hostel for the first couple of nights I was here. Then I met some German students in a pub on Tottenham Court Road. I've been sleeping on their floor.'

'Why didn't you tell me you were sleeping on a floor? You could have come here. Is that where your case is?'

'Yes. Anyway, I thought I'd phone you to see if there'd been any progress with your teacher. Stupidly, I went through the park on my way to a call box. I'd noticed these two guys as I entered the park, but thought it would be alright because it was still light and there were other people around. But the guys caught up with me and pushed me onto the ground behind some bushes. One of them put his hand up my skirt and was trying to get my pants off. The other guy was trying to get my bag. I hung on to it, because it had not only all my money, but my passport and my ticket back to Frankfurt. As I tried to stop the first guy pulling my pants down, the other one yanked the strap of my bag very hard and pulled it out of my hand. Then they ran off.'

'We're going to phone the police and report the theft. It's up to you whether you report the sexual assault or not. I will tell them you're a friend over here from Germany and then hand over to you. You will have to describe the bag and what was in it. They will probably want you to go in to the police station tomorrow to sign a statement. You can give this address and telephone number as your contact details. How much money did you lose?'

'Fifty pounds.'

'No traveller's cheques?'

'No.'

'And your passport?'

'Yes. And my return ticket to Frankfurt.'

'We will have to report the passport to the West German Embassy. We can do that tomorrow. Are you ready to phone the police now?'

She nodded tearfully.

A further twenty minutes later, with the robbery reported, Steve said, 'Right, we'll have a nightcap and then an early night. Tomorrow, I'll go to the bank and get you some cash and I'll give you a spare key to the flat. For the rest of your time in London, you're staying here.'

'I don't want to impose on you.'

'You're not imposing on me. I thought you were with Werner. Didn't you go to Oxford with him?'

'No, I made that up. I didn't want you to think you needed to help me. I feel so stupid.'

'You're not stupid. London is a completely different kind of city from East Berlin. In certain parts of the city there are lots of junkies and down-and-outs.'

Steve poured two large whiskies and said, 'I've made up the bed in the guest room.'

Ulrike smiled sorrowfully at him. 'Thank you, Steve. I'll sleep with you, if you want me to…'

Steve interrupted her. 'The last thing you want right now is to have a man pawing you.'

Next morning, Steve was wakened by the sound of the telephone ringing from a dream in which he was making love to Ulrike. He climbed out of bed, his erection rapidly fading, and stepped into the hall. Bloody Collingwood! He snatched the receiver from its cradle. 'Yes?'

'Mr Percival?'

'Yes.'

'It's Sergeant Harrison, Camden Metropolitan Police station. Miss Schmidt's bag has been handed in. No wallet, I'm afraid, but her passport's there.'

'Thank you, Sergeant. Miss Schmidt will come by later today.'

Over a cup of coffee half an hour later, with Ulrike wearing Becky's dressing gown, Steve said, 'The good news is they've found your bag and your passport is in it; the bad news is the wallet's gone. But I will replace the money. You can pick up the bag later today.'

'Steve, I can't let you give me money.'

'But what else are you going to do?'

'I'll get the Embassy to repatriate me.'

'Don't be ridiculous. I've got enough.'

'I feel really bad about it.'

'Ulrike, I'm happy to help. We'll sort things out in due course. Look, today's a busy day for me. It's press day. You can either meet me in the John Snow after work or you just make yourself at home here and I'll do my best to get back as early as I can. We can speak on the phone in the course of the day. I've left five pounds and the spare key on the kitchen table.'

'Thank you, Steve.'

In the event, press day went smoothly. Sally came down to the typesetters, mainly so they could talk. He told her that Ulrike had been mugged and was going to be staying with him. He did, however, make it clear that they did not share a bed. Sally didn't entirely believe him, but realised that this was what she had agreed to. There was nothing for it now, but for Steve to play out the hand of cards. She was also beginning to worry whether her bravado about being in the IMG had been a mistake. She thought she had put that all behind her. But some things marked you for life.

She wondered what it was that had marked Steve. She liked him, really liked him. He was good company, but there was also something insubstantial or protean about him. He seemed an ordinary product of his educational background, yet there was something provisional, even amoral, about him. Maybe she should put a bit of distance between them until the situation with Ulrike had resolved itself one way other another. She would give the John Snow a miss this week.

But Steve had decided to do exactly the same thing. Once the last pages had been signed off, he headed straight back to Borough. He arrived back at the flat to find Ulrike busy in the kitchen cooking. Whatever it was, the aroma was enticing.

He took his coat off and said, 'How are you feeling?'

'Quite a lot better, thank you.'

'Did you get your passport?'

'Yes, and my return ticket was with it. They clearly just wanted the cash.'

'What are you cooking? It smells delicious.'

'A goulash.'

'Oh, wonderful. Something a bit more exotic than a fry-up. Thank you.'

'It's the least I could do. How was work?'

'It all went quite smoothly today. That's not always the case.'

'But you didn't go to the pub?'

'No. What about you? What did you do, apart from getting your passport back?'

'I spent quite a long time hunting through your marvellous collection of cookery books to find a recipe for goulash.'

'The cookery books are my mother's. I don't think I've ever opened one.'

'Well, don't get rid of them. They're a great resource. I also found some other interesting items on the book shelves, a beautiful hand-crafted book called *Event/Horizon* by someone called Steve Percival, which turned out to be a book-length poem. And right beside it the bound copy of a play script entitled *Palace of Tears,* by the same Steve Percival.'

Steve winced. 'Ah, I've been found out. I should have made sure to hide the offending articles.'

'I'm sorry. I thought that if they were on the shelves of the sitting room, they were for anyone to read. But why would you want to hide them?'

'It's a long story, but they're associated with bad periods of my life.'

'I haven't had time to read either of them properly, but they're both substantial pieces of work. I can't imagine how long it must have taken you to write the poem. And, as you may imagine, I was intrigued by the setting and the theme of *Palace of Tears.* I know it's simplistic to say so, but I was struck by the characters of Freya and Tristan.'

Steve was silent. Why hadn't he foreseen this? This rather gave the game away. Sheena was going to be furious, although it was her idea that he should get close to Ulrike. Nor had it been his idea for her to come to London. 'I'm sorry, Ulrike. I was just trying to make sense of all the things that happened in Berlin. Freya is not meant to be a portrait of you.'

'I'm not angry. If anything, I'm flattered. This is a work of art. It borrows from life, but it obeys its own laws. Those characters are not you and me. And how could you have imagined that we would ever come together again or so soon? I am just overawed by the way you have been able to transmute the nasty reality of Cold War life in a totalitarian state in a divided city into something so beautiful. Did it get performed?'

'It did, by a professional company. It ran for a week, but was basically a flop.'

'Who played the part of Tristan?'

'I doubt if you'd know him, a young actor called John Philpot. He was very good and I think he will go far in the profession.'

'And what about Freya?'

'I think you already know.'

'How could I?'

'Becky, the girl who's clothes you're wearing.'

'Ah, I see.'

'It's not that I hoped to find you in her. That's not how we came together.'

'But it's axiomatic that one does not understand the workings of one's own unconscious.'

'Yes, I suppose that's right.'

'So, who is the female figure in the last part of *Event/Horizon*. Is it Grace?'

'I thought you said you didn't read it.'

'One can get a sense of a work of literature even from a cursory look.'

'Well, no. It's not Grace. I'd rather not unpack the poem right now. That is a complicated subject. But I will at a suitable moment.'

'I noticed that there are a number of notebooks in the little bedroom. I didn't look at the contents of those. Notebooks really are private. But I'm eager to know what you're working on now. You are a versatile writer.'

'I'm not sure I'm working on anything specific at the moment. Of course, I write all the time, but that doesn't mean that what I'm writing belongs to some formal work. I'd rather not discuss the contents of those notebooks, but if things work out between us, I'll consider letting you read them. In the meantime I'll leave it to you not to peek at them. But if you do, you do.'

'Going back to the play, it does seem that there are suggestions that Freya may be a Stasi undercover agent. Is that what you really think?'

'What I was trying to do there was show that there are different views of what or who the key characters are working for, what motivates them. One person's view is not the same as another's. It depends on the angle that things are seen from.'

'So that's like the parallax effect that is talked about in astronomy.'

'Yes, that's a very good image. Anyway, you know my little secret now.'

'Surely there are others who do?'

'Well, Becky knows I wrote the play she acted in because to an extent I built the part around her.'

'And Sally presumably?'

'No, for Sally I'm just a sub-editor. She only recently found out that I was at Cambridge. We haven't got around to my serial failures as a writer.'

'Two of something is a minimal series.'

'Strictly speaking, yes.'

'Well, there must be others who know.'

'Not many. One of those who does is Grace, whose house in Cambridge we will be staying at this weekend.'

Grace & Müller – Cambridge – Thursday

IT WAS THURSDAY AFTERNOON. Grace was in her college room, attending to her correspondence, when the phone rang. It was the switchboard operator. 'I have a call for you from a Steve Percival, Dr Mitchell. He's in a telephone box. Will you take it?'

'Yes, Norman, please put him through.'

A moment later, Steve came on the line. 'Hello, Grace, this is Steve.'

'Steve, it's lovely to hear from you again. Is this weekend okay for you and Ulrike?'

'Yes.'

'And she understands that she will only be seeing Dieter over supper on Friday evening?'

'Yes.'

'Good. Did you find out anything about her field of research?'

'She's interested in the poetry of resistance in Europe in the first half of the twentieth century.'

'Oh, that is interesting. Did she name any particular poets?'

'Yes, René Char and Paul Celan.'

'Even better. She does know that I will quiz her more closely and ask Dieter to confirm that assertion?'

'Well, I've told her that's what's likely to happen. I can't vouch for what she's saying as being true. It's way beyond my sphere of competence.'

'Tut, tut. Enough of that, Percival. And how are you two getting on?'

'Okay, I don't really want to go into it too much on the phone, but she has now moved into my place.'

'I hope that is a positive development.'

'So do I. Anyway, looking forward to seeing you tomorrow.'

Over supper in the rooftop restaurant of the Arts Theatre, Grace said to Dieter, 'Steve phoned me in my college rooms today. They're going to arrive tomorrow and go back to London on Sunday morning. You can come round to join us for supper at Glisson Road tomorrow evening. Steve will show Ulrike around Cambridge on Saturday, no doubt he will be taking her to all his favourite pubs. I hope she likes beer.'

'Of course she likes beer, Grace. She's German. Does she know you and I are close?'

'Yes, I believe she does. And, if she doesn't, we can make it clear.'

'A little show of affection?'

'Yes. And then on Saturday evening they are having dinner with an old friend of Steve's. So you will only have to endure a few hours on Friday evening and then you can escape back to your rooms.'

'Might he not want to show Ulrike St Rad's? It is, after all, his old college.'

'He might, but if he does and you don't want to be taking callers, you can sport the oak.'

'Ah, yes, such a civilised custom. Who is the old friend of Steve's they are visiting?'

'His name is Jon Chapman. He is a rock musician, rather good on the electric guitar, apparently.'

'Not one for me then.'

'Certainly not.'

'You know I am not entirely comfortable with this. Ulrike is highly strung. I was happy to help her get out of the DDR, but I don't want to feel responsible for her in a land and a university system in which I do not feel at home myself. I am not sure that Steve knows what he might be getting into with her.'

'I wouldn't worry about Steve. He likes difficult women.'

'Do you include yourself in that category?'

'Yes.'

'In that case, you must be making an exception for me. I am not sure how I would have negotiated the complexities of the British class system and the academic establishment without your help.'

'It has been a pleasure, Dieter. And it has been beneficial for me. It is not often that a scholar gets the chance of such prolonged contact with one of the great contemporary intellects.'

'You flatter me.'

'But I mean it. Our interests are better aligned. It was a mistake for me to have a relationship with a former student. I don't know what I was thinking of. But Steve is a decent guy and this encounter cannot be easy for him either.'

'I suppose so. And, as you say, he is behaving honourably. But how likely is it that your college will offer her a place?'

'I can't really say. Obviously, I have some influence, but it is not something that I can force through. However, Steve says that her area of research is the poetry of resistance with particular reference to René Char and Paul Celan. Is that correct?'

'Yes, she has done some brilliant work. I helped her get access to material that is not open to the ordinary reader in the DDR. But she has probably had to leave her papers behind.'

'Poor girl. That must be dispiriting. Still, there are materials here that she would not have access to in East Berlin. And that kind of work is exactly the direction I would like to take the faculty in.'

'Would you consider supervising her yourself?'

'I might if she can convince me of the depth and range of her research.'

'I, for one, would certainly be grateful, even if I remain uncertain about having her living in Cambridge.'

'If she does get the studentship, your paths are very unlikely to cross.'

'Even so, Cambridge is a small city.'

'Dieter, let's cross that bridge when we come to it. In any case, from what Steve was saying it seems that he and Ulrike are getting on rather well. And I happen to know that Steve recently ended his year-long affair with an actress called Becky Spalding, which suggests he's clearing the emotional decks. He also has a very nice flat in south London, which Ulrike has now moved into. It may be that Ulrike is starting to enjoy the pleasures of the Great Wen.'

'I am sorry, you have lost me.'

'Cobbett, the Great Wen is London.'

'Ah, yes, *Rural Rides*, I believe.'

'But what I am saying is that London has some fine universities. University College has an excellent department. The sort of research Ulrike is engaged in is a hot topic for them. If Steve and Ulrike really have fallen in love, then she will have somewhere very nice to live.'

Müller was thoughtful. 'That would certainly be convenient.'

Sally & Jeremy – Islington – Thursday

'THANK YOU, SALLY, FOR agreeing to meet me. I hope you haven't mentioned it to Steve.'

'He's in Cambridge for the weekend.'

'No, I mean that I phoned you at the office and asked to meet you without him.'

'Well, we're not in that kind of relationship; in fact I'm not sure we're in any kind of relationship.'

'I'm sorry. My colleagues and I have rather spoiled things for you.'

'Well, now I know a bit more about Steve's life, I'm not sure things would have worked out anyway.'

'Oh, I'm sure that's not true. He's a nice guy and does his best to deal squarely with people.'

'Has he sent you around to make his excuses for him?'

'No, I'm here on my own account. I wondered if I could take you out to dinner.'

'You mean on a date?'

'Well, yes, though I've never really got the hang of that word.'

Sally laughed. 'You mean you fancy me and, while Steve's off saving the empire, you thought you'd sneak in.'

'I don't quite see it in those terms. I think I'm the one who has a rather more onerous role in defence of the realm. But, yes, I find you very attractive and I thought I might chance my arm.'

'Jeremy, that's very sweet of you.'

'I'm afraid I haven't dated many girls, so my approach is probably a bit laboured.'

Sally suddenly realised he was serious. He wasn't really her type, but he had a nice manner and was quite nice looking if he'd just relax a bit. She leant forward and kissed him on the cheek. 'Jeremy, I'd love to. I was being a bit cautious because I thought you were trying to get me to freelance for you as well.'

'Well, of course, it might come to that, but I think we'd want to employ you on a more permanent basis.'

'You're pulling my leg.'

'Not at all, but let's not get ahead of ourselves. Would you be my guest at Frederick's tomorrow evening?'

'I'd love to.'

'Excellent. See you there at seven-thirty.'

'Jeremy, I'm not going to mention this to Steve right now.'

'Much the best. Let's put our heads together at the restaurant about how we deal with that. See you then.'

Ulrike & Steve – Glisson Road – Friday

As STEVE AND ULRIKE walked from Cambridge railway station to Grace's house in Glisson Road, he pointed out the house in Tenison Road that he had lived in before moving in with Grace. 'Nearly as bad as your place in Prenzlauer Berg.'

Ulrike was not convinced. 'It looks very nice. I would have been very happy to live in a place like that.'

She looked carefully at the houses as they turned into Glisson Road. 'These houses look very nice, but it is not the ancient mediaeval city I was expecting.'

'This area is from the later Victorian development of the city. I will show you the older parts of the city tomorrow.'

'And you are certain that it is okay for us to stay for two nights?'

'Yes, and if you're seriously interested in coming here to study, it's worth having a good look at the place.'

'You are right, but I am a bit nervous.'

'So am I. And if it does become unbearable we'll check into a hotel. Don't worry. I'll pay.'

Soon they were walking up the path to the front door of Grace's house which for several months the previous year had also been his home. Indeed, when he had been packing his bag earlier that morning before going to work, he'd realised he still had a key to the house. Grace had probably changed the lock on the front door, but even so Steve had slipped the key into his pocket.

He rang the doorbell. As they stood on the doorstep, Ulrike said, 'Do I look okay?'

'You look fantastic. That red coat and the purple beret really suit you.'

'I have never worn such fine clothes. I am worried that Becky will be angry with me.'

'Leave Becky to me.'

A moment later the door opened to reveal Grace's smiling face.

'Steve, Ulrike, welcome, please come in.'

They stepped into the entrance hall and put their bags down. 'Steve, you know where the coats go. Leave the bags in the hall. You can take them up once you've had a cup of tea or something stronger, if you prefer.'

Grace invited Ulrike to follow her through to the big kitchen-dining room at the back of the house, while Steve hung up the coats and tucked the bags out of the way. Grace said over her shoulder, 'Dieter is not joining us until eight o'clock, so there's plenty of time to unwind and get to know each other before then.'

Steve was relieved. It would give Ulrike a chance to win over Grace before any input from Müller. On his way to the kitchen-diner from which a delicious aroma was emanating, he glanced in at the sitting room. Not much had changed.

By the time Steve caught up with the two women, Grace was already opening a bottle wine. 'We decided against tea. Ulrike is drinking white. Perhaps you would open a bottle of red for you and me.'

Drinks poured, they toasted each other. After taking a sip of wine, Grace said, 'Ulrike, I know that this can't be easy for you, or indeed for Steve, in fact for any of us. But I am sure we can make it work. I am so glad to see you and Steve together. You will probably know – Steve has probably told you – that Steve and I were lovers for a while. Unfortunately, I did not treat him well. There is no point going into the details. But you can imagine that things are still a little awkward between us. I also know that there is some history between you and Dieter. So we are all going to have to be gentle with each other.'

So far Ulrike had hardly uttered a word, but she now said, 'Dr Mitchell, I am so grateful for your agreeing to see us. I am well aware of your academic standing and I understand why you have won Dieter's heart. But I too have lost my heart. After those few hours with Steve in East Berlin, I knew that I was in love with him. It seemed improbable that I would ever get to see him again. But thanks to Dieter's great generosity, I am now in the free world and with Steve. I know too that Steve bears you no grudge. I am hoping to apply to Cambridge to continue my studies and Steve thought I should speak to you. It is, of course, ridiculous to imagine that I might be accepted at this ancient university, but so many improbable things have happened in the last two years that I thought I should try.'

'Absolutely, we should all aim as high as we can. And please call me Grace. What is your area of research?'

'Until I was arrested, I was working on links between the thought and work of Paul Celan and René Char.'

'That's an interesting pairing. We don't often see young scholars working in that subject area. What drew you to it?'

Steve held his breath. Would Ulrike rise to the occasion? Or would she show herself to be a chancer?

'Initially, necessity. Celan was one of the few poets I could read in depth in East Berlin. *Mohn und Gedächtnis* was available, though always framed within an antifascist, state-approved narrative. *Todesfuge* was studied, but only as a condemnation of fascism, never as a reckoning with personal or linguistic rupture. Later, I came across Hans Mayer's *Außenseiter*, which framed Celan as part of a German-Jewish antifascist tradition, but I always felt something was missing in that reading.'

'Char is a French poet. How did you connect with him?'

'René Char became important to me when I realized how deeply Celan himself had engaged with his poetry. I managed to find Celan's German translations of Char – those weren't widely available, but with Dieter's help, I was able to access them.'

Steve hadn't expected anything quite so fluent and assured. Suddenly, he felt rather out of his depth.

Grace, however, wanted a little more. 'That must have been quite difficult in the DDR.'

'Yes. Certain texts were inaccessible, and others had to be read in very particular ways. I read Char's *Hypnos* because it was considered part of Resistance literature, which aligned with the DDR's antifascist rhetoric. But his later works, and especially his poetic mysticism, were viewed with suspicion.'

'How do you see their connection, then? What do you think Celan found in Char?'

'Celan was drawn to Char's vision of poetry as an ethical, almost clandestine act. Char had lived through the French Resistance, and his poetry bears the weight of hidden language, of things that cannot be said directly – which, of course, is something Celan understood all too well.'

'Because of the Holocaust?'

'Yes, his work was shaped by the impossibility of speaking after the Holocaust, by the fracturing of language itself. In Char, he found a poet who had also faced the challenge of articulating trauma, but through a resistance framework rather than a post-Holocaust framework.'

Grace was nodding. 'And yet Char was a Surrealist in his early years. Celan never truly aligned himself with Surrealism.'

'No, but he engaged with its disruptive energies – and particularly with Surrealist techniques of fragmentation and dislocation. His late poems, the *Atemwende* texts, have an almost Surrealist compression, where meaning collapses into itself.'

'Interesting. It is certainly arguable.'

'I suspect Celan admired Char's ability to maintain a sense of secrecy and retrieval in language – words as something fragile, volatile. That idea must have resonated with him profoundly, given his own relationship with German as a language both of poetry and of destruction.'

'You've clearly thought deeply about this. But what about the secondary literature – where do you place Jean Bollack's reading of Celan in all this?'

Ulrike paused, leaning forward slightly, brow furrowed. Steve was proud of her. She had done incredibly well up to this point. It was unfair of Grace to bowl her a googly. But Ulrike was not yet done. 'That's a question I would have loved to explore more freely in East Berlin. Bollack's work – what I could find of it – was illuminating. He argues that Celan resists poetry itself. That *poésie contre poésie* – poetry against poetry – isn't just a method but a necessary breaking of lyricism. He sees Celan's work as a refusal of aestheticization, which complicates any attempt to read him through a strictly antifascist or Surrealist lens.

'I think Char helped Celan maintain the idea that poetry could still carry weight, even if its syntax was shattered. Char, after all, wrote in *Feuillets d'Hypnos* that poetry must be like an underground resistance network – moving in secret, coded, alive.'

Grace was impressed but also perturbed. Ulrike's field of research was extremely close to the subject of the book she had proposed to her publisher and for which she had now been commissioned, a little too close perhaps.

It was true that she had mentioned the book to Steve when they had met in the bar of the Great Eastern hotel and perhaps he had spoken to Ulrike about it. But it was unlikely that she had mugged up what, at first blush, passed for a close knowledge of the subject area in the few days since then. And if she had, she would be, both as a graduate student and as potential collaborator, a person worth cultivating. Grace would have to question this bright young woman a little more closely. With luck, there would be time for that later.

'That's an astute and somewhat pertinent observation. And where would you like to take this research from here?'

'I want to explore how Celan's late works engage with his translations of Char. His translation practice was never merely linguistic – it was a form of re-creation, a dialogue across history and trauma. I'm particularly interested in how Char's idea of a poet as a resistance figure intersects with Celan's idea of the poet as someone who must speak even when language itself is in ruins.'

'And you think Cambridge, not Paris, would be the right place for you to pursue this?'

'I do.'

Steve was looking at the two women in amazement. Not for the first time, he was reminded of what a poor student he had been. God knows why Grace had ever taken any interest in him. Grace caught Steve's eye and gave him a half smile, which he read as saying that Ulrike had passed the test. She stood up and said, 'Look, I've still got a few things to do for the meal. Steve, why don't you take your bags up and show Ulrike where things are in the house? You might want to freshen up before Dieter gets here.'

Steve led Ulrike back out into the hall and picked up both bags. 'Our room is on the top floor, up two flights of stairs.'

A few minutes later he was showing her into the room that his mother had slept in nearly eighteen months previously and, for a moment, felt a lump in his throat. Ulrike looked around, wide-eyed. 'Oh, Steve, what a beautiful house! You actually lived here?'

'Hard to imagine, I know.'

'Grace is wonderful and such a brilliant scholar. Do you really think I could work with her?'

'I don't see why not. Of course, getting funding might be difficult, but some colleges have bursaries.'

'And she was your teacher too?'

'Yes, but not at the level you're operating at. I was one of the bad boys.'

'Which is why she liked you in her bed?'

'I don't think I said that.'

'No, but it's obvious. I can see that you know each other very well. You may not be together anymore, but there is still an energy between you. What happened?'

'It's a long story. I can't talk about it here. But you too have had an intense relationship. Aren't you just using me to get to Dieter?'

'No, I really do want to study here. Dieter was just a means to that end. But I understand now why he didn't want to see me. Why would he want to have me when he has Grace? Of course, that might mean that she will not want me around either. She might feel threatened by me. But so far she has been much friendlier than I ever expected. And I will try to reassure them both that I have no designs on Dieter.'

'How will you do that?'

'By making clear that I am in love with you.'

'What will you do if Grace can't help you or Cambridge won't take you?'

'I would try and persuade you to let me stay with you while I study privately and apply to other universities. Since I will not be able to earn money, I will pay my rent by cooking and cleaning for you and sleeping with you when you want me to.'

'Ulrike, I'm not saying I won't help you, but why does it need to be on those terms?'

'Because I have no money, only the little my aunt has given me.'

'You could get a job. Your English is easily good enough.'

'But surely I would need a work permit and a residence permit? In West Germany, one cannot get a job until one has a *Sozialver-sicherungsausweis*. I know that because I have recently had to go through that process when I moved in with my great-aunt. And presumably I would also have to register at the police station, what we call *Meldepflicht* in Germany. But I am afraid to go to a police station. I do not have a convincing story and I think that Germans are still not very popular.'

Steve laughed. He wasn't sure if Ulrike's earnestness was genuine or feigned. He knew all about the German penchant for what they called *Gummistemplerei*, literally a mania for rubber stamping. He'd had to go through the exact same process she had just outlined when he started work in Frankfurt in 1971. It was probably even worse in the DDR.

'It's not like that here, never has been. You go to the Employment Office, get a temporary National Insurance number and start work. In fact, for jobs in pubs and restaurants, you probably don't even need to do that. No reporting to the police station, no *Meldepflicht*.'

'But I am German.'

'And Britain is now a member of the EEC, and has been for the last three years. We actually had a referendum last year to decide whether we wanted to stay in. It was carried, the result confirming that citizens from the other member states are also entitled to come here to work. So, if you did stay at my place until you could afford your own place, you could pay your rent in a more conventional way. Not that I would ask you to pay anyway.'

'Are you serious?'

'Yes, but London is not Cambridge. Cambridge University has residence requirements. There are exceptions, but generally you have to live in college, licensed college accommodation or within three miles of Great St Mary's church.'

'I don't understand.'

'You couldn't work for your PhD at Cambridge but live in London.'

'I see. But I have heard that the London universities are very good too.'

'They are. I sometimes think Oxbridge is over-rated, even though I enjoyed myself at Cambridge. Anyway, I think we'd better go downstairs.'

'Do I look okay?'

'You look lovely. Becky's clothes look better on you than on her. We'll go over to Werner's when we get back to London and rescue your case.'

'Steve, would you kiss me before we go downstairs?'

Dieter put his glass on the table. 'Grace, that was a magnificent meal. Thank you.'

Steve and Ulrike murmured their thanks too. Grace waved away the thanks. 'It was nothing. I don't often get the chance to cook these days. Far too much High Table dining, and a glass of wine and a packet of crisps the rest of the time.'

Dieter laughed. 'But even then the wine will be of a notable vintage.'

'Not always, Dieter. But I just wanted to remark that this evening's gathering has been a significant event. I do not think it helps for any of us to pretend we weren't a little nervous. Steve and I have not seen each other for more than a year. We parted under somewhat bitter circumstances, which I will not go into here.

'Ulrike, you have spent time in a Stasi jail. When Dieter managed to use his connections to get you ransomed, you must have been hopeful that you would be able to resume the old relationship with him, only to find that he has now found a place in my affections, a fact that might also be painful for Steve.

'But it would seem that you and Steve have found solace in each other. I can tell you from the way that Steve spoke about you when we were in Berlin, that you made a deep impression on him. You make a good couple. And to be quite frank, so do Dieter and I. I am sure with a little bit of good will, we can all get along. After all, we are all on the same side.'

Dieter pushed his chair back, leant over to Grace and kissed her. 'My dear, your eloquence is even better than your cooking.'

'Tush! Enough of this flattery.'

Müller bowed his head slightly in acknowledgment before turning to Ulrike. 'But if I may, I would like to address a few words to Ulrike in this connection before we move on to other matters. I can imagine you were puzzled and upset by my reluctance to encourage you to follow me to Cambridge, even though I had done my best to get you expatriated from the East. I simply did not know how to break the news to you that it would be no longer possible for us to resume the arrangement we previously had.

'Also, although I am accorded the honorific of professor, the truth is I am not a professor here. In Cambridge, professors are not ten a penny as they are in the USA. In the curious way the British manage things, I have no formal position with the university. I am simply an extraordinary fellow at St Radegund's. And who knows how long that will last?

'I am, of course, deeply indebted to the master and fellows of the college. They have made me feel at home. For the first time in many years, I am in a position to finish the monograph containing my mature thoughts on German Romanticism, which has been mouldering in my papers for far too long.

'So, not only am I not teaching, but I have no standing with the university. Grace on the other hand does. If anyone can find you a place on a postgraduate programme here, Ulrike, it is she. She may even be able to organise a bursary. You must understand that this is not a foregone conclusion, but she will do her best, I am sure.

'This is a poor apology for my behaviour, but I hope it will make you feel less angry with me. And, my dear Ulrike, who would have imagined, three years ago when you first embarked on your post-graduate studies with me at Humboldt, that we would one day meet in Cambridge?'

During the course of these two speeches, which Steve had found teeth-grindingly embarrassing, he had been on the point of de-nouncing both Grace and, more particularly, Dieter. He noted, however, that whatever she might really be feeling, Ulrike seemed prepared to go along with Dieter's fawning comments, no doubt in the hope of making a good impression on Grace.

Fixing her gaze on Grace, she said, 'I have been so focused on my own predicament that I failed to realise that the pressure I was putting on Steve to bring me to Cambridge might be painful for others as well. I am deeply sorry. But I also feel so lucky to have been invited into this beautiful house and to have met you, Grace. Thank you for your hospitality and your words of encouragement.'

She now turned to Müller. 'But, of course, I also owe a huge debt to you, Herr Professor Müller, for your efforts in getting me released from prison. It was not my intention to disrupt your peace of mind. I simply wanted to thank you and seek your guidance.'

'Please call me Dieter. Enough of this Herr Professor nonsense. We are now in a much less formal and deferential society. It was my pleasure to help you. The thought that the world of letters might be denied your perspicacious contributions was intolerable to me. After all I was only repaying the part you played in my own escape from repression. And if it has meant that you have been reunited with this fine young man who was also involved in that operation, then I feel that my efforts have all been worthwhile. I wondered at the time whether the hand-over of documents might ignite a spark between you.'

'I do not want to presume too much, but I believe it has.'

He turned to Steve. 'But, Steve, you must have been surprised when this young lady turned up on your doorstep?'

'She turned up in my local actually.'

'I am sorry. I do not understand the term *local* used in that way.'

'The pub near my place of work.'

'And what is your work?'

'I am a sub-editor for a rock music magazine.'

'Steve, this seems an unworthy occupation for one of your intelligence.'

'Actually it suits me very well. I do not have the powers of memory and readerly comprehension that is so evidently available to the other members of this gathering.'

'I do not believe that for one moment, but perhaps it is because you are the only artist amongst us. Grace has shown me some of your work.'

Steve glared at Grace. He thought he had gathered up all his drafts and his work in progress when she had asked him to leave. Was it possible that he had left a copy of the play script? It had certainly gone through many drafts and he might not have kept track of them all. What was Dieter referring to? It would not conduce to a positive outcome for the evening's encounter if Dieter had read an early draft of *Palace of Tears*. The character based on Dieter himself had not been drawn in a flattering light in early drafts.

Grace intervened. 'Steve is unaware that the young woman, who produced the beautiful letterpress edition of his long poem *Event/ Horizon*, gave me a copy of it after Steve moved to London.'

Dieter studied Steve's face carefully. 'I'm sorry Steve. I think I have put my foot in it, as the saying has it.'

Grace said. 'No. It's my fault, but this is the first time that Steve and I have met since we came to the conclusion that our relationship wasn't working out. And since he and Ulrike arrived, much of the conversation has been about Ulrike's work on the poetry of resistance.'

Steve was troubled that Grace and Jude had been in touch with each other. Of course, they were both Cambridge residents. But it was clear that everyone in the room was improvising furiously and this was no time to show his sensitivity on the subject. 'Oh, that. It was just an undergraduate piece I knocked off when I should have been preparing for my finals. Grace would have been within her rights to have refused to teach me. I am grateful to Jude for having produced the edition, but I no longer feel it represents my interests.'

Dieter chuckled. 'Constant reinvention; the mark of the true artist. Always striving for the beyond.'

Steve had disliked Dieter's condescension when he had first met him in West Berlin and had no desire now to be pegged as some latter-day Rimbaud. 'The only mark I recognise is the one I veer away from or cross out.'

'Come, come, my dear fellow, in both cases the mark remains. In the first you leave it behind for others to read; in the second you scratch it through, but it remains legible. *Biffures*, as I think Leiris calls them, signal both the impulse and the afterthought. We get, as it were, a stereo picture, a kind of holism.'

'But that is exactly what I am resisting. A poem is never finished, literature never arrives at a final meaning. It evades resolution. My last word will be a leaving off, not a summation.'

'That may well be, but we are entitled to take your words at face value, even if you repudiate them or cancel them later.'

Grace said, 'Steve was interested in Mallarmé. He wrote an excellent essay on the *Divagations* shortly before his finals, even though he likes to claim he did no work.'

Dieter looked at Grace. 'My dear, perhaps one should go easy on the Mallarmé and Blanchot. Ultimately, Mallarmé's lucubrations were of little use to him.'

Ulrike decided that if she wanted to prove her mettle to Grace she had better make a contribution. 'Steve will not thank me for saying it, but I too have read some pages of *Event/Horizon*. The impression I had of it was that it was a provisional text, opening itself to revision. He explicitly resists in his Afterword the totalising approach of Hegelianism and its aftermath in favour of drift and errancy, as I think he puts it.'

Dieter was proud of his own student, even though he was troubled by her reference to the aftermath of Hegelianism. Presumably, this was a covert criticism of Marx. However, they were no longer in a seminar room in Mitte and he should not pick her up on it. 'Well said, Fräulein Schmidt.'

Steve was immensely irritated. He did not recognise his own poem in anything that had been said. But this was not the time to rock the boat. 'If I may paraphrase something that Goethe said to Schiller with reference to the latter's take on *Wilhelm Meisters Lehr-jahre*: I am grateful to you all for making me better acquainted with my own poem. I would only add that the process has been intensely parallactic.'

Dieter burst out laughing. 'A hit, a very palpable hit. Let us leave the matter undecided and ask Grace if we can end the meal with some of her delicious Hine cognac.'

Grace was already rising to her feet. 'A very good idea, Dieter. Let us move into the sitting room.'

The evening ended without further mishap. Grace asked Steve to be in charge of the drinks and music. He put on Miles's *Kind of Blue* and poured generous measures of Hine. From the expression that had momentarily clouded Dieter's face when Grace had made her request, Steve hoped that Dieter was irked at having been passed over as the substitute host. But any such tensions soon evaporated in the warming glow of the cognac.

Plans were made for the following day. Unexpectedly, Dieter invited Steve and Ulrike to visit him in his rooms in St Rad's at four o'clock for tea. Grace apologised for the fact that she would be out for much of the following day, but hoped to see both Steve and Grace in the evening. If the weather was unkind, they were welcome to spend the day at Glisson Road. But if the weather was fine, Grace hoped that Steve would take Ulrike to see Newnham.

At half past ten, Dieter's taxi arrived. When Müller had gone, Ulrike meekly said that she would like to go to bed. It had been a long day. Steve said he would stay down and help tidy up, but Grace would not hear of it. The two young people went upstairs and Grace sat for a few minutes finishing her cognac, a glistening tear in each eye.

Back in their room, Ulrike said, 'I am sorry. I was trying to enable you to spend some time with Grace without my struggling to understand the difference between what is being said and what is meant.'

'Ulrike, I can assure you that I feel exactly the same. But let me also assure you that you were very impressive. I really feel that you have won Grace over. Not only that, but you looked stunningly beautiful. Müller was devouring you with his eyes.'

'That's sweet of you to say so, but I think it was the effect of the items from Becky's wardrobe that you encouraged me to wear.'

'They fit you like a glove. You could almost be twins.'

'So does it make you feel that you are still with Becky if I put on her clothes?'

'No, not at all. You are beautiful in your own right. Why shouldn't you have nice things? I can straighten things out with Becky. Anyway, I doubt very much she will even bother to collect her things from the flat.'

'Because she wants to hold onto you?'

'No, because she is already moving on.'

'She is another *qui va à la dérive*?'

'You may well be right there. Are you surprised that Müller asked us to visit him in his college rooms tomorrow?'

'No, I think he's rather proud of the fact. I know you do not like Dieter and I understand that. He is Grace's lover. That's why he fears you.'

'He was your lover too.'

'That was purely transactional and, as far as he is concerned, I am with you now. Even though that is apparently what he wants, it must trouble him for all sorts of reasons. No doubt he is worrying about what I might tell you or what you might tell me.'

'Like what?'

'I honestly don't know. I just know that Dieter is always looking over his shoulder. Anyway, let's get some sleep now.'

Steve got up from the chair he was sitting in and opened a closet and started rummaging around inside it. Ulrike said, 'What are you looking for?'

'Trying to find some blankets. I'll sleep on the floor.'

'Steve, you don't need to do that. I know we have been sleeping in separate beds since I came to stay with you on Tuesday. The attack in the park shook me up. It reminded me of the way I was treated in prison, being knocked about by men. But my ribs don't hurt as much as they did. So please share the bed with me.'

'Ulrike, I completely understand. I'm happy to sleep on the floor.'

'Thank you, Steve, for being so considerate. I will do my best to show my appreciation. But I want to take charge of the process.'

Steve, determined not to make any assumptions about what the invitation involved, had absolutely no objection to that.

He undressed quickly and got into bed. For some considerable time, they lay self-consciously side by side with a gap between them like two church effigies until Steve, despairing of any activity in the early watches of the night, rolled onto his side and tried to give himself up to sleep. He had almost drifted off, when he became aware that Ulrike had rolled over too and he became aware of her warm body pressed against his back. Resisting the urge to turn over and embrace her, he felt her reach down in search of his now eager cock. Having ensured that he had a serviceable erection, she burrowed under the blankets and took him in her mouth. It did not take her long to coax a respectable climax from him. After a few moments, he drew her up towards him and reached down towards her vagina, but she pushed his hand away. 'I'm sorry, Steve, I'm not ready for that.'

'I just wanted to reciprocate.'

'No, there's no need for that. I am content with having given you some pleasure. It is the least you deserve for everything you have done for me. Let us now go to sleep.'

As Steve drifted off to sleep, he wondered whether contentment really did trump satisfaction.

Sally & Jeremy – Islington – Friday

'OOH, SALLY, THAT WAS absolutely marvellous.'

Sally laughed. 'It was marvellous for me too. You are a very considerate lover.'

'Beginner's luck, I suppose.'

'What do you mean, beginner's luck?'

'Well, it's my first time…'

'Really?'

'Yes. Does that make it seem less good? Or put you off me?'

'No, it makes me think it's worth taking this further.'

'Do you really mean that?'

'In terms of the physical stuff, absolutely. But in terms of practicalities, who knows?'

'What do you mean by practicalities?'

'Will your job suddenly require you to fuck fifty Finnish bathing beauties?'

'Oh, I see. Take on a Steve lifestyle?'

'Exactly.'

'I don't think the complexities in Steve's life have anything to do with his working occasionally for the intelligence services.'

'I was beginning to think that myself. He seems to be playing a complicated game with three very powerful women.'

'Which doesn't stop him from getting entangled with one or two others along the way.'

'If you're including me in that second list, you can include me out.'

'Does that mean you'd consider throwing in your lot with yours truly?'

'It does, Jeremy. But just to make sure, have you got enough left in the tank for another test drive?'

'I most certainly have, madam. Would you like to get in the driving seat again?'

'I thought you'd never ask.'

Steve & Ulrike – Cambridge – Saturday

STEVE AND ULRIKE WERE having a coffee on the Quayside, opposite the mediaeval splendour of Magdalene College on the further side of the river. Steve said, 'Are you okay? I'm not making you do too much walking, am I?'

'No, this is so wonderful.'

They had already come all the way along Trumpington Street, passing the Fitzwilliam Museum, Peterhouse, Pembroke and St Catherine's colleges before coming to the magnificence of King's and its soaring chapel. Ulrike had said, 'Is that the cathedral?' Steve had laughed. 'Well, it's certainly on the scale of a cathedral, but it's actually King's College Chapel.'

They had then continued past Gonville and Caius, the castellated gatehouses of Trinity and St John's and finally turned into Bridge Street.

Ulrike took a sip of her coffee. 'You said you were going to show me Grace's college.'

'I am if your feet aren't too sore. I thought we'd get there by walking along the river.'

'How far is it?'

'Not too far. Afterwards we can have some lunch at a pub and then we'll get a taxi back to Grace's, after we've had tea with Dieter at St Rad's.'

'Okay. Let's get going.'

Steve led her across Magdalene Bridge. 'This is the college that the diarist Samuel Pepys went to. The college is on both sides of the road, the mediaeval court on the right and Benson Court behind these ancient timber-framed buildings on the left.'

He pointed to the Pickerel pub. 'You asked to see the ancient buildings of Cambridge. That's the oldest pub in Cambridge, something like four hundred years old.'

He led her a little further down the street and pointed at another ancient building which had a large double gate. 'This also used to be an inn, called the Cross Keys, I think, but now it's a part of the college. We're going through here.'

Ulrike was uncertain. 'Are we allowed to?'

'If we look as if we know where we're going, the porter will just think we're students.'

As they passed through the gates, Steve nodded at the porter who was standing in the doorway of his office and said, 'Morning.'

The porter smiled and said, 'Mornin', sir, and a beautiful one it is too.'

They passed into the centre of the court. Ulrike looked around in amazement. 'This does not look like some of the other colleges. There are all sorts of different buildings here.'

'Yes, its official name is Benson Court, but it's often called The Village. We're going to go through here and then through the part of St John's which is on this side of the river.'

They walked along by the gleaming white bulk of the Cripps Building seeming to float over a tributary stream of the river and then into the echoing passageways of New Court and its vaulted cloisters. Turning right, they looked out through the great portal across the huge expanse of lawns towards Trinity College's Wren Library.

Ulrike said, 'Oh, Steve, it's so beautiful. It's like a palace. I can't believe that people get the chance to study here.'

'This is called The Backs. We're going to follow the gravel path to the right of the lawns. There's a gate over there, which will bring us to Queen's Road.'

Soon they were passing the back of King's. Ulrike sighed. 'King's College Chapel looks even more beautiful from this side.'

'It does. The interior is also magnificent. I'll take you to see it, but perhaps not this weekend.'

Shortly thereafter, they turned into Sidgwick Avenue, now both footsore and glowing with the exertion of the morning's walk. Cambridge had unfolded before them – its courts and cloisters, its pale stone and river reflections – until Ulrike felt she was in some kind of dream. She pulled her bright red coat closer against the damp September air, glancing at Steve as they crossed the road towards the main entrance of Newnham College.

'I don't think I can walk much further without some refreshment.'

'Grace wouldn't forgive me if I didn't show you something of Newnham. It's very different, but I think you'll like it. And the pub we're going to is not far away.'

Ulrike sighed theatrically. She wished she'd chosen shoes more suitable for a long walk. Following a couple of paces behind Steve, she looked around with interest at the red-brick sprawl of Newnham College as they stepped through the main gate. It was nothing like the medieval courts they had spent the morning exploring – no battlements or Gothic towers, no great chapel looming over a manicured lawn. Instead, it stretched low and expansive, built for comfort rather than grandeur, its windows large and inviting, its gables rising against the pale sky.

'This was one of the first,' Steve said. 'A women's college, I mean. When it opened in the 1870s, they didn't even give degrees to women. They studied here, sat the exams, but their work was considered unofficial. It took until the late forties for Cambridge to finally grant degrees to women.'

She ran a hand along the iron railing as they walked. 'And now?'

'Now, the number of women at Cambridge is increasing. Two or three of the traditional colleges have started taking women, but there is a long way to go before there is proper equality.' He nodded towards the main entrance, where a student in a long coat, books clutched to her chest, disappeared through the doorway. 'Dorothy Garrod was the first female professor at Cambridge – she was based here. And Sylvia Plath was a student.'

Ulrike studied the red-brick façade, the wide bay windows and the elegant Queen Anne details. It was homely, somehow – grand in its own way but without the weight of centuries pressing down on it. She could imagine rooms filled with books and conversation, laughter filtering through the corridors.

'It's different,' she said at last. 'Less... austere.'

'Yes,' he said, slowing his pace. 'That's what I've always liked about it.'

They wandered further in, past bicycles leaning haphazardly against walls, past a stretch of lawn damp with morning mist. In the distance, the Newnham Gardens spread out behind the buildings, secluded and peaceful.

Ulrike shivered slightly. 'It must be beautiful here in summer.'

'It is. It's always quiet. You can sit under a tree and read, and no one bothers you. At least, no one did when I used to come here.'

'You used to come here?'

'I knew someone who studied here,' he said vaguely.

She gave him a sideways glance, but he didn't elaborate. He turned back towards the gate, clapping his hands together. 'Right. That's your final tour stop. Now, beer.'

They retraced their steps towards Sidgwick Avenue, the morning's *dérive* fading behind them. The prospect of a snug interior, a cold beer and something solid to eat, gave new energy to their steps. They turned right onto Newnham Street and made their way to the Granta pub, perched on the banks of the millpond, the river glimmering dully under the autumn sky.

The pub was already busy when they arrived, students enjoying a lazy Saturday lunchtime, the low murmur of conversation rising and falling over the occasional clink of glasses. Steve found them a spot by the window, overlooking the water, and as they sat down, Ulrike sighed in contentment, taking off her coat and beret, glad that Steve had persuaded her to wear them.

When he had finished his lunch of quiche lorraine, coleslaw and jacket potato, Steve said, 'Dieter invited us to his rooms at St Rad's at four o'clock. Are you sure you still want to see him again?'

'I suppose so. How long will it take us to walk there?'

'Not more than half an hour. It's on the other side of the river from Magdalene.'

'So we could sit here until three-thirty and then go to Dieter's?'

'I'm afraid not. The pub will be closing in half an hour's time at two-thirty. Pub opening hours are a curious and annoying feature of British life. I thought we could break the walk at the Whim in Trinity Street. I pointed it out when we were passing Trinity.'

'The building on the corner with a turret, like a witch's house?'

'That's the one. It's a favourite with undergraduates. We can have tea and cake before continuing to St Rad's.'

Ulrike was delighted by the Whim. They found a table downstairs and ordered from the waitress. Ulrike had coffee and a slice of coffee and walnut cake, and Steve had a pot of darjeeling tea and a buttered scone with jam. When Ulrike had consumed the last crumb of her cake, she said, 'I'd much rather stay here than go to see Dieter.'

'Me too, but if you want him to corroborate your academic claims, you're going to need to keep him sweet.'

'I suppose you're right, but before we do, I have a favour to ask. Would you mind leaving me alone with Dieter for a few minutes?'

Suddenly, Steve was alarmed. 'Isn't that what Dieter was trying to avoid?'

'I think he is reassured now that I won't be a nuisance to him.'

'It will feel like we were misleading him.'

'It is a private matter of no real relevance.'

'Which you can't share with me?'

'Only because it would be embarrassing.'

Steve paid for the refreshments and they set off for his old college, both with a certain amount of apprehension.

Tucked between Thompson's Lane and the Quayside, St Radegund's College – known to all but the most formal dons as *St Rad's* – was one of Cambridge's lesser-known colleges, its reputation veiled in an air of quiet eccentricity. Unlike the grand facades of King's or the sprawling courts of Trinity, St Rad's presented a more haphazard silhouette to the river: a mixture of medieval stone, Tudor timber, and stubborn Victorian brick, each century imposing its own logic on the next.

The college had been founded in the late fourteenth century as a small monastic house dedicated to St Radegund of Poitiers, much like the former St Radegund's nunnery that later became Jesus College. Unlike its larger counterpart, however, St Rad's never quite found its way into the upper echelons of Cambridge's great institutions. It remained a modest foundation, overlooked in favour of its grander rivals, often surviving on the patronage of idiosyncratic benefactors with obscure academic interests.

Its main entrance, a narrow archway half-hidden off a winding lane, gave little sense of the college's true shape. Beyond the main gate lay Front Court, an uneven quadrangle of ancient stone buildings, their windows small and mullioned, the walls leaning slightly inward as if conferring in whispers. The hall was a modest affair, its high-beamed ceiling blackened with the soot of centuries of candle smoke, the long wooden tables scarred by generations of student cutlery. The chapel, tucked away behind the hall, was a peculiar mix of architectural styles, its medieval chancel abruptly truncated by an ugly Victorian addition – funded by a nineteenth-century Fellow who believed a direct, unembellished approach to worship was the only path to salvation.

Down by the river, the College Library occupied what was once a merchant's warehouse, its gabled roof still bearing the old hoist beam where sacks of grain were once lifted from boats below. Inside, the narrow reading room smelt of old books and wax floor polish, the shelves crowded with volumes that no one had borrowed in decades. But, for some, the library was a haven and a place for serious study, though it was also said that the ghost of a seventeenth-century scholar lingered there, searching eternally for a misplaced manuscript.

Beyond the courts, a narrow passage led to the riverside Fellows' Garden, a sloping lawn fringed with willows, where wooden benches provided a perfect vantage point over the Cam. The garden was bounded on one side by the remnants of the old city wall, now little more than a crumbling stretch of stone smothered in ivy. It was here, when the weather was fine, on a bench set into the old wall, that Professor Dieter Müller now liked to sit, book in hand, watching the punts drift by.

St Rad's had always been a college of misfits, attracting scholars who, for one reason or another, never quite belonged elsewhere. It had never sought grandeur, nor had it ever needed it. The students and Fellows who passed through its quiet, shaded courts found something different there – a place where the weight of tradition sat lightly, where conversations stretched long into the night, and where the past was always close.

Approaching St Rad's, Ulrike said, 'It's almost as if your college is hidden away.'

'Yes, it's one of the smaller colleges, rather shy and retiring, but once you're inside the college precincts, it seems much bigger than some of those colleges which have huge quadrangles and enormous chapels.'

As they passed through the main entrance, the door of the porter's lodge swung open and a portly man appeared on the top step. 'Mr Percival, sir, so nice to have you back with us. How are you?'

'Hello, Stan. Yes, I'm sorry I've not been back or taken up my non-resident member's dining rights. Life has been a bit hectic.'

'So I hear from Professor Müller. And this lovely lady in the beautiful red coat must be the professor's former student.'

'Yes, Stan, you've obviously managed to wheedle everything out of Dieter. This is Miss Ulrike Schmidt.'

Stan bowed his head slightly and said, '*Guten Tag, Fräulein Schmidt.*'

Ulrike laughed. '*Hallo Stan, freut mich Sie kennenzulernen.*'

'*Ganz meinerseits, Fräulein Schmidt. Willkommen in St Rad's. Ich hoffe, Ihre Reise war angenehm. Darf ich Ihnen den Weg zu Professor Müllers Räumen zeigen?*'

Steve was more than a little nonplussed to hear Stan conversing so easily in German. 'It's okay, Stan. I believe Professor Müller's set is just across Founder's Court from Dr Doyle.'

'Just so.'

'Do you know if Dr Doyle is in college at the moment?'

'He returned not long ago. I am sure he would be delighted to see you.'

Stan watched the couple cross First Court, Steve pointing out particular details here and there, and then returned to his office from which he and his colleague Sid watched all the comings and goings of college life.

Ulrike slipped her arm through Steve's. 'What a lovely place, so peaceful and quiet. And what a curious jumble of styles. But somehow it works.'

Soon, they had reached Founder's Court. Steve said, 'I'll stay for five minutes of chit-chat and then ask Dieter to excuse me for a few minutes while I call on Dr Doyle. Will that give you enough time?'

'Yes, thank you for being so understanding.'

Dieter's set was on the first floor of staircase G. Steve showed Ulrike how there was a nameplate at the bottom of each staircase, indicating the name of the resident of each room or set of rooms.

'The staircase is the fundamental unit of habitation in Cambridge. The signs get repainted at the beginning of each academic year.'

'Where was your room?'

'On the Jesus Green side of the college. I'll show you if there's time. The room was a bit poky, but it meant that I was able to climb in late at night.'

'Why couldn't you use the front gate?'

'Because all junior members of college are supposed to be in college by midnight. One of the conditions of getting a degree is that you had to have spend sixty nights or so *in residence*.'

'How quaint. Presumably you were coming back from your girlfriend's college or getting her out of St Rad's?'

Steve laughed. 'Yes, and the long skirts the girls were wearing then didn't make climbing in and out of windows easy.'

They were now standing in front of Dieter's door. Steve looked enquiringly at Ulrike. 'Ready?'

She smoothed her hair, tugged the collar of her blouse and nodded. Steve rapped on the door with his knuckle. They heard a muffled '*Herein*'. Steve pushed the door open and indicated with his hand that Ulrike should enter first. Dieter was sitting in an arm-chair, a book on his lap, and a cigar smouldering in an ashtray. He had clearly been dozing.

'Come in, come in, my dear young people. What a splendid time we had last night.'

He rose with some difficulty from his armchair. 'And welcome to my humble but, for me, absolutely perfect quarters. Ulrike, my dear, you can put your lovely coat over there.' He indicated a hatstand in the corner.

'I have laid the table for tea. But I am afraid that I have not yet mastered the art of actually assembling the victuals. I am going to have to call on your services, Steve. I think that we two Germans should be able to manage toasting crumpets, if you will get us started. But you will have to be completely in charge of brewing the tea.'

Steve stole a glance at Ulrike. This was going to delay her plan to have a private word with Müller. She showed no emotion.

Swinging into action, Steve said, 'Dieter, have you got a toasting fork?'

Müller proudly produced a rather ornate toasting fork. 'Excellent. And do you have an electric kettle or is there a gas hob in the gyp room?'

'There is indeed an electric kettle.'

'And finally, we need a teapot and a tea-strainer.'

'I have what I am reliably informed is called a Brown Betty in the kitchen, a tea-strainer and a tin of Fortmason tea.'

'Excellent. Let's light the gas fire and get to work. Ulrike, you be the toaster.' Steve lit the fire and put the first crumpet on the end of the toasting fork. 'Just hold it close to the grille, but not too close. Don't let it burn. Toast both sides.'

He watched Ulrike for a moment or two. 'Good. I will go and attend to the tea.'

Steve made the tea in time-honoured fashion, warming the pot and letting the leaves steep for just under five minutes. He brought the teapot and tea-strainer through to Müller's study and put it on a table mat. 'The one thing missing, Dieter, is a tea cosy. But for now that is not essential. I'll use a tea towel. Right, let us sit at the tea table.'

Steve positioned himself with the tea pot in front of him. Ulrike brought over the plate of crumpets. 'Is the butter salted, Dieter?'

'It is. And it is French. I was told that was better.'

'Indeed. You have put out strawberry jam and honey. That is okay, but purists go for butter only. I will pour. I see you have also provided a jug of milk, which is fine, but a good tea like this doesn't really need milk.'

Dieter smiled. 'We will take it as you recommend.'

Using the strainer, Steve poured the liquid into each of the tea cups. Dieter took a sip of his. 'Oh, that is so delicious. There is a distinct aroma of orange blossom. Is that possible?'

Steve sipped his. 'You're right. Well, Fortmason is one of Fortnum & Mason's blends. I'm not sure of the constituents. But, Dieter, these tea cups are magnificent. Bone china, I imagine.'

Müller glowed with pride. 'They are. Wedgwood in fact. The design is Wild Strawberry and the rims are 22-carat gold. If one is going to perform the British tea ceremony, one should do it properly.'

Ulrike had still not tried her tea. 'Ulrike, my dear, do you think it might taste horrible?'

'No, I just don't think I will be able to respond in the appropriate way.'

Steve tried to reassure her. 'Ulrike, you can drink tea in whatever way you want. Yes, one can fetishise it. But for most Britons, it's an everyday drink made from strong black tea dust. I can put a splash of milk in yours if that will make it more palatable. Or Dieter might have some sugar.'

Müller was annoyed with himself that he had forgotten to put the sugar on the table. 'I do, I do. There are some sugar cubes in the kitchen cabinet.'

Steve went into the kitchen and returned with a small bowl of sugar cubes. Ulrike dropped one into her cup and, when it had dissolved, took a sip. The tension that had been visible on her face evaporated and she said, 'Yes, it is delicious. I am sorry to be so timid.'

Steve said, 'Well, let's get on with the crumpets or they'll be getting cold. They need plenty of butter. And you might note that that butter will probably drip through, so lean over your plate. You don't want to drip it onto your skirt.'

While he had been saying this, Steve had been eating his own crumpet. With his mouth still full, he said, 'Dieter, can I top you up?'

Müller nodded enthusiastically. Steve then filled his own cup up and said, 'I'll brew a fresh pot. Back in a jiffy.'

While he was in the kitchen, he was aware that there was brief, whispered conversation in German between Ulrike and Dieter, none of which he was able to catch. But when he came back with the fresh pot, all Müller's bonhomie had evaporated. He looked diminished. Steve poured the fresh tea, but the atmosphere had changed completely. Müller made an attempt to rally, and while he showed Ulrike some of the books he had found in the college library, Steve cleared the tea things away. Hoping to give Ulrike and Müller a little more time together, he washed up the tea service, drying the cups and saucers carefully with the tea towel. When he re-entered the room, they were sitting in silence, not looking at each other.

As Steve and Ulrike emerged from Dieter's staircase, Steve spotted two older male figures emerging from a doorway in the range that formed the parallel side of the quadrangle, one of whom was very familiar, the other not quite so.

The older of the two looked up and said, 'Well, bless my soul, Steve Percival, and back in the hallowed precincts of St Radegund's.'

'Dr Doyle, I was hoping I might catch you. Stan said you were in, but Professor Müller insisted on giving us a splendid tea.'

'Steve, are you going to introduce us?'

'I'm so sorry. This is Ulrike Schmidt, a former graduate student of Dieter's at Humboldt, through whose good offices she has been able to get to the West. She hopes to continue her studies at Cambridge.'

Steve then turned to his companion. 'Ulrike, this is Dr Doyle, my former director of studies,' and, pointing to the other don, who had so far remained silent, 'This is Jeremiah Flynn, the great poet.'

Flynn bowed his head slightly towards Ulrike, in silent acknowledgment, and then, turning to Steve said, 'So you are the elusive Steve Percival. I have heard great things about your work from Rob Williams and also from Grace Mitchell, but you have managed to avoid coming anywhere near me.'

'Dr Flynn, not only is Rob a good friend, but he is also a better poet than I will ever be. And that is also the case for Grace.'

'I understand that you do not wish to be part of a coterie, but I would be happy to see you outside those channels, for a pint in the Fort St George, for example.'

'That is kind of you, but I am no longer a Cambridge resident. I live in London, and Ulrike and I are just here for the weekend. I wanted to introduce her to Grace. And whilst what you say about being part of a coterie is true, my real reason for avoiding you in person, though I am very familiar with your work, is that my own work is worthless.'

Flynn seemed to grow taller and said in quietly thunderous tones, 'It is not for you to say…'

But at this point, Ulrike intervened. '*Herr Doktor Flynn, darf ich was sagen*? My area of research is the poetry of resistance in the first half of the twentieth century. Naturally, it focuses on German and French texts. I am sorry to say I do not know your own work, access to contemporary texts from so-called imperialist powers is restricted in the DDR. But I have taken the liberty to read some of Steve's work and I am shocked at its scope and poise for one so young. It seems to me that he is also a poet of resistance. It is just that in the postmodern era, or let us say, the late modern era, hegemonizing tendencies operate in different ways. Consequently, the sites and techniques of resistance must adapt too, which is what I think one finds in Steve's work.'

'Well, Fräulein Schmidt, that is a discussion I would very much like to continue next time you are in Cambridge. I do hope we can see you again soon. Perhaps in the meantime you can persuade Steve not to avoid me so determinedly.'

Doyle, who had been following the exchanges with a wry smile on his face, said, 'And, Steve, I just want to say how sorry I was to hear of your mother's death. Please forgive me for not having written, the news only reached me recently, some time after the event itself, I fancy. I would also be delighted if you would be my guest at High Table, the next time you are up.'

With that, the two dons made their way to some more secluded spot in the college, the Senior Combination Room perhaps.

On their way back to Glisson Road, Steve said to Ulrike, 'I'm not sure I've got the energy to go to Jon Chapman's this evening. We've done a lot of walking and had rather more encounters than I was expecting. Why don't we stay in?'

Ulrike didn't need any persuading. 'I'd prefer that too.'

Back at Glisson Road, they found a note from Grace. She wouldn't be back until late. They were welcome to help themselves to anything in the fridge and drinks cupboard. Steve asked Ulrike what she'd like for supper. But she said she'd had more to eat than she was used to and just wanted to lie down for a while. Steve was feeling much the same way. If she wanted to go up, he would be up shortly with some tea. Ulrike said that would be nice, but could she have coffee?

When he got up to the guest room with the drinks, she was already in bed. He put her coffee on the night stand on her side of the bed. 'Steve, I'm so tired after all the walking we did today and with the stress of seeing Dieter.'

'I understand, Ulrike. I will stay up for a while longer if you don't mind. I will try not to wake you when I come up.'

'That's fine, Steve. I'm not sure anything would wake me.'

Steve went next door to the bathroom and ran himself a bath. A few minutes later, lowering himself into the warm water, he allowed himself to reflect on the day's developments.

The walk around Cambridge had been exhausting, but it had been instructive to see the place through the eyes of someone who had very little idea how idiosyncratic England's two ancient universities were. It reminded him how much he missed the place and how his sense of belonging there was already starting to fade. Of course, Ulrike had been enchanted by everything she had seen. It would be hard now to persuade her to complete her thesis in London.

The encounter with Müller had also been much more positive than he had been expecting. Müller had been surprisingly friendly and welcoming. It was clear that he already felt at home at St Rad's. He had finally found a haven in which to complete his life's work. The elaborate tea party had been a bit of a rigmarole, but not without its charm. It had certainly helped break the ice.

But the visit had ended on a curious note with the flustered conversation between Ulrike and Müller when Steve had been washing up the tea things. Whatever she had said, it had certainly had a considerable impact on Müller's mood. He had seemed unable to regain his earlier lightheartedness or retreat to his default pomposity. He had, in fact, seemed utterly broken.

Steve and Ulrike might well have touched on the matter, had they not bumped into Doyle and Flynn in Founder's Court. Steve had not previously been aware of any particular amity between the two. It occurred to him that Müller had let Doyle know that Steve was visiting him and Doyle had contrived to bump into Steve and Ulrike. But to seriously think such a thing he would have to have had a very inflated sense of his interest to his former director of studies. So, no, it must have been pure coincidence.

As he stood up in the bath to reach for the towel, he wondered where Grace was this evening. She was under no obligation to be in, of course. It was they who had changed their plans. Back in the bedroom, Ulrike was still sleeping peacefully. He looked at his watch. It was not particularly late. Perhaps he could have a nightcap. He got dressed and went downstairs. In the front room, he switched a couple of lamps on and drew the curtains. He pulled Coltrane's *Ballads* from the record rack and put it on the turntable. Not wishing to disturb Ulrike's slumber, he kept the volume low, even though he doubted that the sound of the music would reach the top floor. He went over to the drinks cupboard, pulled out a bottle of Glenfiddich and poured himself a decent amount. Pulling a book at random from one of the shelves in the alcove to the left of the chimney breast, he settled down to read. For a short while he felt at home again.

He was on his second glass of Glenfiddich, when he heard Grace's key in the lock. A few moments later she was standing in the doorway of the sitting room. She was in evening gear and looked distinctly tipsy. 'Hello, you're back early.'

'Ulrike was exhausted by all the walking, she's fast asleep upstairs.'

'Did she get to see Newnham?'

'Yes, it was love at first sight.'

Grace threw her coat over a chair and said, 'I need to go to the loo and then I'll join you if that's okay, make mine a large one.'

A few minutes later, she was back, and Steve handed her a large Glenfiddich. She took a sip and said, 'So tell me how it went.'

Steve described their walk in detail, how welcoming Müller had been, and how they had bumped into Doyle and Flynn.

Holding her gaze, he said, 'Did you mention to Doyle that we were visiting Müller?'

She smiled at him over her whisky. 'I might have done, but I think you'll remember that not much happens at St Rad's without Stan or Sid knowing about it. Who needs a surveillance system when you've got those two?'

Steve realised this was much more likely to have been the case. 'Anyway, Flynn was very civil and said that both you and Rob had said good things about my poetry. He wondered why I had been avoiding him. He said he could understand that I might not want to be part of a coterie.'

'He probably thinks all the more of you for that very reason. You know how it is, Steve. Playing hard to get, only makes the desired object even more desirable to the seeker.'

He did know how it was. 'I hardly think I'm an object of desire for Flynn.'

'You know what I mean. Anyway, you'd be surprised.'

'Grace, have you been drinking?'

'I should have thought that was perfectly obvious. I hope you are not expressing disapproval.'

'Of course not, I just wish I was at the same stage of tipsiness.'

'There's plenty more in the bottle, if that's the way you're feeling.'

'Thank you. I might just do that.'

Grace stood up. 'Well, if you're getting stuck in, I'll go up and change into something more comfortable, as they say.'

Steve was about to say something inappropriate, but caught himself in time. Raising an eyebrow, he watched her totter across the sitting room in her heels. In the doorway, she looked back at him and winked.

A while later, she reappeared in a pair of satin pyjamas and a white towelling robe. 'That's better. Nothing seems to fit me anymore.'

Steve said, 'That's nonsense. You looked a million dollars when you came in. Admittedly, in your jimjams, you look more like the Grace I know and love.'

Grace sighed deeply. 'It's lovely having you here, Steve.'

'It's lovely being back, but painful too.'

'And for me. I cried myself to sleep last night.'

'Grace, don't tell me things like that.'

'I know I shouldn't, but I miss you. We had some tough moments, but mostly it was great.'

'I don't think we should be talking like this. It's taken me nearly a year to pull myself together. Becky was just a cover for my loss of self-respect.'

'But now you have Ulrike.'

'I'm just doing a job and I'm pretty sure she knows that. There's not much substance between us. Mainly, I just feel sorry for her.'

'Does she like it here?'

'Cambridge? It's her dream.'

'What does she think of me?'

'She's massively impressed, very respectful.'

'Well, supposing I ask her to stay here for a few days. I could show her around Newnham properly and take her to the UL. That sort of thing.'

'What would be the point?'

'I might find out something that will explain what's going on. With all due respect, Steve, some things can be said between women, which couldn't be said even to the man you are making love to, particularly to the man you are making love to.'

Steve laughed. 'Well, okay, but all her stuff is down in my flat.'

'I can sort her out some clothes and any other female impedimenta she might need. And you could come back next Friday, if your diary isn't otherwise full.'

Grace & Ulrike – Cambridge – Sunday

OVER BREAKFAST, GRACE SAID, 'Ulrike, I'm sorry I was out yesterday evening. Steve told me how much you liked Newnham. Of course, Steve couldn't really show you the parts of the college reserved for members and their guests. But I can. I should have given the matter a bit more thought before you came up. Anyway, I was wondering whether you could stay on for a few more days. I could take you to Newnham and show you around properly. You could be my guest at dinner. I would introduce you to some interesting people. I could also show you around the University Library and if you were here on Thursday, you could attend my lecture.'

Ulrike could hardly believe what she was hearing. 'But what about Steve? He has work.'

'He will have to go back and do his work. Would you feel uncomfortable being here with me on your own?'

'No, but I only brought a change of clothes for the weekend.'

'I am sure I can help you there.'

'Steve, would you mind if I stayed?'

'Of course not. As Grace says she is much better placed than me to show you around. St Rad's was really the only card I could play.'

Talk of St Rad's reminded Ulrike of something. 'Grace, Steve introduced me to a poet called Flynn. Do you have any of his books on your shelves?'

'Pretty much all of them, I should think.'

'Would you permit me to read some of them?'

'Of course. I'll show you where they are after breakfast. So that's agreed then. You'll stay for the week. Steve, can you come back up on Friday?'

Later that evening after Steve had left to catch the London train, Ulrike, who was washing up the supper things, said over her shoulder to Grace, 'Thank you for letting me stay with you a little longer.'

Grace picked up a tea towel and began to dry the crockery. 'It's a pleasure. If you're serious about coming to Cambridge to study, it is worth having a closer look at how it works.'

'I will be very pleased to see it from the inside, so to speak.'

'You probably realise that Dieter was very apprehensive about your coming.'

'But he arranged my release.'

'How do you know that?'

'That's what the authorities at the prison told me.'

'But Dieter says he did not. He says that he only knew about your planned release when the West German authorities asked him to vouch for you.'

'Well, I think that he felt guilty that I went to prison and wanted to help me. But when I decided not to stay with my aunt in Frankfurt, he did not want me to get in the way of his relationship with you.'

'And he also felt guilty because by helping him you had condemned yourself to a prison sentence.'

'Yes.'

'But you knew the risk you were taking.'

'From what I know, no one else was interviewed. It was expected that all his students would be interviewed, but they came for me directly. So someone must have told them.'

'And you think that person was Dieter?'

'Yes, it's possible, but it's also possible that it was someone else.'

'Who else knew?'

'Well, at least two people on the British side, Steve and his handler. And possibly more. I am just trying to think about it logically.'

'You are in a relationship with Dieter and want to protect him.'

'And you were in a relationship with him and now you want to punish him.'

'But I was not in love with him. It was useful for my studies.'

'My situation is not so different. I may be further along in my career, but the knowledge that I am highly-regarded by someone of Dieter's standing might help me become a professor.'

Ulrike nodded. 'So you do not love him either.'

'No, I'm ashamed to say that is the case.'

'Who do you love? Is it Steve?'

'No. I like him, but I know he could never stay with me. When my husband left me, I decided I wanted the baby my husband had denied me for so many years. I asked Steve if he would be the father and he agreed. Things went wrong between us, and in any case I did not become pregnant.'

'Why? Would he not stay with you?'

'There is an age difference between us. I was his teacher and that would eventually have become a problem.'

'But you still like him?'

'I do. But there are more fundamental reasons which I'd rather not go into now. Nothing directly to do with Steve or Dieter. But there was obviously a spark between you and Steve when you met in East Berlin and now you have been able to resume that relationship.'

'But it is also a relationship of convenience. We are just pretending. I hoped that if Dieter thought I was in love with someone else, he would be prepared to see me. And I am not sure a spark is enough to sustain a relationship.'

Week Three

18 October – 24 October 1976

MI6 – Borough – Monday

COLLINGWOOD PUSHED THE PLATE of Marie biscuits across the table. 'Sorry to call you in so early on a Monday morning.'

'I'm getting used to it.'

'How did it go in Cambridge?'

'Fine. Ulrike's still there.'

'Really?'

'Well, that's what Sheena wanted, isn't it? Something along the lines of *assisting her and if she makes her own way to Müller, all well and good*.'

'But she can't be staying with him.'

'Of course not. She's staying at Grace's.'

'I'm not sure that's a particularly good idea.'

'Jeremy, don't be an idiot. Where else is she going to stay?'

'So she and Grace got on? Given your involvement with both of them.'

'Very well, in fact. Ulrike is the real McCoy, academically speaking. She certainly impressed Grace and, I suppose, Müller already knew how brilliant she was. And in terms of my involvement, I'm just doing what I've been told to do.'

'And you saw Müller?'

'Yes, twice. He came to dinner at Grace's. And then he invited us to tea in his rooms at St Rad's.'

'Where are his rooms?'

'Staircase G, First Floor, Founder's Court right opposite Doyle's set.'

'A place you could probably find your way to blindfolded even in the labyrinth of St Rad's?'

'Absolutely. So could you, I imagine. And of course, Stan was standing on the steps of the Porters' Lodge to welcome me back. He must have rung through to Doyle to let him know I was there, because on our way out Doyle miraculously appeared with Flynn in tow and introductions were made.'

'Had you never met Flynn before?'

'I'd been to some of his lectures, but never met him face-to-face. He suggested we meet for a pint in the Fort St George.'

'Quite an honour. How did Ulrike find all this?'

'Well, she's totally sold on Cambridge and Grace. But she was not particularly friendly to Müller.'

'Unfriendly, even though he was instrumental in getting her freed?'

'Well, he's only ever been a means to an end. And he extracted a price for promoting her academic career?'

'What kind of price?'

'Come on, Jeremy. By making her submit to his attentions, if I can put it that way.'

'Oh, I see. But wasn't that the implied quid pro quo for seeking him out in Cambridge.'

'Yes, but she now understands better how Cambridge works, and she realises that he does not have that kind of clout. They did have a whispered exchange of words. I think she offered him a few home truths. Unfortunately, I wasn't able to monitor their conversation. I was being mother.'

'I'm sorry, I don't follow.'

'Müller had laid on tea in his rooms for us, but I was on kitchen duty. Neither of them knows how to make a pot of tea with loose leaf tea. Although he did have a tin of Fortmason.'

'Very nice. No doubt Doyle had given him a few tips.'

'And he had a lethal looking toasting fork.'

'Who was in charge of that?'

'Ulrike.'

'Appropriate somehow. What happens next?'

'Ulrike's going to stay with Grace for the whole week and I'm going back up there on Friday. I have no idea what happens after that.'

'Okay. I'll let the governor know. She's out of the office quite a lot this week. She might want a personal report. This operation is high on her list of priorities.'

'I can't imagine why. Müller is a busted flush and Newnham will snap Ulrike up for their graduate student programme with Grace's backing.'

'We'll see.'

'If that's it, I'll be on my way.'

'There's one other thing I wanted to talk to you about, a personal matter.'

'Personal?'

'Yes. I'm not really sure how to broach it.'

'Oh, come on, Jeremy. You're a top notch operator. I can't imagine what would make you hesitate.'

'But you don't really know me on a personal level.'

'True, but come on, just dive straight in, no background.'

'Well, Sally and I went to bed together.'

It took Steve a moment to connect Jeremy and Sally as being inhabitants of the same social universe. But then the penny dropped. He was about to remark about how underhand certain people could be, but quickly stifled his outrage. His rights vis-à-vis Sally were really rather limited. He laughed as lightly as he could. 'Well done. You two will be good together. And well done for the man to man thing.'

'Thank you, Steve. I told Sally you would be a gent about it. She's dreading seeing you at the office later.'

'She has nothing to dread. She has every right to be wary of further involvement with me. My life gets no less complicated. And you are a very decent man. I'm pleased for both of you.'

Steve – Trinity Church Square – Monday

BACK AT THE FLAT that evening, he poured himself a glass of red wine and set about preparing a light supper. On occasion during the preceding fifteen months, he had wondered what it would be like to meet Inge again. His daydreams had naturally enough focused on the elevated levels of sexual electricity that would be generated. In the event, though, with the exception of the first evening at his flat, that aspect of their reunion had been distinctly tepid. The fact is he knew very little about her. It occurred to him that having travelled to Cambridge with only an overnight bag, she had left her suitcase, which she had rescued from the place she'd been staying at when she went to get her bag from the police station, in the guest room. He knew that it was an intrusion, but perhaps he would find something in the case that would give him some better idea of the real Ulrike.

He brought the case into the living room. It was not locked. He opened it. Inside lying on top of her neatly folded clothes was a small zipped attaché case. He lifted the attaché case out and un-zipped it. There was very little in it: a street map of Cambridge and a small notebook with a pencil tucked under the buttoned clasp. He unbuttoned the clasp and leafed through the first pages. There were pencilled notes in German about Steve, his real name, his address, the location of the *Buzz* offices, the name of his girl-friend. On subsequent pages there were Müller's contact details and the location of St Radegund's College. More surprisingly, there were also details of Grace's house in Glisson Road. But, at first sight, there was no information here that she might not have got from her correspondence with Müller and her own research.

He continued working his way through the notebook. There was a section with facts and brief observations about the poetry of Char and Celan. That was a little more disconcerting, suggesting that she had taken the time when travelling to Britain to memorise details for an academic interview. One might have thought that a graduate student hoping to transfer her studies to Cambridge would be sufficiently on top of her subject not to need a crib. On the other hand, it was also the case that she had spent the last year in prison, with little or no access to relevant texts, which in itself must have been a form of torture.

He put the notebook back in the attaché case and zipped it up again. He then lifted the items of clothing out of the case, making sure to keep them in the same order. She had travelled light. Apart from her underwear, there were only two changes of outerwear and one pair of shoes. Her toilet bag was no doubt up with her in Glisson Road. Apart from that the case was empty. He put everything back in its original order and closed the case. The contents of the case gave very little impression of a real life behind the sparse details of the person he already knew. But God knows what he had been expecting to find. If she really was a trained Stasi agent, she was hardly likely to leave her badge or the contact details of her handler in the case.

But why was Sheena so confident that Ulrike was Stasi? There was nothing about the woman he'd spent the last week with that suggested that to be the case. Nor did anyone seem to be disputing that she had been arrested, spent time in prison and been badly treated. Why would the Stasi do that to one of their own people? Even her release from prison, while no doubt welcome, had involved exile. So there was no good reason for her to be particularly enthusiastic about being with Steve, let alone sleeping with him. Clearly, he was just a stepping stone.

Yet, when they had been together in East Berlin, with no prior obligations on either side, the sexual chemistry between them had been immediate. There had been powerful flashes of that same chemistry when they had gone to bed after the drink in the George. But since then, the flame had almost gone out. Yes, Ulrike had subsequently been assaultcd in the park in Camden, and had picked up an injury to her ribs. This had perhaps triggered a flashback to the sexual abuse she had suffered in prison. Steve had certainly not been insensitive to that possibility and had slept in a separate room at his flat.

Even at Glisson Road, when they had had to share a room in pursuance of the increasingly absurd charade that they were lovers, he had been prepared to sleep on the floor. It was she who had asked him to share her bed. In accepting her invitation, he had done so without expectations, happy to take things slowly, recognising that she might not yet feel comfortable again with the sexual act. But she had been the one to initiate intimate contact, although in her own way and very much in the spirit of getting the whole business over and done with as quickly as possible and making no demands for her own pleasure. It had almost been as if they were an older couple; she uncomplainingly submitting to the grosser demands of a husband of many years. No resistance to the basic act, but no passion either.

Grace & Ulrike – Newnham – Tuesday

GRACE SHOWED ULRIKE INTO her office. 'This is where I give supervisions. And also where I take care of the increasing amounts of administration I now have to attend to. If I want to read in peace, I go to the library or work at home.'

'But it's such a lovely room and it overlooks the college gardens.'

'Yes, that is a bonus. Anyway, we can leave our coats and bags here while we are at dinner.'

'Grace, I am not sure I have the confidence to meet your colleagues. I will feel out of place. Once you have shown me the grounds and the library, I think I should go back to Glisson Road.'

'Oh, nonsense. You will be fine. The skirt and blouse suit you very well. You'll have any men who are at dinner tonight swooning.'

'I don't think I want to be noticed in that way, but thank you for lending them to me.'

Grace was annoyed with herself. What a stupid thing to say! 'What I meant was that they look much better on you than on me. For some reason I think of myself as flat-chested, but that's not been the case for nearly twenty years.'

'You have a lovely figure. Whereas I have no figure at all.'

'Nonsense. You are slim and perfectly proportioned. I am just sorry that none of my bras fitted you.'

'I don't mind going without, as long as it is not too noticeable.'

'No, that silk camisole does a perfect job. I rather enjoyed dressing you up. I haven't had so much fun for years.'

'Me neither.'

'So we'll have no more of these anxieties. I can assure you that in what matters, your reading and your ideas, you are more than capable of holding your own.'

'But I will be very careful with your clothes.'

'There is no need. They are yours now. I've got far too many clothes and most of them no longer fit me. But I do understand that they are not necessarily your style. So why don't we go clothes shopping on Saturday? We can get you some less frumpy outfits.'

'Frumpy? That's a word I don't recognise.'

'It means dowdy and old-fashioned.'

'But the clothes I am wearing at the moment are not frumpy. I feel very comfortable in them. In any case, I don't have enough money to buy new clothes.'

'I will pay.'

'I couldn't possibly let you do that.'

'Ulrike, it would give me great pleasure. I haven't been clothes shopping with a woman friend for years. We can make a day of it and then have a late lunch at the Arts Theatre rooftop restaurant.'

'I can't pretend that I'm not tempted. It's good to have a person with good taste to advise on such occasions. But I'd feel uncomfortable about the money.'

'You're going to need some smart clothes if we manage to get you an interview. You can pay me back when you're in a position to do so.'

'If you're sure.'

'I am.'

'But isn't Steve coming up?'

'Steve will not want to come on a clothes shopping expedition. I can assure you of that. Leave Steve to me.'

Suddenly, Ulrike smiled like an excited child. 'Thank you, Grace. I am so looking forward to going shopping with you.'

'Good, that's settled then. Let's go to the library.'

A few minutes later, Grace pushed open the doors of the library and said, 'I love working in here.'

Ulrike stared in wonder at the perfect proportions and beauty of the space that presented itself to her view: a light blue barrel-vaulted ceiling decorated with stylised white floral patterns floating over a central space, to the left and right of which were bays of gleaming wooden bookcases.

Grace noticed the look of rapture on her face. 'Of course, it can't compete with the University Library, but even so, it is well stocked. And these days I have quite a say in our acquisitions.'

She gestured at some shelves to the right. 'This is the German literature section. Hölderlin, Celan, Bachmann. We try to be as comprehensive as possible.'

Ulrike stepped over to the shelves that Grace had indicated and scanned along them. She pulled a slim volume from the shelf and ran her fingers over the spine of the book. 'You even have Sarah Kirsch. She is one of the bravest poets. Even with Müller's help, access to controversial writers was very difficult for me.'

'No one in this country gets sanctioned for writing poetry. Ignored perhaps, but not ostracised or banished.'

'Whereas in the DDR it is forbidden even to read such things.'

'So it is important that our students are made aware that in some parts of the world writing poetry can be a truly radical act and not just a parlour game. In fact, telling the truth can be a parlous act.'

'Another word I do not know.'

'Parlous or parlour?'

'Both, though I suppose they are related.'

'Not really. A parlour is a room for receiving guests and is actually related to *parler*, whereas parlous is derived from perilous. But sonically parlous does suggest the act of speaking out. And even if that's not actually etymologically correct, we are allowed to make these condensations in poetry.'

'And, of course, condensation is *Verdichtung* in German, while *Dichtung* itself means poetry as in Goethe's *Dichtung und Wahrheit.*'

'In which he is effectively saying poetry is truer than truth.'

'But there are risks in telling the truth.'

'You are proof of that. You have been imprisoned and exiled.'

'But I am not a poet.'

'I am not sure I believe that, but, in any case, you helped one of the world's great literary critics escape to Cambridge to finish his magnum opus. I have never done anything like that. I have only made a fool of myself with a succession of worthless men.'

'Do you include Steve in that?'

'I suppose it was good for my self-esteem to have a younger boyfriend. But I don't see why I should exonerate him.'

'I cannot pretend I was not doing something similar, although in my case I was in thrall to a much older man.'

'It's high time we stopped seeking the approval of men and looking for validation through them. That is what Newnham is really all about.'

'I agree and that's what inspires me. Perhaps it is true that I followed Müller here and used my slight connection with Steve to get to him. But that was before I got to know you and was introduced to Newnham. I now see that it was the place I had always been trying to get to without even knowing that it existed.'

'Well, that is one of the mysteries of life. How do we find the person or the place that we don't know exists?'

'I don't know.'

'But you have done it and with luck I can persuade my colleagues to accept you on our postgraduate student programme. I should warn you, though, that you won't be able to start until next Michaelmas term.'

'What is Michaelmas?'

'The autumn term and the start of the academic year.'

'What will I do until then? I don't want to go back to Frankfurt.'

'Don't worry about that right now. We'll sort something out.'

'Thank you.'

'Right, let's take a turn around the gardens before we go into dinner.'

As they stepped out into the college gardens, the last light had drained from the sky. Grace walked slowly, as if not merely taking Ulrike to dinner but inducting her into a new dispensation. They turned a corner and Clough Hall came into view, golden light flooding out of its tall bay windows.

Ulrike was suddenly nervous again. 'Will there be... introductions?'

'Of a sort. Don't worry, you're my guest. No one will quiz you.'

'Still, I should be able to explain myself. Why I'm here.'

'Just tell them the truth – you're working on Celan and Char.'

They turned right to follow the path around and entered the Champneys building. Grace, who had been carrying her gown over her arm, slipped it on. Ulrike felt uncomfortable. 'Should I have a gown?'

'No, you're my guest, but once you're a member of the college you'll wear a gown appropriate to your academic standing.'

Ulrike was struck by the scent of old wood and floor polish and the women, many of her own age, most wearing gowns, hurrying to take their places. Grace took Ulrike by the arm and squeezed her elbow. 'You'll be fine.'

Clough Hall opened up before them – long, timbered, and softly lit, its tall windows already dark with the early autumn dusk. The warm gleam of candlelight flickered from rows of brass candlesticks set down the length of the dining tables, glinting off glassware and burnishing the edges of cutlery.

High above, the hammer-beam ceiling disappeared into shadow. Arched wooden trusses met like cathedral ribs overhead, giving the room a chapel-like solemnity. Yet there was a quiet femininity here too – less austere than the great halls of the men's colleges. The wood panelling along the walls had a golden warmth, which spoke of care rather than grandeur. At the far end to which they were now heading, the High Table was set beneath four portraits of individuals important in the history of the college.

Grace guided Ulrike to her place. 'I will be sitting next to you and we will be opposite two of my most reliable colleagues. Try not to worry. You will not be out of your depth.'

A moment later the Principal entered. A hush fell, and a senior Fellow intoned a Latin grace. Ulrike didn't catch the words, only the rhythm. Then with a scraping of chairs, the room came alive again with the rustle of sleeves, and the murmur of conversation and quiet laughter.

Someone filled her wine glass. Grace bent her head towards Ulrike. 'Welcome aboard,' she said, her voice low, almost amused. 'Your first step to joining the crew. And your second step is to be introduced to Mme Odette Colombiers and Dr Silke Menken.'

'Silke? One of your colleagues is German?'

Ulrike seemed perturbed. Grace wondered why. She'd thought having a fellow German to talk to would make Ulrike feel more at home. But perhaps she was afraid that Silke might notice something about her that only a native speaker would spot. Somewhat anxious herself now, Grace made the introductions, 'Ulrike, this is Dr Silke Menken – she lectures in German literature. And next to her, Mme Odette Colombiers, who teaches French – specialising in twentieth-century poetry and literary translation. Ladies, this is my friend Ulrike Schmidt.'

For a moment or two further exchanges were interrupted by the arrival of the soup course. While the soup was being served, Ulrike studied the two women. Dr Menken was small-boned and wiry, with dark, neatly cropped hair and a pair of silver-rimmed spectacles perched halfway down her nose. Her face was sharp-featured, alert, the sort that missed very little. She wore a simple black gown over a bottle-green dress and a silver brooch in the shape of a lyre. Mme Colombiers, by contrast, was elegantly dishevelled – tousled dark-blonde hair, a silk scarf knotted loosely at her neck, and a warm, appraising smile.

'So, mademoiselle – Grace tells us you have worked closely with Professor Müller at Humboldt?' Odette's tone was light, but Ulrike felt that there was an underlying note of disbelief in her question.

'Yes, he was supervising my postgraduate studies. My dissertation focused on *Das Romanfragment* – the fragment as aesthetic and political resistance in the Jena circle. Particularly in the writings of Caroline Schlegel.'

That caught Menken's attention. She put down her soup spoon. 'Caroline, not Friedrich? Interesting. Most students begin with the brothers Schlegel or with Novalis.'

Ulrike allowed herself a small smile. 'That's true. But I was interested in how Caroline's editorial work and correspondence challenged the Romantic model of authorship – and how her marginality may in fact be central to the movement's contradictions.'

Grace reached for her wine and took a sip, realising that she too had been tense, worrying how her *protégée* might fare. This was a solid start.

Mme Colombiers turned slightly toward Ulrike. 'And in French? Have you read much of the *poésie engagée* – say, Éluard? Or later, Char?'

'Yes,' Ulrike said. 'Though more recently I've been drawn to the later surrealists – especially the tension in Char between poetic opacity and moral clarity. And to how Celan responds to that tradition in translation.'

Colombiers looked pleased. 'You speak French?'

'Not perfectly,' Ulrike said, modestly. 'But well enough to read critically.'

Menken leaned in again. 'Your English is excellent – for an East Berliner – in the sense that you seem to have none of the horrible American inflections from listening to American radio.'

'No, Professor Müller suggested that I listen to the BBC German Service instead. Of course listening to either is frowned upon and can get you into trouble. That does mean, however, that my command of colloquial English is inadequate. Grace used the term *frumpy* earlier on. That was a new one for me.'

Colombiers laughed lightly. 'I hope that Grace was not referring to anyone here.'

Grace joined in the laughter. 'I was referring to my own taste in clothes. Ulrike and I are going on a clothes buying expedition at the weekend.'

Colombiers raised an eyebrow and exchanged glances with Menken, the sort of glance colleagues share when a quiet consensus begins to form.

As the soup was cleared and the next course arrived – salmon in a delicate sauce, accompanied by small new potatoes and buttered green beans – Grace leaned slightly toward Ulrike and said, 'You're doing well. Odette and Silke are intrigued.'

Ulrike, too, felt she had managed to project an image of modest academic competence and began to relax a little. The probing of her abilities had been gentle but deft. Odette and Silke were now talking quietly to each other and Grace was being engaged in conversation by the diner to her right. Ulrike looked around the room. Was it too much to imagine that she could become a member of the college and come to feel at home in this beautiful place? At that moment, Ulrike's neighbour to her left, a tall woman with silver hair and a strong brow, turned towards her and said, 'And what brings you to Newnham, Miss…?'

'Schmidt. I'm a visiting scholar, working on twentieth-century poetry under constraint. Language under pressure. In the German context.'

'Poetry under constraint, you said? Are we talking Oulipo? Or something more… exogenous?'

'Well, imposed, certainly. Something coercive, rather than freely chosen as in Oulipo. In the latter, constraint is a luxury. Where I come from the Oulipoian approach would be considered decadent.'

'And where is that?'

'East Berlin.'

'Well, that *is* unusual. One hears that it is a difficult place to leave.'

'In practice, I have been exiled.'

'You were a dissident?'

'Just a very junior scholar.'

'Well, welcome to an environment which, I hope, will be more conducive to your studies.'

'Thank you, madam. And you are?'

'Eugenia Waterhouse-Adams, Fellow Emerita in Classics.'

She took a sip of white wine, studying Ulrike with an appraising look softened by an air of mild amusement.

'Poetry under constraint,' she repeated. 'You know, I spent a long time sifting fragments of Sappho from the sands of Oxyrhynchus. Not literally with a brush and a sieve, you understand – though I did once knock over a tray of papyrus and was nearly strangled by an irate epigrapher. No, my contribution was in the reading, the reconstructing, the deciphering of what barely remains. You'd be astonished how much ancient literature survives only by accident – if that's the right word – and a different kind of constraint.'

Ulrike leaned slightly closer. 'The vicissitudes of history?'

'Well, of course, none of us can escape the vicissitudes of history, but, in Sappho's case, I think there was something more systematic at work. Let's say I've grown wary of attributing silence to chance. Sappho's work was never forgotten – only neglected, disapproved of, quietly untransmitted. And the voices of women, in particular, have a habit of being mislaid by history when they are no longer convenient to remember.'

Ulrike hesitated a moment, then said carefully, 'Do you think the disapproval... was primarily aesthetic? Or was it something more – moral?'

Eugenia's eyes glinted. 'Ah. You mean, was it the content, or the company it kept?'

Ulrike gave the faintest of nods.

Eugenia set down her fork. 'Let's say this: lyric poetry is tolerated when it decorates the margins of acceptable feeling. But Sappho didn't decorate – she inhabited. She gave desire a grammar. And not just any desire – female desire, directed toward other women. That, my dear, is an unpardonable clarity.'

She paused, letting the words settle in Ulrike's consciousness.

'For centuries, men anthologised her for her metre and quoted her for her flowers. But they copied other poets. They preserved what they could use. Sappho... was harder to use.'

Ulrike was fascinated now. 'Do you think there's any chance more of her work might come to light?'

Eugenia swirled the wine in her glass thoughtfully. 'Have you heard of the scrolls from Herculaneum? Carbonised by the eruption – entire libraries of ancient philosophy turned to charcoal. We know they're there, line after line of reasoned thought, held tight inside themselves like secrets. But unrolling them means destroying them. The paradox is exquisite.'

She glanced at Ulrike, noting her attentiveness.

'I sometimes wonder whether someone, someday, might find a way to read them without tearing them open. Light, perhaps. Or some method we can't yet imagine. I doubt I'll live to see it – but wouldn't it be something?'

She paused, then added, more quietly, 'A library of fragments, waiting to be deciphered. Like so much of what survives. Like Sappho. Like history. Like us.'

She glanced down at her plate, then added, almost idly, 'It teaches one to read absences. Sometimes the gaps are where the truth is hiding.'

Ulrike was spellbound. Eugenia turned towards the younger woman and smiled. 'But I am monopolising you. Grace will disapprove, perhaps. But if you would like to continue this discussion, Grace will tell you where my rooms are. I hope you will soon be able to shoulder the gentler yoke of Newnham on an official basis.'

'Thank you, Eugenia. I would very much like to be instructed by you in these matters.'

Grace could hardly fail to notice how Ulrike was hanging on Eugenia's every word. In concentrating on arranging for Ulrike and herself to sit opposite Odette and Silke, Grace had given no thought to who might be sitting on Ulrike's other side. Grace reached for her wine, nodding vaguely at something the geologist beside her was saying about Devonian strata. But she was really more interested in trying to catch what Eugenia was saying. She did not have to strain much. Eugenia's voice rose, unmistakable – wry, precise, utterly at ease. Ulrike was leaning towards her, intent, a faint flush at her throat. Something in the angle of her head – deferent, curious – gave Grace pause.

Eugenia was speaking of Sappho again – of desire sharpened by absence, of voices mislaid by history. Grace knew the lines, but not like that. Not with that weight. Not with that freedom.

A strange flicker passed through her. Not quite irritation. Not disapproval. Something more private. Envy, she realised, startled. Not of Ulrike. Of Eugenia. It lodged low in her chest, unfamiliar and oddly tender. How long had it been since she'd let herself want anything that clearly?

Oblivious to the fact that Grace's thoughts and attention were elsewhere, the geologist had asked her a question and was now waiting for Grace's response. Suppressing the irritation she felt, Grace said apologetically, 'I'm sorry, I lost you at subduction.'

Ulrike, conscious now that Odette, Silke and Grace had all been observing her conversation with Eugenia, turned back to them, just as the next course was being brought out – a tart of spinach and Gruyère. Colombiers lifted her glass slightly toward Ulrike. 'To those who read between the lines,' she said, a playful smile on her lips.

Ulrike raised hers in return, though her hand trembled slightly. 'And to being able to speak freely.'

Grace said nothing, but her fingers tapped once on the linen tablecloth. Just once.

On their way back to Glisson Road in the taxi, Grace said, 'That wasn't so bad, was it?'

'Grace, I can't tell you how grateful I am. It was so much better than I could ever have imagined. It is almost as if I have been born again. Thank you, thank you, thank you.'

'You seemed to be getting on very well with Eugenia?'

'She was telling me about the carbonised scrolls of Herculaneum and the hope that one day they might be read. What an amazing woman!'

'She is, but she also has a bit of a reputation.'

'She did say you might disapprove.'

'I don't disapprove. I'm envious.'

Ulrike turned to look at her, surprised. 'Envious?'

Grace kept her gaze on the passing terraces, their windows lit like miniature stages. 'Not of you,' she said, too quickly. Then, more softly: 'Of her. It's just… Eugenia has always known who she is. She never hid it. Never pretended. Even when it cost her friends. Or promotions. Or – other things.'

The taxi slowed at a junction. Grace traced a circle on the knee of her skirt with one gloved finger.

'And you don't?' Ulrike asked.

Grace let out a breath that wasn't quite a sigh. 'Know who I am? No. I grew up in a world where clarity came with consequences. So I learned ambiguity instead.'

They drove in silence for a few moments. The city outside was quiet now, only the occasional student walking under the lamplight.

Then Ulrike said, very gently, 'But ambiguity can be its own form of prison, can't it?'

Grace didn't answer at first. Then she turned to Ulrike with a smile that tried to be light and failed. 'Perhaps. Or a library of unread scrolls.'

Later as Grace was getting ready for bed, there was a tap on the door of her bedroom and Ulrike entered the room in the dressing gown Grace had lent her.

'Is this a good moment for you to look at the bruising on my ribs?'

Grace wiped the cleansing cream off her face and said, 'Yes, it is.'

Ulrike took the dressing gown off and laid it on the bed. She was naked.

Grace studied the bruise beneath her right breast. 'What happened here?'

'The doctors in Frankfurt said that I'd broken two ribs.'

'But that was several weeks ago.'

'When I was mugged in London, the two guys couldn't decide whether they were going to rob me or rape me. They threw me on the ground and one of them got on top of me. I was in quite a lot of pain. I think those two ribs got injured again. When I got to Steve's flat, he had to help me get in and out of the bath.'

'What's this other mark under your left breast, then?'

'It's a birthmark. Something that will always be with me. But it's the other side that hurts, particularly when I breathe deeply.'

'I can imagine.'

'Steve has found it frustrating. I think he was expecting a degree of enthusiasm in our love-making that I find difficult to offer, even at the best of times.'

Grace was surprised. She'd understood from Steve's description of how things had gone in Prenzlauer Berg that Ulrike had performed in a highly enthusiastic manner. But, after all, Steve was a self-admitted fabulist with a decided tendency to braggadocio. The reality had probably been somewhat more prosaic.

'I hope he has not complained. If he has, I will have words with him.'

'No, he has been very considerate. Please don't raise the matter with him.'

'Right, first thing tomorrow morning, I will make an appointment for you with Rebecca, my GP. I think we need a second opinion.'

'Thank you, Grace. I'm sorry to put you to so much trouble.'

'It's no trouble. Thank you for being brave enough to show me.'

Ulrike put her dressing gown back on and went up to her room. Grace sat down on the edge of her bed. She had found the sight of Ulrike's beautiful but fragile body unsettling. After a moment or two she continued with her bedtime routine.

Steve & Müller – St Radegund's – Saturday

As STEVE WALKED FROM Glisson Road to St Rad's, the sense of irritation he had been feeling since he had arrived at Grace's the previous evening started to lift. The conversation over supper had been full of Ulrike's breathless accounts of the people she'd met and the places she'd been with Grace. It particularly irked Steve that she had been Grace's guest at Newnham High Table, something that Grace had promised to Steve but had never got around to. Grace beamed with pleasure at Ulrike's evident excitement. Clearly she had relished presenting this brilliant young scholar to her colleagues. But apparently there remained one or two people who had not been available. So Grace had suggested that Ulrike stay a further week. Steve wished that they'd come to this conclusion before he'd set off from London. Still, another weekend in Cambridge might soften the blow to his self-esteem occasioned by the news of Sally and Jeremy's sudden romance.

At bedtime, Steve had felt a little awkward joining Ulrike in the guest room. It was as if it was now her room and he was an intruder. But she had been less distant than she had been the previous weekend. She said that she had had an x-ray at Addenbrooke's Hospital at the instigation of Grace's GP. Two of her ribs were fractured, but would heal in due course. There was no particular treatment other than pain relief. She was already feeling less worried. As a consequence, intercourse while still being far from energetic was rather more satisfying, at least from Steve's point of view.

Then over breakfast the next morning, Grace had announced that she was going to take Ulrike clothes shopping that afternoon. Apparently not many of Grace's clothes were a good fit for Ulrike. Steve was somewhat bemused that it had taken the two women a week to discover that fairly obvious fact. He had not been invited to join them, for which he was heartily grateful.

Finally, to cap the feeling that he was having his agenda set for him, Grace had asked him to drop in on Müller while they were shopping. Müller had something important to tell him. And would he mind picking up Ulrike's red coat, which she had still not retrieved? Steve had felt like saying that the coat was actually Becky's and that he had lent it to Ulrike, but he had somehow managed to stifle giving expression to his general sense of being fucked around.

But now as he walked across Parker's Piece, having parted company with the two women, his mood lifted. It was actually great to be back in Cambridge and, to an extent, at a loose end. With luck the conversation with Müller wouldn't take long and he could then find a corner in one of the pubs he used to frequent and have a contemplative pint or two.

Soon Steve was passing through the gates of St Rad's and, not entirely unexpectedly, Stan emerged from the Porters' Lodge with an amused look on his face. 'My goodness, Mr Percival, a second visit in as many weeks.'

'Professor Müller asked to see me. And none of this Mr Percival malarkey, Stan. My name's Steve, as you well know.'

Stan chuckled. 'I don't hold with all this informality, sir. There's the commissioned class and there's the squaddies. Admittedly, nothing would work in society without the NCOs. And as for your professor friend, for a new Fellow and a somewhat retiring gent, he certainly gets a fair few visitors.'

'He's a world-renowned intellectual, Stan.'

'Oh, they all are, they all are, Mr Percival. No doubt you will be yourself before long.'

'Not a chance.'

Steve was just about to continue on his way to Founder's Court, when a thought occurred to him. 'But Professor Müller doesn't take students, does he?'

'Quite right. His visitors are mainly civilians, as you might say, although Dr Doyle is in and out of his rooms like a jack in the box. And he even gets the occasional female visitor.'

'Not the girl I came with last week, the one in the red coat?'

'She came alright, but weren't wearing no red coat. Then he had a visit from Dr Mitchell, which between you and me is not the first time she's been to his rooms.'

Steve laughed. Not much escaped Stan's notice. It was unsurprising that Grace had visited Müller, but the same could not be said for Ulrike. Considering the way that the tea party visit had concluded, a return visit by Ulrike only a few days later struck Steve as being odd.

Stan noticed the thoughtful look on Steve's face. 'Not what you were expecting, sir? I don't imagine the Professor is one to indulge in hanky-panky. And the girl seemed cheerful enough when she passed the Porters' Lodge on the way out.'

Steve would have felt her visit more explicable, had she been weeping bitter tears on her exit from the college.

Despite Steve's errant ways, he'd always got on well with Stan, who'd turned a blind eye more than once to his escapades. 'I daresay there's life in the old dog yet.'

'Not sure about that, Mr Percival. His ticker's none too good. And he's puffing on those cigars like he's making up for lost time. There's not many weeks when he don't get a delivery of Cohibas from Bacon's in the Market Square.'

'I think that's exactly what he's doing. He didn't have access to the real thing when he was in East Berlin.'

'Well, I'm glad he knows enough about cigars to choose Cuban and Cohibas at that. I don't know whether Dr Doyle tipped him the wink, but that is the preferred brand among the Fellows.'

Steve was aware that there were any number of codes and markers of social class or affiliation in British society: matters of language, how you handled your cutlery, but he had never thought it extended to cigars.

'Is there much difference between one cigar brand and another?'

'There certainly is. I can see you are no smoker. Cohibas, the St Rad's favourite, are creamy and aromatic. Montecristos, though perfectly decent are rather more robust and slightly earthy, and will result in silently raised eyebrows in the SCR, as will Romeo y Julieta with its floral and cedar notes, despite Winston's endorsement of the brand.'

'Isn't that all a bit pretentious?'

'Mr Percival, I can see I'm going to have to take you in hand.'

'It sounds like you're a bit of a cigar smoker yourself, Stan.'

'You're not wrong there, but it would be inappropriate for me to go around the college trailing clouds of Cuban delight. However, some of the dons are aware of my partiality and I am sometimes lucky enough at Christmas or on my birthday to be given a box of Cuba's finest.'

'I thought there was an embargo on Cuban cigars.'

'In the USA, not here in Blighty.'

'So is it easy to tell one cigar brand from another?'

'Well, of course, you have to have smoked a few. It's like wine and port. You can't be a connoisseur without having done an apprenticeship.'

'So you personally can distinguish between the different cigars you mentioned earlier just by smell?'

'I reckon so. For instance, yesterday an older lady dressed up like a film star from years gone by, big dark glasses, hair done up in a scarf, beautiful clothes, asked if she could look at Magdalene from the Fellows' Garden. Bit of a cheek really. Strictly speaking the Fellows' Garden is not open to members of the public. Anyway, I could smell that she was a Montecristo smoker.'

'Surely she wasn't puffing as she crossed the quad?'

'No, I could smell it on her clothes when she stepped into the Porters' Lodge.'

'I'm impressed. The only cigar I could infallibly detect is a Hamlet. The bloke who showed me the milk round I was doing for a few weeks after my Finals chain-smoked them.'

'Them's no cigars, Mr Percival. They're abominations.'

'Well, they certainly made me feel sick and I wasn't even smoking them.'

'Serves you right. What on earth a graduate of St Radegund's was doing on the milk is beyond me.'

'I know I was letting the college down, Stan. That's why I haven't been back until now.'

'But here you are hugger-mugger with Professor Dieter Müller, formerly of Humboldt University. I imagine East Berlin has changed from my day.'

Steve was taken aback. 'You were in East Berlin?'

'Well, we didn't call it East Berlin then. It was the Russian sector. Yeah, I was there with the military from late 1945 to early 1950. When I first saw Humboldt, it was a mess, but amazingly the facade was still standing. The whole of Unter den Linden was devastated. But the Soviets got to work patching things up pretty quickly.'

So that explained Stan's fluency in German when he had greeted Ulrike the previous week. Steve suddenly saw Stan in a very different light. 'Unter den Linden and Alexanderplatz look pretty good now. But I went up to Prenzlauer Berg and plenty of the buildings there are still pock-marked with bullet holes and shell damage.'

'And that's where you met the professor?'

'No, I met him in West Berlin at my mother's funeral.'

'I'm so sorry, Steve. I should have offered my condolences before. Dr Doyle did tell me.'

Steve was touched by the use of his first name. 'Thank you, Stan. I miss her terribly.'

'Steve, next time you're up, let's have a longer chat over a pint of something nice.'

'I'd like that, Stan, but you're never off duty.'

'It might seem like that, but it's not strictly true. Sid's not actually my identical twin, but he's as good as.'

Steve laughed. 'You're right there. Anyway, lovely talking to you, Stan.'

'Steve, two things before you go. Please pop in and see Dr Doyle. He would appreciate it. And please know that you can count on me if things get rough.'

What on earth was Stan talking about? Was Doyle going to tear him off a strip? 'Do you think it might?'

'I can feel it in my water.'

With that, Stan disappeared back into the Porters' Lodge.

A few minutes later, Steve was once again entering Professor Müller's G staircase rooms in Founder's Court. Müller was sitting in his armchair as he had been the previous week with a half-smoked cigar on the go, Cohiba presumably. 'Thank you for coming to see me again, Steve.'

'It's a pleasure, Dieter. Grace is worried about you and wants you to see a doctor. I promised that I would add my voice to that suggestion that you cut down on the Cohibas.'

'Ah, I did not have you down as a connoisseur of cigars.'

'I'm not. Stan told me that you've practically cleared out all Bacon's stock of Cohibas.'

'Not much escapes Stan's notice.'

'That's true, but Grace is worried about you too.'

'That is very sweet of both you and her. But there is no need to worry. The doctors know all about me. I'm already taking an alarming cocktail of drugs. I am not sure that any more are really going to help.'

'They might be able to adjust the dosage to be more effective.'

'Thank you for your concern, but I would rather medicate myself with this nice bottle of claret from the St Rad's buttery. Would you care to join me in a glass? I will take a glass myself whether you join me or not.'

It seemed niggardly to deny Dieter a convivial drink even if he was dying. 'Thank you, Dieter, as long as we can drink to your health.'

A few minutes later having toasted each other, Dieter said, 'First of all, how are Grace and Ulrike getting on?'

'Like a house on fire.'

'Another curious English expression. It rather suggests that situation is not entirely desirable.'

'I suppose it does, but I certainly didn't mean that.'

'No, but you can't really do the job you have been asked to do if you are in London and Ulrike is here in Cambridge?'

Steve did not reply.

Müller continued. 'I know you don't want to depart from protocol, so we can simply take that for granted. But I may also say that I know that the reason you and Grace have not been together since Berlin is that she also has been tasked with keeping an eye on me. I am thought to be a Stasi asset. But if I tell you I am not, you will probably not believe me.'

'I do not really know what to believe. I certainly do not believe half of what I am told, whoever's telling me.'

'Even if it comes from Sheena Ferguson?'

'Particularly if it comes from Sheena.'

'I would say that is a sensible stance. But which half?'

Steve laughed. 'Yes, that is the problem.'

'And what do you think about Ulrike?'

'I think she is a brilliant scholar. I also think she has been abused, particularly by men. And I think she feels more comfortable as a student of Grace's.'

'But do you think she's a Stasi asset?'

'Obviously that has crossed my mind, but on balance considering the treatment she received at their hands, I would say not. What is your own feeling?'

'Based on the fact that I got to know her quite well as my student and the ideological niceties of her writing, I would say she is not Stasi.'

'So we are at one that Ulrike is not Stasi.'

Dieter took a mouthful of wine and considered how best to say what was on his mind. 'The fact is I don't think your mother's death was an accident.'

Steve shrugged. 'Collingwood has always thought that quite probable, but in the absence of proof it was impossible to do anything to bring anyone to justice.'

'Of course. Well, a week or two before her accident and your arrival in Berlin, Mavis and I attended an academic colloquium in Leipzig. She came across in an official car and was able to get some of my papers out to the West under diplomatic rules. As you probably know, I was well connected in the higher echelons of the party and I had had a drink with one of my oldest friends a few days before this trip with Mavis. My friend was a comrade from the anti-fascist days, but had in the meantime risen to the rank of colonel in the Stasi. We'd had a big drinking session. But he'd never been much good at holding his drink. Had a tendency to become indiscreet. Anyway, on this particular occasion he told me that the Stasi were cock-a-hoop at having turned a senior MI6 officer, to whom they'd given the codename *Tollkirsche*, the German for deadly nightshade.'

'From what one hears MI6 is riddled with traitors. How is that relevant to my mother's death?'

'The particular individual had been caught in a honey trap and there was a lot of gay *kompromat* material.'

Steve was suddenly on full alert. How many people knew that his mother and Sheena had been lovers? 'It happens.'

'I mentioned it to Mavis and her whole demeanour changed. She became quite agitated. Little more than two weeks later she was dead.'

Steve knew now that he had to tread carefully. 'You don't think the two things are connected, do you?'

'I think what I'd told her was enough to enable her to identify the mole.'

Everything pointed to Sheena. Steve was now making the same deduction his mother must have made. She must also have confronted Sheena, who had then arranged for the hit and run accident, absenting herself at the crucial moment. 'And you think the mole became aware of this and arranged for her liquidation.'

'Yes, it is hard to resist that conclusion.'

'Do you feel threatened too?'

'When you've done what I've done, you always feel threatened. The Stasi are unforgiving. I hardly dare cross the road.'

'Surely, they're not going to do a hit and run job on you, not here in Cambridge?'

'Probably not, but the mind plays tricks on you once the paranoia gets hold.'

'Yes, I can imagine. But why are you telling me this?'

'Well, to begin with, in a certain way you are the son I never had. I would like to help you avenge your mother's death. But also I am afraid for you.'

'Surely the Stasi or their servants here don't care about me.'

'I am not so sure about that. You are Mavis's son. You were involved in getting me out. And you too may be privy to Mavis's deduction.'

'Anyone who thinks that clearly didn't know Mavis very well. I had no idea that she worked for the intelligence service until she was knocked over and then she was in a coma until she died.'

'These are ruthless people.'

'Well, thank you, Dieter, you know how to unsettle a chap.'

'I'm sorry, Steve, but if some unfortunate accident befalls me, perhaps you could bear in mind what I've just said.'

'And having borne it in mind, what should I then do? Take my suspicions to Collingwood?'

'Perhaps.'

'Why don't we do that now? You can tell him everything you've just told me.'

'Because I fear that Ulrike is being used as a diversion or is being set up.'

'By whom? Not Collingwood?'

'By the Stasi.'

'What makes you think that?'

'It seems to be accepted that I am the person who initiated the ransom process with the West German Government. But that is not the case. I was only asked to vouch for Ulrike as her former teacher. The process had been started elsewhere.'

'Perhaps the West German authorities initiated the process themselves.'

'They knew nothing about her.'

'The Stasi?'

'Much more likely.'

Steve was having difficulty processing all this information. 'If all this is true, why did she contact me first?'

Müller reached across to his desk and picked up a light blue aerogramme envelope and waved it around. 'She wrote to me from her aunt's in Frankfurt saying she was going to come to the UK and asking to stay with me. I wrote back to say I didn't think it was a good idea and in any case I couldn't put her up because I lived in a men-only college.'

'And so you gave her my real name and address, which is how she landed up in the pub near my work?'

'I'm sorry. I hoped you would understand.'

Dieter stood up. 'Back in a second. Nature calls.'

While he was in the lavatory, Steve went across to the table and quickly read over the aerogramme. Dieter had not been lying. On an impulse, Steve jotted down the address of Ulrike's aunt in Frankfurt in his notebook. He replaced the aerogramme on the desk and was back in his chair by the time Dieter returned.

'Sorry, not the least of the indignities in the ageing male is the incompetent bladder. Even so, I imagine we could both do with another glass.'

Steve nodded and while Dieter was filling the glasses said, 'What am I supposed to do with this information?'

'I don't know, Steve. I like you and trust you. I don't want to see you getting into trouble and perhaps it will help you figure things out in due course, especially if something happens to me. And if it does, you must watch out for yourself. You probably know more than is good for you.'

Steve, partly under the influence of the wine, suddenly felt warm towards Dieter. He now saw him as a scared, old man whose days were numbered. In the light of everything he'd just said, it was extremely unlikely that he was a Stasi asset. Nor did it feel like he was putting the moves on Steve. But wasn't that precisely the way a sophisticated operator put the moves on you?

As he walked across the court a little later, he realised that he had once again forgotten to pick up Becky's red coat. He wished he'd never suggested that Ulrike borrow it. He had no great desire to go back up to Müller's. Perhaps he could ask Stan to retrieve it on his way out of the college.

Steve & Doyle – St Radegund's – Saturday

STEVE TAPPED ON THE door of Dr Doyle's rooms. A moment later the door was flung open and Richard Doyle said, 'Steve, my dear chap, thank you for dropping by. Come in, come in.'

Steve stepped into the room in which he had had weekly supervisions over the three years of his undergraduate career and other meetings to discuss his results and academic progress or lack thereof. It was a room in which he felt very much at home. Doyle invited him to take one of the armchairs in front of the fireplace and Doyle took the other.

'Grace tells me you are working on a music magazine.'

'Yes, but as the lowliest sub on the production team.'

'I am sure your contribution is a valued one.'

'Well, my failure to properly appreciate the titanic range of Goethe is not a matter of comment. The world I now work in has never heard of him.'

'I hope you didn't think I was pulling you up when we spoke of Goethe.'

'No, I didn't. I could not have hoped for a more patient teacher. As was Grace Mitchell.'

'Ah, yes, Miss Mitchell. You know you could still climb back in the saddle.'

Steve wondered for a moment what Doyle meant. 'How would I do that?'

'I could probably get you into Freiburg for a year. There might even be a bursary involved. Then you could be back here in a couple of years to do your PhD. You would have my support with the governing body.'

'Are you serious?'

'Perfectly.'

'But my degree was rather middling.'

'There were mitigating circumstances.'

Steve wasn't sure what those were in his case. 'And I haven't been keeping my hand in.'

'That's not quite what I hear. A book-length poem in an exquisite limited edition, a collaborator on Grace's highly successful book on the existentialists, a full-length play at the Festival Theatre, and a little bit of jiggery-pokery in Berlin on both sides of the Wall.'

'None of that was academic work.'

'So much the better. I am not sure it is particularly useful for people to go straight from their undergraduate course to postgraduate work. There was a ten year gap between my first year and the final year of my Tripos.'

'That was because a world war intervened, I imagine.'

'It was indeed. But I learned more in the army than I would ever have learned in these hallowed cloisters. I was a callow youth supposedly commanding battle-hardened men. I would never have survived if Stan hadn't put me right on more than one occasion.'

'Stan? Stan Mallory?'

'Yes, he was the senior NCO in the unit of the Intelligence Branch I was supposedly commanding. But I was just a wet-behind-the-ears lieutenant. On one occasion when we were moving up through Italy, Stan challenged my decision to take a particular route through an olive grove that the map from HQ said was safe. We'd already lost a couple of good men getting to a ruined farmhouse which was our shelter for the night. Stan was adamant that the map wasn't accurate. How did HQ know it was safe? We were closer to the front than they were. He thought we should take the more difficult route over the mountain pass rather than through the grove.'

'Was this in front of the men?'

'No, it was just the two of us having a bevvy before turning in. I was about twenty-three or four, just about the age you are now. He was thirty or so, had been around a bit. All the men respected him.

At that stage, I am sure they had their doubts about me. For a moment I considered tearing a strip off him and putting him on charge when we got back to our own lines. But deep down I knew he was not the sort of man to challenge authority lightly and that he was trying to save me from making a terrible mistake. So I agreed to the route he was recommending.'

'What happened?'

'He was completely right. We got through without losing anyone else. Another unit that was coming up after us went through the olive grove before we could radio back the safer route and was practically wiped out.'

'I think I would have been useless in the same situation.'

'That's not what I hear from Collingwood.'

Steve was not entirely surprised that some version of his East Berlin escapade had got back to Doyle. 'The situations hardly compare.'

'I'm not so sure. But the point I want to make is that as Stan was leaving the command post, with me still poring over the map, he said that I had made a good call. I said, rather truculently, I suppose, that it was *his* call and he said: *Mine to offer. Yours to make.* I knew at that point that he was a true leader of men. He remained my senior NCO for the rest of the war and subsequently for our time in Berlin. Then when I came back here and got my junior fellowship and he'd returned to civvy street, I arranged for him to become the senior porter. So in a sense we're still together. I trust his judgement completely. And he thinks highly of you.'

'Dr Doyle…'

'Please call me Richard.'

'Richard, I like Stan enormously, but he doesn't really know me that well.'

'I'm not sure that is actually the case. Stan and I did nearly eight years together in the Intelligence Branch. He has a sixth sense and he has intuited that something is afoot, something in which you are deeply involved.'

Steve stared at the carpet, unsure what to say. Doyle rose from his chair. 'Let's have a small Fino.'

He half filled two tulip glasses with a pale, straw-yellow liquid from a dark green bottle and handed one to Steve, who sniffed it and then took a sip. 'Most certainly not Bristol Cream.'

Doyle sipped his own. 'La Ina, actually. What do you taste?'

Steve took another sip. 'Off the top of my head, I'd say salt and maybe almonds, and something I can't quite define.'

'Flor. The yeast that covers the wine as it ages. Starves it of oxygen, keeps it lean. All the best Finos have that ghost of the sea. Austerity in a glass.'

Steve laughed. 'Richard, you haven't asked me to call on you to upgrade my knowledge of sherry.'

'That is correct. So where to begin? Well, you know that I taught Collingwood a few years before you. But perhaps you do not know that I am also quite close to Sheena Ferguson.'

'No, I did not know that, but somehow I am not surprised.'

'I did not know your mother, but I knew who she was. And she knew that I was something more than your director of studies. So when she and I spoke at your graduation, that was something of a masquerade.'

'At that stage, I still didn't know what my mother did, but I do recall that when we went out to dinner that night she was rather well informed about events in Cyprus.'

'Well, I'm sure you're learning that it can be difficult sometimes to remember which register you are in, if I can put it that way.'

Steve laughed. 'I certainly do.'

'I also got to know Dieter slightly during the Airlift. And afterwards, as we both started publishing, we communicated by reviewing each other's work favourably, especially after 1961, when Dieter's freedom of movement ceased almost completely. However, he was well connected in the higher echelons of the party and his area of expertise could hardly be considered subversive. Of course, I did not know that he was passing information to us for several years and that your mother was his case handler.'

'He tells me that he and my mother were lovers in the Airlift years and that she tried to get him to return with her to England to continue his studies here.'

Doyle nodded. 'Ah, yes, I see. Anyway, I was a bit slow off the mark when he was exfiltrated and Edinburgh got their paws on him first. But I managed to get the master and the fellows to appoint him as an extraordinary fellow.'

'So you could keep an eye on him for Sheena?'

'That was a factor.'

'Even though Sheena had asked Grace to do the same thing?'

'Well, I couldn't very well go to bed with him. Well, I could have, but you know... In any case, he preferred the more monastic environment of St Radegund's.'

Steve had to suppress a guffaw at the thought of Doyle and Müller in bed together. 'But I suppose you know that I had been having a relationship with Grace, which Sheena's intervention brought to an abrupt end.'

'Yes, I did gather that. Sheena can err on the side of overkill. Grace is in all respects a delightful woman and a fine scholar, but one feels you have other options. The lovely German girl you introduced to me and Jeremiah last week perhaps.'

'Ulrike was the one who paid with her freedom for the operation I was involved in. She has only recently been released from a Stasi jail in which she was beaten and raped. But in the same way that Sheena thinks that Dieter has been turned, she thinks Ulrike is a Stasi asset and I have been asked to get close to her and assist her to make contact with Dieter – '

' – who wishes to have nothing to do with her, even though she was his star student.'

But it seemed that Doyle could sense that there was something odd in Müller's reaction. 'I think Dieter fears Ulrike. It seems to me that he shares Sheena's view that Ulrike is being controlled by the Stasi.'

'No doubt I am entirely the wrong person to be given the task of establishing whether that is true or not. But in the time I have been pretending to be her lover she has given me no reason to suppose that she is being controlled by the Stasi or capable of harming Müller.'

Doyle emptied his glass, and reached for the bottle from the sideboard. 'Another tot?'

Steve was not so naïve as not to realise that Doyle was hoping that alcohol would render him less guarded. But he fancied that he could hold his drink rather better than an elderly don. Even as he entertained this thought, he felt that he was probably making a mistake.

Glasses replenished, Doyle said, 'Perhaps you are wondering what the point of all my questions is?'

Steve allowed himself a small laugh. 'What puzzles me is that my position seems to be utterly informal with little guidance or structure. To begin with, I didn't really warm to Dieter, but as I have got to know him better, I find it harder to believe that he has come to rest in the bosom of St Radegund's in order to undermine the English way of life. That may just show how gullible I am. As for Ulrike, if you were to speak to her about these matters, you too would find it hard to believe that she is a Stasi asset. But then again, I am probably lacking in the key skills required of an intelligence officer.'

'My dear fellow, I hear what you say. You are the young subaltern in the field. I and, a fortiori, Sheena are the duffers at HQ intent on making you walk through a minefield. You have every right to take the mountain pass.'

'Dr Doyle, why are we having this conversation? What is your stake in the game? Are you trying to protect Müller or bring him down? Are you acting in concert with Sheena or against her? Do you see me as an enemy or an ally?'

'All good questions, Steve. I'm not sure I can answer them as explicitly as I'd like, but if I could, I wouldn't wish you or your young lady any ill.

'I thank you for your concern. I wish she were my young lady, but the pretence is not exactly convincing. And I am the last person who needs protecting.'

'Steve, that is certainly not the case. Danger may be the wrong word, but you do need to take seriously the idea that there is trouble ahead, and even more so for Ulrike, whether she is your young lady or not. I think you should get her back to London as soon as possible.'

Week Four

15 October – 31 October 1976

Müller & Mrs Nairn – St Radegund's – Monday

MÜLLER WAS SITTING IN his favourite armchair reading, with one of his Cohibas on the go, when there was a tap on the door. He looked at his watch and realised that it must be Mrs Comberton, his bedder. He put his book down and said, 'Come in.'

The door swung open and a middle-aged woman he did not recognise entered the room. 'Good morning, Professor Müller, my name is Mrs Nairn. Mrs Comberton has come over a bit funny this morning, and I have been asked to clean your room. I hope you don't mind. Where would you like me to begin?'

'Thank you, Mrs Nairn. Please do the bedroom and bathroom first and the gyp room. No need to touch this room.'

'Certainly, Professor.'

Mrs Nairn took her cleaning things into Müller's bedroom. It didn't take her long to make his bed, hoover the floor and clean the bathroom. When she emerged, she said, 'Could I make you a cup of tea or coffee while I'm doing the gyp room?'

'Thank you, Mrs Nairn. A cup of tea would be most welcome.'

A short while later Mrs Nairn brought Müller a cup of tea and an arrowroot biscuit. Müller took a sip of the tea and put the cup and saucer on the table beside him. 'Is Mrs Comberton alright?'

'Just a virus I should say. I'm sure she'll be back in a few days.'

'Will you be coming in the meantime?'

'It depends on what the arrangement is between the agency and the St Radegund's superintendent of housekeeping. But I'm available.'

181

'Well, you certainly make a fine cup of tea. I much prefer it strong with only a splash of milk.'

'The best way, if I may say so.'

'Forgive me if I remark that your accent does not sound like a local one.'

Mrs Nairn laughed. 'Nor does yours Professor Müller. I was born and brought up in Edinburgh. And your accent, if I'm not mistaken, is German.'

'Spot on. I suppose the name is a bit of a give-away. I am a Berliner.'

'I seem to recall President Kennedy saying we were all Berliners now.'

'He did indeed. And perhaps something of Berlin's schizophrenic nature has infected the rest of the world.'

'Schizophrenic, Professor Müller?'

'In the way that the city is divided.'

'I see. I must say that I don't give much thought to all this Cold War business. I just like to keep an eye on my young, and not so young, gentlemen.'

'I imagine you must see all sorts.'

'My lips are sealed, Professor, but, yes, one has to be somewhat broadminded. On the other hand, quite a few of my young men are actually homesick and are missing a mother's touch.'

'It is not only the young ones who are homesick, Mrs Nairn.'

'But not many of the young ones smoke Cuban cigars, Cohibas, if I am not mistaken.'

'That is, indeed, very perceptive of you. Surely you are not a smoker yourself?'

'No, Mr Nairn, God rest his soul, was fond of a puff in the evening. Mind you, I did make him go and smoke them outside.'

'I take it that Mr Nairn is no longer with us?'

'No, he's been gone a good ten years now, but the aroma of a corona never fails to bring a tear to my eye.'

'Oh, my dear Mrs Nairn, I am sorry to have been the cause of a painful memory. I will extinguish my cigar.'

'Please do not, Professor Müller. I believe that they are not quite as nice when they are relighted.'

As they were talking, Mrs Nairn, despite Müller's request not to bother with the main room had been bustling around it with a yellow duster, cleaning surfaces, stacking newspaper and magazines, and putting the coats and hats scattered around the room on a hat stand in the corner of the room. She picked up the red coat, which Steve had forgotten to retrieve at the weekend and said, 'I do not imagine this is your coat, Professor Müller, even if it is in Cambridge scarlet.'

Müller laughed. 'No, it belongs to a young friend. She will be missing it. Nor, might I add, am I entitled to wear Cambridge scarlet academical dress.'

'I am sure it will not be long before you are awarded an honorary doctorate. But I will not detain you any longer. I will let you get back to your book and cigar.'

'Thank you. Mrs Nairn. It has been a great pleasure talking to you.'

As she picked up her cleaning things and let herself out, Müller felt sure he had seen her face somewhere before, but he couldn't quite place the context.

A little while later, there was another tap on Müller's door. It was Doyle. 'Thank you for your note, Dieter. I hope this is a good time for you.'

Müller rose from his chair. 'It certainly is, Richard. Please come in.'

Doyle stepped into the room, closed the door behind him and looked around. 'My goodness, it's all spick and span in here. It looks like Mrs Comberton did a thorough job this morning. She seems to have missed me out.'

'It was not Mrs Comberton who put everything in order, but a Mrs Nairn. Mrs Comberton was feeling unwell this morning and Mrs Nairn, a lady with a delightful Scottish accent, whizzed around. She was even a connoisseur, by proxy, of my cigars. The only thing that troubled me was that she was oddly familiar.'

'Well, I hope she manages to get around to my rooms while I am out. Anyway, I am sure you do not want to talk to me about the relative merits of the bed-making staff.'

'No, indeed. But before we begin, may I offer you something?'

'Thank you, old boy, but a little too early in the day for me.'

'I am becoming quite adept at brewing a pot of tea.'

'No, thank you all the same.'

Müller invited Doyle to take a seat and said, 'I am thinking of making a short trip to Germany.'

'Surely not to Berlin?'

'No, to Frankfurt. What I am about to tell you is extremely sensitive information. I know I can rely on your discretion.'

'Of course, Dieter.'

'It has to do with Steve Percival's young friend.'

'Miss Schmidt?'

'Indeed. She was probably the most able student I ever taught. And she volunteered to help me get out of East Berlin at great risk to herself, a risk for which she paid a harsh penalty.'

'Yes, I know something of this, but you did your best to get her ransomed by the West German government and, in fact, succeeded.'

'Well, let's not go into the precise details of all that. And yes, here she is in Cambridge.'

'Having been taken under the wing of Grace Mitchell, it would seem.'

'Yes, Grace is kindly putting her up, while she explores the possibilities for Ulrike to continue her studies at Newnham.'

'A very satisfactory outcome, I should say. I believe Ulrike shone the other night at Newnham High Table and impressed a number of fellows, including Eugenia Waterhouse-Adams.'

Müller laughed. 'Ulrike has an unerring sense of where power lies. And in another time and another place, I was one of those who wielded a certain amount of power, which I am ashamed to say I abused from time to time.'

'That is, of course, a matter of regret, but Miss Schmidt is perhaps worldly enough to forgive and forget.'

'Perhaps. And, yes, I am the one with the stricken conscience.'

'Dieter, if I could offer you absolution, I would, but only she can do that.'

'Which brings us to the reason for my trip to Frankfurt. Ulrike says she is my daughter…'

Doyle gasped. 'Not in a spiritual or intellectual sense, I assume?'

'No, you immediately see the doom that is hovering over me.'

'But, I presume, this is not something you knew at the time of the transgression?'

'No, so I need to speak face-to-face to the woman with whom I had a brief affair in 1949 or 1950 and whom Ulrike knows as Tante Elisabeth, but who now claims to be Ulrike's biological mother.'

Doyle nodded gravely. 'I see. And Ulrike knows this?'

'Yes. A little over a week ago, I gave Steve and Ulrike a little tea party. Towards the end of the visit when Steve was cleaning up the tea things, she told me *sotto voce* what Elisabeth had said. We were unable to discuss it in detail because of Steve's presence, but it certainly cast me down. So I asked her to come back on her own later in the week. We had a longer talk then and I am convinced that she is telling the truth, at least as she understands it.'

'But this is news to you too. You were never her father in any practical terms.'

'No, but quite understandably she blames me for breaking this ancient taboo.'

'Dieter, any blame here is surely venial compared to the apocalyptic transgression you have just been invoking.'

'I wish I could see it like that, but to my further discredit, I am not sure I believe the story. It is possible that Elisabeth herself has been deceived or in some way induced or coerced by other actors.'

'Our friends in East Germany?'

'Yes.'

'But surely Ulrike is telling you what she believes.'

'I am not even sure of that. Perhaps my trip to see Elisabeth will change nothing; perhaps it will make matters worse. I do not feel I have much time left and I would like to try and get to the bottom of the matter.'

'Dieter, we are both philologists and we both know that the search for certainty in the transmission of a text can lead to madness.'

'You are right, but I must at least try before I exhaust Bacon's supply of Cohibas.'

'If you don't mind me saying so, I think it is the Cohibas that are exhausting you.'

As if to prove the point, Müller attempted a wry laugh, but ended up coughing painfully. Having got his breath back, he said, 'While I am away, I would be grateful if you would take into your care my two Zettelkästen.'

'Of course, but surely you do not fear that they might be *borrowed* or tampered with?'

'Not by members or staff of St Rad's, but by outsiders with rather more sinister intentions.'

'I see. I would be happy to look after them in your absence.'

'Thank you, Richard. And I also have here a letter for Steve Percival. In the event of my death I would like you to give to him.'

'I will do as you ask, but if that is how you are feeling, I beg you not to return to Germany at this juncture. Stay here. Despite your justified fears, this is a much safer place.'

'I am grateful for your concern, but I cannot settle down to my work with these issues swirling around.'

'In that case, I will go and put your Zettelkästen under lock and key right now.'

MI6 – Borough – Tuesday

STEVE WAS IN THE *Buzz* offices working on the pages for the current week's issue, when the phone on his desk rang. It was Grace.

'Steve, Dieter is dead.'

'What happened?'

'He seems to have had a heart attack. We'll have to wait for the post-mortem to know for sure.'

'How is Ulrike?'

'Beside herself.'

'I can imagine. Would it help if I came up?'

'There's nothing you can do right now. I can look after Ulrike. I will keep you posted.'

Sally noticed the troubled look on Steve's face as he replaced the receiver. 'Steve, are you okay?'

Steve leaned across to Sally and said, 'Müller is dead. Heart attack, it seems. Everyone has been telling him to go easy on the booze and cigars.'

'Oh dear, that's sad. Will you go up?'

'No. It's not really my responsibility. I'll try to go to the funeral, of course.'

'Ulrike must be in shock.'

'Yeah.'

'What are you going to do?'

'Well, right now, I'm waiting for Jeremy to ring.'

And, as if on cue, the phone on Steve's desk rang.

'Thanks for coming in, Steve. How was Grace?'

'She sounded okay. As you know, her relationship to Müller had very little sentimental content.'

'And how is Ulrike taking it?'

'Not very well, I believe.'

'One can imagine.'

'On the other hand she seems to have made a positive impact on Grace and her colleagues at Newnham.'

'And when did you last see Müller?'

'On Saturday.'

'How was he?'

'Rather down in the dumps.'

'Why do you think that was?'

'Well, having said that he didn't want to have Ulrike hanging around, I think he was a bit hurt when she took him at his word.'

'Because Grace had taken over as her mentor?'

'Quite.'

'Without all the messy stuff?'

'Presumably. Not that Müller's up to that kind of thing. I thought he looked pretty ropey. Definitely had some kind of bladder or prostate problem and possibly a heart condition, too.'

'Oh, poor chap.'

'Curiously, it was the first time I've ever felt sympathetic towards him. He seemed very sad. To be honest, I do not think the Cambridge establishment had taken him to its collective bosom.'

'One can see that.'

'I also think that talk of his magnum opus was a pipe dream. He no longer had the energy. So, sad though this is, it is probably for the best.'

'Yes, but we do seem to have put a lot of effort into something and got no outcome.'

'It seems nuts to regret that he hadn't had enough time to establish a network of DDR sympathisers in British academia.'

'The thing is those people still exist; they just remain undercover.'

'Jeremy, you ought to get out a bit more. The DDR is a tiny country. It is not going to undermine open enquiry in the British university system.'

'The price of freedom, Steve, is constant vigilance.'

'Perhaps it's worth reflecting that Jefferson was thinking about how to evade the might of the British crown. The Brits in that formulation were the bad guys.'

'Steve, I am not used to this more assertive aspect to your personality. Is there any special reason why you have had this change of heart?'

'There is something that doesn't feel quite right about this whole business. Right from the start it has felt wrong. I am not going to allow myself to be sucked into the paranoia and double-dealing that seems to be pervasive in your world. I am not blaming you personally. I know you are constrained as to what you can say. But that path leads to one's own thinking being constrained too.'

'There may be something in what you say, Steve. If there is something you wish to share with me, please feel free to do so. You can trust me to use my discretion.'

Steve scoffed. 'As one St Rad's alumnus to another, I suppose.'

Collingwood looked hurt. 'Well, yes.'

Steve realised that he had gone too far. 'I'm sorry, Jeremy. I suppose the smoke and mirrors are getting to me.'

'You are not alone. It happens to all of us. But we are where we are. Do you know whether Dieter had any visitors on Monday or Tuesday?'

'No, I came back down to London on Sunday. I am sure Stan would have a pretty good idea of the comings and goings in Founder's Court.'

'In which case, I too will be on the list.'

'How come?'

'I went up to see Doyle yesterday.'

'But not Müller?'

'No.'

'I hardly think that every person who passed through Founder's Court need be considered a suspect. There are quite a few undergraduates on Founder's Court staircases. I doubt if many of them have even heard of Müller.'

'Well, with luck we will have the results of the autopsy tomorrow, and that should enable us to draw a line under the whole operation.'

Steve & Grace – Cambridge – Thursday

JUST BEFORE STEVE LEFT the office on Thursday evening, the phone on his desk rang. It was Grace.

'Steve, we've had Special Branch officers here all afternoon, turning the house over. They have arrested Ulrike and taken her to Paddington Green police station. They believe she poisoned Dieter.'

'That's preposterous.'

'I know. Can you come down here tomorrow, so we can work out what to do?'

'Wouldn't it be better if I go to Paddington Green and get her a solicitor?'

'I'm pretty sure they won't let you see her and they will have applied to have more time to question her until she's allowed a solicitor. Come to Cambridge. And bear in mind you might be on the receiving end of a visit from Special Branch yourself.'

'Well, they won't find anything at Trinity Church Square.'

'Steve, I need to talk to you.'

'Okay, I'll get the train after work tomorrow.'

'Thank you.'

Steve and Grace were sitting in the kitchen-diner of the Glisson Road house. Grace took a sip of her wine. 'How long were the police with you?'

'Not long. They clearly already had a good idea of the layout of the flat. They could have made a nuisance of themselves and gone through all the cupboards and the attic space, but they confined themselves to Ulrike's possessions, which are not many. The only thing that they went through in my presence was her case. It was in the sitting-room where they had asked me to wait. I had put it out to bring it up here. They found something in it which interested them.'

'Did you see what it was?'

'Not closely, but it looked like a small phial.'

'A lipstick?'

'I don't think so. I actually went through her case myself after we first came up here.'

'Steve!'

'Don't be silly, Grace. It's not as if this was a normal situation even then. Normal rules of conduct didn't apply. Anyway, the point is I didn't expect to find anything and I didn't. The contents of the case were remarkable in being completely unremarkable, apart from the fact that the underwear all looked new.'

'You're an expert in women's underwear?'

Steve shrugged. 'To an extent. But there was definitely no phial in the case.'

'Perhaps you overlooked it.'

'I did a slow and very thorough search, took everything out, felt each individual item of clothing, the lining of the case. There was no phial.'

'Did they ask you whether you recognised the phial?'

'No, they didn't refer to it. But after that, they didn't hang around for very long. How long were they here?'

'Hours. They went over the house with a fine-tooth comb. Had us both sitting down here. A female officer gave us both a full-body search before we could use the loo, which we had to use with the door open and the officer standing outside.'

'That was a bit oppressive. Were you questioned here?'

'Only to answer when each of us had last seen Dieter.'

'How did Ulrike cope?'

'I think she's been through worse. She just went into herself.'

'Was she upset or surprised that they didn't take you to Paddington Green as well?'

'I don't know. We weren't really able to say much to each other.'

'Has Collingwood been in touch?'

'Yes, he said they'll probably want me to go down and speak to them next week.'

'Same for me. He said the official position is that we're still waiting for the results of the autopsy, but that in the meantime there's no reason not to suppose that Müller had a heart attack. In effect there's a news blackout.'

'You can understand why.'

'I suppose so, but it doesn't feel quite right. Dieter had a feeling that something like this might happen. Anyway, I'm going in to see Doyle tomorrow and then I'll head back to the Smoke.'

'Steve, I can understand that you want to get home, but I'd really appreciate it if you could stay with me for the weekend. I'm feeling really scared.'

'I'm not sure I'll be much good at fighting off the Stasi assassins.'

'It's not them I'm worried about.'

'Come on, Grace, you're not in the firing line.'

'I know that I have no right to ask you, but I feel completely out of my depth.'

'You feel out of your depth! That's a laugh.'

'Steve, please.'

'Okay, I'll think about it. I'll see what Doyle's got to say first.'

'Thank you, Steve.'

Later in bed up in the guest room, Steve was feeling somewhat pissed off. He hadn't really wanted to come up to Cambridge again. Müller was dead and Ulrike was in custody in Paddington Green police station. Really, there was not much he could do. Perhaps he'd read too much into Grace's need to talk to him. When he'd arrived, her greeting had been the peck on the cheek that she'd been offering him since that Sunday in the Great Eastern, friendly, but not close or passionate. It was therefore unreasonable to suppose that just because she was shaken up by events that she would invite Steve into her bed. But when she'd told him she was scared and wanted him to stay for the weekend, he'd read it as a message to that effect. So he'd been considerably put out, indeed dismayed, when she'd made it clear that he would be sleeping in the guest room.

Dr Doyle rose from his armchair as Steve entered his room.

191

'Steve, thank you for coming to see me. Poor Dieter, he had so little time to enjoy Cambridge and to complete his work.'

Steve was, of course, aware that Doyle had connections to MI6, but was not sure how much he knew. So he would have to tread carefully. 'Yes, I feel very sad. You and I both knew he had a bad heart and how reluctant he was to give up his cigars.'

'You are quite right to proceed cautiously. But let me stop you there and tell you what I know. Yes, the public, those who have any interest in an obscure German intellectual, are being told that he died of a heart attack. But I know from certain contacts we share that the autopsy revealed traces of a substance often used by the Stasi and that is why your young friend is being held at Paddington Green police station.'

'I wondered if you were in the loop.'

'I imagine you yourself also received a bit of a grilling.'

'Not really. Or not yet. They searched my flat. Not very thoroughly and seemed to find what they were looking for.'

'And what was that?'

'I don't know, but I'm guessing it's something that ties up with the substance the autopsy revealed.'

'Do you think she did it?'

'Frankly, no. But things certainly look bad for her.'

'You seem to have become close to our friends in Borough.'

'Not intentionally. It is proving difficult to disentangle myself.'

'But you and Jeremy get on?'

Steve was hesitant. 'Ye-es'

'There must be a bond of trust between you, both being alumni of St Rad's.'

'We get on well, but there is a huge amount of distrust in the department because of the recent spate of leaks. Everyone is watching everyone else.'

'Yes, I see. And Dieter was never entirely trusted?'

'Not at all.'

'Yet if his death was a Stasi hit, it suggests that the Stasi did not trust him either.'

'That is the fate of the double agent, but Jeremy does not believe that. Though I do understand that what's thought and what's shown or communicated can be two entirely different things.'

'Sadly, that is the case. But I can tell you that Dieter trusted you and, I suppose, in anticipating that something like this might happen gave me a letter to pass to you in the event of his death.'

Doyle handed Steve a large envelope. 'Don't open it here. He also wanted you to have his two card index files, Zettelkästen as they are called. I'm afraid they're a bit cumbersome, but I've put them in this bag.'

Doyle pushed the bag across the floor with his foot.

Steve looked at it blankly. 'I'm surprised that the Special Branch boys didn't want to cart that off.'

'Let's just say that I somehow forgot to mention that I had them in my rooms. My interview was even less cursory than yours. I'd be obliged if you were careful with the information that I had them in my keeping.'

'Of course.'

'Where are you staying in Cambridge?'

'At Grace's.'

'Is that wise?'

'Probably not, but I've given up trying to be wise.'

'Well, in that case, please be careful.'

Inevitably, on his way out of the college with the bag containing Müller's Zettelkästen, Steve bumped into Stan.

'Morning, sir. How was Dr Doyle?'

'Pretty shaken up.'

'I can imagine. Rum goings-on. From what I hear things don't look too good for your girl.'

'Stan, I just don't think she did it.'

'Well, she certainly called on the professor the afternoon of the evening he died.'

'I am sure that she was not the only visitor that he had that day.'

'Well, you are, of course, correct. Dr Doyle visited the professor. He does most days. I did myself, to take him his mail. His bedder must have been in too, but Mrs Comberton wouldn't harm a fly. And Dr Mitchell round about four o'clock. There may have been others, but I doubt it.'

'I am surprised that Ulrike had been in to see him. The previous time she'd seen him hadn't gone very well.'

'She'd come in to retrieve her beautiful red coat, I would say. She had it on when she was leaving. Hadn't been wearing it on her arrival.'

'Oh, thanks, Stan. I wasn't aware of that, but even so.'

'Remember, Steve, things aren't always what they seem.' He nodded at the bag that Steve was carrying. 'Dr Doyle give you an assignment?'

Steve laughed. 'Yeah, some things don't change.'

Stan tapped Steve on the chest with his forefinger. 'Make sure you do this one.'

Steve gulped, 'I will, Stan.'

Rather than read the letter in the street or back at Glisson Road, Steve turned right at the end of Thompson's Lane, crossed Magdalene Bridge and dropped into the Pickerel. He got a pint, found a seat in the back and opened the letter.

Dear Steve,

If you are reading this, it will be because something unfortunate has happened to me. In the short time that we've known each other, I have very much enjoyed our encounters. But at the same time I am aware that you probably feel that my appearance in your life has coincided with a series of unfortunate events. I am sorry if that is the case. It was not anything that I intended.

Your mother and I lived through difficult but exciting times. You will find with this letter two black and white photographs from those days in postwar Berlin. You will see what a handsome woman your mother was and remained.

Of course I regret that I wasn't brave enough to join her in London. But had I done so, you would not now exist. So in some sense it was for the best. In a way you are the son I never had. In saying this, I do not want to write your own father out of the story. It is merely one of those oddities of fate.

I do not even know if you and Ulrike are really together or were just putting on a show for my benefit. If the former, I could think of no better partner for her. And in her, I think you would find a partner who has a fine intellect and is capable of great things.

My next request to you is, I hope, not as onerous as it might sound, since I have very few possessions and little money. But I do own a considerable number of copyrights. I have therefore appointed you the executor of my will and, in particular, my literary executor. I am sorry that I did not discuss this with you first. I understand that in British law you do not need to accept this duty, but I sincerely hope you will take it on. I am vain enough to think there will be interest in my work for many years to come, and I see no reason why you shouldn't benefit from any proceeds. I also trust your judgement when it comes to publishing contracts and any distributions to deserving individuals and causes.

And finally, as you perhaps have already noticed, you will also now be in possession of my master Zettelkasten and its less academically important but surprisingly fertile offspring in the black leather box. I would like you to have them. I know you resist being a scholar, even so I think you could make good use of the material in both of those rather battered boxes. But my real purpose in bequeathing them to you is that they contain some information that might help you better understand the situation you are currently in. In deploying that information, bear in mind that there will never be a point at which everything is completely clear. Schlegel (F) and Novalis understood this all too well. And that is the only hint I am going to give you. You will have to find your own way through the maze.

With respect and affection,

Dieter Müller

Back in Grace's kitchen-diner, Steve took the two Zettelkasten boxes out of the bag that Doyle had given him and put them on the table. Grace gasped in wonderment. 'Dieter's Zettelkästen.'

'You're familiar with them?'

'He never really stopped talking about them. When he first arrived in Cambridge, they had still not caught up with him. For his first months here he had a temporary set on the go. When finally the department released them, he spent a happy time revisiting them and sifting his new cards into the mother lode.'

Steve was curious. 'The department had them?'

'Yes, they were with Mavis's official documents.'

Steve relaxed a little. That fitted with what Müller had told him, but he was still slightly troubled by the line of transmission. 'Müller only recently gave them to Doyle for safekeeping, otherwise I imagine that they'd already be back at the department.'

'I really don't think they have time for notes on German Romanticism.'

'Well, in his letter, Müller, is very keen that I should familiarise myself with them and suggested I focus on Friedrich Schlegel and Novalis.'

'Maybe he's just trying to help you catch up with all the work you didn't do for Doyle.'

Steve laughed. 'That's a rather elaborate way to get someone to do their studies.'

'Not everyone is as resistant to being taught as Steve Percival.'

'Well, I'm glad I have you on hand to guide me through Müller's labyrinth.'

Steve opened the drawer of the bigger box and pulled out the front card.

ZK 2.11.4 → NOVALIS / Romanticisation / cf. Benjamin 9.6.1
ZK 3.1.1 → SCHLEGEL / Irony as Wound ← see also 5.6.3
ZK 3.14 → C. SCHLEGEL / Anti-idealism / "nicht bloß Idee"
ZK 3.18.2 → W. von HUMBOLDT / Bildung & Coercion → cf. 4.7
ZK 4.4.1.3 → HÖLDERLIN / Das Heilige ↔ aura theory
ZK 4.7 → FICHTE / Freedom as pre-political idea
ZK 5.6.3 → SCHELLING / Wound-consciousness theory
ZK 6.9 → Günderrode / Goethe letters / under review

ZK 7.2.19 → Kierkegaard / pseudonyms / marginal irony
ZK 8.3.2 → xxxxxx / xxxxxx / xxxxxx → Withdrawn 76
ZK 9.6.1 → BENJAMIN / Aura / reproducibility
ZK 10.2.5 → SAUSSURE / langue as Bildung system
ZK ?.?. → DUMAS / Montecristo / "Withdrawn = Misplaced ≠ Discarded"

Scribbled in the upper margin was a handwritten note: *Man sieht nur, was man weiß zu sehen* – W. v. Humboldt. (One sees only what one knows how to see.)

He handed the card to Grace. 'My God, what am I meant to do with this? How is it going to help us work out who killed Müller, or my mother, or who the mole is?'

Grace studied the card in silence for a couple of minutes, then put it back on the table. 'Steve, Müller has done you the greatest honour a scholar can accord to another scholar. He has bequeathed you the fruits of his life's work. This is the seed, the DNA of the book he was hoping to write before he died. It would have been his crowning achievement.'

'That simply can't be the case. He knew I was no scholar. It would be a different matter if he left it to you or to Ulrike.'

'But look at the line of transmission. He gave it to Doyle to give to you.'

'Then it must be for another reason. Most of the lines on this card mean little to me. I recognise some of the names, but the notes might as well be in cuneiform.'

Grace picked up the card again and said, 'Let me have a stab at outlining his argument.'

Grace proceeded to improvise what she saw as the thesis of Müller's unwritten book. Steve listened in admiration, amazed at how each of the lines on the card unlocked successive stages in the argument. When she had finished, Steve said, 'I wish I'd been in a relationship with you when I was writing essays for Doyle on German Romanticism.'

Grace laughed. 'That would have been inappropriate on several counts.'

'Well, thank you for the refresher. But I notice that you have omitted to say anything about Dumas. Is that a gap in your reading?'

'No, I love Dumas. *Le Comte de Monte-Cristo* is a great yarn. All those aliases: Lord Wilmore, Number Thirty-Four.'

'And betrayal, imprisonment, rebirth, identities within identities.'

'So you've read it too. But I just don't see how it fits into Müller's thesis. I would have to study his notes in detail to explain how it figures in his argument. Dumas is simply not a significant figure in the Frühromantik.'

'Nor are Kierkegaard, Benjamin or Saussure.'

'But they are theorists whose ideas Müller can use to advance his case.'

'Well, the reference to Dumas can't be accidental.' He picked up the card and studied it for a few moments. 'Actually, I'd say that line was added at a different time to all the other lines. It's at a slight angle to them and it looks like it's been typed on a different typewriter.'

Grace took the card from Steve and peered at the bottom line of the card. 'I think you're right. This line has probably been added since Dieter's been in the UK. You can also see that the subject matter, theme and note have all been heavily crossed out.'

'And it's rather different from the other entries in another way. To begin with it has no index number, so we can't even look up the card it refers to.'

'That's right. But it does share something with the other anomalous line – ZK 8.3.2. That card has an index reference but no subject or comment other than that it was withdrawn this year. The Dumas card also has the word *withdrawn*, but as a term in a logical proposition which equates *withdrawn* with *misplaced* and not with *discarded*.'

'So, assuming that all this has been done on purpose, it's as if we're being directed to card ZK 8.3.2 or the card which has replaced it, and which, in turn, is misplaced. But there must be hundreds of cards in this box. It'll take us hours to find a misplaced card.'

'But it's definitely not an impossible task. We could split the collection at the point where ZK 8.3.2 should be and, assuming it's not there, one of us works forwards from that point and the other works backwards. Maybe a glass of wine will help.'

Steve laughed. 'On that we can agree.'

A few minutes later, with a bottle of red wine between them, Grace said, 'It's so lovely having you here, just the two of us.'

'Don't say things like that. We can't go back.'

'No, but we could go on.'

'We can discuss that once we've got Ulrike home and we're all safely out of the clutches of Special Branch.'

'The evidence looks very much against her.'

'But it doesn't make sense. She does time in a Stasi hellhole, gets bashed about, gets freed with Müller's help, to some extent, and then decides to murder him because he'd made her sleep with him on a number of occasions. And somehow she had access to a poison favoured by the Stasi.'

'But she was the last person to see him alive. She had traces of the poison on her coat and a phial of the same poison was found in her case at your flat.'

'Well, that last detail, as I said before, is cobblers. There was no phial in that case.'

'How did it get there?'

'The two Special Branch officers must have put it in the case.'

'The plods wouldn't have access to a phial of Stasi poison.'

'Well, in that case, one of Jeremy's boys broke into my flat and put it there. In fact, they wouldn't even have had to break in. They could have borrowed Sheena's key.'

'You don't think Sheena would get involved in something like that, something which could go terribly wrong?'

'I think that's exactly the sort of thing that makes Sheena tick.'

'She's your guardian, Steve.'

'I don't need a guardian, not in that sense anyway. I'm old enough to go to hell on my own.'

'Okay, I can see we're not going to agree on this.'

'I don't see why you're so unconcerned about Ulrike.'

'I'm extremely concerned about her. I just think the evidence is against her.'

Neither of them spoke for several long moments. Finally, Steve said, 'I'm sorry, Grace. That was uncalled for. I appreciate your help.'

'That's okay. This is a stressful situation. Let's get on with going through Dieter's Zettelkasten cards one by one.'

Grace flipped through the deck of cards to the point where ZK 8.3.2 ought to have been but was not and handed Steve the batch of cards onward from that point. As she did so, she said, 'Don't get them out of sequence.'

Steve grunted his assent and started working through his cards. Grace then picked up her batch and set to work too.

They found the card even before they had finished their glasses of wine.

> ZK 8.3.2 → Montecristo / Envelope S.F. / Intended reader: S.P.
> ↳ Interpretive keys:
> Compare Box C, bundle 5e (re: Wound-consciousness / eroticised ritual)
> IRG 3.6.4.7 (withdrawn: "Uniformity and Eros")
> Not pornography. Tactical but also real. The real always leaves a bruise.
> Further interpretation: see me (not as you imagined)
> Not to be copied.

Beneath the text on the card was a small polyester envelope of the type for storing photographic negatives and contact prints, marked S. F. in blue pencil.

Steve said, 'Maybe Müller read Dumas when he was a boy and he uses it as a key to his ideas.'

'He never once mentioned Dumas in my hearing. There's something else going on here. I think S.F. is Sheena, Sheena Ferguson and S.P. is you.'

'Sheena?'

'Well, you said just now that planting Stasi poison in Ulrike's case is just the sort of thing that makes her tick. Dropping a few cards into Müller's Zettelkasten would be a piece of cake for someone like that. Perhaps she's the aficionada of *The Count of Monte-Cristo*.'

'But it seems so far-fetched.'

And then suddenly, it struck Steve. 'No, I think you're right. It's Montecristo at the top of the card. Not Monte-Cristo, as in the novel. Montecristos are a brand of cigar favoured by Sheena. They are named after the novel. She was smoking them when I went around to supper with her recently.'

'You've had supper at Sheena's home?'

'Yes.'

'Well, you are in a very select group of people. And so I am even more of the opinion that whatever is in the envelope is for you.'

Carefully, Steve detached the envelope from the card and noticed that there was a message in tiny spidery writing on the card where it had been covered by the envelope:

"Zugang nur im Ernstfall - oder wenn du's nicht mehr lassen kannst."

He paused, momentarily daunted by the Dantesque admonition: *Access only in case of emergency – or if you simply can't help yourself.* Then with a shrug he opened the flap and pulled out four contact print strips, four images per strip. He looked at the top strip and blinked at the improbable images: a bare-breasted, middle-aged woman was administering a cane to the shapely buttocks of a naked young woman, restrained on a wooden frame, her arms and legs spread wide. The flagellant's face was turned away from the camera, but even on a contact print the identity of the flagellator was all too apparent. It was Sheena Ferguson.

He shook his head and passed the first strip to Grace. The next two strips were much the same with the participants in a variety of poses of domination and submission. In these images the submissive was wearing a black half-mask. The final strip showed the girl released and the two women, now both fully naked, embracing, the flagellant's back to the camera, the marks of the beating visible. Both Grace and Steve were silent for a long while.

Finally, Steve said, 'This is the gay kompromat that Müller was talking about. And that means that Sheena is the mole.'

Steve instantly regretted giving to voice to his thoughts, because Grace said, 'Müller obviously shared something with you that he did not feel comfortable sharing with me. But given how explosive this material is, you're going to have to tell me more.'

A little later they had moved to the sitting room. Some Oscar Peterson was playing quietly on the hifi. Grace ran her finger around the rim of her glass, mulling over what Müller had told Steve, both in person and in his letter. 'So let's assume that Müller was telling the truth about the way he acquired this material. Why didn't he go public with it when he got to Britain?'

'Because he hadn't been reunited with the Zettelkasten until quite recently. And he must have wondered at times whether one of Collingwood's analysts had already come across it.'

'I'm sure Collingwood has some very bright people working for him, but it would be very easy to dismiss the overwhelming majority of this stuff as academic nonsense. Also you can't compromise someone who's not afraid to be known as a lesbian dominatrix and who's had half the women in the intelligence community and others besides.'

'Including my mother, it would seem.'

'I get the impression that what they had was a bit more enduring.'

Steve was grateful for Grace's sensitivity. 'But Müller's story is that Mavis either saw this material or felt she knew enough to raise the matter with Sheena. And shortly afterwards she was involved in a fatal accident in West Berlin on the same day that she was being visited clandestinely by Sheena herself.'

'Yes. But we don't know that it was this material. So it would be unwise simply to confront Sheena with these photos.'

Steve shrugged and took a sip of his wine. 'We can hardly give them to Collingwood. Sheena could whip him with one hand tied behind her back.'

'You could have used a less tasteless expression, but you're right. There's something troubling about those photos though, apart from the content.'

'What do you mean?'

'Did Dieter use the term kompromat, or have you made that assumption?'

'I'm pretty sure it was the term he used.'

'I assume you've never seen kompromat material before.'

'No.'

'Well, I have and it is generally much more blurry with odd or oblique framing because of the fixed position of the hidden camera.'

Steve was thoughtful. 'Yes, I think I understand what you mean. It's almost as if Sheena and the girl know the camera is there and are posing for it.'

'Much as you did with Inge in Prenzlauer Berg.'

'It's true. I hadn't thought of that.'

'Whose idea was all the rigmarole with Inge, getting her to give you a blowjob in front of the window with the curtains drawn back?'

'Not mine, I can assure you. Collingwood told me in general terms what I was expected to do and Inge explained the choreography.'

'So, there had been some prior collusion.'

'I suppose so.'

'Choreography seems a very appropriate term for these images. Perhaps there were many more frames and we're only seeing the best ones, but these look like a lesbian S&M burlesque act.'

'Yes, and Sheena is making absolutely no attempt to hide her identity, whereas the girl is masked or her face is turned away.'

'Exactly, as if this is something that the participants know is going to come to light.'

'Do you think the girl is enjoying being beaten? She doesn't seem to be crying.'

'You'd have to ask her.'

'We can hardly do that.'

'True, but if we'd seen these images sooner, we might have been able to.'

'What do you mean?'

'Don't you think that's Ulrike under the mask?'

'Well, the body shape and size, and the hair colour are about right.'

'Oh, come on, Steve. Look at the mark under her left breast.'

Steve peered at the clearest print showing the girl's torso. 'The mole or birthmark?'

'Yes, it's a birthmark exactly where Ulrike has a birthmark.'

'How do you know?'

'I noticed it when she was showing me the bruising on her ribs on the right side of her body. You've been sharing a bed with her. Didn't you notice it?'

'No. Since she was assaulted in Camden, I've had to be very careful how I touched her and she's been very shy and modest compared to how she was to begin with.'

'I am beginning to think that this so-called kompromat is not something that was captured by hidden cameras more than a year ago in Berlin.'

'I'm not sure I can follow the implications of what you're saying.'

'What I'm suggesting is that it was staged by Sheena and Ulrike with a photographer or with a camera on a timer shortly before Ulrike re-appeared in your life a few weeks ago.'

'You mean that Sheena has had dealings with Ulrike quite recently?'

'Exactly.'

'But that doesn't make sense. Müller said he got the photos in East Berlin before he fled.'

'No, we're making that assumption. We're adding two and two and getting five. These are a different set of photos.'

How did they get into Müller's Zettelkasten, then?'

'I suppose, using Occam's Razor, Sheena herself put them in the box somehow.'

Grace suddenly had an idea. She turned the cream envelope over to show the handwritten note on it and then put the first content card with the quote from Wilhelm von Humboldt beside it.

'Look, the handwriting on the envelope is different. Because the sentence is in German, it's easy to make the assumption that it's Müller's. But it's not.'

'Whose handwriting is it, then?'

'I'd say it's Sheena's.'

'Why would she put something like that in Müller's Zettelkasten and when and how did she do it?'

'It's hard to guess the when and how, but the why is so that the beneficiary of the bequest should find it.'

'You mean me?'

'Yes. The reason that Collingwood's analysts didn't find the photos is because they weren't in the Zettelkasten when they had access to it at the department. Which means that they have only been put there quite recently and in the knowledge, probably, that both Zettelkästen were destined for you.'

'I would never have found them without your help.'

'I'm not so sure about that.'

He frowned. 'You think it's a message?'

'I do. From Sheena.'

He shook his head. 'Why not just call me in?'

'Because she didn't want others to be party to the message. Or because she has a special purpose in mind for you. She probably didn't expect me to be involved in the process.'

'Well, that didn't work then. Anyway, she's the boss.'

'But she's also aware that there's a leak in the system.'

'But why trust me? I'm not sure that I trust her.'

'That doesn't matter. You're the person on the ground. You are to hand. And she has a personal link with you. You're her boy. You've dined at her board and inhaled the aroma of her cigars.'

'Well, that all sounds very weird and I'm not sure I like the thought that she considers me her boy.'

'Only in a manner of speaking, Steve. She is prepared to reveal herself to you. Look at the interpretive key on the card that the envelope was attached to – *see me (not as you imagined.)*'

'She doesn't figure in my imagination to any extent, and certainly not in an erotic capacity. In any case, it's an absurdly elaborate form of revelation. It's like a mime troupe presenting a weather forecast.'

'That's exactly what it is. It's a charade as memo.'

'Why to me?'

'Because she knows you will use the information wisely.'

'In that case, she knows more than I do.'

'She does. What is the hidden message in that image?'

'That she's a lesbian dominatrix?'

'That's the surface. But look at how it's *made*. The half-mask. The girl's birthmark. The lighting. The staging. This isn't surveillance. It's theatre. And again, look at the interpretive key – *Not pornography. Tactical but also real. The real always leaves a bruise.*'

'Who's being bruised?'

'Ostensibly the girl, but perhaps the viewer too.'

'So she's putting on a show?'

'In McLuhan's terms, yes. The *medium* is the message. It's not what's in the frame – it's *why* the frame exists. What it *does* to you, seeing it?'

'Makes me suspicious. Uncomfortable.'

'Good. So ask yourself – why show her breasts? This is Sheena we're talking about.'

'That's all part of her lesbian S&M persona.'

'But the message is for you and you are not a submissive lesbian. So there must be another meaning. There are only a few contexts where women bare their breasts without erotic charge: life modelling, medicine… and suckling a child.'

Sullenly, Steve said, 'Yeah, I suppose.'

'You are that child, Steve. She is offering you her breasts as a form of sustenance, not to excite you.'

'Grace, that's absolutely bonkers. You're saying Sheena's my mother now?'

'Not literally. Morphologically. If your actual mother had died before you were of age, she'd have been your guardian. It's the underlying dynamic of the relationship.'

He felt uncomfortable. 'Not a dynamic of my choosing.'

'You don't get to choose archetypes, Steve. They come with the script.'

'Okay, but what has McLuhan got to say about a girl strapped to a frame being beaten?'

'The frame is a situation the girl can't escape from. We believe that Ulrike was beaten in prison, so the girl in the picture represents Ulrike. At the end of the sequence, she and Sheena are shown embracing, reconciled, loving.'

'So… Sheena is saying: I have Ulrike. I trust her. You should too?'

'Close. She's saying: *I* trust you enough to show you this. So trust me – and, by extension, trust Ulrike.'

'Well, I don't trust her, and I'm going to confront her with this material and challenge her to explain why this isn't the kompromat that Müller was talking about.'

'Steve, don't do that. Haven't you been listening to what I've just been saying. This material doesn't pre-date Mavis's death. It's very recent. So Müller couldn't have been referring to it.'

'No, I'm determined to have it out with her.'

'Sheena will crucify you. Let's take our time to think our way through this. We've got the rest of the weekend to go through Müller's archive. There's another box we haven't even looked at yet.'

'No, I'm going first thing in the morning.'

'Steve, stop it. Come to bed with me.'

'I'm sorry, Grace. It's too late for that.'

Grace blushed and bit her lip. 'There's no need to be so truculent.'

'Apparently I'm noted for my truculence.'

'This is a difficult time for all of us. I thought we could have comforted each other.'

But Steve was already heading for the door. 'I'll bring you some coffee in the morning.'

That night, Steve had a wet dream. He had had them quite frequently as a teenager, but they had become rarer in recent years, no doubt because he actually had a fairly active sex life. But that had not been quite the case recently. In his dream, a naked girl wearing a mask had turned her back to him and bent over from the waist, showing him her beautiful vulva. He had read this as an invitation to penetrate her, but as he stepped forward to do so, another figure had interposed itself between him and the girl. He realised as he came that the person who had taken him in her mouth was a bare-breasted Sheena in the persona he'd seen in the photos in Müller's Zettelkasten. He woke gasping, and more than a little horrified.

Sheena – Kennington – Sunday

NOW THAT HE WAS standing in front of Sheena's front door, Steve wasn't sure that he actually had the courage to go through with the encounter. He looked at his watch. It was nearly eleven o'clock.

Four hours earlier when he had been getting ready to leave Glisson Road, a tearful Grace had come downstairs in her dressing gown and begged him not to go, when he'd told her he was still determined to have things out with Sheena. She'd put her arms around him. But he'd been adamant and shrugged her off. He'd been lucky enough to board the next fast train just as it was pulling out and was back at his flat by nine o'clock. He'd then had a quick shower, put on some clean clothes and phoned Sheena on the number she'd made him memorise. She hadn't seemed in the slightest bit surprised to receive a call so early on a Sunday morning and had told him he should come round at five o'clock that afternoon, but Steve, surprising himself, had demanded to see her immediately. Sheena, sounding faintly amused, had agreed to his demands.

So now here he was on her doorstep and all his anger and confidence had evaporated. He should have listened to Grace. He didn't entirely buy into her McLuhanite media theorising, but she was surely right about his hasty misidentification of the S&M images as kompromat. It was too late now, though. With a trembling hand, he rang the bell. A couple of minutes later, the heavy door swung open to reveal the tiny figure of Sheena in grey trousers, collar and silk tie and a cashmere V-necked sweater. 'Steve, come in.'

She led him into the living room. 'It's a bit early in the day, but I've made us a couple of Bloody Marys.'

She handed him one of the glasses and said, 'Cin, cin!' And touched his glass with hers.

For a moment, he wondered whether she might have put poison in his drink, but immediately dismissed the thought. It was too late for such worries.

Sheena looked at him steadily. 'Poor Professor Müller. And poor Ulrike Schmidt. What an unexpected outcome!'

Steve took a deep breath. 'Hardly unexpected.'

She raised an eyebrow. 'That the Stasi sent an assassin to punish a traitor and we let him slip through our fingers?'

Steve was immediately wrong footed. 'Him? But you've arrested Ulrike.'

'It is not our function to make arrests. But yes, to keep her out of harm's way.'

Steve was speechless.

Sheena took another sip of her drink. 'She speaks warmly of you.'

Steve's mind was racing, trying to find a handhold in the conversation. Sheena smiled at him. 'Was it comforting to be back in Miss Mitchell's embrace? She has rather more to comfort a chap of your disposition than someone of my build, though I thought my breasts didn't look too bad in the photos.'

Steve had no idea how to answer that statement. 'What do you mean?'

'You found the envelope I put in Müller's little bag of tricks by following the hints I added to a couple of cards and left it at that. You didn't seem to notice the difference in handwriting. And you were so distracted by a picture of me baring my breasts and a naked girl who could almost have been Ulrike that you stopped thinking.'

'We found the kompromat and we *did* notice the difference in the handwriting. That's why I'm here.'

'What? To expose me? Didn't the little tableau I presented you make you realise that you can't expose me? No doubt you have worked out that I'm the mole and that, therefore, I must have murdered Müller.'

Steve remained silent.

Sheena tapped the arm of her chair. 'Well?'

'Yes, I did think that.'

'You have obviously left your brain in Miss Mitchell's bed.'

'I have not slept with Grace for more than a year, since, in fact, the point when you broke up our relationship.'

'Well, I give you credit for that. But those photos are not so-called kompromat. You will see some real kompromat in due course. It is generally artless. And even if those images were kompromat, I am immune to attempts of that nature to compromise me. I am a well-known lesbian dominatrix. Furthermore just because you have pictures of me caning a naked young woman with my tits out, it does not make me a murderer. On that basis, the pictures I have of you receiving oral pleasuring standing in front of a window in East Berlin would make you a murderer too.'

Once again, she had thrown him. He spluttered as he tried to find a way to parry the observation. 'The situation was preventing me from performing normally.'

'Steve, I'm not talking about your rather pathetic erection in that picture. I'm sure you can do better when no one is looking. I'm saying you can't use distaste as grounds for supposing someone to be a wrongdoer. Anyway, how do you know Müller is dead?'

'That is what people are saying.'

'And that is just where you are going wrong. It does not help to believe what people are saying. You need to make sure that the person telling you something can account for the source of the knowledge. Provenance is all.'

'But what about the young woman who was the recipient of the beating?'

'Oh, she wasn't forced to do anything against her wishes. Steve, I am not trying to persuade you that sadomasochism has something to be said for it. I wanted to see how you would react in the context of the Müller and Ulrike situation. I give you credit for not going to Collingwood, and also for insisting on seeing me immediately. You are not short of courage. I make much tougher chaps than you quake in their boots.'

'I thought I might wet myself.'

'Well, yes that happens. But you didn't. However, I am sorry to say you fell at the first hurdle. You have not really worked out what is going on here. You have allowed yourself to be bamboozled by a whole bunch of women. Really, I'm beginning to feel you shouldn't be allowed out on your own.'

'So what do you want me to do?'

'Ideally, you should crawl across the floor and kiss my shining brogues. But I will remit that part of your penance. Go home and try to use Müller's infernal machine to better purpose. I cannot stop you letting Miss Mitchell, or whichever willing female you have to hand, help you. I would rather you just used your own brain.'

'Don't you like Grace?'

'Let us not go there. There will be time for that later.'

'She told me I was making a mistake.'

'Yes, well she is a good deal more experienced than you.'

'Should I trust her?'

'In intelligence matters, yes. In matters of the heart, I am not so sure. But your heart is yours to give as you please. I make no demands on your heart.'

'What about Collingwood?'

'He is your handler. He has a certain amount of power over you. But with him you need not reveal all until I tell you it is alright to do so.'

'Doyle?'

'Of course. But in the first instance, Stan Mallory is a better choice. He is a person of vast experience.'

'I love Stan.'

'That is the first bit of good sense you have spoken.'

'And Ulrike is alright?'

'She is fine, but for reasons you may come to appreciate, this is the end of Ulrike Schmidt.'

'I don't understand.'

'I am not going to spell it out, you fathead. In the days to come, think about what I have just said.'

'Am I still working on this operation?'

'You most certainly are and you haven't come up with a solution yet. So get on with it. Try your best to activate your brain.'

'Is that it?'

'Yes, unless you want a good thrashing. Get the hell out of here and let me enjoy the rest of my weekend.'

Sheena rose from her chair to indicate the interview was over. Steve got to his feet and turned to go. But Sheena said, 'Steve, you've forgotten something. You don't need to crawl, but as your guardian, I would like a kiss from you.'

Steve – Trinity Church Square – Sunday

STEVE PULLED THE TWO Zettelkasten boxes out of the bag in which he had carried them back from Cambridge and put them on the kitchen table. He withdrew the drawer of the black box and noticed that as with the grey box the first several cards served as a kind of table of contents. He took the frontmost card out and studied it carefully. The first thing that struck him was that the card was new, not as yellowed as the other cards. There was also a handwritten sentence at the top of the card in what he now recognised as Müller's handwriting: *The truth is what one is not allowed to say -M.*

Presumably, M was Müller, though the sentiment felt like something Steve had stumbled across elsewhere. Then below that was an index of serial numbers, names, comments and further references, very much like the German Romanticism index in the grey box.

He scanned down the list of name and realised he recognised nearly all of them. The only one that didn't make sense was the very first one: MORGAN, M with a reference to a wedding affair.

> 1.4.2 → MORGAN, M. / airlift liaison / Wedding affair ← see 9.7.3
> 2.8.1 → PERCIVAL, M. / MI6 recruitment / U. cut-out
> 3.3.9 → SCHMIDT, U. / twin disclosure → see 6.6.6
> 3.4.2 → SCHMIDT, K. / Müggelsee event / libidinal asymmetry ⚠
> 4.1.1 → STASI / surveillance begins / K. retribution ↩ bundle 7b
> 4.7.2 → COLLINGWOOD / restraint & coercion / blackmail protocol.
> 5.5.5 → FERGUSON, S. / domination ritual / Montecristo!
> 5.8.3 → MITCHELL, G. / ethics compromised / seduction & redemption arc ← cf. 3.3.9, 6.6.6
> 6.6.6 → K. as U. / body double / Who? game
> 6.7.1 → PERCIVAL, S. / Muttermal → SP / cf. my Verdichtung & Verklärung (Condensation & Transfiguration)

Conscious of Sheena's jibe that he gave up too easily in trying to figure things out, he flicked forward to card 1.4.2 and pulled it out. The title on the obverse side was *Der Luftbrückenkorridor* (the airlift corridor), beneath which, glued to the card, was part of a sketch map of Berlin during the Airlift in 1948 with the air corridors marked in red pencil. Steve turned the card over. There were three sentences in Müller's handwriting.

> I remember her fingers tracing the Tempelhof runways on this map, murmuring about logistics. Mavis Morgan, she was called then, clear

eyes, incredible energy, and unshakeable belief. I fed Berlin. She
nourished me with her love.

She asked me to go to London with her. But I had books to read, and
the ruins of Humboldt to haunt. I thought history would wait.

And in a different coloured ink.

What I fool I was! In love, be bold, take what is on offer.

Of course, Morgan was his mother's maiden name. This was
Müller thinking about when he and Steve's mother had been lovers
during the Soviet blockade. She had been a liaison officer for the
British administration and he had been a SPD councillor for the
borough of Wedding. So *Wedding affair* did not mean a fling at a
marriage ceremony. Reassured that he was at last accessing material not relating to German Romanticism, Steve slipped the card
about his mother back into its place and returned to the main
index card.

The next item, 2.8.1, related to M. Percival, clearly his mother,
now bearing her married name. The comments this time seemed
reasonably transparent. Wind forward many years and Mavis had
re-connected to Müller and recruited him as an agent, using Ulrike
as a cut-out. That was practically common knowledge. He flipped
through to the designated card. There was a small transparent
envelope glued to this card. He opened the flap of the envelope
and pulled out a business card from the British Embassy in Bonn,
to which a small pressed flower was taped. The name on the card
was M.Percival (Liaison Officer). Steve turned the card over.

She said: 'We never really said goodbye.' I said: 'We never really said
yes.' We were older, but not wiser. She didn't mention MI6 straight
away. Just that she needed a favour. It was Ulrike's flat we used. She
thought it was a kindness. Perhaps it was. Or perhaps that was part
of the price.

Steve knew that Mavis and Müller had had their assignations at
Ulrike's apartment. But who was the payer of the price?

Towards the bottom of the card there was an annotation in a different ink.

> Some debts accrue interest over decades. Others are repaid in
> secrets and sweat.

Moving on to Ulrike's card (3.3.9), he was puzzled by the short sentence on the obverse.

> A page torn from Hölderlin's Hyperion, underlined in violet ink:
> "Doch uns ist gegeben / Auf keiner Stätte zu ruhn…"

He turned the card over, to find a short essay in tiny script filling all the white space.

> Instantly aware of U. Not for her looks. She was a shy little mouse,
> but for her brain. The best graduate student for years. Braver than
> she seemed, though. Didn't flinch when I touched her. Looked better
> with her clothes off. Reluctant to allow vaginal sex. Preferred to take
> me in her mouth. The quality of her work never faltered. Spoke of
> Katrin, her twin. Away in Leipzig at the Stasi training school. She
> said they were identical. I demurred. No one else could have a brain
> like hers. She said I'd be surprised.

Steve flinched at the vulgarity, but what was most shocking was the mention of a twin. And not only a twin, but one who was a Stasi trainee. This immediately opened up a series of dizzying perspectives. But at least it explained the reference to Schmidt, K which had puzzled Steve on his first glance at the table of contents card.

Apprehensive as much as curious, he flipped through to card 3.4.2, the Schmidt, K card.

The obverse simply said:

> Twins ≠ reflections. Similarity ≠ sameness. There is always some
> divergence.

There was no attribution. Beneath the handwritten line a polyester photographic pocket was taped to the card. There was a contact print in it. Steve fished it out. It was a side-by-side portrait of the Schmidt twins from the waist up, bare-breasted staring fixedly at the lens, not the least hint of a smile. If there were any *divergences*, it was impossible with the naked eye to discern them at the scale of a contact print or to say which was Ulrike and which was Katrin.

He turned the card over to find another short essay.

> That summer, U. Told me she was going with her sister to the Freikörperkultur beach at the Müggelsee. I took it as a dare. Didn't take long to find them. Might I join them? Neither seemed embarrassed. Identical. The breasts a little heavier in K., the bush more luxuriant in U. Back to Prenzlauer Berg for a drink. I had my Praktica with me. They let me photograph them, side by side barebreasted. It was only later when I developed the film that I noticed the birthmark under U.'s left breast. I had them both, of course. U. indifferent as usual, K. surprisingly willing, even though I was unable to satisfy her. I should have taken her first. That was not my only mistake.

Steve squinted at the contact print, but it was impossible to resolve a birthmark on either of the girls.

He moved onto the Stasi card.

> K. must already have been an IM (Inoffizielle Mitarbeiterin). Maybe I was just a Stasi school project at first, but that soon changed. I became the subject of full surveillance, the price to be paid for eating of the tree of knowledge.

It was hard to say what period the notes about Ulrike and Katrin related to, but probably two or three years earlier because Ulrike had only just started her PhD. But might not Katrin by now be a fully qualified Stasi officer? The implication of card 4.1.1 was that by engineering a threesome with twins he had brought himself to the Stasi's full attention. It was Katrin's revenge.

On an impulse, Steve put the contact print of the double topless portrait in his wallet. He would see if he could get it enlarged in the office darkroom tomorrow.

Steve now pulled out the card on Collingwood. This also had a photo pocket taped to the card. Inside were four prints of Collingwood in a state of arousal with a younger man, who was trussed in such a way as to give Collingwood easy access to his hindquarters. There was also a card from a hotel in Leipzig with a room number and a date in March of the previous year. The card had been dusted with fingerprint ink, leaving a clear impression of two prints. He put the photos and the card back in the polyester pocket and turned the card over.

> The colonel - an old drinking companion from before the Wall - was careless. He was so elated about the future deployment of Tollkirsche that he didn't even notice some of the material was missing.

So this was the gay kompromat that Müller had mentioned. And now it was abundantly clear to him that, as Grace had suspected, he had been barking up the wrong tree. The mention of a gay honeytrap had directed him towards Sheena because he had not known that Collingwood was gay. Of course, he'd had his suspicions, but these had been allayed by the blossoming of the romance between Collingwood and Sally.

But if Collingwood was Tollkirsche, why hadn't Müller exposed him?

Then he noticed the note at the bottom of the card.

> To be useful to a system is dangerous. To know its secrets is fatal.
> But the right secret can mean survival.

Suddenly, all the pieces slotted together to form a coherent picture. He saw it all. The Stasi had become aware of the purloined kompromat photos on Collingwood in Müller's possession and had instructed Collingwood to liquidate Müller. Which was why Sheena had referred to the Stasi assassin as *him*. And which meant that Collingwood was also responsible for Mavis's death. At last he had the answer that Sheena had been helping him towards.

Now feeling more confident in his ability to decode Müller's archive, he turned to Müller's notes on Sheena. The line on the index card read:

5.5.5 → FERGUSON, S. / domination ritual / misdirection op.

Well, no one was going to quibble with the *domination ritual part* of it. But *misdirection op*, what did that mean? Steve picked up card 5.5.5. Once again the card was a carrier for a polyester photo pocket, otherwise bearing only the card's serial number. Steve slipped the photo out of the pocket. This seemed to be the torn corner of a larger photo. All that it showed was an Oxford brogue and a pale shoulder. On the back of the scrap of paper were the words:

Ein ganz gewöhnlicher Trainingstag für die englische Offiziersklasse.

Just another training day for a member of the English officer class. This must be Müller's take on Sheena, the way she worked, the way she trained her people. It was the British way; one learned on the job, with a side order of fagging. The German way was much more systematic, though Steve doubted humiliation was entirely absent. The British were inherently anti-systematic. No wonder Müller had found it difficult to establish himself at Cambridge. He was the supreme professional; Doyle, his sponsor at St Rad's, the gifted amateur. Müller bridged the worlds of philology and espionage; he had a foot in both camps. Sheena was a purist master of espionage. And *master* was the correct epithet.

Steve moved on to 6.6.6.

6.6.6 → K. as U. / body double insertion /'Who?' game

This was another knotty one. The initials presumably referred to Ulrike and Katrin, the Stasi twin. But Katrin *as* Ulrike? Had Müller concluded that the woman presenting herself as Ulrike that night at Grace's was in fact Katrin? Perhaps. But according to Müller's earlier note, it was Ulrike who had a birthmark beneath her left breast. And Grace had been adamant that the woman who had been staying with her had such a birthmark. Steve, on the other hand, had noticed no birthmark, even though he had slept with her on several occasions during that time. Admittedly, both he and she had been more concerned about the bruising on the ribs on the right side of her body. And, apart from the first evening in Borough, Ulrike had been distinctly modest and reserved, indeed, to use Müller's own formulation, indifferent.

There was also the fact that Ulrike had impressed everyone she had come in contact with at Cambridge with the breadth of her reading and her intellectual poise. It was unlikely that a Stasi officer, even if she were an identical twin, could fake that sort of knowledge. This, at least, was an example of *divergence*.

Steve extracted card 6.6.6 from the box.

> The birthmark is a fake. It is some kind of makeup. They use it to deceive me. U. sends K. When she can no longer bear my urgent fumblings. I try to guess which one is sharing my bed from the slight differences in sexual technique and response. I call it the Who? game. I look forward to K's turn. I never let her know that I know she is not U. I fully exploit the prestige of my position. Very little is off limits. I know I am heaping up trouble for myself. She will have her revenge. But I don't care.

Was he saying that Katrin was in the habit of making the area under her left breast look like a birthmark with stage makeup? Or was he saying that neither of them had a birthmark? It didn't really matter. For the purposes of submitting to his attentions, the birthmark signified Ulrike. In which case the twins had been manipulating him right from the start, from the Müggelsee event. Katrin had been sparing her sister some of the violation she was having to endure in order to make her way in the academic world. And planning her revenge.

Steve turned his attention to the handwritten note at the bottom of the card. It was faint, as if written in haste: *Only someone who has worn a mask knows how to be another.*

The girl in Sheena's S&M photos had been masked. Grace, for one, had been certain that the masked girl had been Ulrike. Steve wasn't so sure. But if what distinguished Ulrike from Katrin was the birthmark, then the *K. as U.* could not apply to the girl in Sheena's S&M photoshoot. Müller must have meant something else in his note because it was highly unlikely that he had seen the photos or knew of them. To complicate matters, Sheena had said something like *this is the end of Ulrike Schmidt*. What had she meant by that? She had also used the phrase: *a naked girl who could almost have been Ulrike*? That was a curious phrase too, leaving open the possibility that it wasn't her.

Steve was not sure how much more of this he could absorb, but the one thing he did know was that he wanted to avoid another dose of Sheena's derision. He needed to find some ledge he could settle on before he was hauled in by Collingwood. He picked up the next card, the one Müller had devoted to Steve himself.

6.7.1 → PERCIVAL, S. / Muttermal → SP / cf my Verdichtung & Verklärung (Condensation & Transfiguration)

Steve pulled out card 6.7.1. He was pretty sure he was not going to enjoy reading Müller's private comments about himself. So he was at first surprised to read the single line on the front of the card.

The son I never had. Or perhaps he is my son. The timing is equivoc-al.

That was a shock. Was it in fact possible that he was Dieter Müller's son and not Harry Percival's? Once he was out of this mess, he would try to recreate the chronology of his mother's pregnancy. But would that be a good idea? He turned the card over. There was a single word *Muttermal* typed in the middle of the card. Lower down there were two short handwritten sentences.

Steve too bears a birthmark, a psychological one, and perhaps not just one. Steve has been fatherless for most of his life, but it is a mother he seeks.

He'd forgotten, perhaps never known, that the German for birth-mark was Muttermal – the mark from the mother. But was it true that he had been marked by his mother, or indeed by her absence?

Would that explain why he was drawn to women like Ginny, Grace and, God forbid, Sheena?

Steve sat very still, the final card still in his hand. Outside night had fallen. He drew the curtains shut with a shiver. The Zettelkasten wasn't just an inheritance. It was a test, a trap, a slow-burning fuse.

Week Five

1 November – 7 November 1976

MI6 – Borough – Monday

STEVE SPENT A RESTLESS night, imagining the various ways in which he might unmask Collingwood as Tollkirsche. But they all ended up with him confronting Collingwood man to man with the kompromat material from Müller's Zettelkasten in the Borough offices. As Collingwood wept piteously, Steve would pick up the phone and call for security, watching impassively as he was dragged down to the cells. But even as this scene looped through his dreams, small details undermined it. What number would he ring? Were there even security staff with powers of arrest in the building, let alone cells? Wouldn't Collingwood just laugh at him rather than weep? Wouldn't Steve be the one dragged away to Sheena's S&M dungeon for a severe thrashing? By the time he awoke, he knew that he would do none of those things. He would act as if he had no knowledge of what might have gone on in a Leipzig hotel room. Which was precisely what Sheena was expecting of him.

His thoughts were suddenly fractured by the sound of the telephone ringing. Steve stumbled out to the hall to answer the phone. It was Collingwood.

'Steve, could you come in on your way to work?'

Affecting a brighter tone than he felt, Steve said, 'With you in a jiffy.'

A little while later in a meeting room at the department's offices in Borough, Collingwood said, sipping his scalding coffee, 'How was your trip to Cambridge?'

'Not very enlightening. Müller didn't take students. Not many people knew him. Those who did knew he had a dicky heart. A couple of lines in the Cambridge Evening News. And as for Ulrike, she was just a visitor. Grace had introduced her to a few people at Newnham. There was no expectation of her staying. No one knows she is suspected of murdering Müller.'

'And no one need know. She has not actually been charged. It may be in our best interests to keep that under our hats.'

'But she's confessed to killing Müller?'

'No, she hasn't, nor, with her training, would one expect her to.'

Steve remembered that, of course, Collingwood had no idea that it was Ulrike's twin, Katrin, who was the Stasi officer. He wondered why his handler hadn't informed him of this crucial fact. Once again, it was probably the blanket application of the need-to-know principle.

'But we're sure she's the murderer?'

Well, the toxicology report shows that there were traces of the toxin that killed Müller on her coat.'

'The red one?'

Steve felt the urge to shout triumphantly at Collingwood that the red coat had been lying in Müller's room for more than two weeks and that in all probability Ulrike hadn't touched it in all that time. But then he remembered that Stan had said that Ulrike had been into St Rad's to visit Müller and had left wearing the red coat. Instead he said, 'I thought it was a bit heavy-handed getting your guys to find a phial of the poison in her case at my place. Surely the trace on the coat would have been enough?'

'Truthfully, the traces on the coat were not completely convincing, Steve. So it was belt and braces. But none of that matters now because we don't expect this to end in court. Of course, it matters that she continues to think that that is a real possibility.'

'So, she's putting up a bit of a fight?'

'We don't understand why she's being so uncooperative.'

'You've interrogated her?'

'The way things work, that is our sister organisation's remit. I have been allowed to sit in, though.'

'What did you think of her?'

'Rather drab and listless. I can't imagine what you see in her.'

Steve laughed. 'Shows how much you know about me.'

Collingwood narrowed his eyes, trying to estimate the amount of spin in that riposte. 'I wouldn't be quite so blasé, if I were you, Steve.'

'I'm sure that's something we could all bear in mind.'

Collingwood didn't smile. 'So that means you can get back together with Grace Mitchell.'

'I don't think that's on the cards.'

'That's not the impression I'm getting.'

'Time to call off the watchers and listeners, Jeremy. Müller's dead and his killer is in custody. The operation has disappeared up its own arse.'

'I wish that were so. I can't help feeling that Müller left one or two booby-traps.'

Steve stiffened. 'What makes you think that?'

'It all went too smoothly.'

'Intelligence work must be the only business in which when things go smoothly people are suspicious.'

'Yes, I suppose you're right. Well, thanks for coming in. As ever, keep me posted if anything changes.'

Buzz – Soho – Monday

STEVE WAS FEELING DISGUSTED with himself as he caught the bus to Soho. He had wanted to blow Collingwood out of the water. But he had managed to master his anger and tell himself, as Sheena had pointed out, he had no proof that Collingwood was responsible for his mother's death. It was not the right moment to fire all the guns. If anyone was going to blow Collingwood out of the water, it would be Sheena.

When he got to the office, Sally was already in and, as was usually the case on a Monday morning, none of the editorial staff had shown up yet, and nor were they likely to be for some time. Steve put the coffee he had brought up for her on her desk and said, 'How was your weekend?'

'Nice, thanks. Spent most of it with Jeremy.'

'Things going okay on that front?'

'Yes, but I'd rather not go into details.'

Steve took the lid off his styrofoam coffee cup and sipped the hot, bitter liquid. 'I'm not asking for any. I'm just pleased for you that it's working out.'

Changing the subject abruptly, Sally said, 'So, what's the position with Ulrike?'

Steve looked around the room. 'I shouldn't tell you this.'

'Steve, tell me or don't tell me, but, for God's sake, stop prefacing everything with a Secrets Act warning. Jeremy doesn't seem to feel the need to do that.'

'He has been at it rather longer than me. But you're right. Sal. All this stuff is doing my head in. Well, basically, the German professor is dead.'

'Wow!'

'Jeremy didn't mention it?'

'No. What happened?'

'Officially, he died of heart failure, but unofficially he was poisoned.'

'By whom?'

'Ulrike.'

'Bloody hell. So, where is she now?'

'She's been arrested by Special Branch.'

'But not charged yet?'

'Not as far as I know.'

'They're putting the thumbscrews on her?'

'I guess.'

'Poor girl. Why did she do it?'

'She's Stasi or they've got their hooks into her. Well, that's the view in-house and she did have the poison that was used to kill him.'

'Blimey. So you were right to be scared when she turned up in the John Snow.'

'I'm scared of all sorts of things.'

'And you really haven't seen her?'

'Not for ten days or so.'

'So if the Prof is dead and she's in clink, what are you doing up in Cambridge?'

'Müller's made me his executor.'

'What's that involve?'

'Sorting out the stuff he was working on when he died.'

'Like what?'

'Notes on German Romanticism.'

'Are you still up on that?'

'Not really. I asked Grace to give me a hand…'

Even as he was saying it, he knew he should have kept Grace out of it. But like a flash, Sally said, 'Back to mummy?'

'Yeah, pathetic, I know. That's something like what Sheena said.'

'I think I'd like to meet Sheena.'

'Be careful what you wish for. I think she'd have a lot of fun with you. She's a little eccentric. You'd be right up her street.'

'What do you mean by that?'

'She's a lesbian dominatrix.'

Sally shook her head in mock disbelief. 'What's wrong with you people?'

Steve bridled. 'I'm not you people. And anyway, there's much more to her than that.'

'So the show's coming to an end, then?'

'I hope so, but I really don't know how these things end.'

'And then you expect to pick things up with me again?'

'I don't expect anything.'

'Well, buster, now I know a bit more about the world you move in, I will be expecting to walk across your back in my stilettos.'

Steve finally relaxed. 'It would be my pleasure.'

Sally leaned forward and kissed him on the cheek.

Steve & Grace – Trinity Church Square – Wednesday

IN THE AFTERNOON, AS Steve was signing off pages at the typeset-ters for that week's issue, Stacey from the admin office came into the production office and said that there was a phone call for him. He followed Stacey back to the admin office and picked up the receiver lying on the desk. It was Grace.

'Steve, Sally, your colleague at your office, gave me this number. I know this is short notice, but could I stay at your place this evening? I've got to get an early train from Paddington tomorrow. If it's inconvenient…'

Steve was puzzled by the somewhat vague reason given, but said, 'No, that's fine. What time do you expect to get to Borough?'

'Seven-thirty. I'm sorry to do this to you.'

'It's not a problem. Are you okay?'

'Yes, I'm alright. Thank you. I'll tell you everything later.'

Steve sat there for a few moments trying to imagine what lay behind the request. *Alright* was not *fine* or *well*. Grace seldom did things off the cuff. Her timetable was far too unrelenting. Well, he'd find out soon enough. Thank goodness this week's issue was going smoothly. But he'd need to get off sharpish and pick up a couple of bottles of wine and something for supper on the way home. And once there, he was going to have to do an emergency tidy up. He couldn't remember the last time he'd blitzed the bathroom and kitchen or changed the sheets on the beds.

By the time the doorbell rang, Steve was exhausted. Thankfully, Grace was later than predicted. He pressed the entry buzzer and went down to meet her. Back inside the flat, he took her coat and hung it in the closet in the hall.

He clapped his hands together in a vague impression of a welcoming host and said, 'Right, what do you want first, a cuppa or a glass of wine?'

In a very small voice, Grace said, 'Do you think you could give me a hug?'

Steve looked at her carefully and noticed that she looked pale and strained. He took her in his arms. 'Grace, are you alright?'

She put her head against his chest and said, 'No.'

He held her for a few moments and then moved her gently to the sofa. 'What's happened?'

'Mummy's dead.'

'Oh, Grace, I'm so sorry.'

'She didn't want to go on without Gideon.'

'No, I can see that.'

'I only got the news a little before I phoned you at the office. Even if I'd set out immediately, I wouldn't have got to Castle Cary until about now. Difficult to get a taxi from the station at this time of night.'

'Of course. What happened?'

'Heart attack, it seems.'

'So it was sudden?'

'Yes. She managed to get to the phone, but she was dead by the time the ambulance got her to the hospital.'

'Will you be able to see her?'

'I hope so.'

'Will you be okay on your own?'

'Yes.'

'Are you sure? I could see if I could get the rest of the week off and come down with you.'

Grace hesitated and then said, 'Do you think you could?'

'I'll need to phone Sally, but Thursdays and Fridays are our slack days.'

'I don't want to put you in difficulties with your work.'

'I won't be. Let me get you a drink and then I'll phone her.'

Ten minutes later, Steve rejoined Grace who was now hunched on the sofa sobbing. She wiped the tears from her eyes. 'What did she say?'

'It's fine. We're ahead of the game for next week's issue.'

'Oh, that's very nice of her.'

Steve nodded. In fact, Sally had been more than a little outraged at first, especially when Steve told her who the bereaved person was. But as the conversation developed Sally had softened her stance and was mannerly enough to express her sympathy and concern for Grace.

'Right, let me get some food on the go.'

'I'm not hungry, but I could do with an early night, if you don't mind.'

'Okay, you can have Mavis's room. There are clean sheets on the bed. I'll sleep in the guest room.'

Grace seemed relieved and said, 'Thank you.'

While Grace went about her bedtime routine, Steve made himself a cheese sandwich. He'd been planning another evening with the

Black Box, but in view of Grace's bereavement, it would be tasteless to focus on Müller's puzzles. He might as well have an early night too. After brushing his teeth, he tapped on the door of the room Grace was sleeping in. There was no reply. He pushed the door open gently and saw that she was already fast asleep, her beautiful auburn hair spread out on the pillow. He listened for a moment to the gentle rise and fall of her breathing, then went next door to his childhood bedroom and was soon asleep.

Grace & Steve – Somerset – Thursday

GRACE LAY IN THE bath and soaked away her grief. It had been a long day: the train journey down from London, the taxi ride to Shepton Mallet Hospital, the viewing of her mother's waxen, lifeless body, another taxi ride to Lane End, and then getting a fire going in the cold house. Steve had been marvellous, gentle, kind, helpful. She didn't know what she would have done without him. He had managed to get Gideon's Morris Traveller going and had driven to the supermarket and picked up some supplies. She could hear him now downstairs in the kitchen preparing something for supper with the radio tuned to Radio 3, making the house feel lived in again.

So why had she been keeping him at arm's length since they'd started seeing each other again, but particularly since Ulrike's arrest? She couldn't say. And it was not just her. She thought he'd been somewhat standoffish and awkward too. Maybe they had both come to believe in their cover stories too much and with the sudden disappearance of their targets had become disorientated. But she was also aware that she had been a highly disruptive force in his life and she feared that if they resumed an intimate relationship, she would end up hurting him again. But if there was one thing that she had come to understand about Steve, it was that he was resilient.

She stepped out of the bath and wrapped herself in a towel. She wiped the steam off the mirror over the hand basin and looked at herself. She would be thirty-seven in a few days. Little lines were already forming at the corner of her eyes. She was starting to look more like her mother. Time was running out. Not for the first time she felt how empty her life was, how pointless her academic achievement had been. In many ways, she was still the impulsive, selfish teenager who had caused her mother so much grief twenty years previously. Yes, she had been busy, but that didn't justify the way she had not made time for her parents. She had only seen her mother twice since her father had died the previous year.

She unwrapped the bath towel and looked at herself in the long mirror. She slapped her belly and lifted her breasts with her hands. She'd put on some weight in the last year. That was partly a consequence of having done very little running and partly because of the relationship with Müller, which had focused more on food and drinking than on physical passion. It was as if he had been encouraging her to match his corpulence. On the few occasions they had tried to copulate it had been more like something from a natural history film, two blubbery beasts heaving themselves onto and off each other. Not much *jouissance* there. For that, other techniques had been needed, a process which she preferred not to think about too much now.

Knowing Steve's preference for androgynous, stick-thin or waif-like women, she couldn't imagine what Steve had ever seen in her. Maternal comfort perhaps? Was that so bad? What a strange boy he was! In many ways, still not a man, curiously innocent. But kind and, as she had noted earlier, resilient. Clearly Ulrike had got under his skin when he had encountered her in East Berlin.

Still, when it came to positive reactions, Ulrike had triggered them in Grace herself. She reached down with her hand and, touching herself gently, looked at herself in the mirror. Was that why she was now feeling the urge to masturbate? Here of all places and now of all times! If her father could see her, he would be appalled. Well, if her father could see her, she'd be appalled! But not so her mother, she thought. June had once told Grace when she was still a teenager, that she herself occasionally masturbated when she needed to comfort herself. She had indicated that Gideon found the whole business of sex too troubling and as a consequence there had been a distinct lack in that area of June's life. Grace realised now that June had been giving her permission to explore her own body. But at the time, she had been deeply embarrassed at the thought of her mother masturbating and grateful in a way that her parents *didn't* have sex. She had been at an age when the thought of people as old as her parents were then, interacting in that way, disgusted her. She had still been only vaguely aware of what an erect penis was like and had had no great ambition to give one admission to her body. In any case women's bodies were so much neater and more convenient, the monthly bleed aside.

She removed her finger from her clitoral fold and, turning sideways on to the mirror, smoothed her hand over the pent of her belly, tracing the curve of her breast with the other hand. How sad that she would never see her body with child! Even worse in some ways was that she had also denied her mother a granddaughter. June had even accepted, indeed positively welcomed, the possibility of Steve being the father of Grace's baby, despite his tender years.

In fact, June had taken quite a shine to Steve. She had connected with him on an almost psychosexual level. He'd told Grace after they stayed with June and Gideon early in their relationship that June had touched him and he'd felt a charge go through him. She had then told him to go and lie with Grace. She had obviously been deploying her wise woman skills on him, something of which Gideon seriously disapproved. Perhaps Gideon, wary of June's ways, had managed to neutralise the magic she was trying to cook up with an intense bout of prayer, because Grace failed to conceive that weekend, despite Steve having poured himself into her on several occasions. Not that the willing lad had complained, surfeits of sex were what he lived for.

Grace put her towel in the laundry basket and padded next door to her room. She took some clean underwear from the neatly folded pile in her chest of drawers and slipped the knickers on and then hooked the rather virginal bra she had picked up over her shoulders. As she tried to close the clasp behind her back, she realised that the bra was too small. Maybe there was one in her mother's room, which would be a better fit. She went into the room, which had been her parents' and which had not changed in the slightest since her father's death the previous year, and searched in her mother's closet for something that might be a better fit. But while she might now be slightly bigger on top than when she had

been a young woman, she was not yet ready for the highly struc-
tured underpinnings that her mother had been wearing recently.

For goodness' sake, why did she need a bra anyway? They wer-
en't going out. Steve was hardly going to object if she wasn't
wearing one. The way they were interacting with each other at the
moment, he probably wouldn't even notice. Grace considered
herself a feminist but had never felt the need to join the bra-burn-
ing brigade. Being a little bigger on top, a bra had helped her keep
things under control. But there was a time and a place for
everything. In fact Steve might find the sway of her untethered
upper torso rather alluring.

Did that mean that she would rather like to arouse him? Yes, if
she were being honest. Whether they should be having a relationship and whether she still turned him on were completely different
questions. She cast her mind back to when she had tracked him
down in his grotty bedsitter nearly two years previously. To get
things moving, she had had to make the first move, which had
involved an element of what many would consider demeaning
behaviour; she had stripped off in front of him.

The more serious mistake she had subsequently made was to
frame the relationship in terms of his willingness to provide her
with a baby. She would have been better advised to have kept that
under her hat. It had become a bit of a running joke between
them. Was it the fertile part of her cycle? In some ways he had
taken the contract, if you could call it that, more seriously than she
had. Why hadn't she just treated the whole thing as a fling? Kept it
light and fun? Admittedly other realities had supervened, not to
mention the fundamental internal contradiction between her
competing ambitions: motherhood and professional success.

Grace suddenly caught sight of herself in the cheval mirror in
the corner of the room, becalmed, bare breasted, wearing a pair of
schoolgirlish, primrose-patterned knickers. She laughed. What did
she look like? She went back to the closet and soon found the
djellaba that she had bought in Marrakech in her student years and
which her mother had subsequently requisitioned as a kind of
dressing gown. She removed the only recently donned knickers and
pulled the djellaba over her head. If anything was going to happen,
it might as well be as close to a zipless fuck as possible.

Having solved the problem of what to wear, Grace looked around her parents' bedroom. Her intention had been to not disturb the parental place of repose; for her to sleep in her child-hood bedroom and for Steve to sleep in the guest room. But now that she had spent a few minutes in her mother's room, she realised that her mother would be the last person to disapprove if she and Steve slept in the bed she herself had slept in for the last time only a couple of nights before. No, Grace was now certain that June would want them to sleep in her bed and to make love in it. She was not going to discuss it with Steve, because she was still uncertain where things were heading. But she would change the bedding before she went down.

Ten minutes later having put fresh linen on the double bed, she finally joined Steve downstairs. He had got a roaring fire going in the inglenook fireplace in the sitting room and had just got a casserole bubbling away on the top of the Aga. He washed his hands and dried them on a towel and then said, over his shoulder, 'Feeling any better after the bath?'

'Yes, I am. I'm sorry I've left everything to you.'

'Not at all. I've enjoyed getting the place warmed up and getting some food on. I'm afraid the casserole is going to take a couple of hours, though.'

He turned around and saw the djellaba she was wearing. 'Wow! You look amazing.'

'Thank you, Steve. I bought this in Marrakech years ago.'

Steve took a couple of steps towards her as if to embrace her and then seemed to remember the present rules of engagement. Grace smiled at him. 'Please give me a hug, Steve. I feel in need of a bit of comfort.'

'Of course, Grace, I didn't want to presume or cause any upset.'

'Thank you. I'm grateful for your sensitivity. Just hold me for a moment.'

He wrapped his arms around her. Noticing her unstructured top as he clasped her to his chest, he said, 'Nice.'

Grace smiled. 'Yes, I thought they needed liberating this evening.'

'We all do. Would you like a glass of wine? I've opened a bottle of Côte du Rhône.'

'That would be lovely. Let's take it into the sitting room, seeing that you've got the fire going so well.'

A few minutes later, sitting in front of the roaring fire, Grace said, 'Steve, I'm so grateful that you came down with me. I was dreading the whole thing, seeing June, but also coming here on my own.'

'I'm glad I was able to make the arrangements at short notice.'

'Was your boss pissed off?'

'She was a bit. We're a very small production department.'

'I thought you sounded apologetic.'

'She was okay. Thursday and Friday are our easy days. Even Monday is not so bad. It's Tuesday and Wednesday that can be a scramble.'

'That makes me feel a bit better. Do you think you'll be able to come down in a couple of weeks for June's funeral?'

Steve wasn't sure how things would be in a couple of weeks, but how could he not agree? 'Of course. You will need support then more than ever.'

'I'm dreading it actually.'

'Put it out of your mind for now. We can deal with it.'

'Do you mean *we*?'

'You helped me in similar circumstances, didn't you?'

'I suppose I did.'

'There'll be Müller's funeral too.'

'Presumably St Rad's will organise that.'

'But you and I will have to be there. Do you think they'll let Ulrike attend?'

'I can't see that happening.'

'But if they don't charge her with murder, how can they hold her?'

'Believe me. There are ways.'

'Well, when I got back to London I spent a long time going through the black Zettelkasten. The first surprise is that Ulrike has a twin sister called Katrin and there are cards for both of them. Ulrike starts as a graduate student with Müller and he instantly recognises her talent. He calls her a shy, little mouse, but he is impressed that she doesn't flinch when he gets her to give him a blowjob. She tells him she has an identical twin sister at the Stasi training centre in Leipzig. Müller is intrigued. He finds out that the two sisters are going to a nudist beach at Müggelsee and decides to bump into them there.'

'Oh, how horrible!'

'It doesn't get better. He asks if he can join them. Presumably he is starkers. He studies them, Katrin's breasts are a little heavier, Ulrike's pubic hair more luxuriant.'

'What an awful man! Anything else?'

'They go back to Ulrike's place, possibly the same place I went to. He had his camera with him and took a photograph of them side by side, with their tops off. He then says that he only noticed Ulrike's birthmark when he developed the film.'

'It's a pity we don't have that photo.'

Steve stood up and opened his shoulder bag. 'We have. There was a contact print attached to the card. I got it enlarged in the office darkroom.'

Steve handed the print to Grace, who studied it for a few moments. 'Well, seeing them side by side, one does notice other small differences. Have you spoken to anyone else about this?'

'No. But there's a little more. Müller persuades the two girls to have a threesome with him. He describes Ulrike as indifferent, but Katrin as surprisingly willing even though he was unable to satisfy her, as he puts it. Clearly, he was already running out of steam. He says he should have taken her first.'

'I really don't want to hear any more.'

'I'm sorry, but there's one more detail you need to know. After he says that he should have taken Katrin first, he says that was not his only mistake. Katrin must have already been an IM, *inoffizielle Mitarbeiterin*, in other words an informant.'

'I know what it means, Steve. I was one myself.'

Steve was put off his stride. 'What do you mean?'

'I'll tell you later. Just finish your analysis.'

'He says that sometime after the threesome when this photograph was taken he realised that he was now subject to full-scale surveillance. He had brought it on himself.'

Grace picked up the photograph of the sisters again and said, 'In some ways, it's a very beautiful photograph. But when one understands the circumstances in which it was taken, one feels very differently about it.'

Steve nodded. 'I'll just go and check the casserole.'

He had been about to explain to Grace that the hints in Müller's cards about the divergent sexual responsiveness of the Schmidt sisters had led Steve to speculate whether he himself had had dealings with both, albeit not in a threesome context. But he concluded from Grace's somewhat incurious reaction to the revelation that Ulrike had a twin that this was not a good moment to advance that theory. In any case, there was a good deal more to talk about that was of more immediate relevance.

He returned a few minutes later with the bottle of wine and refilled their glasses.

'There's something else you should know. Ignoring all your warnings, when I got back from Cambridge, I went around to Sheena's place and confronted her with the S&M photos.'

'Oh, Steve. I asked you not to do that. What happened?'

'She wiped the floor with me.'

'I'm not surprised. How did you talk yourself out of that one?'

'It was a very weird conversation. She said she hoped I was safely back in your embrace, that you had rather more on top to comfort a chap than she had, as I might have noticed from the photos.'

'My God, she's brazen.'

'You can say that again. She more or less said that the whole thing with the photos was to see how I reacted. It was she who'd put them in the Zettelkasten.'

'Do you believe that?'

'I'm not sure.'

'When could she have done it?'

'I don't know and at the moment I don't care. She said she gave me credit for coming to see her directly and not taking the matter to Collingwood.'

'That's odd. He's your handler.'

'She'd told me to report to her directly.'

'When?'

'I told you I'd had dinner with her a couple of months ago. When I was leaving, she gave me her direct line.'

'Not only dinner, but her direct number too. There's not many people who are accorded that privilege.'

'Well, she's also kind of my step-mother.'

'Yes, I suppose she is.'

'Anyway having given me credit for my bravery, she then said I'd fallen at the first hurdle. I hadn't noticed that the handwriting was different. I must have been so distracted by her naked breasts that I stopped thinking.'

'Golly, not the type of conversation that you usually think of a ward and his guardian having. And we did notice that the handwriting was different.'

'Well, you did and I told her that. She said that just because I had a photo of her with her tits out caning a young woman didn't mean she was a murderer.'

Grace laughed. 'Well, she has a point.'

'I asked her what I should do. She said ideally I should crawl across the floor and *kiss her shining brogues*. But instead she wanted me to go home and try to work out the secret of Müller's infernal machine. She wanted me to use my own brains, not enlist your help. She said I could trust you in intelligence matters. She wasn't so sure about matters of the heart. But that was up to me.'

'What a bitch! Don't I get a say too?'

'Well, I'm paraphrasing. What she actually said was that my heart was mine to give as I please. She made no demands on my heart.'

'I'm glad she made that distinction. She really gave you a going over, didn't she?'

'She then said how did I know Müller was actually dead. I said that was what I'd heard. She said that was just where I was going wrong. I shouldn't take too much notice of what was being said.'

'What did she mean by that?'

'I don't know. I asked her if Ulrike was alright. She said she was, but this was the end of Ulrike Schmidt. I would understand what she meant in the days to come. Which I find very worrying.'

'And that was it?'

'Yeah, except she asked me to give her a kiss.'

'Oh, Steve, it's like I was saying the other night. You really are her boy.'

'I feel even less comfortable with that thought than I did after my mother died.'

'None of us gets to choose our parents, not even our surrogate parents, it seems.'

The last thing that Steve wanted to discuss right now was the thorny issue of paternity, and certainly not his own as hinted at in the black box.

'True, but our supper awaits us. We can return to these matters later.'

'Steve, that was delicious. I feel almost human again. But I'm also feeling rather tired. Could we leave the washing up until tomorrow and go up to bed.'

'It's your home, not mine.'

'It was my home and no doubt once the formalities are concluded, it will be my house. But it's not really been my home for a long time.'

'Well, your call.'

'If it's my call, then I'd like you to join me in my bed. I know we've been tiptoeing around each other, for understandable reasons. But I need you now. I'm not going to hold you to anything. If Sheena can ask you for a kiss, I don't see why I can't ask you for something a little more full-blooded.'

Steve raised an eyebrow. 'Lead the way.'

A little later at an appropriate break in proceedings, Grace said, 'Not bad Percival, you've learned a few more moves.'

Steve chuckled. 'I hoped it wouldn't be that obvious. Was it when...'

But Grace had put her finger to his lips. 'I do not want a sexological seminar. And I do not want to know where you have acquired these new skills. Suffice it to say, they hit the mark. No disenchantment, please.'

'As did your new moves, as you so cunningly put it. Although to be perfectly honest, I was fine with the old moves.'

'Less of the old, please. Anyway, while we are catching our breath, I want to have a serious chat.'

Grace noticed that Steve tensed a little. 'Don't worry. I'm not about to put other kinds of moves on you. I hope I have learned the error of my ways.'

'What do you mean by that.'

'I mean I don't want to put either of us under any obligation. I don't know where we go from here and I don't want to talk in those terms. I am just happy to be with you. If things change, they change. Let's see how it goes.'

Cautiously, Steve said, 'Okay, but there's some pretty painful history between us.'

'Yes, and I want to talk about that. Firstly, I want to apologise as sincerely as I can for having been such a disruptive force in your life.'

Steve was about to say something, but she stopped him. 'Just hear me out because this is not going to be easy for me to say. And I have to accept this might not make things better between us. But it will help you understand why I behaved as I did.'

Grace took a sip of her tea and tried to order her thoughts. 'Earlier when we talking about Katrin and the fact that one of Dieter's cards identified her as an IM, I said I too had been an informant.'

'Yes.'

'And your assumption may have been that that was one of the things I've done over the years for the British intelligence service?'

'Something like that.'

'But in fact I was an informant for the Stasi?'

'What?'

'Yes, I fell in love with a boy when I was working for the escape committees. Remember the Wall had only just gone up and people were stuck on both sides. This boy was an enthusiast for the DDR and persuaded me it was a noble project. I was captivated by his ideas and when he asked me to tell him something of my activities, I did. I named names and gave dates and locations. People were arrested and imprisoned. Worse may have befallen some, though I have no proof that anyone I betrayed was executed.'

'Grace, you don't have to tell me this.'

'I *do* have to tell you. I probably would have done a lot more damage, but I was detained shortly after I started passing information to my Romeo and interrogated.'

'Who detained you?'

'SIS.'

'Oh no, I think I see where this is going.'

'Maybe you do; maybe you don't. It was put to me that if I wanted to avoid legal proceedings, I should stay in place, but pass along with real intelligence, details that would show where the leaks were elsewhere in the system. I, of course, agreed to do what I was asked. Fortunately, the operation didn't run for very long, partly because I was due to move to the Sorbonne and partly because several people were rounded up thanks to my efforts. You probably won't be totally surprised to know that the person who interrogated me and who was then my handler was Sheena.'

'I wondered. Did that involve a bit of S&M?'

'Let's not go into that, but you're not far off the mark. So when I got to Paris I used my radical German contacts to infiltrate the student Left and passed back reports to Sheena. Then when I came back to Cambridge, my job was both to inform about certain individuals and to identify promising people who might be a good fit for the service.'

'So you didn't recommend me?'

Grace laughed. 'No, I stopped doing all that years ago. Unfortunately, when Mavis came to stay with us, I as good as told her that I was occasionally debriefed by the department. She said she would have to check me out and consequently I came up once again on Sheena's scanner. That is how I came to be Dieter's watcher.'

'Okay, but I don't really see where this is going.'

'I was reluctant to take on the job because you and I were together and we were trying to have a baby. When I put this to Sheena, she said that if I didn't break with you, not only would she let you know that I had worked for the Stasi, the very agency that had probably murdered your mother, but that she would make sure senior colleagues in the University knew as well, thus stymying my chances of becoming a professor.'

'What a bastard she is.'

'Well, that's her job. Also she had calculated that I would put my reputation above our relationship. And she wasn't wrong. I feel utterly ashamed of myself. To make matters worse I was forbidden from letting you know anything of this. Which was why I manufactured the slander about your using violence against me. I eventually told Gary that this had been a lie. He was disgusted with me, felt that as a consequence he had cut off from you and torpedoed your play. I have lost his trust completely and he has ceased to be a friend.'

'Grace, this is all Sheena's fault.'

'No, it is my fault. She has just exploited the situation. I should have confessed to you and risked your hating me for having worked for the organisation that killed your mother. And I should have told her to do her damnedest to ruin my name with my colleagues. I have finally come to the conclusion that I don't deserve to be a professor and I am not going to put myself forward.'

Tears were now streaming down Grace's cheeks. Steve took her in his arms and said, 'Grace, I don't hate you. I don't think any the less of you. I love you more than I ever did.'

'You're just saying that, Steve, because you're kind and you know I have had a bereavement. But it will gnaw away at you and I will be diminished in your eyes. It's what I deserve, but it makes me feel so sad. I've screwed up one of the few good things that has come into my life.'

Grace was soon asleep, but Steve's mind was racing and he was unable to give himself up to sleep. He slipped on a dressing gown and went downstairs. The fire in sitting room was still glowing. He sat down on the sofa and stared into the embers.

What a strange evening. After Grace's confession about her treachery in Berlin in 1961, she had asked him to spank her. Steve had been reluctant to join the subculture of which, to his mind, Sheena Ferguson was the chief exponent, but, on reflection, he accepted that in many respects he was already a denizen of that world. He had awkwardly agreed, his reluctance tinged with mild amusement, but realised almost immediately that his defensive jocularity was at odds with the earnestness of Grace's mortification. She'd said that when she had misbehaved as a girl her father had called her a disgrace. Steve felt this explained a lot about her, not that her father might have smacked her bottom – he hoped he hadn't – but that Disgrace was an apt reification of shadow aspects of her personality. She'd asked Steve to call her a naughty girl and wanted to feel the flat of his hand on her rump. Only then would she feel shriven.

But putting a grown woman over one's knee was not a simple matter and had required a good deal of co-operation, during which Steve had had to stifle a powerful urge to laugh. Once securely in position, his first effort had amounted to little more than a rather dainty slap, provoking a quickly stifled giggle from Grace. The next rather more forceful blow had resulted in a sharp intake of breath. Having now found his range, he'd smacked her several more times while calling her a disgrace until her bottom had developed a nice glow, whereupon they'd made love, collapsing on the floor of Grace's parents' bedroom in a sweaty, exhilarated tangle of limbs.

So once again the invisible stage hands who managed his life had set the stage for a new scene even before the current one had come to an end. Here he was sitting in what was in effect Grace's country cottage. The ritual spanking seemed to have been Grace's way of offering herself to him again, this time without the elaborate conditions that she had asked him to accept nearly two years previously. In the meantime other things had changed too. They had both lost their parents. Both were in some sense orphans and both without siblings. What they lacked in close relatives, they made up for in property. Between them, they had three properties: his flat in Borough, her house in Glisson Road, and now this cottage in Somerset.

But many things remained the same. They did get on well. He liked being with an older woman; she liked being with a younger man. They shared a body of cultural knowledge: she as an expert, he as a knowledgeable amateur. She remained indescribably beautiful; he made up in youthful vigour what he lacked in classic good looks. They were, for the most part, comfortable with each other sexually.

The chastisement business had been a new development. It was not a mode of intimate relations Steve felt particularly comfortable with. Possibly, it was something that her time with Müller had awakened in her, or more probably, as she had suggested, the dynamic in her relationship with her father which had come to the fore since his death. Steve couldn't pretend that he hadn't got a bit of a kick out of it, but it didn't seem to fundamentally connect with something deep or veiled in him. In fact for much of the time, he had had to stop himself from laughing. On the other hand it did seem to mark a change in the balance of power between them. And maybe that is what she had wanted to express in a way that was not contaminated by the recuperative powers of language.

But even if, this time, she wasn't setting conditions, he would still be taking on obligations. But so what? Wasn't it childish to imagine that any relationship came without obligations? And wasn't willingly accepting obligations actually the best way of protecting oneself from the destructive energies deep in the human heart?

In her typically enigmatic way, Ginny had told him all this when they'd been together in Ainsworth Street. She'd said on more than one occasion that he could have whoever he wanted, other than her. It must have become abundantly clear to her by then that the only woman he wanted was her. So she'd done her best to gently explain to him that the disappointment attendant on unrequited love was less destructive to the human psyche, than the hedonic deficit created by the fulfilment of one's desires. Desire itself had to be protected from the banality of satisfaction. Not that she'd put it quite like that. He was still reformulating in his own terminology many of the things she'd said in those days. And still marvelling at how she had known such things.

And, deploying that same terminology, didn't that mean, if he and Grace did resume their relationship, that Grace would be in some sense a consolation prize, second best? Maybe. But maybe he'd be her fifth place consolation prize, or worse. And mightn't they be a stronger couple for that very reason? Or did it make them more vulnerable to unexpected temptations?

Well, one could hardly make a life on the basis of the least likelihood of temptation. Surely, Oscar was right when he said that he could resist everything but temptation. Wasn't temptation the uniquely coincident package of conditions guaranteed to undermine the falsely positive image of self?

And then there was the fact that the previous scene was still playing itself out. Müller was dead, but unburied. Ulrike was in prison, but, so far as Steve knew, had not yet been charged. Sheena had asked him how he knew Müller was dead? How did one know anything that one had not personally witnessed oneself, other than by trusted channels of information flow? He and Grace had seen June's lifeless face. It was not beyond imagining that this was some kind of terrible hoax. The mind in despair sometimes clutched at such ludicrous thoughts. But it was even further beyond any kind of meaningful probability that it was the case. On the other hand, simply witnessing Müller's burial or cremation in a sealed casket would be no more proof than they already had that he was actually dead. So what had Sheena been driving at?

And there was the equally puzzling comment that although Ulrike was alright, this was the end of her. Sheena might have been saying that this was the end of her activities as a Stasi agent or her presence in their lives, but Sheena did not use language in that loose way.

There was also the matter of Collingwood which Steve had not raised with Grace and was minded not to. The problem was that Steve didn't see Collingwood as a killer. But mightn't that be exactly where he was going wrong? And, as with the S&M photos of Sheena, the existence of such images didn't make him a murderer. And, finally, there was Müller's speculation that he might even be Steve's father. This was something that he was definitely going to keep to himself. Even if it was true, it changed nothing. And yet, in some way, it changed everything.

Steve woke late the next morning to find Grace getting back into bed, having brought up some coffee.

She rolled over and snuggled up against Steve.

'Oh, this is lovely. Wouldn't it be nice if we could just stay here?'

Steve wasn't entirely out of sympathy with the sentiment, especially in the light of his midnight brooding.

'Yeah, let's make it happen.'

'What give up work? Give up London and Cambridge?'

'Give up the crap work, not the good work. I've got a novel to write. And I bet you've got dozens of books to write.'

'I thought you liked working on the magazine.'

'Yeah, I do. But when I took it on, I thought it would leave me plenty of time to work on my book, but that doesn't seem to be the case. And I get paid peanuts.'

'What would you do for an income?'

'Well, my mother left me a bit. And the life insurance payout means that the mortgage on the flat is paid off. I could let the flat and live off that.'

'But it's handy having a London base.'

'Yeah. But you know.'

'You're a bit young to be thinking of retiring.'

'I'm not thinking of retiring. I'm thinking of doing something worthwhile with my life.'

'Are you going to let me see the novel?'

'Yeah.'

'Promise?'

'Promise.'

'Well, we could let out the Glisson Road house instead. And live here and in London.'

'Are you serious?'

'Well, since we're talking about these things, we might as well consider all the permutations. I could probably take a sabbatical. We could see how it goes.'

'Well, it does appeal. It'd get us out of Sheena's clutches.'

'Lane End is a bit off the beaten track. It drove me crazy growing up here.'

'But neither of us is a teenager desperate for the bright lights.'

'Okay, let's think seriously about it. It's not something we can do overnight.'

'No, and talking of which when are you thinking of heading back to Cambridge?'

'I've got a week's compassionate leave. So at the moment I'm thinking of staying here until Saturday or Sunday next week. There's a lot to arrange, funeral, sort out things with the bank and so on.'

'Of course. The thing is I need to go back to London *this* Sunday at the latest.'

'I realise that.'

'I could possibly come back down on Thursday if it's cool with Sally.'

'And then we could travel back together the following Sunday.'

'Yeah. Will you be okay here on your own?'

'Of course, I will, Steve.'

'I don't mean safe from Stasi nasties, but you've suffered a bereavement. You need support.'

'Don't forget Gideon was the local vicar. He might have been retired for quite a few years, but there are plenty of people in the village who remember him. There'll be a stream of visitors coming up the garden path, you mark my words.'

'Okay. So what are we going to do today?'

'I've got a few phone calls to make, funeral directors, solicitor and so on. But apart from that the day is open. If the weather remains nice we could go for a walk and have supper in The Bull.'

'Sounds great. I've got one call to make, but I can fit it in around yours.'

'Sounds like a plan. That means we can have a nice lazy morning in bed.'

'Couldn't think of anything nicer. But no more chastisement, unless you do something really bad.'

'Ooh, that's the kind of challenge I like.'

Grace had finished her calls by eleven-thirty. She said she'd drive into the local supermarket while Steve made his call. Once he'd heard the Morris crunching out of the drive, Steve rang the Buzz offices and got put through to Sally.

'Hi, Sal. How's it going?'

'Okay. Remember, I used to do the whole thing on my own before you joined us.'

'I never doubted you could cope. I meant you personally.'

'Can you talk?'

'Yeah, Grace has gone to the supermarket. Can *you* talk?'

'Yes, it's like the Mary Celeste here.'

'Good. Not about the Mary Celeste, but that we can talk.'

'What's there to talk about?'

'I just want to assure you that I'll be in on Monday.'

'Okay.'

'But I was wondering if I could have next Thursday and Friday off again. I can take it as holiday.'

'Why do you need more time?'

'The funeral needs to be organised. And stuff do with the house and the bank.'

'Can't Grace do that on her own? She's a grown-up.'

'She can, but she could also do with some support.'

'Okay, fine. Did you tell Grace about you and me?'

'I did.' This was a slight bending of the truth.

'Are you two back together again, then?'

'Well, there are no public pronouncements being made, no plighting of troths, but we are sleeping together.'

'Haven't you been doing that for some time?'

'Sal, until last night I haven't had an active sex life since I last slept with you.' Again this was a distortion, but did, he felt, put the insipid sex he had had with Ulrike in its proper perspective.'

'I see. Is that meant to make me feel better? You seem to forget that I am with Jeremy now and it is a matter of little or no concern to me who you are sleeping with.'

'Sorry, Sal, I'm just trying to tell you as honestly as I can what the situation is. I'll be back at my flat on Sunday evening. We can talk further then if you want.'

'No, let's just have lunch at the Coffee House on Monday and you can tell me how you see your job with Buzz going from here.'

He was still sitting on the sofa brooding when he heard the sound of the Morris pulling up on the drive. He jumped up and quickly filled the kettle. A few moments later Grace appeared at the back door with bags of shopping. He gave her a kiss. 'That was quick. Coffee?'

'Please.'

Putting the things she'd bought on the kitchen table, she said, 'No point getting a lot if we're going out this evening.'

Steve nodded. 'And we can reheat the remains of the casserole for lunch.'

Grace pushed her hair out of her eyes and said, 'Perfect.'

Steve – London Train – Sunday

GRACE DROVE STEVE TO the station at Castle Cary on Sunday morning. The rain was lashing down. They sat in the car holding hands until a couple of minutes before the train was expected. As Steve reached for his bag, Grace said, 'Steve, it's been lovely.'

Steve nodded. 'It has. It's how it should be. I'll phone you when I'm back at the flat. What are you going to do with yourself?'

'I am not short of reading matter.'

'Okay, take care.'

'You too.'

She watched him walk up to the platform. The train pulled in. Just before he climbed aboard, he turned and waved at her. And then he was gone.

She sat there for a few minutes. Despite the sadness of her mother's death, it had been a delightful couple of days. She realised, however, that she was once again stampeding Steve. That was how she was. But this time she would try to give him more space. It wouldn't be easy. Perhaps she was deceiving herself, something she was very good at, but it did feel to her that there had been a rebalancing of the dynamic between them. Not because she had encouraged him to chastise her, though that had been fun, but because he now seemed more secure in himself. It helped that he was now, to an extent, financially independent and had his own place. She must persuade him not to give the flat up. It would somehow be easier for her to maintain her affection towards him if he was not always with her. And she must resist her tendency to try and organise him. Steve had his own way of going about things and she must allow him to do that. She must stop trying to be his teacher and become his partner.

On the way back to London, Steve's thoughts returned to the card devoted to Collingwood in Müller's Black Box. He was pretty sure this was the key to what had happened, but he couldn't see how. He needed to step carefully through the pieces of information in his possession. Clearly, this had all begun before Steve himself had become involved.

Maybe it was something like this? Shortly before his exfiltration, Müller had filched kompromat photos of Collingwood from a senior Stasi acquaintance. That meant that at the time of Mavis's funeral, when Steve had first met him, Müller already knew that Collingwood had been compromised. Reasonably enough, he had not used this information while his own position was so precarious. And presumably, Collingwood didn't, at that stage, know that his identity had been uncovered. But at some point, he must have become aware of the fact and must have recognised the threat that Müller posed to him. How had he come to this realisation?

Perhaps the Stasi had identified that the photos were missing and alerted Collingwood. They then devised a plan to free Ulrike in the confident expectation that she would make her way to Müller. Once established in his circle, she could be blamed for his murder. The hit itself, of course, would actually be carried out by one of their agents on a signal from Collingwood, who would also make sure that Ulrike's clothing bore traces of the poison used. Or was it no such thing? Because something else was afoot?

It seemed to him now that the new element that he had yet to integrate into any explanation was the role of Katrin, Ulrike's identical twin. Not only was Katrin a serving Stasi officer, but she also seemed to have been the person who had initiated the close surveillance of Müller leading to the urgent need to exfiltrate him. Admittedly, the only source of these facts was Müller himself or to be precise his Zettelkasten, which, now Steve came to think of it, was also the source of the theory that a birthmark under the left breast was the only reliable way of distinguishing one sister from the other.

The assumption that he and Grace had been making was that the woman with the birthmark was Ulrike. Yes, there were photographs showing the birthmark, if you looked carefully, but there was no caption on Müller's photographs to link the birthmark to a named woman. On the one hand, Grace was certain that the woman whose body she had examined when booking an appointment for her with the GP had a birthmark in just that position. On the other hand, Steve, who had slept with the same woman on several occasions, had noticed the bruising to the ribs on the right side of the body, but not the birthmark.

But in any case the reliability of the birthmark as an identifier had been undermined by the disclosure of the Who? game. It was now entirely conceivable that the woman he had been dealing with, at least at certain crucial points, was the Stasi officer. It was a modern variant of one of those ancient conundrums loosely gathered under the heading of the bed trick. In the dark or in the intimacy of the bed chamber, could you reliably know that the person you were making love to was your regular bedmate? The existence of an identical twin only made the task of identification that much more difficult.

Week Six

8 November – 14 November 1976

MI6 – Borough – Monday

'THANKS FOR DROPPING BY, Steve. Anything to report?'

'Not operationally. Grace's mother died last Tuesday and I took a couple of days off to help her sort things out at her parents' place in Somerset.'

'Oh, poor Grace. Were they close?'

'Not particularly, I'd say, but in some ways that makes it more of a blow. All sorts of regrets and self-recriminations.'

'Yes, I think I recognise that.'

'You've lost a parent?'

'Both.'

'Recently?'

'Fairly.'

'So all three of us are in the same boat. I thought average longevity was on the increase.'

'Averages can be locally deceptive. Is Grace back in Cambridge?'

'No, she's taken a week's compassionate leave.'

'Will you go down for the funeral?'

'If I can. Talking of funerals. Is there a date for Müller's yet?'

'Not yet.'

'Why's it taking so long?'

'I don't know. Of course, he has no family here, so it's down to St Rad's to sort things out. Will you go?'

'Yes. You?'

'I hope so. Things are rather busy at the moment.'

'I imagine that Müller and Ulrike are not your only concerns.'

'Very true.'

'Whereas there's nothing for me to do now with Müller dead and Ulrike under arrest. So I'll get back to my normal life.'

'Oh, I don't think it's all wrapped up yet.'

'It's a pretty open and shut case with Ulrike, isn't it?'

'As I mentioned last week, Fräulein Schmidt is proving to be rather uncooperative.'

'Maybe she's putting her hopes in the British reputation for fair play?'

'We would like to disabuse her of that idea.'

'How?'

'By making her believe in the threat of a lengthy term in a British prison and accepting that if she were a little more helpful, she might be able to go home. One can see this whole business as an internal settling of scores within the Stasi itself. To an extent we have no problem with that, other than that they chose to settle the score on our patch. So we have to clean up the mess.'

'Müller wasn't Stasi.'

'He was, as good as.'

'What would she have to agree to?'

'We'd like her to give us a detailed picture of where she fits in the organisation, who she reports to, who reports to her, her training, and so on. We would get her out of Paddington Green and take her to a safe house. Life would be nicer for her. She'd be out of the hands of the screws, wouldn't have to eat prison slop again.'

'Perhaps she can't because she's not actually a Stasi operative but really is a brilliant scholar.'

'That is not how we see things. In fact we have reliable sightings of her in full Stasi uniform.'

Steve was convinced now, more than ever, that Collingwood did not know that twins were involved and he was conflating aspects of the two women. Or if he did know, it was, for some reason, in his own interests to pretend not to.

'Okay, assuming she is Stasi, even though she actually spent some time in one of their prisons, we just toss her back to East Berlin and let her take the consequences there, knowing that they will never trust her again or that this time they will lock her up for good.'

'There is no real evidence that she actually was in prison. We think it much more likely that the period of incarceration was faked as part of the plan to set her up as a long-term sleeper agent. In any case, we would prefer to keep her out of our justice system.'

'Why would that be a good thing?'

'She is determined to plead not guilty. There are certain things we can do, in the event of a trial, to limit the amount of sensitive information that is made public, but there is still a risk that we could get the wrong verdict. And furthermore, one never likes to wash one's dirty linen in public.'

'But isn't that the whole point about a liberal democracy that those accused of crimes have a right to adequate representation and an impartial tribunal.'

'Of course, but in matters of state security, it's not always so easy to furnish those rights.'

'Jeremy, rights inhere. They don't have to be furnished.'

'That's a somewhat utopian view.'

'Well, anyway, why are you telling me this?'

'I thought maybe *you* could talk to her. We know that you and she connected, if I can put it like that, in Prenzlauer Berg. And we know she trusts you. A friendly face might help her come round to seeing things our way.'

'Jeremy, I don't want to be the one to persuade her to go back into the lion's den.'

'I'm afraid you're going to have to. I've already cleared it with the governor and with MI5, who can get a bit territorial about these things. They don't normally like us to do these interviews, but have agreed on the basis that Ulrike would be a useful asset back in the DDR. So please meet me here tomorrow at nine o'clock and we'll go over to Paddington Green in an official car. They will bring her to an interview room. I won't come in with you. She seems to have taken against me somewhat.'

'Jeremy, I have a job.'

'I'm sure that Sally will understand. I'll put in a word for you.'

Steve laughed. 'There are surprising advantages to having both my bosses going out with each other.'

'There may come a time when it doesn't work in your favour. Anyway, I'll see you tomorrow. With luck the Percival charm will coax the icy maiden down from her tower.'

On the walk to his flat, Steve went back over the conversation with Collingwood. It really went without saying that Steve was dreading the prospect of conducting an interrogation with Ulrike. She would surely feel that he had been deceiving her all along and was now revealing his true colours. It seemed unlikely that she would even be prepared to talk to him. But he also felt that Collingwood had been franker with him than he ought to have been. There was clearly no appetite in the department to bring Ulrike to court. The deal to drop charges in exchange for information was clearly a fig leaf. Somehow, he had to persuade her of that fact without explicitly pointing out the weakness of Collingwood's case. This would be difficult because Collingwood and, more problematically, MI5 would be listening in. And Ulrike would assume something of the sort too. But at that moment, he had little idea how he could manage such a thing.

He also wondered whether Sheena really was in the picture about his being deployed in this way. He could easily call Collingwood's bluff by ringing Sheena, but he was not entirely sure of his ground yet. The last thing he wanted right now was another psychological thrashing.

Paddington Green Police Station – Tuesday

STEVE AND COLLINGWOOD SAT in the back of the official Rover P6 as it wove its way through the rush-hour traffic. Sally had been exasperated when Steve phoned and asked for the morning off and had only been placated by his offer to work late.

'Jeremy, I'm really not clear why you think I would be a better advocate for Ulrike providing us with an organisation chart of her bit of the Stasi than you or someone with some experience of negotiating with opponent operatives.'

'Because you and she are already acquainted, not just in East Berlin, but she also stayed at your place, and in your bed one imagines.'

'All the more reason to hate me, I would have said.'

'Well, I'd like you to give it your best shot. We can give you two hours with her.'

'That sounds like a lot. I'm not sure we've got enough shared experience to sit there for two hours.'

'Just chat about any old thing. You took her around Cambridge and took her to St Rad's.'

'A place she'll never be able to return to again.'

'You're the writer. Use your imagination. Look, she's obviously been trained to control herself in the face of threats of violence or violence itself. But a friendly face might help her to be more pragmatic.'

'So you want me to be the soft cop.'

'If you want to put it like that.'

'Presumably you are the hard cop. I can imagine it comes naturally to you.'

'I say, Steve, that's rather hurtful. Anyway, we don't use those terms.'

'I'm sorry. I'm not sure being thought of as a soft cop is any more beneficial to the self-esteem.'

They were now passing in through the sliding steel gates into the drop-off area. Collingwood leant forward and said to the driver, 'Drop us off here, Paterson, and park up in the underground garage. Go and get yourself some breakfast in the canteen. And then be ready to pick us up at midday.'

Collingwood got out of the car and headed towards the main reception doors. Steve followed him in and waited as they were both signed in and given badges. Collingwood said, 'The officer will take you up to the interview room. A female officer will bring Ulrike to you and will remain in the room. She will only be there to restrain Ulrike should she become violent. I will be listening in, as will Harry Larkin, a colleague from the security service.'

Steve nodded. His mouth was dry and the oppressive atmosphere of the high security police station was already making him feel claustrophobic. An officer came around from behind the desk and said, 'Please follow me, sir.'

As Steve went through the security door, he saw Collingwood give him an airy wave and settle himself on a seat in the waiting area. After passing through several more security doors and going up a couple of flights of stairs, Steve and his guide arrived at a door which the officer unlocked. 'This will be the room you're using, sir. There is a plastic jug of water, a pot of coffee and a couple of plastic cups. If you need the coffee or water topping up, please ask the officer who will sit with you. It is up to you whether you want the interviewee to have some. There is a lavatory in the corner of the room. I'm afraid it doesn't have a door, but it is out of direct view of anyone sitting at the table. The table itself is screwed to the floor. The red button on the wall is a panic alarm, should something happen that the officer can't deal with. Any questions?'

'Any chance of some biscuits?'

'Yes, sir. Rich Tea?'

'Perfect. And can I invite the interviewee to smoke. I have brought a packet of Marlboro with me.'

'Yes, sir, entirely up to you.'

'Thank you, officer. In that case, I am ready when you are.'

Steve sat down, took the cigarettes and a yellow plastic BIC lighter out of his pocket and put them on the table. He then poured himself a cup of coffee and tried to empty his mind. A few minutes later the door swung open and Ulrike, wearing handcuffs, stepped into the room, followed by a female officer. Ulrike looked directly at Steve, but did not show any surprise or emotion. The officer, tapping her on the shoulder to indicate she should stop, unlocked the cuffs and pointed to the chair opposite Steve. Ulrike sat down and put her hands on the table. Steve opened the packet of Marlboro and pulled a cigarette up and offered it to Ulrike. She shook her head and Steve returned the cigarette to the packet.

Steve tried to relax the muscles in his face and smile. 'Have they been treating you properly in here?'

'Yes. It is not much better than a Stasi prison, but I haven't heard anyone being tortured.'

'Perhaps you are surprised to see me?'

'No, not much surprises me. I had always supposed that the much-vaunted British system of fair play in which a person was innocent until proven guilty was a myth.'

'Perhaps we all live by myths.'

'Yes, I think that is probably the case. Your myth is that you are a writer or a student, but the reality is that you work for the state security apparatus.'

'That applies to both of us. But it didn't feel like that in Prenzlauer Berg.'

'It does not apply to me. It should be easy enough to check unless your famous intelligence services are as deficient as your sense of fair play. And how could I possibly know what it felt like for you to take advantage of me sexually? What would you care, anyway? If there is a body to use, why not use it? A free ride.'

Steve felt winded, but also angry because that was not how things had been. 'If you recall, I said that I didn't think it was necessary for us to have sex. We could just simulate it. You were the one who said that it was harder to simulate sex than to perform it.'

Ulrike was silent for a moment and then said quietly, 'Maybe I did. It was an awkward situation.'

'It was and perhaps you are confusing what happened in reality with what you recently read in the draft of my play that you found when you were staying at my flat. That draft was a version of the play that wasn't produced because the director said we would not be allowed to show those scenes on stage. The character called Tom in that draft does take advantage of the girl and ties her up before having sex with her. But that didn't happen in reality, did it?'

Steve could tell from the movement of Ulrike's eyes that she wasn't sure why he was describing an event that she did not recognise from the encounter in East Berlin or from the draft of the play. After a moment, she said in a small voice, 'No.'

'Before we move on to what really did happen, you will have noticed that in the play text I called the girl Katrin.'

Steve noticed another flicker pass over Ulrike's face. Again she would not have seen this in the manuscript however much she had read of it because that name did not appear in the draft. But she would now realise that he knew the name of her twin. This time she did not reply.

'At the time, of course I called you Inge, which was your cover name.'

'Yes.'

'But when the play went into production, the director wanted more mythic names. So we ended up calling Katrin Freya and Tom Tristan.'

'I did not know that.'

'No, because you didn't see the play. But getting back to the actual encounter between you and me in Prenzlauer Berg that day, I didn't tie you up and there was no coercion, was there?'

'No.'

'So perhaps you could tell me what did happen, Ulrike?'

'Why are you asking me these questions? You were there?'

'To begin with that is my job in this encounter. In the same way that I didn't want to have sex with you that day, not because it wouldn't have been lovely, but because I didn't want you to be in a situation in which you were being forced to do something against your will – in the same way, I don't really want to be asking you these questions. But my understanding is that you are being offered a deal that will see you avoiding prison and arrangements made to get you back to the DDR, but you are painting a picture in which you were the one being abused in Prenzlauer Berg. You said, why would I care about you. If your body was there for using, a man like me would just do whatever he wanted.'

'No, I am not saying that.'

'Well, tell me, what was the first thing that happened when we got back to your room?'

'I went down on you.'

'Yes. Did I make you?'

'No.'

'What happened?'

'The usual thing.'

'In your mouth?'

'Yes.'

Suddenly Steve was on the alert because, much to his chagrin, that was decidedly not what had happened. Ulrike had done her best to play out the stupid charade they had been asked to perform. But nerves and the thought that they were being observed had impeded Steve's part in the performance. Not only had he failed to come; he had not even had a functioning erection.

Was it possible then, that in East Berlin he had had sex with the Stasi sister not the woman who was Müller's student and that Ulrike in attempting now to answer his question was extrapolating retrospectively from their lovemaking at Glisson Road to the earlier encounter which had been with her sister?

But if that was the case, when had they changed places and which sister was he now dealing with? Perhaps all along he too had been involved in a decidedly awkward version of Müller's Who? game. Whatever the reason for their changing places in Prenzlauer Berg, they could not have then imagined that Steve would eventually be the interrogator following the arrest of one of them for Müller's death.

The problem now for Steve was that he needed some further proof of his speculations without alerting Collingwood and the other listeners to the possibility of a twin.

Proceeding with caution, he said, 'And what happened next?'

'We had sex on the bed.'

That much was true. 'How was that for you?'

'It was transactional. Our encounter in Prenzlauer Berg was sordid, but in your play you make it beautiful.'

Casting his mind back Steve thought that their lovemaking on the bed had actually been rather beautiful and Ulrike had said as much at the time. Yes, the set-up had been transactional, but his memory of that stage of the operation was that they had opened up to each other. But, no doubt, his interviewee was also presenting matters not just for him but for the wider audience of listeners, including those in East Berlin.

'Perhaps I should take that as a compliment. Writers always hope to transform raw reality into something finer. We seldom succeed. But nor do I think what we did was sordid. We were careful with each other.'

'Yes, perhaps we were. But the situation was impossible.'

'It was. But that is exactly why I have been asked to talk to you today. We *were* careful with each other. And I have tried to be sensitive to your situation since you have been here.'

'That is true. And I am trying to help you as much as I can today. What happened to Tom and Katrin in your play? I did not read to the end.'

For a moment, Steve was encouraged by her use of the names of Tom and Katrin. One way or another they would have considerable resonance for her. 'There was no hope for my characters. The political situation crushed them. That's why the play was called *Palace of Tears*.'

'That makes me sad.'

'It was and is sad.'

'I also read some of your notebooks.'

Another discrepancy. She'd said she hadn't looked at the notebooks. But it was to no one's benefit to call her out on these discrepancies. 'Go on.'

She must have noticed the look that crossed his face and realised that she'd made a mis-step. 'I am sorry. I lied when I said I hadn't. I realised that the material in the notebooks was personal and deeply private.'

Steve sensed that she was now telling the truth. 'It's fine. I don't mind. There's no point in writing if you don't want people to see what you write, even if you feel that those same people will disapprove of what you have written. You can only write by allowing your words to have a life of their own, which is given to them by the reader. You are the only person to have read those notebooks. So you are the one who has really given birth to them.'

'That's beautiful.'

'Thank you. Did you read the section about the two girls who go to the Müggelsee and an older man joins them?'

'I don't remember that part.'

'I explain to the English reader that the Müggelsee is a lake where people indulge in *Freikörperkultur*, what we would call naturism or nudism in English. The man studies the girls' bodies, as they are sun-bathing. The man and the girls go back to the flat of one of the girls. The man asks to photograph the girls as they were at the beach, naked and side by side. He has brought his Praktica camera. The girls agree. After the photoshoot, the man takes his clothes off too and the three of them make love, what we call a threesome in English. The man finds one of the girls very giving, but the other withholds herself.'

Steve had been on the point of mentioning that the girls were twins and including the detail of the birthmark, but had decided that he should continue to withhold those details from the listeners. Even so, Ulrike was floundering again. How did he know this?

Steve took a sip of his coffee and studied her face. She could not hold his gaze. She said, 'I don't remember reading that. I felt guilty about looking at your private notebooks and only looked at certain pages.'

'What do you remember from the pages you did look at, then?'

Thankful for being allowed to move on, she said, 'I read your retelling of the Schneeweißchen and Rosenrot tale from Grimm, the one in which the miller's daughters are stolen by an ogre called Tollkirsche, but eventually freed by Gräfin Johanna von Christen-burg.'

Steve felt quietly triumphant. Of course, neither scene was in his notebooks. But Ulrike's own improvisation showed that she had understood that Steve knew that she had an identical twin and had had a close relationship with Müller. The fact that she also knew Collingwood's Stasi codename was a little disquieting. Did that mean that the girl he was interviewing really was the Stasi sister? More worryingly, if Collingwood himself knew his own internal codename, he could hardly fail to smell a rat. Steve would soon find out.

He and Ulrike sat in silence looking at each other for several long moments. Eventually, Ulrike said, 'What do you want me to do?'

'Ulrike, I'm no one around here. I don't want you to do anything. But I understand that my colleagues want you to help with organisational information. No one will know it came from you.'

'How can I be sure of that?'

'I don't think you can. But if you agree, you won't have to stay in this prison. You will be moved to a safe house. You will be debriefed. It might take some days.'

'I am afraid they will kill me.'

'Why would they kill you? You are worth more alive than dead. It is information they want. And they want to swap you for someone the Stasi are holding. So they will keep you alive.'

'If they move me, will I be able to see you?'

'I do not make the decisions.'

'I will not provide information unless you are involved in the debriefing. I realise, of course, that everything will be recorded. I am not so naïve as to believe that they will let me talk to you without others being able to hear what is being said, but those are my terms.'

As the Rover eased out of the gates of Paddington Green police station, Collingwood said to Steve, 'We'll give you a lift back to your office. It's the least we could do.'

'Thanks. I'm starting to get a bit of a reputation as a part-timer.'

'Well, it looks like you've got an alternative career as an interrogator, if sub-editing begins to pall. You did an excellent job. You have a unique approach.'

'Mainly because I didn't have the foggiest idea what I was doing. It was fortunate that I'd had some previous with Ulrike.'

'Yes, it was intriguing. I was struggling to keep up.'

'But you heard her conditions at the end?'

'I'm not sure that the powers that be will allow that to happen. I'm not even sure if they did that it'd be a good idea. The main point is that she showed some signs of being willing to shift her position.'

'I'm not sure I'd be able to fit it in with my work, anyway.'

They fell silent for a while and peered out the windows at the London traffic. Collingwood seemed to be considering his next conversational sally. 'What was all that stuff about the Müggelsee and the naked sun-bathing leading to a threesome? Not quite what one might expect in a novel by a St Rad's alumnus. Does the novel have a title yet?'

'The working title is The Burnt Edge.'

'A striking title, but what does it mean?'

'I'm not really sure, to be quite frank. The image I have in mind is someone burning a letter which contains personal or sensitive information. But the flames do not fully consume the paper. Some lines are still legible in the charred fragments that remain, but peter out where the paper has been reduced to ash.'

'Rather a good image, but fairy tales and phantasmagoric accounts of erotic dreams are not really my thing. I never could get on with the Grimms.'

'I find the tales useful for sketching out the bones of a story. My notebooks are full of all sorts of nonsense. I suppose, as a German literary scholar, Ulrike was struck by my using that kind of material.'

'But why go to those lengths at all, in the interrogation I mean?'

'I wanted to avoid the encounter just being me asking questions and her playing with a straight bat.'

'Which, as we who have been raised to the thwack of leather on willow know, counterintuitively means to avoid answering questions.'

'Quite. So I thought I'd engage her in a different way.'

'A somewhat psychoanalytical approach, I would say.'

'I'll take that as a compliment.'

Collingwood bowed his head graciously. 'One does wonder, though, whether you have anything other than sex on your mind most of the time.'

'Not much. It seems to me a subject of endless fascination. And like most people I think about it more than I do it.'

Steve turned his head towards Collingwood to see his reaction to this sweeping generalisation. But Collingwood sidestepped this thrust by saying, 'If I didn't know to the contrary, I would say that you and Ulrike had thoroughly rehearsed the whole little perform-ance.'

Steve smiled to himself. 'I don't know what you mean.'

'You seemed to be speaking to each other in some pre-arranged code.'

'I can assure you that there has been no collusion. I haven't spoken to Ulrike since before Müller's death.'

'Which, fortunately for you, I can confirm. So it must have been some arcane form of flirting.'

'I suppose there may have been something of the sort going on.'

'Did you really want to tie her up and have your way with her?'

'You know how these things sometimes cross your mind.'

'No, I really don't. I thought you had a higher regard for women.'

'Well, as I was saying to Ulrike, one cannot persuasively disown what one has put down on paper. And even if you do manage to burn the offending text, some of it may well remain legible. It's as well to be reminded that our sins will find us out.'

As Steve let this sentence hang in the air, the Rover pulled up outside the *Buzz* offices. Steve opened the door to climb out, hoping that none of his colleagues were in the immediate vicinity. Before closing the door, he leaned in and said, 'Thanks for the lift, Jeremy.'

'My pleasure. And once again, well done.'

By the time Sally got back from her lunch, Steve had pulled together everything for the afternoon session at the typesetters and was ready to get the bus to Clerkenwell.

Sally put her bag on her desk. 'Is the realm secure for another few hours?'

Steve laughed. 'Yeah, I think so.'

'I don't suppose you can enlighten me further?'

'Maybe tomorrow after we've signed off the new issue. For now all I can really say is that the whole thing was a very public session of psychoanalysis.'

'Your strong suit, I would have thought.'

'Pretty much what Jeremy said.'

Sheena – Kennington – Wednesday

SHEENA STOOD IN THE open doorway of her imposing house and said, 'Steve, come in.'

She led him into the front room and said, 'I'm sorry to make you come around at this ungodly hour. I was somewhat tied up earlier on. Though you may think it was I who was doing the tying up.'

Steve laughed uncomfortably. 'Sorry, Steve, that joke was not in good taste. And I can see that you have come to have a serious talk. What can I offer you to drink?'

When Steve demurred, she said, 'For goodness' sake, man, at least have a small whisky and water.'

Steve realised that he was going to have to go through the motions. But, in fact, the drink helped him relax a little and reminded him to let the conversation develop naturally.

Sheena lit a small cigar, and exhaling a mouthful of smoke, said, 'I was sorry to hear of Grace's loss. Please send her my condolences.'

Steve thought that the condoler ought really to express her sympathy to the bereaved in person. But it was pointless expecting Sheena to be conformist.

'I gather you have been helping her with the arrangements in Somerset.'

'She has taken care of the arrangements. I have just tried to support her.'

'Which we all need at times.'

'I am going down again tomorrow. The funeral is on Friday.'

'Did you know her mother?'

'I met her once. We got on surprisingly well.'

'Of course. It is Steve Percival we are talking about.'

Steve laughed. 'I am not sure that Grace's father was quite so approving. Although he remained extremely civil and friendly.'

'Fathers and daughters, fathers and daughters, Steve.'

Steve nodded and took a sip of his whisky. Sheena drew contemplatively on her cigar. 'I have read the transcript of your interview with Ulrike Schmidt. I was so intrigued that I listened to it again with the transcript in front of me. I presume Collingwood was delighted with the result.'

'I think so, though he was also somewhat suspicious. He seemed to feel that Ulrike and I had cooked up some kind of code in the event of our having to communicate certain things with other people listening in.'

'Which, in a manner of speaking, you had.'

'We had no code and we had not envisaged the circumstances.'

'No, but through your shared experience, partly with Müller and partly during the time she stayed in your flat, you had an arcane set of facts and ideas which you could manipulate in order to send each other secret messages.'

'Is that what Collingwood thinks?'

'No, I don't think he has conceptualised it that way. But he is uneasy about the way that you achieved your goal. Or, let us say, his goal.'

'I am not surprised he is uneasy and...'

Sheena cut across him. 'We will come back to Collingwood and his Discontents shortly. But you know, as I do, that there are certain details of which he is unaware. He is unaware that Ulrike has an identical twin called Katrin. By your cunningly wrought précis of the Müggelsee events which ended up in a threesome, you were able to indicate to her that you knew this.'

Steve wondered how long Sheena had herself known twins were involved. Was it since having tampered with Müller's Zettelkasten or did it pre-date that? He felt, however, that there was not much to be gained by asking her.

'I didn't work it out in advance. I was improvising wildly.'

'And very effectively. But then you introduced this idea that in the draft of your play the Katrin character is tied up and coerced sexually. From the euphemistic language used, I imagine an unconventional form of sex was implied. I do not see how that follows from the Prenzlauer Berg scenario, unless the information we had of that event was incomplete. It seems gratuitous.'

'It was a message for someone else.'

'Now, that is a very bold thing to say. The only people you categorically knew would hear the audio or read the transcript were Collingwood and me. We can discount the sleeping police officer and Larkin, the MI5 berk who was listening in.'

She looked pointedly at Steve, who remained silent. Sheena gave an almost imperceptible smile and drew on her cigar. 'Well, I do not think the message was for me directly. You already know something about my foibles. So I have to suppose this was a signal of some kind to Collingwood.'

Steve shrugged. 'Yes, I wanted to let Collingwood know that I had him in my sights.'

'Do you think he realised that the message was for him?'

'Probably not, though he was more than a little puzzled by the exchanges with Ulrike. I think he disapproves of my way of life and considers me a rather grubby individual.'

'An easy and perhaps fatal mistake to make. But it was wrong of you to try and provoke him. In the future, I want you to show more restraint. But let us leave that to one side for a moment. Don't worry, we will gather all the material relating to Collingwood for a separate discussion. Let us move on instead to what I consider your stroke of genius. You invited Ulrike, in the spirit of your own approach, to improvise something, which was supposedly an extract from the notes to the book you are working on, as a way of letting you know a detail about Ulrike herself which you might be able to corroborate in other ways.'

'Yes, I rather liked her little tale of miller's daughters stolen by the ogre.'

'Well, I do not think we need spend too much time on working out the identity of the girls. I think I can guess who the ogre is, but I lack the stepping stones to reach that conclusion securely. Maybe you can help me there.'

'Collingwood was compromised in a hotel room in Leipzig with a very young man. Kompromat was obtained. Müller got this information from an old friend who was an alcoholic colonel in the Stasi and at the same time stole a couple of the images. The Stasi had given Collingwood the codename *Tollkirsche*, which translates as belladonna or nightshade. I have photocopied the card and copied the photos in the darkroom at work.'

Steve took the copies from the pocket of his jacket and handed them to Sheena. She glanced at them and put them to one side. 'Is there more?'

'Yes. Initially, I thought that was all. But then I realised that there was an additional index reference on both Collingwood's entry and Mavis's entry. I tracked down the card and was horrified but not surprised to see that the location of the bar that you and Mavis were in just before the hit and run was provided by *Tollkirsche*. Presumably, you were meant to take the hit as well.'

Steve handed Sheena a copy of this second card, which she put with the other card and the photos.

'Thank you, Steve, this is first class work. Let me just say that I am sorry that it was Mavis who took the hit. Let me also say that I had a strong suspicion who the mole was. Of course, you are entitled not to believe me on that particular point. But what I am now going on to say will not please you, I fancy. So I think we need a top up.'

She poured some more whisky and lit another cigar.

'I imagine you feel we should move against Collingwood imme- diately and get him to confess all, then put him in prison and throw the key away, but we are not going to do that. You have every reason to hate him. And I have similar reasons not to wish to see his face again. But we have to play the hand out.'

'And what does that mean?'

'Mr Collingwood will stay in place for the time being and you will assist him. We will arrange to have Ulrike moved to a safe house. She will be properly looked after. You and Collingwood will debrief her.'

'Sheena, I have a job.'

'You will have to tell them to let you have the time off. Or else you will have to tender your resignation.'

'How much time?'

'A week. Put a bag together for five days away. A car will pick you up on Monday morning. You will be driven to The Grange, a nice place in the country. You will spend the week debriefing Ulrike. At the end of the week, Ulrike will be taken somewhere else and you will be brought back to London.'

'I don't know how to debrief someone. I won't know what questions to ask.'

'Don't worry. We will give you some pro forma material.'

'Will there be other people there?'

'Yes. There'll be the housekeeping staff. People to make your meals and keep the place clean and tidy.'

'Will I be able to contact you if I need to?'

'Cicely Durrant runs the place. She lives on site. She has the means to contact me or the emergency services. There are no public telecommunication facilities there for what we might call *guests*. If you have a problem or need something sorting out, talk to Cicely. She and I are close.'

'How will I identify her?'

'Cicely will greet you when you arrive and show you the facilities. She will hold Ulrike's passport while she is at The Grange. Do not make the fact that she has a twin a point of discussion during the debriefing sessions. I cannot stress this enough. It is vital that the fact that Ulrike has a twin must not become common knowledge.'

'I understand. Will there be other people there?'

'Well, not other guests. There are some technical staff on site to set up and maintain the recording equipment. And, of course, some security staff. Don't worry, it won't be like Paddington Green. It's much more like a rather nice country hotel. The rooms are comfortable. There's a nice sitting room, stocked with plenty of books. The food is rather good. If the weather is fine, there are some nice walks. Obviously, Ulrike will not be permitted to leave the site. The perimeters of the site are under observation. If, in an emergency, *you* need to go off site, you will need to arrange it through Cicely.'

'Will Collingwood be staying as well?'

'No, but he might drop by. He will not like it but he will be kept busy elsewhere for most of the time. We cannot cut him out completely because he will technically be in charge. Which means you will have to make a report to him and he will see the daily transcripts.'

'What is the point of all this?'

'I should have thought it was obvious. She may not be a Stasi officer herself, but her twin sister is. It is clear that the two women are very close, even for twins. Ulrike will have gleaned all sorts of things about the context in which her sister works. I want you to get her to provide as much information as you can. We will compare what she says with our manuals and see if they need updating. But don't limit your questions to Stasi operational matters, information about staff and students at Humboldt will also be invaluable. In fact get as much information about East Berlin as you can, including her prison experience.'

'Can we talk about other things during the debriefing sessions?'

'I think it's almost impossible not to.'

'And outside of the formal debriefing sessions, can we socialise?'

'Of course, that would be much the best thing. You don't have to take your meals together, but it would be better if you did. If you wish to discuss with Ulrike matters that you do not wish to be overheard, confine those discussions to occasions when you are outside and some way from the house. If anything of significance emerges from those discussions, you will report them to me in person. Do not commit anything of that sort to writing.'

'Okay. Will there be other *guests* there?'

'No, that is never a good idea. So anyone else you encounter works for the firm. You, of course, are not a guest in the sense we have been using that term.'

'I'm going to have to say something to Grace.'

'I appreciate that, but please do so in the most general terms. Do not name names, even if you think it must be obvious to her. And do not say anything to anyone else. You can tell your work that the week off is to support Grace in her bereavement.'

'What will happen when the debriefing is finished?'

'Let us not rush our jumps. One final point: the rooms you and Ulrike will have access to do not lock. This is to avoid unfortunate accidents. It does mean, however, that there is a lack of complete privacy. Normally, I would caution against intimacy, but in this case I think it is unnecessary.'

Steve was puzzled by this last statement. It was curiously equivocal. And what was meant by unfortunate accidents?

Grace & Steve – Somerset – Sunday

IT WAS SUNDAY EVENING. Grace and Steve were on the train back to London from Somerset. The previous few days had been intense. Even though the funeral had been a small affair, it had still taken quite a lot of organising. Only two immediate family members had attended, cousins on her mother's side. The rest were mainly neighbours from the village or former parishioners of Gideon's. There had also been an atmosphere of quiet disapproval that not only had there been no funeral service at the church, but there had also been no burial. At some point in the future, June's ashes would be interred beside her husband's grave.

To make matters worse, Emma, one of the cousins, had stayed over. Steve had driven her to the station after lunch on the Saturday. Only then were Grace and Steve able to fall into each other's arms. It was also then that Steve had told Grace that he was going to be away for a week on departmental business. Grace had tried to wheedle details out of him, which Steve had managed to resist. The only thing that he was prepared to say was that his trip didn't involve a passport.

When he'd phoned Sally to tell her he needed to take the week off to support Grace in her bereavement, he had expected her to be outraged, but she had just seemed resigned to the way things were developing. No doubt Collingwood had already smoothed the way. The one note of criticism she had sounded was to ask Steve to reconsider whether he had longer-term expectations at *Buzz*. She had not been convinced by his assurances that he was fully committed to the project.

The only untoward moment in the four days he'd been at Grace's was a phone call Grace had received from Richard Doyle, informing her that Müller's funeral would be on the following Wednesday. He hoped that Grace and Steve would be able to attend. Steve was in fact upset that he would have to miss the funeral. It crossed his mind that Sheena might have had prior notification of the date from Doyle, but he dismissed this. Even if it was true, there was not much that could be done about it now.

Sitting opposite each other now in the window seats of an otherwise empty compartment, Grace said, 'Thank you, Steve, for all your help. I don't know how I would have got through it without you.'

'I'm glad I could be with you.'

'I wish you could come back with me to Cambridge.'

'That would be difficult even if I didn't have this week away on departmental matters. Sally is getting pretty fed up with me.'

'I presume she has even less idea of what you're up to than I do.'

'Grace, it's better if I don't say anything right now. There may be time for that later.'

'I know it may ring hollow coming from me, but I really don't like the idea of your getting deeper into Sheena's world. Please be careful.'

'I will. I promise.'

Week Seven

15 November – 21 November 1976

Steve & Ulrike – The Grange – Monday

AS THE OFFICIAL CAR turned in through the gates of The Grange, Steve was mildly amused to note that he actually had a fairly good idea of its location. He had imagined that a secure facility for the purposes of debriefing and perhaps interrogation would be some way out of London and in a remote area. But it seemed that not only was The Grange not much more than an hour's drive north of London on the way to Cambridge, but the premises were reasonably visible from the road. Admittedly, the gates they were turning through were formidable and electrically powered, and there was a security post immediately inside them, manned by two guards in uniforms with no insignia. The driver of the car wound down his window and spoke to the guard who had emerged from the security post with a clipboard in his hands. The driver and the guard were obviously well-acquainted and exchanged a bit of banter, after which the guard peered in through the open window at Steve and said, 'Welcome to The Grange, sir. Miss Durrant is expecting you.'

Five minutes later, Steve was standing in the lobby of the main building, surprised to find that the front door had been standing open. He looked around and noticed that there was a small brass bell standing on a side table in the reception area. After waiting a further couple of minutes to see if Miss Durrant or someone else might magically appear, he rang the bell tentatively. A few moments later, a door off to one side of the lobby opened and a statuesque woman of indeterminate age entered and said, 'Mr Percival, I am sorry to have kept you waiting. I was just settling in our other guest. I am Cicely Durrant and The Grange is my fiefdom. I hope the journey up was stress-free.'

'Please call me Steve. The journey up was very smooth, thank you.'

'But no doubt you could do with a cup of coffee.'

'That would be most welcome.'

'Well, let's go into the lounge, but first I will get someone to bring a coffee. How do you take it?'

'Black, no sugar, please.'

Before guiding Steve into a room on the right, Cicely rang the bell and a younger woman appeared. 'Marianne, could you please bring Mr Percival a black coffee, no sugar?'

Cicely invited Steve to sit. 'So you are with us until Friday?'

'Yes.'

'And Miss Ferguson explained how things work here?'

'She did, but I'm not sure I took it all in. You are no doubt aware that I am a new recruit and really feel somewhat out of my depth.'

'Well, it is brave of you to admit it. If you have any doubts or worries, please do not hesitate to find me. I have an apartment in the building and I am here most of the time. If I do need to be away, I will do my best to give you plenty of notice. In my absence, Marianne will deputise for me.'

'Thank you. You mentioned that you were settling in the other guest. Would that be Ulrike Schmidt?'

'Yes, Miss Schmidt is having a little lie down before lunch or perhaps tidying herself up. It is not easy to make yourself present-able in a place like Paddington Green.'

At that moment, Marianne arrived with the coffee and put it on the small table next to Steve.

She turned to Cicely. 'I'm going into the village, ma'am. Can I pick up anything for you?'

'Yes, please, Marianne. A couple of packets of Benson & Hedges.'

She opened her purse and gave Marianne a five-pound note.

'And put the change on Zeta's Son to win in the Gold Cup at Newbury on Saturday at the bookmakers in the high street. I'll pay the tax on the winnings.'

'Yes, ma'am.'

When Marianne had left the room, Cicely said to Steve, 'I like to have a flutter once a week. It's good to have an interest, don't you think?'

Steve smiled. 'Yes, I am sure it is, but I am completely ignorant about horse racing.'

'Well, if there is time this week, I would be happy to indoctrinate you.'

Steve laughed. 'I look forward to that.'

Cicely raised an eyebrow. 'But you have weightier matters to attend to.'

'Yes, and I believe the first session is scheduled for two-thirty this afternoon.'

'It is. When you have drunk your coffee, I will show you to your room. On our way, I will show you the dining room and the interview room. Don't worry if you feel you don't get very far during the first session. It often takes a while to get into the swing of things.'

'That is reassuring to know.'

'There are two sessions a day: nine-thirty to twelve-thirty in the morning and two-thirty to five-thirty in the afternoon. There will be no afternoon session on Friday.'

'Miss Ferguson said that the sessions will be recorded and transcribed.'

'That is correct. We have technical and administrative staff here. Generally speaking, you will not come into contact with them. The idea is to reduce the number of interactions with others. But the transcript of the morning session will be put in your room before the start of the afternoon session and the transcript of the afternoon session will be in your room after dinner.'

'That's quick.'

'Well, things have speeded up since we started using audio-typists, but I am afraid you will probably not be able to read the morning session in full before the afternoon session starts.'

'It will just be useful to refer to.'

'Quite. Breakfast is available between eight and nine in the morning. It is not obligatory to take it, but I would recommend you do. And Mrs Bedwin is a very good cook. Lunch is at one o'clock and dinner is at seven-thirty. I would also recommend trying to get out for a breath of fresh air. The grounds of The Grange are really quite pleasant.'

'Is Miss Schmidt allowed to take walks?'

'She is, but she must check with me or Marianne in my absence before doing so, even if it is to accompany you. If you are going out on your own, you, of course, do not need to seek permission.'

Half an hour later and the guided tour complete, Steve was hanging up his shirts in the wardrobe of his room. There was an hour until lunch. He lay down on the bed and reflected on the turn of events. It was almost as if he was a new teacher at some kind of quaint private school of which Cicely was the headmistress. There was a certain level of comfort combined with a strict timetable and restrictive rules. God knows what Ulrike had made of it. It would be useful if he could speak to her privately before the first session started.

Cicely had remarked as she had shown Steve to his room, that the room opposite was Ulrike's. He would see if she was in her room and propose a pre-lunch walk. He crossed the landing and tapped on the door of her room. A moment later the door opened a little and Ulrike's face appeared. She was smiling, not quite the expression he had been expecting.

'Steve, you've arrived.'

'Yes, I was wondering if you'd like to get a breath of fresh air before lunch.'

'That would be nice. Let me get my coat.'

She emerged a few moments later wearing a smart grey coat. Steve said, 'Did Grace lend you the coat?'

Ulrike looked puzzled for a moment and then, drawing the coat more tightly around her, said, 'I'll explain shortly.'

They made their way to the main entrance and, having checked with Cicely first, they stepped out through the front door onto the portico of The Grange. As they stood there, trying to work out the best route to take, Ulrike took a packet of Marlboro from her pocket, extracted a cigarette and lit it. Exhaling a mouthful of smoke, she said, 'Let's just follow the main path.'

Steve pulled up his collar. 'You're smoking?'

'Well, we're outside now or as good as. I didn't think you objected.'

'No, of course not. That's fine.'

They set off along the path that bisected the extensive lawn in front of the house, an awkward silence interposing itself between them. Eventually Steve said, 'Have you recovered from Paddington Green yet?'

'I had a bath after Miss Durrant showed me around and I'm feeling quite refreshed.'

Steve was surprised at Ulrike's positive tone. He turned his head to look at her, in an effort to see if her facial expression matched her tone. 'I wanted to clear a few points with you before we do the first session.'

She nodded. 'Good.'

'And you realise that everything we say in those sessions will be recorded?'

'Of course.'

'But it's possible that our rooms, the lounge, dining-room and so on are also under some form of surveillance.'

'That is very likely.'

'So we should confine anything that we want to keep to ourselves to conversations out here.'

'Understood. Who are we putting this show on for?'

'Collingwood, the guy who originally interrogated you at Paddington Green and asked me to come in.'

'I wondered.'

'But we've got to make him feel he's getting good information.'

'Yes, I can do that.'

'We've also got to realise that this information will get back to East Berlin.'

'Of course.'

Steve was struck by Ulrike's matter-of-factness. 'So whatever goes on the tape has got to make sense to them and it has to make sense to Collingwood.'

'I agree.'

They had reached the end of the lawn and the path branched left and right. They took the left-hand path and soon came to a small gazebo. Ulrike said, 'Let's step in here out of the wind.'

She opened the door and looked inside. There was some wicker garden furniture and deck chairs and a parasol stacked in the corner. She stepped inside and motioned to Steve to join her. 'Shut the door.'

He did as she asked and when he turned back she smiled at him and said, 'Please kiss me, Steve.'

He was hesitant. What was going on here? This was not like the sullen and reticent person he'd been trying to pretend to have a love affair with in the last few weeks. And just when there was no longer any need to pretend. Perhaps the time she had spent in Paddington Green had softened her attitude towards him. He took a step towards her and kissed her experimentally. She pressed herself against him and slipped her tongue into his mouth. After a long passionate kiss, he detached himself from her a little and said, 'Ulrike, what has brought this on? I can only imagine that you're relieved to be out of Paddington Green.'

Ulrike smiled mischievously at him and unbuttoned the grey coat and laid it over one of the wicker chairs. She then unbuttoned her blouse and took it off. She wasn't wearing a bra.

Steve had that feeling he often had that his brain had stopped working. He stared wonderingly at her beautiful breasts. Holding his gaze, she covered her breasts with her hands and said, 'What are you thinking?'

'It's a bit cold to get undressed.'

'Steve, I am not going to take all my clothes off here. That can wait for later. What I want you to do is to ask yourself why I'm doing this?'

Suddenly, the penny dropped. There was no birthmark. She noticed his eyes growing wider in realisation. 'Feel the skin under my left breast if you want to make sure.'

He shook his head slowly. 'You're Katrin?'

'Yes, no birthmark.'

'But a packet of Marlboro instead.'

Katrin laughed. 'I wondered if you'd notice.'

'I'm not sure I had really. But I found it strange that you refused my offer of a cigarette when I was interviewing you at Paddington Green.'

'I wondered if that might happen. Cigarettes are the currency of prisons. But I couldn't get a message through to Ulrike.'

'Where is she?'

'She's safe. We swapped places on the drive here. Sheena arranged it.'

'You've met Sheena?'

'Yes, she told me you knew that Ulrike had a twin sister. Now give me a hug and warm me up.'

Steve undid his own coat and took Katrin in his arms. They kissed again. After several long moments, Katrin pushed him away. 'I'm sorry, Steve, it really is too cold in here.'

She put her blouse and coat back on and said, 'Let's sit down and I'll do my best to answer your questions.'

'How long have you been in Britain?'

'Ulrike and I travelled at the same time, but by different routes. She came via Harwich. I came on the Dover ferry. It was I who tracked you down in the pub in Soho and then came back to your flat the first time. But since then you have been dealing with Ulrike. She is the scholar; I am an officer in the *Staatssicherheitsdienst*.'

Steve wasn't quite sure if he believed her. 'Why have they allowed you to come to Britain?'

'I am here on an official mission.'

'What is the mission?'

'It's better I don't tell you.'

'But how do you explain to your handlers that you have taken Ulrike's place?'

'They don't actually know that I have taken her place. They think I am lying low until the heat has died down from the reaction to what I was sent here to do.'

'Who else knows about the swap apart from Sheena?'

'No one. I don't think Cicely knows. The driver certainly doesn't. Nor does Collingwood.'

Steve was still feeling that some elaborate hoax was being played on him. 'You know I think this birthmark business is a bit of a red herring. I've never seen both of you together. I wonder how many people have.'

'I'm not sure how I can prove that I am the other one.'

'You said you made contact with me in a pub in Soho called the John Snow. Who was I with?'

'You were with a girl called Sally. She was protective of you. She didn't like me and Werner turning up on her patch.'

'Okay. On what other times have we been together?'

'I met you the next day in a beautiful old pub near London Bridge and then went back to your flat and we made love.'

'Did I suggest that we go to bed?'

'No, you asked me to take my clothes off, but only after I'd prompted you. I didn't mention it, but I wanted you to see that I didn't have a birthmark.'

'Well, I suppose I didn't know that I was meant to notice its absence. What happened then?'

'You undressed, and we just stood there looking at each other.'

'I was suffering from the same nerves I had in Prenzlauer Berg?'

'No, you weren't. You were ready for action.'

'So, I asked you to perform oral sex on me, to make up for my failure on that previous occasion?'

Katrin laughed. 'No, you picked me up in your arms, laid me on the bed and went down on me.'

'What then?'

'We made up for lost time, but I didn't stay. I had to be somewhere else the next day.'

'Where did you go?'

'At the time, I told you I was going to Oxford, but that's not actually where I went.'

'So where did you go then?'

'I can't tell you. It was to do with my official reason for being here.'

'But aren't your people going to think something odd's going on?'

'If they get sight of the transcripts of Ulrike's interviews via a certain person, they won't know that these ones are actually from me.'

'So it wasn't you in Paddington Green?'

'No.'

'But it was *you* in Prenzlauer Berg. I wondered why Ulrike's recollection of what happened there was so vague when I interviewed her in Paddington Green police station.'

'We didn't have much time together at the start of all this. It didn't occur to me to go into great detail with her about my sexual interactions with you.'

'Is she a lesbian?'

'Yes, that is her preference. Not that she has ever had a special friend as far as I know. Of course she has had to put up with expectations from certain men in positions of influence. I have helped her out from time to time in such cases. I do not think, on the whole, that they were disappointed or, indeed, noticed that there had been a swap.'

'I'm not so sure about that. Müller seems to have been aware of the switch. He called it the Who? game.'

'Yes, well, he was a wily old dog.'

'He felt that one of you was indifferent to his efforts, while he was unable to satisfy the other.'

'That is a subtle distinction. Perhaps he was a connoisseur after all, but one lacking in male vigour because of his age. When did he tell you this?'

'He didn't tell me. I read it in his personal Zettelkasten.'

'And do you detect a similar difference?'

'I would prefer not to answer that right now.'

'And does Müller's Zettelkasten contain other details about me, about us?'

'It does, extremely personal ones.'

'Should I be worried about what he has to say?'

'He thought he had brought himself to the attention of the Stasi by contriving to have a threesome with you and Ulrike.'

'Ah, after Müggelsee. Yes, there may be something in that. Once again, I was just trying to help Ulrike out.'

'And aren't you just helping her out now too?'

'In one way, yes, but this is also on my own account.'

'I can't believe that you taking this enormous risk just to get back together with me.'

'I have wanted to be with you since we met in East Berlin. We are sexually very compatible, but I can't pretend there aren't other reasons.'

'What are they?'

'I want to help change things.'

'How?'

'By going back to the DDR and passing information to your organisation.'

'But at the cost of your liberty or, even, your life?'

'There is risk in everything. One can be killed crossing the road, as you know.'

'Why not just defect and then you and I can be together all the time?'

'Because I need to make sure that Ulrike remains safe and is properly looked after.'

'How are you going to ensure that.'

'I can't tell you right now, but it will soon become apparent.'

'How did you feel about being involved in the arrest of your twin sister?'

'Not good. I was told that if I took her place, they would go easy on her. What else could I do?'

'How did they know that travel documents were being delivered to Ulrike?'

'Someone betrayed her.'

'In that case, how did Müller get out?'

'Your run was just a ruse. The Nietzsche book contained no documents. Someone else had delivered the real documents to him earlier and he had already crossed.'

That aspect of the operation had Sheena's fingerprints all over it. 'Why did they put Ulrike in prison then?'

'For ideological reasons as much as anything. They found her essays and the draft of the book she was writing on the poetry of resistance. But they also treated her as a scapegoat for the failure to stop the exfiltration.'

'On that run to East Berlin, I had very precise instructions about what to take with me, where to meet you, and so on. How were those agreed?'

'I don't know. I was briefed by a case officer. Somebody on your side must have been in touch with Müller.'

'The person who was handling Müller was killed in a hit-and-run accident a few days before I made the crossing. That was why I was brought in.'

'That was a tough assignment for a first operation. Why did they choose you?'

'Because it was my mother who was killed.'

The colour drained from Katrin's face. 'So Siebenschläfer was your mother…?'

'Siebenschläfer?'

'Dormouse. Because it hibernates for so long. It was our code-name for Müller's British handler.'

'I'd come out to be with her in her last hours and it was put to me that I wouldn't have a profile with the Stasi. So I agreed to do it.'

'Oh, Steve, I had no idea. I'm so sorry.'

'Within the Stasi, was it regarded as a liquidation or an accident?'

'I don't know for sure. I wasn't close to the operation. But I think it was seen as a hit.'

'What about in Cambridge? Did you take Ulrike's place then?'

'No, I know nothing about her academic subject. She did give me a few notes in case I had to try and convince you.'

'You probably know more than I do about German Romanticism. Anyway, I think it's time we got back. Let's see if Mrs Bedwin's cooking is as good as Cicely says it is.'

On the way back to the house, they worked out what they would cover in the first session later that afternoon. Katrin made it clear that she would only give him the kind of information that Ulrike might be thought to have. If it was too detailed it might raise suspicions. But she did say that she would provide extensive material on the current state of the DDR socially, politically, economically and culturally. He would see that all was not well in the socialist republic. It survived at the pleasure of Podgorny or Brezhnev or whoever was in the General Secretary's chair of the Soviet Union and as long as the West German state was prepared to supply hard currency in the ransoming of dissidents.

The lunch was, in fact, extremely good and Steve, for one, was not really in the right frame of mind to conduct the first debriefing session. In the event, however, he was pushing at an open gate. Katrin played her part superbly, hesitant at times, truculent when being pushed on particular details, caustic about the workings of the British justice system. Steve felt that she had missed her vocation and should have been an actress.

Both were somewhat subdued over the evening meal, conscious that they needed to be careful about how they interacted, and decided to turn in early. Later in bed, Steve did his best to concentrate on his book, but his thoughts kept straying to Katrin, knowing that she was sleeping across the passage from him. He wondered if he dared creep into her room and join her in her bed. But it seemed improbable that there weren't some kind of sensors in place. While he was turning the matter over in his mind, his door opened silently and a small figure swathed in a towel as far as he could make out crept across the room and, discarding the towel, slipped into his bed. She pulled the covers over their heads and whispered in his ear. 'I gave up waiting for you. Thought I'd take matters into my own hands.'

He gathered her in his arms and said, 'I'm glad you did.'

A short while later as they were climaxing for the first time that night, Steve was struck by the oddity of the situation. Eighteen months previously they had also made love in somewhat unusual circumstances, with specific instructions to make as much noise as possible, both conscious of the Stasi listening into their lovemaking. Now it was the British intelligence service who might well be listening to their coupling, only this time they were trying to make as little noise as possible. Once they had both regained their breath, Katrin whispered, 'Oh, Tom, that was lovely.'

Steve stroked her cheek. 'Darling Inge, it was for me too.'

'Can I stay with you all night?'

'Yes, I'll set the alarm for six.'

When she came in to say good morning the next day at breakfast, if Miss Durrant noticed that her two guests were considerably less talkative than they had been the previous day, she didn't remark on it. Steve invited her to join them, but she said she'd take her coffee to her office and get started on the day's correspondence. Steve vaguely wondered if his and Katrin's indiscretions of the previous night would be on her agenda. But in truth he didn't care. He had fallen in love with Katrin once again, as she had with him it seemed. Whatever their respective organisations did to them it wouldn't change that simple fact.

The only moment of disquiet had been when they were tearing themselves from each other's embrace at six o'clock in the morning, Katrin had started to cry. In their short time together this was not a mode with which he associated her. He'd asked her why she was crying. She'd said she'd tell him during the break before lunch. She needed to take a shower and get herself tidied up before breakfast. He'd watched her wrap herself in the towel she'd arrived in and creep softly across the room. When she reached the door she turned and smiled sadly at him, tears staining her face. A moment later she was gone.

The morning session was hard work. It was difficult to keep the pretence going that Katrin was actually Ulrike. Both Steve and Katrin were listless and less fluent than they had been the previous day. It was a relief to get to the break for lunch. Once again, having first checked with Cicely, they put their coats on and walked to the gazebo. Once inside with the door shut against the biting wind, they embraced fiercely. But after some minutes, Katrin pushed Steve away and said, 'There's something you don't know.'

Steve laughed. 'What I don't know dwarfs what I do know by a mile.'

'I mean about us and what's happening here.'

Steve was suddenly on his guard. Was the scenery about to change again?

'Tomorrow night I, as Ulrike, will appear to commit suicide by hanging myself in my room. An ambulance will be called, but it will be too late. I will be dead. My body will be removed to a morgue. The coroner's report will say that I took my own life in remorse for what I had done to my former teacher and lover.'

'Why wasn't I told this before?'

'You know how it is, Steve. I shouldn't be telling you now. It means you are going to have to do some acting, some simulation in your terms, to make it look authentic.'

'What's the purpose?'

'My superiors will be pleased that Müller has been eliminated, that Tollkirsche has lived up to expectations by framing Ulrike for his murder. It also means that they will be reassured that Tollkirsche has not been detected. This will provide Sheena with a channel for disinformation. And, most importantly, they have no idea that I have been turned.'

'And then what?'

'I will make my way back to East Berlin.'

'I will come with you.'

'You can't.'

'I want to be with you.'

'And I want to be with you, but it is not possible. At least, not right now.'

'Why don't you just defect?'

'Because there's work to do, as I told you yesterday.'

'Oh, fuck the cloak and dagger stuff.'

'It would be more dangerous for me to end this operation abruptly, and possibly dangerous for you too, than to play out the hand.'

'Is this another of Sheena's harebrained ideas?'

'Sheena knows what she's doing. It's a sensible way to resolve the situation. I can't tell you all the details.'

'Why not?'

'You know why not. I've already broken an important part of the protocol. I was asked not to tell you. Your responses would be more natural if you did not realise it was a ruse. But I wanted to soften the blow so we could both enjoy this last night together. That means you will have to be brave about things and act the part of someone in deep shock.'

Steve was silent. He felt like simply walking out of the stupid performance they were putting on. He felt like going down to London and smashing Collingwood's face in and giving Sheena a piece of his mind. He felt rage at the insane machinery they were caught up in. But even as he felt this violent impulse sweep through him, he knew that he would do none of these things, if only for Katrin.

She looked into his eyes. 'We will work out ways to communicate.'

'But I want to see you, to be with you.'

'Maybe that can happen, but we can't count on it for the foreseeable future. We will both have to get on with our lives. There will still be people watching us.'

'But our time together will always be fleeting.'

'Life is like that. Let's not think ahead too much. Let's enjoy what we have right now.'

He didn't know how he got through lunch and the afternoon debriefing session. He kept losing his train of thought and just staring at Katrin, trying to fix her image in his mind. He felt certain that Cicely must realise something was up, but, if she did, she didn't say anything. It then occurred to him that even if she didn't know that Ulrike was Katrin, she must be in on the fake suicide stratagem. The paramedics in the ambulance would be department people. He himself would be treated as one of those being deceived. But clearly the performance was primarily for the benefit of Collingwood and his handlers.

At the end of the afternoon debriefing session, he suggested to Katrin that they skip dinner, but she thought that was not a good idea, even though neither of them had much of an appetite. Cicely affected not to notice how little they ate. They took their coffee in the lounge, chatting listlessly. Eventually, Katrin tapped her watch to indicate that they could now turn in. She stood up and, enunciating clearly, said, 'I'm exhausted. I think I'll have an early night.'

As previously arranged, he sat there for another fifteen minutes, staring at his book but unable to read it, before, yawning theatrically, heading off to his own room. He completed his ablutions rapidly and, eschewing pyjamas, got into bed and switched the lights out. He did not have long to wait before the door of his room opened and a slim figure glided across the room and climbed in beside him.

If the previous night had been one of surprise and exhilaration, what now unfolded was one of intense urgency and desire, as much on Katrin's part as on his own. Even after they had climaxed, she seemed to want to hold him inside her. They both wept. She kissed away his tears and traced with her lips what felt like every inch of his body, eventually sucking from him the most intense orgasm he had ever had. He doubted that he could do the same for her, but her own orgasm was profound and copious. They held each other for a long time before falling asleep.

When the alarm went, she said, 'Well, this is it. I won't be down for breakfast. They will wait until towards the end of breakfast before checking my room. There will be a carefully orchestrated panic. You will be asked to wait somewhere out of the way. Paramedics will arrive and take me away. You will not be allowed to look at me. Arrangements will be made to get you home.'

Steve nodded mournfully. He knew it was a ruse, but it did feel in some way as if she was dying. She kissed him. 'I have your address and telephone number. I will be in touch, but I can't say when. Ulrike's apparent suicide will release her to become the great scholar she really is. But remember, neither of us is actually dying, not yet at any rate.'

'What about you and me?'

'We will have to go on with our lives. We have to accept that we may never meet again, but let's never give up that hope.'

She kissed him again and then quickly left the room. He lay there, grieving already at losing her for a second time.

Things unfolded very much as Katrin had predicted. Clearly Cicely and several other operatives were privy to the plan. Once the "body" had been removed, Cicely turned her attention to him. She was solicitous and not quite as brisk as usual, but he detected that she knew that he and Katrin had spent both nights together and that he was probably aware, at least in outline, of what was going on. She brought him tea and said that she would organise transport for him once she had the go-ahead from the department. A little later, she appeared in the lounge to say that there was a call for him in the office. It was Collingwood.

'Steve, I'm sorry. You must be in a state of shock.'

Steve felt that he could honestly say he was, but that it might not be for the reasons that Collingwood supposed it was. 'I am. I thought things were going well. I wasn't being too demanding.'

'No, you did a great job. There is some excellent material there. But she had clearly run out of road. You mustn't blame yourself. A car is coming for you. Go home and take a few days off. You're booked out at *Buzz* until next week.'

'Thanks, Jeremy. I don't think I'm really cut out for this sort of thing.'

'Nonsense. These things happen. If you do manage to right yourself over the next few days, let's have a drink. But only when you're ready. And by the way, the governor asked me to send her commiserations but also her congratulations.'

Steve sobbed softly. Responding to the sound of Steve's emotion, Collingwood said, 'You know what she's like.'

Steve said, 'Yeah, but really, she is a piece of work.'

'But she's also the best in the business.'

Steve would have liked to have scoffed at Collingwood's complacency, but said instead, 'As I am beginning to realise.'

Steve – Trinity Church Square – Wednesday

THE DEPARTMENTAL CAR DROPPED Steve off in Trinity Church Square a little after two o'clock. He felt drained. He let himself into the flat and ran a bath. While the bath was filling, he put the kettle on for a cup of tea. A few minutes later, he was taking his first sip of tea when the phone rang. It was Sheena. 'Well done, Steve. Cicely, let me know how the operation went. It was a tough one for you, especially as I hadn't let you know what was going on. Though we realise that you must have got a tip-off from the horse's mouth, so to speak. Completely reasonable under the circumstances. But, please, utter discretion elsewhere. Lives are at risk.'

'Hi, Sheena, thanks for the call. Yes, I understand. Do you want me to come in?'

'No need for that. We'll catch up at my place when the dust has settled down. I just wanted you to know that your work is appreciated by a number of people.'

'Thanks, it does make a difference to know that.'

'I won't keep you, but I'll be in touch soon.'

She hung up, which was as well because the bath was on the point of spilling over. He was about to undress for his bath when it occurred to him that it was press day and Sally might be having a tough time at the typesetters. Perhaps he should offer to come in, if only for a couple of hours. He phoned the typesetters and asked to be put through to Sally. A few moments later, he heard her voice. 'Steve?'

'Hi, Sally. The project I was working on has collapsed. I'm back in London and could come and give a hand.'

'Thanks, Steve, I appreciate your asking, but I got a temp in. Her name is Kate and she's very experienced. She's got things nicely under control here. You might as well take the rest of the week off as originally planned.'

'Okay, but only if you're sure.'

'Steve, I've got a vague idea from Jeremy that you've had a tough time. So recharge your batteries.'

'Thanks. We could meet up over the weekend.'

'I'm going away for the weekend with Jeremy. Going to meet some of his old friends, maybe one or two other St Rad's alumni.'

'Great. Have a nice weekend. See you on Monday.'

'Steve, before you go, I've got Kate booked in for another week, just in case your operation overran. I gather from Jeremy that you might be asked to get more involved at the department. I wonder if we could go out for a coffee on Monday and talk about where you see things going.'

Steve didn't need a crystal ball to see that this was a none too subtle attempt to move him out. And maybe that would be the best thing. But Collingwood's contribution was not exactly helpful and, as far as Steve knew, without substance. Trying to keep his tone as even as possible, he said, 'Yes, of course, good idea.'

Steve now got into his somewhat cooler bath and soaked for a while. Overcome with weariness again, he was now pleased that Sally had not taken him up on his offer. A little later, he realised that if he didn't get out of the bath soon, he would probably fall asleep in it. A few minutes later, having dried himself, Steve went next door to his bedroom and slumped onto the bed. He was soon asleep.

It was just gone four o'clock when he woke. As he got dressed in fresh clothes, he wondered whether Grace would be back in her office yet. It was the time of day she normally liked to catch up on her admin. He went out to the hall, dialled Newnham College and asked to put through. A few moments later, he heard her lovely, low voice saying, 'Steve, are you okay? I wasn't expecting to hear from you until the weekend.'

'I'm fine. The operation didn't run as long as expected.'

'Is that good?'

'Who knows!'

'It was Dieter's funeral today. I only got back a little while ago.'

'Oh, God. I'd forgotten. How was it?'

'A little downbeat. No one was really expecting a big turnout. But St Rad's did him well. Richard Doyle delivered a very well judged eulogy. Jem Flynn read one of his less enigmatic poems. Stan Mallory was there in his best suit with medals clipped to his breast pocket. And even Collingwood put in an appearance. You were asked after. I explained that your work couldn't accommodate letting you have a day off. I didn't say what kind of work. I noticed Collingwood smirking when I was covering for you…'

'Cunt!'

'Steve, please don't use that kind of language.'

'I'm sorry, Grace, but I get the feeling that Collingwood seems to take every opportunity to put a spoke in my wheel.'

'You may well be right, but please don't use vulgar language, at least not in my hearing.'

'Okay, sorry. Well, if I haven't blotted my copybook too badly, shall I come up to Glisson Road? They're not expecting me back at work until next Monday, so I could come up tomorrow.'

'That would be lovely. Sorry, I was a bit snippy. We've both had a lot on our plates.'

Steve & Grace – Cambridge – Thursday

GRACE TOUCHED STEVE'S GLASS with hers. 'So, how is Ulrike?'

'She's fine, as far as I know.'

'Haven't you been with her?'

'No. I've been dealing with something else. It's best I don't go into details.'

'Is she still in Paddington Green?'

'No, they've moved her somewhere safe.'

'They don't believe she killed Müller, then?'

'I don't know what they believe. Perhaps they think that it's beside the point.'

'Aren't you concerned?'

'I am, but I've been stood down.'

'Ha! Believe that if you want to. I'm pretty sure they'll want to deploy you again before long.'

'Maybe, but I'm relieved this phase of things is over. Let me reassure you that I really do care about Ulrike. I've done what I can to help her. Even if I knew where she was, I couldn't bust in and bring her back here.'

'I realise that, Steve, but you probably realise that I've developed feelings for her.'

Steve took a second or two to process this statement. 'You'd better give me a bit more information.'

'You may think you had sex with Ulrike in East Berlin, and perhaps you did. And you may have had sex with her recently to help convince Müller that she would not be a burden to him. But even if you did, you must have realised that sex with men is not her true sexual orientation.'

'And you know this because she told you and because you and she have become lovers?'

'Yes, I am sorry if that is a disappointment to you.'

'Why would I be disappointed if someone is true to their inner-most feelings? I just didn't know you had those same tendencies yourself.'

'I wouldn't call myself a lesbian, but going to bed with Ulrike wouldn't have been the first time I'd been to bed with a woman. It's just that, as with so much about me, I kept it a secret. And in truth none of the women I went to bed with in the past were the sort of women I would have felt comfortable presenting to the world as my partner. I suppose I am what you'd call bisexual. I do not find making love to you distasteful. You are a sensitive lover, but I have other needs and desires.'

'And Ulrike is someone you could contemplate being out with?'

'Yes.'

'And she feels the same about you?'

'Yes.'

'I see. Well, I have no wish to make you do anything you don't want to do. I can check into a hotel.'

'Steve, don't get angry. I don't want you to check into a hotel. I want you to stay here and share my bed with me. I want to make love with you as often as we can. But ultimately I dream of being with Ulrike.'

'Okay, but that is not something I can do anything about at the moment. The fact of the matter is that if there is any public announcement about Ulrike Schmidt it will be to the effect that she hanged herself in her cell when she was being interrogated in connection with the murder of Professor Dieter Müller.'

Grace gasped, somewhat theatrically, Steve thought.

'Grace, you're the old hand in this game. That is not actually what happened. Ulrike is being kept safe and given a new identity. At some point she will re-enter the world. But you must keep this to yourself because if you are still in touch with your old Stasi chums and you pass this on, you will get her and perhaps other people killed.'

'How dare you!'

'Look into your own heart, Grace. You have betrayed others in the past. You can run rings around me. I'm as gullible as they come. In telling you this, I have done what Sheena has said I should on no account do. I've done it because I do believe that you have genuine feelings for Ulrike. I think I had already come to that conclusion. It does not make me angry or bitter. But if I ever feel that you have repeated elsewhere what I have just told you, I will never speak to you again and you will have made an enemy of me.'

'Okay, you have some justification for saying that, but you *are* angry with me.'

'I'm not angry. I am tired. But I'm also relieved. We needed to have this talk. I have been very confused about what's been going on.'

Grace put her arms around him.

'I know you think I'm just another one of the women in your life who is continually trying to put the moves on you. But couldn't we try and have a more fluid, open relationship? For goodness' sake, it's the twentieth century.'

'Yes, I could probably be happy with something like that, but what would Ulrike think of such an arrangement?'

'I don't know. She's not here to put her case, but until she re-emerges, can't we continue to be lovers? And the whole point about a fluid relationship is that it's always up for re-negotiation. We are lovers, but not till death do us part lovers.'

'Okay. And in that spirit I have brought Müller's grey Zettelkasten with me to give you. It is something you can make better use of than I can. I am not a scholar and never will be.'

'Steve, that's incredibly generous of you, especially after I have been so horrible to you.'

'You haven't been horrible; you've been honest. In a way, you've freed me.'

'I'm not sure what you mean by that.'

'You introduced me to a world I could never have entered on my own. Even after I left formal education, I have had the benefit of your deep learning. Some of my friends think I must have sold my soul to the devil to have lived with such a beautiful and brilliant woman. But you have also taught me to grow up and take responsibility. And paradoxically that's an ultimately liberating experience.'

'With that pretty bit of nonsense, you've just ensured another torrid session with Miss Disgrace later on.'

Steve laughed. 'That was not my intention. But if she puts in an appearance, I'll do my best to accommodate her needs.'

Week Eight

22 November – 28 November 1976

Buzz – Soho – Monday

STEVE GOT THE COFFEES and rejoined Sally at the table in the coffee bar. 'Kate's incredibly well organised and fits in really well.'

Sally took a sip of her scalding coffee and pulled a face. 'She is and does.'

Steve laughed. 'She didn't go to the London College of Printing, did she?'

'You guessed it. Whether she can spin deceptively brainy filler paragraphs out of nothing is another matter.'

'Nothing will come of nothing, Sal.'

'Stop it, Steve. I know you've read everything.'

'Hardly.'

'Look, this is a bit difficult…'

'Let me make it a bit easier. Kate is a real pro. *Buzz* can't afford a subbing crew of three. Especially when one of the team keeps asking for days off. So I will tender my resignation. If there are days when you are stuck, I can come and help.'

'Steve, are you sure? Jeremy hasn't been putting pressure on you, has he?'

'I've hardly spoken to him. I'd been coming to a similar conclusion. And now you've found Kate, it gives us both an easy way out without anyone feeling let down. I will just miss you.'

'We can socialise. After all, you and Jeremy have known each other longer than I've known either of you.'

Steve doubted that he would want to do that, at least not with Collingwood still in the picture. In fact, ever since he had turned up Collingwood's card in Müller's Black Box, he had been regretting having brought Collingwood and Sally together. But how was he to alert Sally to the darker side of Collingwood's personality without jeopardising Sheena's strategy or just making it look as though he was suffering from sour grapes? He would have to find a way, but in the meantime it would be cruel not to respond positively to her proposal. 'Yes, of course. That would be great.'

'What will you do?'

'I don't know. I've got a novel to finish. I haven't done much to it since I've been at *Buzz*, but I've got some idea of how to proceed with it now.'

'Is that to do with recent events?'

'Yes, I suppose it is.'

'What's it called?'

'Generally, with the things I write, the title is the last thing to crystallise. But at the moment it's called *The Parallax View*.'

'Steve, you're no Warren Beatty.'

Steve laughed. 'Don't you think so?'

'Only if I'm Faye Dunaway.'

'Damn, that means we're in a different film.'

'Sadly, I think that's probably the case. What will you live on while you're writing this book?'

'I'll manage.'

'Haven't you been earning at the department?'

'If I have, I've yet to see any of it.'

'I don't want to make you destitute.'

'I will be far from destitute, at least not in financial terms.'

Sally looked at him closely. She now noticed the grief in his face. 'Steve, what's happened? You look drained.'

'Nothing. Or nothing I can tell you. Quite a lot of people in my circle have died recently – '

'I'm sorry – '

An uncomfortable silence interposed itself.

Eventually, Steve said, 'How much notice, do you need?'

Not meeting his gaze, Sally said, 'End of the week, if it's not too much of a hit financially?'

'Yes, that's fine. Drinks on me at the John Snow on Wednesday.'

'You're sure?'

'Yes, it's a bit of a liberation actually.'

As they walked back to the office, Steve wondered how much more freedom he could take.

In the end, it was decided that it was pointless for him to continue beyond the Wednesday, the day the current issue would be put to bed. When he and Kate got back from the typesetters, he put some money behind the bar at the John Snow. Pretty much everyone from the office came by. Even Greg came for half an hour to wish him well. In fact, there was soon quite a party atmosphere in the main bar. Early on, Sarah cornered him and insisted on a long and sloppy snog. She said she'd heard from Sal that he was single again. How about the two of them going on somewhere else after the John Snow? Steve laughed and thought he might just take her up on the suggestion. But after squirming provocatively against him for a while, she went off to the loo. When she re-emerged, eyes sparkling and gabbling about her recent interview with The Stones, she'd forgotten the invitation she'd made and without more ado headed off to the first gig of the evening.

Phil, the magazine's editor, who, on the whole, had had very few interactions with Steve in his time at the magazine, was complimentary about his work. He said that he'd like Steve to submit the occasional gig review and from time to time to do round-up reviews of current releases. Steve thanked him for his kindness, but privately thought that he would be unlikely to take up the offer.

As the bar filled up, he managed to have a few words with nearly all his colleagues, even those with whom he'd had little to do. But there was one person he hadn't spoken to, and that was Sally. She was sitting with Kate at the table that he and Sally had been sitting at when Inge and Werner had turned up two months previously. Of course, Inge had not been her real name. And he now also knew that, on that particular evening, it hadn't been Ulrike either. Even so, he'd been absolutely certain that same evening that the woman, who'd waltzed into the John Snow with a bulky minder in tow, was the same woman he'd made love to in Prenzlauer Berg. And even though in the intervening weeks he'd come to doubt his initial certainty, it turned out that he'd been right. Because on that first night and the following one too, it had not been Ulrike he'd been dealing with but Katrin her identical twin. As he was reflecting on the sequence of enchantment and disenchantment, he noticed Kate getting up from her chair and putting her coat on. A few moments later she left the pub.

He went over to Sally's table and said, 'May I join you?'

She patted the chair which Kate had just vacated and said, 'Of course you can. Kate asked to apologise on her behalf that she had to leave early. I think she was finding the evening a bit uncomfortable.'

'I understand. Actually we had a quick drink at the Sekforde before we came over here.'

She looked at him carefully. 'Are you okay?'

'Yes. I wasn't looking forward to this evening. But everyone's been very nice.'

'Even Sarah. She looked like she was going to have you in the corner.'

'That's what it felt like. But then she went off to powder her nose and somehow forgot all about it.'

'That's Sarah for you.'

'Or not for me, it seems.'

'Count yourself lucky. The only thing you'd be picking up if you went down that route is a dose of the clap.'

'Yeah, I suppose. But what about you? Are you okay?'

'Yeah, I suppose too.'

'Things working out with you and Jeremy?'

'Yes, he's a nice man. Courteous, tidy, but a bit wet behind the ears, and slightly nervous about sex. He seems to need quite a lot of encouragement.'

'That's the effect of public school. I am sure you can educate him out of that reaction.'

'Not a response I noticed with you.'

'Yes, well, I was a scholarship boy at CLS and it isn't a boarding school. So not the real thing.'

'He's slightly obsessed with you.'

'Well, technically I'm meant to report to him, but I don't do much reporting. So I guess he's often wondering what I'm up to.'

'No, it's more that he wants to know what makes you tick?'

'I'd like to know the same thing. If he finds out, ask him to let me know.'

'To be quite honest, I don't see things lasting between us – Jeremy and me, I mean. I prefer a bedfellow who takes matters in hand, if you know what I mean.'

'I think I do.'

'Would you be disappointed in me if I were to give him his marching orders?'

Actually, Steve was relieved to hear of the direction her thoughts were taking, but he ought not to express himself too enthusiastically. 'Of course not. It's entirely up to you. But I won't be crossing you off my Christmas card list, if you do.'

'Thanks, Steve. How's Grace?'

'Confused, upset.'

'Was she close to her mother?'

'I don't think so, but that's probably why she's taking it so badly.'

'Jeremy talks quite a lot about her too.'

'Well, she's eminent in her field. She'll probably be a professor before long.'

'Is she still trying to have a child?'

'Not as far as I know. Or anyway, not with me.'

'But she still likes to hang out with scruffy old Steve Percival.'

'It's not quite as simple as that.'

'Things seldom are in your life.'

'If it was just a matter of scruffiness, I'd be home and dry.'

'But you're still with her?'

'Kind of, for the moment.'

'Which of you is limiting the relationship?'

'We both are.'

'Steve, please be careful.'

'I will, but thanks Sally.'

'Can we stay in touch?'

'I'd like that. You've got my contact details.'

'I still haven't seen where you live.'

'Well, we'll have to fix that once the dust settles.'

'It'll never settle, so let's do it before that.'

'Okay, ball's in your court.'

Sheena – Kennington – Thursday

SHEENA FERGUSON DREW ON her Montecristo. 'Steve, I can't tell you how proud of you your mother would have been, were she still alive. I am afraid you will have to settle for unstinting praise from me instead.'

'But I didn't really do anything.'

'Oh, but you did. You kept the show, with all its elaborate deception, on the road.'

'For whom?'

'For Mr Collingwood and those who control him.'

'How did I do that?'

'Collingwood couldn't monitor everything without the risk of showing his hand, but he could monitor you and interpret the twists and turns of the situation you found yourself in. Also he very likely had some SIGINT relating to your activities.'

'Isn't that something that needs your approval?'

'Technically, yes. But there is the old saying about giving a person enough rope to hang themselves. If Collingwood had got the slightest hint that we were watching him closely, he would have shut up like a clam.'

'But now that we know for sure that he is Tollkirsche, why don't we bust him?'

'Because he is more use to us un-bust.'

'But he's responsible for this whole terrible mess.'

'I'm not sure that's quite right. He certainly thinks he poisoned Müller. Perhaps he is even a teeny bit proud of himself. I hope not. Of course, he knows that the public position about Müller is that he died of a heart attack. But he does not know, as we do, that Müller really did die of a heart attack. We just exploited that sad turn of events to encourage Collingwood to show his hand by framing Ulrike.'

'He also thinks Ulrike hanged herself.'

'And so, therefore, do the Stasi. They must feel he's proved his mettle by carrying out an assassination and at the same time successfully blaming someone who was already on their hate list.'

'And where is Ulrike now?'

'I could tell you, but I don't think there's much point. Ulrike is in a safe place being given a new identity. She will re-emerge in due course and next year take up the graduate student place at Cambridge that she longs for.'

Steve laughed. 'Well, I am re-assured. But what about Katrin?'

'Firstly, remember Collingwood has absolutely no idea of Katrin. Secondly, Katrin has come over to us, as I think you already know.'

'Yes, how was she turned?'

'To be honest, and as we told you to begin with, it was Ulrike who we thought was a Stasi asset. We had no idea that there was a twin. So when Ulrike was released, we tracked her to her aunt's in Frankfurt and then out of the blue her identical twin, who really is Stasi, turns up at the aunt's. We realised from the tapes that not only was Katrin remorseful about what had happened to Ulrike and was starting to doubt her commitment to the regime, but that she was also on a mission to Britain.'

'You were bugging the aunt's house?'

'You're surprised? Don't be. Anyway, I had Katrin arrested when she landed at Dover and brought to me. Then, over several days, she and I came to an understanding. We would help her carry out her assignment to raise her profile with her superiors and she would help us neutralise the situation around Müller. You've seen some of the photos from one particular phase of those encounters.'

'But that was Ulrike, the twin, the one with the birthmark.'

'No, it was Katrin. She and I used theatrical makeup to counterfeit the birthmark.'

'But she's not a lesbian.'

'These are just labels, Steve. I was told that you worked in the theatre. Acting is not the only domain in which that skill is deployed.'

'Why were you trying to make her seem like Ulrike?'

'That was purely for your benefit. You knew nothing about Katrin. The Stasi plan had always been to frame Ulrike for Müller's murder, which would actually be carried out by Collingwood. With the result that Ulrike would in effect swap a prison sentence in East Berlin for a much longer one in Britain. Of course, we had no intention of letting Müller be murdered. The original idea was to pretend he'd been poisoned and create a new identity for him. So it was ironic that he had a real heart attack, but I think he knew his race was run. It did force us to improvise a bit. Fortunately, Doyle and Mallory were on hand to hold the fort until we were able to get our own emergency services team in.'

'Why did you have to swap Katrin for Ulrike between Paddington Green and The Grange?'

'We needed to test that Katrin was acting in good faith. But we also needed to create a context in which you would have some time to understand which woman we wanted you to develop a rapport with.'

'Well, I'm very grateful for that consideration, but I prefer to be the one to decide who I develop a rapport with.'

'Of course, in your personal life that is entirely how it should be, but in your professional life it is up to us – well, me actually.'

'I don't really understand what you're saying. Where is Katrin now? She told me she was going to return to East Berlin.'

'That is exactly the case.'

'Isn't that dangerous for her?'

'Of course, it's dangerous. That's what she's chosen. She completed her Stasi-sponsored mission here rather successfully, with our help, and will very likely get a commendation.'

'What was her mission?'

'That is beside the point and will not be helpful for you to know. But she is one of us now and will be a first-class penetration agent. If things get too hot, we will do our best to get her out. But we don't want to get ahead of ourselves. For now we are letting her settle back in.'

'I was hoping I might see her again.'

'Oh, but you will.'

'I don't understand what you mean.'

'I've decided that you will be her handler.'

'Me? But I don't know how to do that kind of work.'

'I am of the opinion that with a bit of training, you will be well suited to the job.'

'Seriously?'

'Seriously. In April, you will be taking up your post in West Berlin with full diplomatic accreditation. Before that you will be at our training centre. Congratulations, you passed your probationary period with flying colours.'

'Sheena, I don't know if I want the job.'

'Too bad, you've got it. You will report directly to me. Of course, Collingwood will be your colleague, but you no longer need to report to him.'

'But isn't he implicated in Mavis's death?'

'This is the last time I say this: Because we have photos of him about to penetrate a German boy in Leipzig trussed like a Christmas turkey, it doesn't make him a murderer. Nor, as it turns out, did he murder Müller. If you and Katrin can come up with more robust evidence of his wrongdoing, then we will act accordingly.'

Steve sat there for a few minutes, trying to make sense of what Sheena was saying. She watched him with a small smile playing across her severe features. After a while, he said, 'So you had the whole thing planned out from the start?'

'Not in detail. You will find that in our business flexibility and improvisation are more important than meticulous planning. In this case it was a matter of responding with the pieces at my disposal to the situation as it developed.'

'By pieces you mean people?'

'If you like. It'd be very much the same if one were running a factory or a business. It was, of course, also a way of testing your abilities. Does it surprise you that I sometimes take advantage of people in anomalous positions?'

'No, I suppose not. It makes a kind of sense.'

'I'm glad to hear it. Do you have any other questions?'

'Yes. Clearly Müller was onboard with the plans because he wrote a letter for Doyle to give me in the event of his death together with his Zettelkästen. Presumably, you communicated with him directly?'

'Yes, I impersonated an elderly American film star and talked Stan Mallory into letting me into Founder's Court. And subsequently, I was Müller's stand-in bedder when Mrs Comberton was feeling poorly.'

'Do you think Stan recognised you?'

'I think he did. He had a twinkle in his eye.'

'He noticed the aroma of your Montecristos.'

Sheena laughed. 'I'll have to be careful of that in future. It might be my undoing. Thank you for the observation, Steve.'

'And what about Müller?'

'He and I had never met before, but I fancy he had an inkling.'

'And I presume you got access to the Zettelkästen while they were with Doyle after Müller's death?'

'Yes, and to Müller's typewriter.'

'This is not the first time you and Doyle and Mallory have worked together?'

'We all go back a long way. The only one missing is poor Mavis. Any more questions?'

'Not about this operation, but going back to my run to East Berlin. Katrin says that the package that I carried over was empty. My run was a ruse. Ulrike was already under arrest and, as I now know, it was Katrin I interacted with, not Ulrike. But the real documents went by another courier and Müller succeeded in getting out. Is that your understanding too?'

'Well, yes, it is.'

'Was it you who made the alternative arrangements, but kept Collingwood and me out of the loop?'

'Of course, but Collingwood must never know this. Understood?'

Steve nodded.

Sheena closed her folder. 'Well, I think we are done here now. On your way out, Emily will give you details of where and when the next phase of your training starts. There's also quite a large cheque for you to pick up and some documents to sign.'

'Can I speak to Grace about this?'

'You know my views on Grace. I do not think it a suitable attachment for you. And I think you might find her an encumbrance once you resume contact with Katrin. But that is for you to decide. I think when you tell Grace you are being posted to West Berlin, she will understand exactly what is happening. Even so, please do not mention the name of your agent.'

'Of course not.'

'There's no *of course* about it. Grace is a subtle woman, very much more experienced than you in these matters. You would be making a mistake if you did not consider that to be so. The worst mistake a case officer can make is to think he or she understands the motivation of a subject, informant or agent.'

'Which of those categories does Grace fall into?'

'For your purposes she's a subject, unless you hear from me to the contrary. Of course, these categories are fluid.'

Reflecting on his recent conversation with Grace, fluidity seemed entirely appropriate to his situation. 'Okay.'

'You have to be prepared to let your conclusions about everyone you deal with remain in suspension. And that includes me.'

'How does one do that?'

'You need to cultivate what Keats called negative capability, which we might redefine for our purposes as the capacity to embrace uncertainty, mystery, and doubt without being driven to seek immediate answers or explanations; to exist in a state of ambiguity, allowing for the exploration of diverse perspectives and experiences without the need to impose a single, definitive truth. I am confident that you already possess those skills in some considerable measure.'

Appendix

Editor's Note

THE FOLLOWING FRAGMENTS WERE retrieved from what appears to be a secondary index appended to Professor Müller's *Schwarze Zettelkasten*. Their provenance is uncertain. The numbering aligns imperfectly with the surviving boxes; several entries are plainly interpolations by an unknown later hand. A few cards are marked **unverortet** – items without fixed location – suggesting a refusal of sequence itself. Whether these fragments represent Müller's own retrospective annotations, a subsequent reader's marginalia, or a deliberate act of misfiling is impossible to determine. They are presented here without emendation.

Week Zero

ZK 0.0.1
Oversight / Blind Spot
"No one has no secrets." (Sheena → Steve)
Theme: surveillance + intimacy blurred.
Tag: TRUST / SECRECY / COLLUSION
Echo: Prefigures Sheena's own blind spots later (Montecristo "tell").
UNVERORTET: Who watches Sheena?

ZK 0.0.2
The Cigar as Sign
Montecristo ritual: "More honest than people."
Theme: objects as signatures (taste, aroma, habit).
Tag: AURA / HABITUS / RECOGNITION
Echo: Stan the porter's nose; Müller's Cohibas; Collingwood's slips.

UNVERORTET: Does a cigar smoke the smoker?

ZK 0.0.3
Ulrike / Inge
Released, renamed, ransomed.
Theme: double names, doubled selves, translation as camouflage.
Tag: IDENTITY / MASK / EXCHANGE
Echo: Prenzlauer Berg → The Grange swap; birthmark vs. fake mark.
UNVERORTET: When does a person become their alias?

ZK 0.0.4
Amelia as Gift
"She's very special... She loves your voice, Steve."
Theme: children as legacy, paternity concealed/revealed.
Tag: PATERNITY / GIFT / FUTURE
Echo: Steve unknowingly holds his child; Grace's frustrated maternity.
UNVERORTET: Whose child is whose?

Week One

Chronology of first contact (Borough → Great Eastern):

ZK 1.0.1
→ SHEENA's diktat: "assist, not thwart."
→ Cover = Buzz (ink-stained alibi).
→ Collingwood silent, lips pursed.

ZK 1.2.4
→ Pub as stage: John Snow encounter.
→ Tom resurfaced; Sally = witness.
→ Werner = shadow / minder.

ZK 1.3.7
→ ULRIKE unveils name.
→ Ransom ≠ rescue? Gratitude → Cambridge.
→ "Practise before performance."

ƵK ∅.1.9 – UNVERORTET
→ Alias circulates: Inge / Ulrike / Tom / Steve.
→ Names unstable, files smudge.
→ (margin hand: "Identity = currency.")

Week Two

Chronology of the test (Soho → Cambridge):

ƵK 2.1.3
→ MUGGING or STAGING? Passport lost, then found.
→ Bath as baptism; bruise as cipher.
→ Red coat enters play.

ƵK 2.2.6
→ SHELVES at TCS: Event/Horizon & Palace of Tears exposed.
→ Freya = Becky? Tristan = Steve?
→ Parallax named, denied, embraced.

ƵK 2.3.4
→ Grace's parlous catechism: Char / Celan cross-examined.
→ Ulrike delivers, dossier fluent.
→ Müller displaced, yet watching.

ƵK ∅.2.9 – UNVERORTET
→ Two writers at one table, one text divided.
→ / Witness / Double.
→ (margin hand: "All readings provisional.")

Week Three

Chronology of the confidences (Cambridge → St Rad's):

ƵK 3.0.2
→ COLL-OP: biscuits, Borough desk.
→ Sally transferred, Jeremy's pride.
→ Cover stories swapped with ease.

ZK 3.1.4
→ PORTER'S CLUB: Stan's ledger > Fellows' files.
→ Aroma as code: Cohiba / Montecristo.
→ Mallory ≠ Collingwood.

ZK 3.2.8
→ Doyle's sherry catechism.
→ "Mine to offer. Yours to make."
→ War memory = field lesson ≈ Steve's own test.

ZK ∅.3.9 - UNVERORTET
→ Suitcase = dossier; notebook = mask.
→ Who is Ulrike? Who is Inge?
→ (margin hand: "Evidence ≠ proof.")

Week Four

Chronology of the bequest (St Rad's → Kennington → TCS):

ZK 4.0.1
→ Mrs Nairn ≠ Mrs Comberton.
→ Cigar smoke recognised, red coat displaced.
→ Bedder as cipher, "housekeeping" as cover.

ZK 4.2.7
→ MATERNAL TRACE: Tante Elisabeth named.
→ Müller = father? Ulrike = daughter?
→ Confession deferred; absolution withheld.

ZK 4.6.3
→ Black Box handed via Doyle.
→ Letter to S.P. = executor's charge.
→ Grey cards: Frühromantik / Black cards: kompromat.

ZK ∅.4.9 - UNVERORTET
→ Archive ≠ coffin / coffin ≠ archive.
→ , presence persists.

→ (margin: "The truth is what one is not allowed to say –M.")

Week Five

Chronology of the unmasking deferred (Borough → Somerset):

ƵK 5.0.3
→ COLL-OP briefing: toxin trace + phial planted.
→ Red coat as exhibit A.
→ Belt & braces = shaky case.

ƵK 5.1.2
→ Grace bereaved, Lane End reopened.
→ Steve as comforter ≈ heir apparent.
→ Djellaba reclaims bed / parental place.

ƵK 5.2.7
→ Black Box yields photo: twins at Müggelsee.
→ Birthmark noted only after exposure.
→ Surveillance invited = trap sprung.

ƵK ∅.5.9 – UNVERORTET
→ Bed trick revived: Who enters which bed?
→ Birthmark ≠ proof.
→ (margin hand: "Identity collapses under touch.")

Week Six

Chronology of the interrogation (Borough → Paddington → Kennington):

ƵK 6.0.2
→ COLL briefing: Ulrike ≈ Stasi uniform sighting.
→ Rights deferred = fig leaf.
→ Percival volunteered as "soft cop."

ƵK 6.1.5
→ Paddington Green: coffee, Marlboro, Rich Tea.

→ Prenzlauer replay ≈ palimpsest.

→ Birthmark withheld, twin implied.

ƵK 6.2.4

→ Sheena reviews transcript: arcane code decoded.

→ Tollkirsche exposed via card + photo.

→ Collingwood retained: mole kept in play.

ƵK ∅.6.9 – UNVERORTET

→ Debrief ≈ confession ≈ theatre.

→ Who plays whom? Interrogator / lover / son.

→ (margin hand: "Privacy never total. Locks removed.")

Week Seven

Chronology of the Grange (Paddington → Gazebo → Glisson):

ƵK 7.0.2

→ CICELY as chatelaine: Benson & Hedges, Ƶeta's Son.

→ Debrief ≈ boarding school timetable.

→ Grey coat ≠ red coat.

ƵK 7.1.8

→ Gazebo embrace: birthmark absent.

→ Marlboro offered, mask dropped.

→ "Please kiss me, Steve" = twin revealed.

ƵK 7.3.4

→ Stratagem announced: suicide staged.

→ Body removed, report sealed.

→ Collingwood deceived, Sheena satisfied.

ƵK ∅.7.1 – GAƵEBO

→ Müggelsee précis deployed as key.

→ Twin unnamed, only implied.

→ (margin: "Bleed = Glisson / Prenzlauer.")

Week Eight

ƵK 8.0 - Buzz → Exit

→ Coffee with Sally; Kate proves seamless; Steve resigns.
→ "I'll manage" → novel retitled The Parallax View (title as stance).
→ Party at John Snow; Sarah's false start; quiet compliments; Steve drifts loose of newsroom gravity.

ƵK 8.1 - Sally Vector
→ Bench talk: Collingwood "courteous, tidy... a bit wet."
→ Sally hints at ejecting him; asks to keep Steve in orbit.
→ Steve bites his tongue re: Tollkirsche, chooses patience over warning.

ƵK 8.2 - The Grange Afterimage
→ Return shock hangs on him; Sheena's call, then the cheque.
→ Official story set: Ulrike = suicide, Müller = heart, Collingwood believes both.
→ Sheena's reveal: Katrin turned, makeup birthmark, Dover arrest, staged swap; Müller plan long-game, Doyle/Mallory complicit.

ƵK 8.3 - Appointment in Berlin
→ Steve to be Katrin's handler; training → April posting, West Berlin (diplomatic).
→ Collingwood left in place - more useful "un-bust."
→ Doctrine: negative capability as tradecraft; people as "pieces," plans as jazz.
→ Grace status: "subject," relationship must stay fluid; no agent names.